ONLY THE DEAD

*The Investigation of a Kidnapping
and Murder*
A Novel

MARTIN R. REGALADO
SPECIAL AGENT, RETIRED
FEDERAL BUREAU OF INVESTIGATION

ISBN: 979-8-7142-3274-9
Cover Design by Pixel Studios
Edited by Kathryn F. Galán, Wynnpix Productions

Lines quoted or paraphrased from *Apocalypse Now,* screenplay by John Milius and Francis Ford Coppola with original narration by Michael Herr. © Omni Zoetrope and United Artists. 1979.

This is a work of fiction. Names, characters, places, brands, media, and incidents are either the product of the author's imagination or are used fictitiously. Any resemblance to similarly-named places or to persons living or deceased is unintentional. The manuscript of this book was reviewed by the Federal Bureau of Investigation, Office of Prepublication Review, and no objections to publication were made. The Federal Bureau of Investigation has not endorsed this book, and any views or opinions expressed in this work should not be taken as those of the Federal Bureau of Investigation.

This book is dedicated to Erasmo and Visenta,
Whose love made many beautiful things possible

What is this thing called love?
This funny thing called love?
Just who can solve its mystery?
Why should it make a fool of me?

—Cole Porter, "What is this thing called love?"

This is the end, beautiful friend…
The end of our elaborate plans…
The end of everything that stands…
The end…
I'll never look into your eyes again…
Can you picture what will be…
So limitless and free…

—Jim Morrison, The Doors, "The End"

Ensanguining the skies
How heavily it dies
Into the west away;
Past touch and sight and sound
Not further to be found,
How hopeless under ground
Falls the remorseful day

—A. E. Housman, "How Clear, How Lovely Bright"

CONTENTS

Author's Note

Raymond Chandler and the Detective Mystery Story

In *The Simple Art of Murder*,[1] Raymond Chandler, author of the noir classics *The Big Sleep* and *Farewell, My Lovely,* shared his thoughts on the art of the detective novel. Then, as now, many did not consider the genre serious literature worthy of an intelligent mind's attention. As Chandler pointed out, however, the good detective story is difficult to write well because, while intended to be realistic, most authors of the genre failed in their attempt to make it so. "Good specimens of the art are much rarer than good serious novels," he opined. I would agree.

> *The main trouble with most detective stories, as I see it, is that the people who write them are bad writers ... the mind which can produce a coolly thought-out puzzle can't, as a rule, develop the fire and dash necessary for vivid writing.*[2]

The detective novel was (and is) usually attempted by less talented writers whose language and vocabulary stilted the story, whose lack of real-life experience made for improbable if not preposterous storylines, and whose lack of imagination resulted in a glaring lack of internal logic, resolved only by a fatuous denouement. These egregious flaws are made more obvious if the untalented but lucky novelist's work is transformed into film. Chandler himself was guilty of several of these flaws, most notably his failure to educate himself about the laws and regulations pertaining to private investigators. He didn't bother to do so until he

---

[1] Chandler, Raymond, "The Simple Art of Murder," *The Atlantic Monthly,* December, 1944.

[2] Letter to Charles Morton, July 17, 1944. Frank MacShane, *Selected Letters of Raymond Chandler,* 1981.

consulted an attorney in 1950—long after he became famous for his
literary detectives.[3]

Despite these many problems, the detective novel remains a mainstay
of Western culture. How could this be so? Chandler may have answered
this question when he pointed out that, while even Conan Doyle suffered
from the afflictions common to mystery writers, he was saved by one
Sherlock Holmes—in other words, by an inevitable and brilliant character:
inevitable because both the real and literary worlds needed such a
character; brilliant because the character is both larger than life and yet
very much a part of ordinary life.

The detective, a unique character in fiction, is both *in* the world but,
unlike Christ, *of* the world, also. He must, therefore, deal with his own
demons as well as the demons thrust upon him by fate, all while
remaining a hero unto himself. It is in his dealing with those demons—the
story—that we come to know the detective, who, in fleshing out the
mystery, fleshes out his own character and reveals his character to the
reader.

If the detective is well and honestly drawn, a hero as unashamed to
show his flaws as he is unafraid to take a bullet, he can save not only the
damsel in distress but a contrived and poorly thought-out and weakly
written story, as well. Just think how unlikely the events in Chandler's
own novels are to occur in real life, and it is easy to see how it's Philip
Marlowe who carries the story—and the reader—along from beginning to
end. Much more so in the case of Doyle and Holmes, whom any intelligent
and educated reader of serious literary fiction would dismiss as sheer
contrivance and buffoonery. As Chandler himself said:

> *Nobody reading the Sherlock Holmes stories at this time can think
> anything about them except that as stories they are pretty thin milk.
> But that does nothing to diminish the character of Holmes himself. He
> rises above them and becomes a person people want to read about even
> when he is being silly.*[4]

The well and honestly drawn detective overcomes the limitations of
the genre because he has been imbued with a vitality that first draws the
reader into the story by force of will—the noble detective's need to solve

[3] Letter to Leroy Wright, April 12, 1950. Frank MacShane, Ibid.
[4] Letter to Hamish Hamilton, October 5, 1949. Frank MacShane, Ibid.

the mystery and get to the truth. He then draws the reader out of the story by force of character—the chivalrous detective's heroic actions. The reader reads and continues reading, despite any shortcomings in the story, because they are compelled to believe in a hero who has all the qualities and flaws Chandler pointed out so well:

> ... *down these mean streets a man must go who is not himself mean, who is neither tarnished nor afraid. The detective in this kind of story must be such a man. He is the hero, he is everything. He must be a complete man and a common man and yet an unusual man. He must be, to use a rather weathered phrase, a man of honor, by instinct, by inevitability, without thought of it, and certainly without saying it. He must be the best man in his world and a good enough man for any world.*
>
> *I do not care much about his private life; he is neither a eunuch nor a satyr; I think he might seduce a duchess and I am quite sure he would not spoil a virgin; if he is a man of honor in one thing, he is that in all things. He is a relatively poor man, or he would not be a detective at all. He is a common man or he could not go among common people. He has a sense of character, or he would not know his job. He will take no man's money dishonestly and no man's insolence without a due and dispassionate revenge. He is a lonely man and his pride is that you will treat him as a proud man or be very sorry you ever saw him. He talks as the man of his age talks, that is, with rude wit, a lively sense of the grotesque, a disgust for sham, and a contempt for pettiness. The story is his adventure in search of a hidden truth, and it would be no adventure if it did not happen to a man fit for adventure...*[5]

Chandler complained much about the writers of detective fiction of his day. He acknowledged, however, despite the poor writing, the authors of his time found success with the detective novel because, as he put it, "the average 'educated' American has the all-round mental equipment of a fourth-form boy in an English public school."[6]

Were he still around, Chandler would have much more to complain about today. In our dumbed-down America of high school drop-outs and the intellectually lazy who allow the Internet and social media to do their

[5] Chandler, Raymond, *The Simple Art of Murder*, Ibid.
[6] Letter to Hamish Hamilton, January 9, 1946. Frank MacShane, Ibid.

thinking for them, detective fiction now doesn't even need a modicum of reality, so long as the protagonist detective can posture like a bodybuilder, spew epithets like a convict, and has an arsenal of weapons, technology, and automobiles of which MI-5 and the CIA would be envious. Who needs a fictional character with moral character when he has guns and overwhelming firepower at his trigger-fingertips? Who even needs a credible storyline, when the entertainment-seeking masses are easily kept in rapt attention with successive high-speed chases and gigantic explosions? The current deluge and success of films based on comic book superheroes make this point irrefutably.

But Chandler also recognized the danger of writing something that might challenge the typical reader of detective fiction. In attempting to "make an art of a language" that a "semi-literate" public could understand, it would be easy to fall into the trap of what he called "a certain literary pretentiousness."[7] Chandler ridiculed a writer who made such an attempt by describing that writer's work as "a springboard for a sermon on How Not to be a Sophisticated Writer."[8] An author who is genuinely "engaged in the effort to do something with the mystery story which has never quite been done"[9] must remain faithful to the basic principle governing the detective story genre, i.e., the detective must remain a common man with uncommon virtue, one who not only talks the ordinary talk but walks the ordinary walk while unraveling the mystery without the aid of special effects, computer-generated imagery, or *deus ex machina*. Most of all, the author must let his creation—the detective—do the talking and walking and not allow his ego to jerk the story away from the reader by attempting to show his literary sophistication with pretentious prose.[10]

In addition to Chandler's irritations,[11] my pet peeve concerns the obsession mystery writers have in leaving their intellectually lazy and

---

[7] Letter to Hardwick Moseley, April 23, 1949. Frank MacShane, Ibid.

[8] Letter to James Sandoe, April 14, 1949. Frank MacShane, Ibid.

[9] Letter to Hardwick Moseley, April 23, 1949. Frank MacShane, Ibid.

[10] Letter to James Sandoe, April 14, 1949. Frank MacShane, Ibid.

[11] To be fair, Chandler was not merely a harsh critic of bad writers and complacent readers. He also offered advice, as well. In his notebooks, unpublished during his lifetime, Chandler provided twelve commandments for avoiding those errors common to most writers of the detective mystery story and an additional thirteen

half-witted readers with no questions unanswered. My experience as a lawyer and investigator taught me there is no case in which every question is answered and every mystery solved. An unknowable universe and the vagaries of human nature are such that, even when every perpetrator, victim, and witness can be rounded up and interrogated, there will remain many unanswered questions and unresolved mysteries. Yet, every third-rate best-selling author will contort logic to an extreme in order to satisfy the simple-minded reader with answers to questions that could never be answered in the real world. While the "willing suspension of disbelief"[12] on the reader's part is a necessary element of every novel, most authors these days rely much too much on a compliant or mindless readership to accept a story with little internal logic. But the reality is there simply are things that can never be known in this life, things only the dead can know.

Keeping all this in mind, I offer this story of a crime and the man who resolves that crime. The story unravels as it would in reality, with only bits of truth gleaned over time, bits that often appear contradictory and subject to interpretation. However, for the reader who needs more, I also offer more of the truth—the truth only the dead could know.

---

considerations for the writer to keep in mind. See, *The Notebooks of Raymond Chandler*, edited by Frank MacShane, 2015.

[12] Coleridge, Samuel Taylor. *Biographia Literaria*. 1817.

Chapter 1

The End is Where We Start From

There could be no more majestic and scenic vantage point along the California coast for a peaceful idyll than the grassy knoll just off the Pacific Coast Highway, between Los Angeles and Santa Barbara and overlooking the vast Pacific Ocean, where the bodies of Rachael Ginsberg-Marino and her unborn baby would rest for eternity. A variety of California conifers, primarily the iconic cypress-pines, along with a few live oaks and palo blancos, graced their resting place impeccably, as did an elegant assortment of colorful native flowers planted with flawless design along the walkways and around the trees.

I took in the scene from a distance. It was a picture-perfect Southern California day, the kind that makes thousands of people flee the rest of the country and migrate here every year, as soon as they have money for bus fare. A gentle breeze wafted in from the sea with just a hint of brine that mixed pleasantly with the non-native citrus and honeysuckle, planted here and there to provide comfort to the grieving. The cool sea air and a few passing clouds tempered the heat of the bright morning sun.

After Rachael's body was recovered, the news media had reported the Ginsberg clan was grief-stricken and had gone into seclusion to mourn their loss. Overwhelming sympathy and support were shown them by the society elite of Southern California. Condolences had been received from celebrities, politicians, judges, and even the White House. The prime minister of Israel sent the Ginsbergs a handwritten note with a massive floral arrangement, delivered by the consul himself. The media also reported that, after Rachael's body was found and the forensic results released, Richard Marino had been so devastated and unable to cope with the loss of his wife and unborn child, he was driven to suicide. Law enforcement officials and a suicide note confirmed this, although his body was never found.

The funeral was attended by the appropriately large number of family, friends, and other notables who had come to pay their last respects, including many well-known personages from the political/legal, business/financial, and film/entertainment worlds that comprised the Ginsberg and Marino milieu. Perhaps many were here simply to be seen as part of the scene, which was being videotaped and photographed extensively by the vultures of the news media, who provided the only discordant noise to disturb the peaceful setting, when their helicopters, seeking to record the event from above, swooped inconsiderately close. Yet, Shakespeare would say Caesar himself would've approved, as the ostentation of the event left no doubt as to how deeply the departed had been loved.

Despite my own long and intimate connection to Rachael, our relationship had remained a secret, so I'd remained an outsider and therefore stood an appropriately discreet distance from the center of activity. I didn't mind not being nearer her gravesite. It wasn't so long ago that the only people of my ethnic background allowed into this elite private cemetery were just here to dig the graves. What did bother me was the tangled web of deceit and hypocrisy and the painful secrets behind the deceit and hypocrisy—the overwhelming and unnecessary sadness of it all that began long before the kidnapping.

Since I was intimately involved with Rachael and had something to do with her being brought here to rest, this is my story, too, and I should introduce myself. You can call me Mig. Everybody does. It's much less pretentious than Miguel Hidalgo Dehenares. But I'm not above a little pretention myself. I've always refused to go by Michael or, worse, Mike, despite all the efforts made throughout my school years and my time in the Army and FBI to force me to accept the Americanization. That out of the way, allow me to take you to the beginning of this end.

Chapter 2

The Kidnapping

On the surface, there was nothing out of the ordinary for this type of crime—nothing to indicate it was anything other than a well-planned kidnapping.

On a chilly Monday morning, December 12, 2016, wealthy socialite Rachael Ginsberg-Marino and her two children, seven-year-old David and five-year-old Sarah, were kidnapped as they left their Holmby Hills estate on their way to the children's private school in Beverly Hills. The kidnappers' spokesman claimed they were military-trained members of the Palestinian Hezbollah intifada and were executing this action on the Prophet's birthday, in his honor. They had targeted Rachael Ginsberg-Marino because her parents, Aron and Magda Ginsberg, were wealthy Jews who had been financial supporters of Israel for decades and because Rachael's husband, Richard Marino, was a wealthy businessman and Jewish sympathizer. The targets and motives were clear and simple to understand. The parents and husband took the kidnappers at their word and feared the worst; following the kidnappers' instructions, they didn't contact law enforcement until it was too late.

FBI Special Agent Bart Keyes prepared a narrative report that provided a summary of the information obtained from the victims and witnesses and analyses of the physical and documentary evidence and forensic reports. The report was a synthesis of all the known facts and circumstances and became the basis of the Letterhead Memorandum the Bureau provided, at the conclusion of its investigation, to the U.S. Attorney's Office in Los Angeles, FBI Headquarters, the Department of Justice in Washington, D.C., the Los Angeles Police Department, and L.A. County District Attorney's Office, and to all the politicians who asked for information—in short, all of the people the Ginsbergs, Marino, and their lawyers would call upon to demand information and action.

A narrative report isn't evidentiary and often contains information that wouldn't be admissible in court, such as opinions, assumptions, hearsay, and conclusions based on the known information. But it provided a chronology of events and verbatim accounts of conversations, where available and corroborated. The following is my very dry and "just the facts" summary of Bart's narrative report of the kidnapping, so you'll know what we knew when the investigation began:

Richard Marino left his estate Monday morning about 7:15. On Sunday, he had told his wife, Rachael, this was going to be a busy week for him, with meetings and telephone conferences concerning his new downtown L.A. development project. Because he was in a hurry, he'd skipped breakfast with the children and given his wife and kids a quick kiss before leaving. For no particular reason, he drove his Jaguar sedan that day instead of his Porsche 911.

Everything seemed normal as he pulled into the private parking area of the underground garage below his ten-story retail and office building in downtown Los Angeles. He'd bought the old building five years prior, refurbished and remodeled it, and used the top floor as the Marino Properties Corporation headquarters. He took the private elevator up to his penthouse suite and got to his office about eight. His longtime secretary, Susan Russo, informed him of his day's schedule as she walked with him into his office and then waited for any immediate instructions. He asked her only for his usual coffee and began to go through his written messages and mail.

While this was happening, the kidnapping was taking place. The security cameras at the gate to Marino's estate showed that Rachael Ginsberg-Marino's Cadillac SUV was blocked on the street by two cars as soon as she drove past the gate. Another vehicle, a van with a side door open, pulled alongside the SUV. Several men, all wearing keffiyehs and some with AK-47-type assault rifles and pistols, surrounded the SUV. Rachael Ginsberg-Marino and the two children were forcibly removed from her vehicle and placed in the van. One of the men got into the SUV while the others returned to their cars, and all the vehicles left the scene. The kidnapping took ninety-six seconds.

The first of the kidnapper's calls came in on Richard Marino's cell phone about forty-five minutes later. Caller ID indicated his wife was calling from her cell phone.

"What is it, honey? I'm already swamped this morning. I told you I would be," Marino said while taking a file his secretary had just brought him. Russo had remained standing by the desk, awaiting any further instructions.

"Are you alone in your office?" the heavily accented Arab voice asked.

"What? Who is this?" Marino asked, as he checked the caller ID again.

"Are you alone in your office?" the voice repeated.

"No."

"Then get everyone out. Now!"

Richard was unsure of what was going on but turned to his secretary and said, "Can you give me a minute, Susan? I need to take this call privately."

"Yes, sir," she replied, noticing the troubled look on his face. She walked out of his office but left the door open.

As soon as Russo was out the door, Marino asked again, "Who are you?"

"We are Palestinian Hezbollah. We have kidnapped your wife and children. We took them as soon as your wife drove her Cadillac SUV through the gate of your estate. If you want to see them again, you will do exactly as I say," the kidnapper said.

"What is this? What's going on? Who are you?" Marino demanded.

"Do I have to spell it out for you? We kidnapped your wife and children. You and your father-in-law are going to pay us a lot of money, or we will kill them, one by one."

As the kidnapper spoke, Marino walked to the door of his office and said, "Susan, call my house and get my wife on the line, please." He walked back behind his desk and told the kidnapper, "I just saw them a little while ago. How do I know you really have them?"

Marino heard movement at the other end, and the Arab voice shouted, "Talk to your husband!"

"Rick, they've got David and Sarah," came his wife's voice, followed by a muffled scream. She sounded frantic.

The kidnapper came back on the line. "Now do you believe me?"

Susan appeared in his doorway. "Your housekeeper said your wife left with the children about an hour ago." Marino knew his wife insisted on taking the kids to school herself, even though their private school offered transportation. She asked, "Is everything all right, sir?"

Marino appeared stunned for a moment then answered her, "Yes. Yes, fine. You can go. I need to finish this call." He asked the kidnapper, "What do you want from me?"

"Get all of the cash from the safe in the cabinet beneath the bookcase in your office. Put it all in a briefcase. Tell your secretary that an unexpected meeting came up and you will be out all day. Tell her to cancel all your other appointments. Take the briefcase with the money to your car, the Jaguar you drove this morning. There is a cell phone on the floor of your car now. Go to your father-in-law's bank. Leave the briefcase in the Jaguar, and go tell the Jew Ginsberg what has happened. You will receive instructions there on the cell phone.

"Do *not* make a note of the cell phone number or try to trace it. Do *not* call the police or the FBI. We will know, if you do. You have all been under surveillance for months. We know all about you and your normal routines. And we will know every move you make and everyone you contact. Your wife and children will be killed if you do not do everything we tell you."

Marino asked again, "Who are you? Why are you doing this?"

The kidnapper scoffed. "For the money, of course. Today is the Prophet Muhammad's birthday, Alhamdulillah-Allah be praised, and we are executing this action in his honor and for his greater glory. It will be ironic justice to take the Jew Ginsberg's Zionist money to fund Hezbollah. He's been gathering money from his Jew friends and sending millions to Israel for years. Now it is time for Palestinians to get some of his Jew money."

"How do I know you'll let my wife and children go, if I do what you say?"

"You don't know. But I promise you they will die if you *don't* do what we say. We are dedicated professionals, we are well trained, and we are prepared to die for intifada. We have been to America many times, and we know what we are doing. We have been planning this action for months, and we will kill your Jew wife and children, if you do not give us what we want. Enough talk. Now go!"

The call was ended. Marino wondered how they knew about his office safe. How much did they actually know about his family? Had they really all been under surveillance? Was he being watched now? He did as the kidnapper ordered. Marino appeared obviously distressed to Susan Russo, when he left the office.

Marino went to his car and found the cell phone. He then drove to his father-in-law's bank.

His father-in-law, Aron Ginsberg, was the president and CEO of the bank he and his wife, Magda, had founded thirty years ago. The bank had been originally named the Bikkurim Bank of Los Angeles and began by serving the large Jewish community of the greater Los Angeles area. Over the years, the bank had grown and expanded both its clientele and business activities, so much so that Ginsberg and the rest of the board members had felt it necessary to change the name to reflect its prominence. The bank was now called the First International Bank of Los Angeles. However, the bank continued to serve as a major conduit for financial transactions between the local Jewish community and financial interests in Israel and other countries with large Jewish populations, and for donations to charitable causes in Israel and elsewhere.

Margaret Milstein, Aron Ginsberg's personal secretary of thirty years, told Marino that Aron was in a board meeting in his conference room and had given her instructions he was not to be disturbed. Marino told her to interrupt the meeting and tell Ginsberg he was there on an urgent matter and would wait in Ginsberg's office. Marino appeared to be greatly agitated, according to Milstein.

Aron Ginsberg was surprised by his son-in-law's unscheduled visit– the first such visit in the ten years they had known each other.

"Richard, what an unexpected surprise," Ginsberg said as he walked into his office.

Marino told Ginsberg to close the door and then said, "Rachael and the children have been kidnapped."

Ginsberg instantly went ashen and looked ill.

"You'd better sit down." Marino helped Ginsberg make his way to a chair.

"What happened? What's going on?" Ginsberg asked.

"I got a call shortly after I got to my office this morning. It came from Rachael's cell phone. I thought it was her, but a man spoke, an Arab. I could tell from his accent. He said Rachael and the kids had been kidnapped. He said he was with the Palestinian Hezbollah intifada, and Rachel and the children would be killed if I didn't do what he wanted. He said he wants money and told me to come here."

"Did you try calling Rachael at home?"

"Yes, of course. The housekeeper said Rachael and the kids had left for school. The man put Rachael on the phone, and she screamed that they had her and the children."

"*Oy vey iz mir!*" Ginsberg cried.

"He told me he'd put a cell phone in my car and to come here and wait for instructions." Marino removed the phone from his coat pocket and showed it to Ginsberg.

"What do they want?" Ginsberg asked, still shaken.

"All he said was they wanted money for Palestine. He said to come here, tell you what'd happened, and wait for instructions. He didn't say anything else, just hung up."

As if on cue, the cell phone rang. There was no caller ID.

"Are you and Jew Ginsberg alone?" asked the same Arab voice.

"Yes," Marino answered.

"Put the phone on speaker, so Jew Ginsberg can hear."

"It's on speaker. Go ahead," Marino said.

"What do you want?" Ginsberg asked.

"Shut up and listen. Little Sarah is on the floor in the back seat of your wife's SUV. She is tied up and sedated. There are explosives strapped to her, and she is chained to the front seat. There are more explosives in the back of the SUV. You have four hours to complete the first part of your assignment. All of the explosives can be set off by cell phone, so don't even think about calling the police or FBI. And don't make any attempt to identify or try to trace the telephone number of the cell phone we gave you. We will know if you do. We are trained in espionage and military intelligence, and we are experts with explosives. The sedation will wear off just in time for the child to wake up and be blown to bits, if you don't do exactly as you are told. Do you understand everything I've told you so far?"

"Yes," Marino said.

"Yes," Ginsberg said, adding under his breath, "*Meshugene klovim.*"

But Ginsberg's comment was heard, and the Arab voice said, "You Zionist dogs have been killing Palestinian children for years. Now it is your turn to know how it feels to see your children suffer. If you don't do exactly as I say, without any more of your Zionist bullshit, there won't be enough of the girl left to fill a thimble, much less a coffin."

"Please, we'll do whatever you say," Marino said. "Just don't hurt them."

"You and Jew Ginsberg will put five million dollars in cash in briefcases. You will put nothing inside but the money—no marked bills, no tracking devices, no dye packs, nothing. Marino will take the money in his car to your wife's SUV. You will put the money in the back seat, along with the briefcase with the money you brought with you from your office. Jew Ginsberg will stay in his office, and Marino will start driving the SUV around Los Angeles. When we are certain you are not being followed, we will tell you where to drop the money and how to release your daughter. If we think you are being followed, we will set off the explosives, and you and your daughter will be blown to bits."

Marino asked, "But where is my wife's car? I don't know if we can get that much cash so quickly."

"Don't make the mistake of thinking we are stupid or that we don't know what we are doing. I told you, we know all about all of you and have been planning this for months. We know that Jew Ginsberg can get the money from his own bank in less than an hour. We will tell you where your wife's SUV is when you have the money ready. The sooner you get the money together and deliver it, the sooner little Sarah will be safe."

The kidnappers obviously knew Aron Ginsberg was the founder, president, and CEO of his bank. They were counting on him using his authority to bypass standard procedures to get the cash from his vault.

Ginsberg spoke up. "But people will see us. They'll know something is going on. Someone is bound to ask questions. Someone may call the police."

The kidnapper answered, "You must be careful. If anyone calls the police or FBI, your daughter and grandchildren will die. If anyone asks, you will say that Marino needs the cash immediately for his downtown project, and that is why he came to see you. Say all the paperwork is being prepared and everything is being handled properly. We will call you in two hours and give you further instructions. Never try to call us."

Marino and Ginsberg did as ordered, trying to be casual about it, but unable to avoid having to explain that they needed to go into the vault to get the cash as a down payment on Marino's downtown project. They said the consortium of major banks funding the multimillion-dollar project wanted cash up front as a sign of good faith, seed money, before proceeding with the financing for the project.

Exactly two hours after the first call, the kidnapper called and instructed Marino and Ginsberg to take the money to Marino's Jaguar.

Ginsberg was told to move his car from his reserved parking space nearest the door at the back of the bank and then return to his office. Marino was to take the cell phone, get in his car, and start driving, with additional instructions to follow.

Marino began to drive. After about fifteen minutes, the kidnapper called and gave him driving instructions intended to reveal if he was being surveilled by law enforcement. After another thirty minutes of confused driving all over Los Angeles, Marino was eventually directed to a long-term parking lot near LAX, the Los Angeles International Airport. There, he found his wife's SUV and saw his daughter under a bedsheet on the floor behind the front seat. Her hands and ankles were zip-tied, and she was chained to the front seat with what appeared to be an explosive device strapped to her chest. He was told to look under a blanket in the back cargo area, where he found another, much larger explosive device chained to the back of the second-row seatback. This device had two cell phones attached. There were also two five-gallon gas cans strapped on either side of the device.

"Leave the keys to your Jaguar and the parking receipt under the front seat. Put the briefcases with the money on the back seat of the SUV and get in. The keys are under the driver's seat. Start driving. We will tell you when to stop."

He drove randomly for fifteen minutes, before he was called and given additional driving directions, again designed to determine if he was being followed. He was finally directed to pull into a parking garage in Century City.

"There is a hood in the glove compartment. You will lie down on the floor and put the hood on. Someone will come and take the money. If you make any attempt to see who comes, you and little Sarah will be shot, and then the explosives will be detonated to destroy any possible evidence. After we have gone, we will call you. That is when you can remove the hood. You will start driving again. After we have counted the money, we will tell you where to go and how to remove the explosives from your daughter safely. Now, get on the floor and put the hood on."

Marino did as ordered and, fifteen minutes later, heard someone drive up, open the back door, and remove the briefcases with the money. He assumed there must have been at least two people, because he heard a car running and the briefcases being handed from one person to another. After another ten minutes, the cell phone rang. He was told to start driving again. After another twenty minutes of random driving, he was directed to a parking garage near his father-in-law's bank. After he parked, he received another call.

"Follow these instructions exactly or you will set off the explosives. There are five toggle switches on the bottom of the device strapped to your daughter. Flip the middle toggle marked with the number three to the other side, and the anti-tampering switch will be deactivated. Do not touch the other switches or you will detonate the device. There are scissors in the glove compartment. Cut the zip ties around your daughter's hands and then remove the vest from your daughter. The vest will still be chained to the front seat. Leave it that way, and cover it with the sheet. Take your daughter and go back to Jew Ginsberg's bank. Park in Jew Ginsberg's reserved parking space, and wait for more instructions in his office."

Marino did as ordered and removed the zip ties from Sarah's wrists and ankles. When he arrived at the bank, he parked in Ginsberg's space and carried the still-sedated Sarah up to his father-in-law's office. Everyone they passed just assumed the child was sleeping.

"Is Sarah all right?" Ginsberg asked.

"I think so," Marino answered.

Ginsberg took the child in his arms. "We should call a doctor."

"I don't know. Maybe we should wait until they call again. We can ask them. I don't want to do anything that might cause them to harm Rachael or David."

Ginsberg only nodded as he laid the child on the sofa.

Margaret Milstein walked in and asked, "Is everything all right, sir? Is there anything I can do?"

Ginsberg looked exasperated and answered incongruously, "Yes, yes, everything is fine. Please, leave us. We need to discuss something privately."

Milstein couldn't help but notice the worried looks on both men's faces and the fact that the child didn't appear to be sleeping normally. She shot Ginsberg a worried look of her own.

"We're fine. Please, leave us," Ginsberg repeated.

She walked out, certain everything was not fine.

Marino closed the door behind her and told Ginsberg about the explosives in Rachael's SUV. Just then, the kidnapper's cell phone rang, and Marino put it on speaker.

"You have carried out the first part of your duties well. Now for your next assignments. You will deliver ten million dollars in cash by Wednesday, 5:00 p.m., or little David will die. Then you will deliver twenty million dollars in cash by Friday, 5:00 p.m., or Rachael will die."

"I can't get that kind of cash that quickly," Marino said.

"Nor can I," Ginsberg said. "Please, give us more time."

"That is all the time you have. It is enough. You can sell all your securities and your wives' jewelry quickly, and you can sell your properties quickly, if you set the price low enough."

"That will ruin us. Bankrupt us," Ginsberg said.

"That's your problem, Jew. Get the money, or little David and Rachael will die horrible deaths, just like Palestinian wives and children have died because of Israel."

"How do we know they're still alive?" Marino asked.

"We will call you tomorrow morning with more instructions and let you speak with them then."

"What am I supposed to do about the car full of explosives in my parking lot? You can't expect me to just leave it there."

"That is exactly what you will do."

"It's not safe for my employees or customers. Surely you can understand that. You have to let us move it, so innocent people won't be in danger."

"There are no innocent people anymore. Not after the Israeli army began bombing Palestinian homes and refugee camps and killing women and children. If you try to move the car, we will immediately set off the explosives, and the building will be destroyed. Many people will die."

"You can't be that evil," Ginsberg said.

"I am tired of your hypocrisy, Jew. Thousands of innocent Palestinians have been killed without anyone caring. Your daughter's car packed with explosives is more insurance for us, in case the lives of your daughter and grandson aren't enough to get you to do what you are told. You can have one of the bank guards keep watch on the car, but don't tell anyone about the explosives or let anyone get in the car."

"I'll have to call my wife to come take care of Sarah," Ginsberg said as Marino nodded. "She'll demand to know what's going on."

"Yes, do that, Jew. But don't tell anyone else or you know what will happen. Now, get to work and get the rest of the money."

Marino and Ginsberg again did as ordered. Ginsberg called his wife and asked her to come to the bank immediately. When she arrived, they explained the situation and had her take the child home then have a doctor come to the house. Magda Ginsberg returned to the bank, leaving her granddaughter with a trusted housekeeper, and remained there with her husband and son-in-law for much of the following week.

The Ginsbergs and Marino discussed the situation. The kidnappers seemed to have thought out their plan very well and now had them entirely at their mercy. Marino seemed particularly intimidated by the kidnappers, repeating several times how much they knew about him and the Ginsbergs, and how well they had planned everything down to the last detail, operating with seeming military discipline. Marino made both Aron and Magda promise not to call the police or FBI. They agreed to do whatever the kidnappers wanted for the sakes of Rachael and David.

They immediately set to work, gathering and arranging for the sale of or loans against their stocks, bonds, jewelry, and artwork. Obtaining cash against their real estate and other less fungible assets was more difficult.

True to his word, the kidnapper called them Tuesday morning and allowed Rachael to speak to them, but only to tell them she and David were still alive. Marino and Ginsberg, not sure they'd be able to gather the full ten million in cash by Wednesday, also pleaded with the kidnapper to give them more time to come up with the money. The kidnapper refused and warned them to have the ten million ready by Wednesday afternoon or David would be killed. They somehow managed to have the money by the deadline.

The kidnapper called Wednesday afternoon with instructions. "Put the money in briefcases like before, and put the briefcases in the back seat of Jew Ginsberg's Cadillac. Marino will begin driving and wait for more instructions. Jew Ginsberg will make sure the parking space next to his daughter's SUV is clear, so Marino can park there when he returns. Now go!"

Again, they did as ordered, and Marino was directed around Los Angeles. After nearly an hour of seemingly aimless driving, Marino was directed to a different long-term parking lot near LAX. He found his Jaguar and, under a bedsheet on the floor in the back, the sedated David with another explosive device strapped to his chest. Marino was given the same instructions as before but warned not to touch the vest strapped on the child, because it was wired differently. He was also informed of another explosive device in the trunk and warned not to open it or the device would go off immediately.

Again, Marino was instructed to leave the Cadillac keys and parking receipt under the driver's seat and to put the briefcases with the money on the back seat of his Jaguar. He was again told the Jaguar keys were under the driver's seat and to start driving.

He drove randomly for fifteen minutes and was then given driving directions to again determine if he was being followed. He was finally directed to another parking garage in Century City, where he was told to put on the hood in the glove compartment and then lie down on the floor.

He put on the hood, lay down on the floor, and waited for the kidnappers to come for the briefcases. Again, he sensed there were at least two kidnappers transferring the money and possibly a third acting as driver. After the kidnappers left with the briefcases, Marino waited for their call before removing the hood and beginning to drive, while the kidnappers counted the money. After another hour, he was directed to a different parking garage near Ginsberg's bank and given instructions on how to deactivate the anti-tampering switch and remove the vest from David. This time, it was the second and fifth toggle switches that had to be moved, in that order. He was again told to leave the device in the car, under the sheet, and then return to the bank and park next to his wife's SUV.

When Marino returned to Ginsberg's office, the Ginsbergs wanted to use the automatic callback feature to call the kidnappers and ask for more time. They knew they couldn't come up with all the money the kidnappers wanted in cash by Friday.

But Marino refused, reminding them the kidnappers had warned them not to try to call them. They were able to ask for more time when the kidnapper called Thursday afternoon to make sure Marino and Ginsberg were working on getting the money. When they pleaded for more time, the kidnapper refused.

"That is all the time you have. We have our own deadline, and we must return to Palestine. We don't have any more time to give you."

"Look, we'll give you everything we can get, but we just can't come up with twenty million dollars in cash by tomorrow," Marino told him.

"Please, give us more time," Ginsberg begged.

"Why don't you take me, instead?" Marino offered. "I'll deliver everything we can come up with by Friday. When I deliver the money, just let Rachael go, and take me instead."

"That may be very brave of you, but it would be foolish for us. We already have the only hostage we need."

"I promise I won't cause you any trouble. We just need more time for the paperwork to go through," Marino said.

"We know you own property all over the United States. It isn't hard to sell property, if the price is right. And you can sell your yacht and other boats and your private jet quickly," the kidnapper replied.

Ginsberg and Marino answered at the same time. "You don't understand how the real estate market works," Ginsberg said, and Marino added, "Our properties don't belong to just us. Most of what we own belongs to partnerships. What we do own on our own is mortgaged and has liens that make it difficult to sell quickly. My boats and jet are mortgaged to the hilt. I couldn't get a penny out of them. We can show you the paperwork. If you've been planning this as well as you say you have, then you should know all this already."

"Enough! No more excuses. Just get to work and get the money. And don't try to call us. We will call you when we are ready to give you more instructions. And don't even think about calling the police or FBI. We will know if you do. The Jew woman will be killed, and the explosives will be detonated. And everyone will know you've already given fifteen million dollars to Hezbollah."

Friday afternoon came, and they had only about nineteen million dollars in cash. Even that had been difficult to come up with and had required the personal guarantees of both men to back the completion of their transactions. The Ginsbergs and Marino had quarreled several times, and their arguments had been overheard by family, friends, and business associates. By this time, more than a little suspicion had been raised at Marino's office and Ginsberg's bank. Both Ginsberg and Marino had had to fend off many questions from their business associates.

When the kidnapper called, they admitted they had only the nineteen million. "Give us until next Friday, and we'll have the twenty million," Marino told him.

"No. Bring what you have now," the kidnapper demanded.

"Will you let Rachael go?" Marino asked.

"No."

"Then what will you do? And how do we even know she's still alive?"

"If you don't bring what you have, she will be killed immediately. You are only buying her a few hours of life. We will have to talk this over with our superiors. We will decide what to do with her after we have counted the money."

"Will you let her go?" Ginsberg asked.

"What we will do is kill her, if you don't bring the money now. Put what you have in briefcases like before, and put the briefcases in Ginsberg's wife's Cadillac. Marino will drive and wait for instructions. Now go!"

"Why must it be my wife's Cadillac?" Ginsberg asked. "We have other cars here we can use."

The kidnapper got angry and yelled, "Don't argue with me! We know what we are doing. We know your Jew wife's Cadillac is already at the bank. Just put the money in it, and tell Marino to start driving."

Obviously, the kidnappers knew the Ginsbergs had matching Cadillacs—Aron's black, Magda's white. They wondered if they had been watching Magda, also.

With the briefcases in Magda's Cadillac, Marino began to drive and was ultimately directed back to long-term parking near LAX again, where he found Aron Ginsberg's black Cadillac. He followed instructions and found Rachael's purse under a bed sheet when he transferred the briefcases to the back seat. Marino was told another explosive device had been placed in the trunk and not to open it or the device would immediately detonate.

He followed instructions and drove Aron Ginsberg's Cadillac around Los Angeles until he was directed to a parking garage in Mid-City, where he was told to get on the floor, don the hood, and wait for the briefcases to be removed. Again, he sensed there were at least two kidnappers transferring the money and possibly a third acting as driver. After the kidnappers left with the briefcases, he waited for their call before removing the hood and beginning to drive, while the kidnappers counted the money.

After the money was counted, Marino was told to return to the bank, park next to his Jaguar, and wait for instructions in Ginsberg's office. They received a call as soon as Marino entered Ginsberg's office.

"You are a million dollars short," the kidnapper told them.

"We told you what we had. We gave you all we could come up with in such a short time," Ginsberg told the kidnapper.

"I'm sure knowing that will make your Jew princess feel better before we kill her," the kidnapper answered.

"We've done the best we can. Please let my daughter go," Ginsberg said.

"Give us more time," Marino asked.

"We should have killed her already. The longer we have to hold her, the more dangerous this becomes for us. Your delays have put us in more danger."

"Give us more time, and we'll get you more money," Ginsberg said.

The kidnapper was silent for a moment then said something to an accomplice in Arabic. He then asked, "How much more?"

Marino and Ginsberg stared at each other, and Ginsberg answered, "We can get you another ten million by next Friday. That's nine million more than you were asking for. Just give us time, and we'll get you the money."

There was silence at the other end.

"Did you hear me? Ten million dollars more, if you give us until next Friday," Ginsberg repeated.

"I will have to call you back. I cannot make this decision. We have to contact our superiors." Abruptly, the kidnapper ended the call. Thirty minutes later, he called back and said, "You have until next Tuesday noon to deliver ten million dollars."

"I said Friday. Give us until next Friday," Ginsberg said.

"You wanted more time, now you have it. Four more days to deliver ten million dollars. That should not be hard for the two of you."

Both Ginsberg and Marino said nothing.

The kidnapper broke the silence. "The price for your Jew princess has gone up because of this delay. You will deliver ten million by next Tuesday, or the Jew bitch will die."

"Let me speak to her," Ginsberg demanded. "I have to know she's still alive."

"Wait." After a moment, the kidnapper came back on the line and said, "I will call you back later," and then hung up.

The kidnapper called back an hour later, and they heard him say, "Here. Talk to your husband and father."

Rachael spoke, frantic and in obvious distress. "Daddy, Rick, please, do whatever they ask. Give them what they want. I can't take this anymore. Please—"

The phone was taken from her, and the kidnapper spoke as Rachael screamed in the background. "That will be the last you hear from her, if you don't deliver ten million dollars by next Tuesday."

"We'll get you the money," Marino said.

"We'll get you the money," Ginsberg affirmed.

"I will call you every day. The sooner you get us the money, the sooner we let her go. We are anxious to get out of the country as soon as possible. But if you don't have the full ten million by next Tuesday, you will never see her again. No more excuses. I told you, we have our orders and our own deadline, and we will have to detonate all of the explosives if we don't get the money by Tuesday."

"We'll do our best to get the money," Ginsberg said, trying to reassure the kidnapper.

"And don't even think about going to the police or FBI. You must know by now we know every move you make. The Jew bitch will die and the three cars full of explosives will be detonated, and the world will know you've given millions to Hezbollah. Don't try to call us. We will call you when we are ready."

Marino and Ginsberg were able to come up with the ten million by Tuesday morning. They had also been able to keep the kidnapping a secret and conceal the reason for their bizarre maneuverings. But they knew it would be only a matter of time before the major players in the Southern California financial and real estate markets began asking questions and federal bank examiners and investigators from the SEC and state department of real estate came calling. They'd have to explain the reason for their unusual and apparently ruinous activities. They hoped Rachael would be returned before then, or the kidnappers would undoubtedly assume that law enforcement had been brought in.

Late Tuesday morning, as they counted the money to be sure they had the ten million, the kidnapper called them. "Do you have the money?"

"Yes," Marino replied, "but we need to know she's still alive."

Marino and Ginsberg heard Rachael crying and the kidnapper say, "Talk to them," and then the sound of a face being slapped and, again, "Talk to them!"

Rachael continued crying and said only, "Daddy... Rick..."

The kidnapper came back on the line. "Marino will get in his Jaguar with the money and begin driving, same as before. He will get more instructions."

Marino began to drive and was ultimately directed to another long-term parking lot near LAX, where he found Magda Ginsberg's Cadillac. He didn't find Rachael in the car. Nevertheless, he followed instructions and transferred the briefcases to the Cadillac. He was told another explosive device had been placed in the trunk and not to open it or the device would immediately detonate.

He followed instructions and drove Magda's Cadillac around Los Angeles until he was directed to a parking garage downtown, where he was told to get on the floor, don the hood, and wait for the briefcases to be removed. Again, he sensed there were at least two kidnappers transferring the money and possibly a third acting as driver. After the kidnappers left with the briefcases, he waited for their call before removing the hood and beginning to drive, while the kidnappers counted the money.

After the money was counted, Marino was told to return to the bank, park between Aron Ginsberg's Cadillac and Rachael's SUV, and leave the cell phone in the back seat of the Cadillac. He was to wait for instructions in Ginsberg's office for picking up Rachael. They waited and waited for the kidnapper's call. When the kidnapper finally called Marino's cell phone, there was no caller ID, and he was obviously very angry. Marino immediately put the call on speaker.

"You were told not to call the FBI. You have made a very big mistake."

"*What*? None of us called the FBI. I don't know what you're talking about," Marino said, adding, "I swear to you, none of us called the FBI."

Aron Ginsberg also screamed that nobody called the FBI.

"Someone called the FBI. You will be sorry," the kidnapper threatened.

"Wait! *Wait!*" Ginsberg shouted. "Give us a chance to prove it to you. We'll do anything you ask. Give us more time, and we'll get you more money. None of us called the FBI. If somebody else called them, we won't tell them anything or cooperate with them. Richard, tell them!"

"Yes, we'll do anything. Just give us a chance to prove it to you," Marino said.

"We'll get you more money, anything... I'll set up a charity for Palestinian children. Whatever you want... *Anything!*" Ginsberg begged.

"I will need to talk to my superiors. I will call you back." The kidnapper ended the call.

They were exhausted and exasperated, angry at the kidnappers and one another. Ginsberg and Marino waited at the bank. Magda Ginsberg left, returning to the bank later that afternoon. The kidnappers never called back.

Chapter 3

Rachael Ginsberg-Marino – Deceased

This is how I remember it.

I remember mumbling, "Damn gate," to myself, because I didn't want the children to hear as I waited for the slow estate gate to open so we could leave. I was running late, as usual. If I really hurried, I'd just barely get the kids to school on time. But I knew I wouldn't be able to avoid another dirty look or maybe even another scolding from the parking lot security guard, who'd warned me before about arriving late, just as the school doors were about to be closed and locked. Security at the kids' private school is taken seriously, and the school was shut tight once classes began.

I had another doctor's appointment to get to immediately after dropping off the kids and was in too much of a hurry for that damn slow gate. I gunned the engine as soon as there was just enough room for my car to fit through the partially open gates. I didn't even bother to look for other cars coming—there never were any at this hour, anyway. As I turned sharply west, to my right, my tires squealed, and a car parked along the curb pulled out in front of me, forcing me to slam on the brakes to avoid a collision.

"What the fuck!" I shouted, unable to restrain myself this time. I was angry and honked the horn several times. Then, I lowered the window to yell at that idiot driver. "What the hell is the matter with you? Why don't you watch where you're going?"

Distracted by this jerk, I didn't notice the other car parked on the east side of the gate. It pulled in directly behind me. Then, several men wearing nylon masks under black-and-white keffiyehs and carrying guns jumped out of the two blocking cars and ran to my SUV.

One of the men came up to my window, pointed a gun at me, and said in a heavily accented Arabic voice, "Unlock the doors and get out of the car, or you will all be killed."

This was the first time anything like this had ever happened to me. I was too shocked to respond at first, and I just sat there, stunned. The man slammed his gun in my face and repeated his commands. The jolt of the gun on my cheek woke me up and brought me back to reality. I said, "Okay, okay. Don't hurt us." I unlocked the doors, and I was pulled out of my car, along with the children.

A van had pulled up beside us with its side door open, and the children and I were shoved inside. Then, we were blindfolded and gagged, and our hands and feet were tied with those plastic zip-tie thingies. From the sound of things, one of the kidnappers must have gotten into my SUV, and then all four cars started to move. It happened so fast. It couldn't have taken them more than a minute from the time they stopped us to when we were all going again.

David and I were quiet, but Sarah never stopped crying. They played loud Arabic music as they drove, and I couldn't tell where they were going. After what seemed like about forty-five minutes to an hour, they stopped and made me talk to Richard, but only for a second. Just to tell him what had happened. Then they started driving again. After another hour or so, we arrived at their destination.

I could tell we were indoors somewhere. They cut off the zip ties around our ankles and walked us around. The man removed the blindfolds, and I could see we were inside something like a very big tent, like one of those heavy military tents you see in the movies. The only other person in the room was the man who had hit me with his gun and spoken to me. He was still wearing the nylon mask under his keffiyeh.

That man said to me, calmly and matter-of-factly, "You are being held in a tent inside a room that was made to be soundproof, inside a noisy factory. No one can hear you, even if you scream. This tent has video cameras, and there are more cameras in the outer room. In the outer room and factory, there are armed guards who have guns with silencers. The guards have orders to shoot, if you try to escape. Do you understand what I have told you?"

I was still too frightened to respond at first. The man shouted, "*Do you understand?*"

"Yes," I answered, trembling. My whole body was shaking. I had never been so scared in my life.

Then the man said, "Your only hope of survival is to cooperate and not cause any problems. We do not want to hurt you, but we will kill you, if we have to."

I said to him, "I'll do whatever you say. We won't cause any problems, I promise. Please, just don't hurt my children."

"Good," the man said. "We are well-trained soldiers with the Palestinian intifada. Today is the Prophet Muhammad's birthday, and we are executing this action in his honor and for his greater glory. The Ginsbergs were chosen because you are Jews and your parents have been financial supporters of Israel for many years. This operation has been planned for months, down to the last detail. If you do not cause any problems, and if your parents and husband pay the ransom, you and the children will not be hurt. This is just a business transaction to obtain money for the intifada and to send a message to those who support Israel. We have no desire to kill women and children, and dead bodies are hard to get rid of. It is in everyone's best interest for you to cooperate and for your parents and husband to pay the ransom as soon as possible, so you can be released and we can return to Palestine."

"I promise to do whatever you want, just don't hurt my children," I repeated. "I won't try to escape, and I'll tell my parents and husband to do whatever you want. I promise I won't even cooperate with the police or tell them anything, if you don't harm my children."

This man was the only person who came into the tent and spoke to us. He always talked as if he had been coached and told exactly what to say. He always wore a nylon mask and keffiyeh. The tent was bare except for a mattress, a bucket, a picture of Yasser Arafat, the flag of Palestine, and another yellow flag with a green logo. There was a boom box in the outer room that played the same very loud Arabic music over and over.

I told David the man in the picture was Yasser Arafat, the leader of the Palestinian people, and the black, white, green, and red flag was the Palestinian flag. I didn't recognize the other flag, the yellow one with the green logo, but told David to remember it. I told him that Israel and Palestine were fighting a war and Grandpa and Grandma had sent money to Israel to help them win the war. I reminded him how, when we had visited Israel, we'd seen Palestinian people wearing the same kind of clothes as the men who kidnapped us.

I also told David the men who kidnapped us were from Palestine and were angry at us because Grandpa and Grandma had sent money to their enemies. That's why the kidnappers wanted to take Grandpa and Grandma's money now. I told David the man said that today was the birthday of the Prophet Muhammad, who was a very important person in their religion, like an important rabbi at our synagogue. I told David the music was the kind that Palestinian people liked. I remembered the video cameras at the gate to our estate and told David to remind Daddy about them.

Several times over the next week, the same man and another one took me for a drive to make a call to Daddy and Richard. The second man never spoke. Each time they took me to make a call, I was blindfolded and gagged, and my hands and feet were zip-tied. I think they used the same van and always covered me with a sheet. I think it was the same van because I could hear the side door slide open before they put me inside on the floor and covered me with the sheet. Then I could hear the van door slide shut.

They always drove for at least an hour, it seemed, and in a different direction each time, I think, before I was ordered to talk to Richard or Daddy. After each phone call, they gagged me again. And then they raped me before taking me back to their hideout. They raped me every time they took me out to make a call and before they killed me.

Chapter 4

The Thin Woman

To say it was a shocking surprise would be putting it mildly, I thought, as I drove to meet Magda Ginsberg for a midafternoon cocktail. She had called me, she would soon tell me, after leaving her husband and son-in-law at the bank to wait for the kidnappers to phone again, after the last ransom payment of ten million dollars had not resulted in Rachael's return.

She and I had first met when I was an undergrad at USC and her daughter, Rachael, introduced me to her parents. I hadn't spoken to Magda in over three years—the last time we'd run into each other was by accident, in the federal court building, when she had stopped by to see one of her sons, a judge, and I was there to testify before the grand jury. Other than that, I'd kept up with the Ginsbergs only by catching glimpses of them in posed photos on the society pages.

Magda had disapproved of Rachael's relationship with me, not because she disliked me, but because I had no place in her gilded plans for her daughter's future. She'd been afraid her daughter's youthful, foolish, and romantic ideas might cause her to defy Mommy and Daddy's wishes and run off with the son of wetbacks from the wrong side of the tracks. Magda had worked hard to achieve her place in society, and her family's social status was as precious to the matriarch as her soul.

Magda had called me a half-hour earlier and said she wanted me to meet her for drinks at La Belle Aurore on Rodeo Drive. She'd tried hard to sound casual about it, which instantly made me realize something catastrophic was happening—something concerning Rachael. Magda was one of those people who never asked if you were busy, never said *please*, and just took it for granted you welcomed the opportunity to serve her and would come when she called you. She said she might be a little late and told me to tell the maître d' to seat me at her table, if she wasn't there when I arrived.

Although I'd been to Rodeo Drive several times while on surveillance, this was my first time inside this elegant restaurant, and I was impressed. Each table had an orchid centerpiece surrounded by an abundance of swanky crystal, china, and silverware on white linen. A fresh-cut rose rested on each carefully folded napkin. I estimated that merely being seated at such a lavish table exceeded the government's daily meal allowance fourfold, so I gave up on the idea of submitting a voucher for reimbursement.

I told the maître d' whom I'd be meeting and was seated at a table by large picture windows. Magda arrived five minutes after me, carrying bags from Fendi and Dior. I stood when I saw her and waived politely; she remained expressionless. At about five-two and a hundred and five pounds, with silver hair and pasty white skin, she hadn't aged well; a colorless little bird, but one with sharp and deadly talons. I remained standing until the maître d' had seated her.

"Have you ordered?" she asked politely with a life-long smoker's gravelly voice that seemed much too heavy for her tiny frame. A waiter drew near.

"Just water."

"Well, we must get you something more substantial." She flashed an effortless plastic smile. "Double gin and tonic for me," she ordered and then threw her gaze at me, commanding me to follow.

"I'll stick with the water," I said. Magda saved the polite drinking for her society affairs. Despite her diminutive size, she could drink most men under the table, and I knew better than to try to out-drink her or even try to keep up. She hadn't removed her oversized dark glasses, but I knew she was taking in every minute detail with those piercing, predatory eyes.

"Your employer can't be that anachronistic. Surely, you're allowed one drink?"

"The water will be fine," I repeated, looking at the waiter, who nodded to Mrs. Ginsberg.

"Very good, madam," he said, as if I weren't even there, and then walked away.

Fully recalling Magda's demand for propriety under all circumstances, I knew better than to get right to the point, which was my own preference and standard method of operation. "So, I see you've done a little shopping this afternoon, Mrs. Ginsberg," I said with a false smile of my own as I took in her designer attire. When it came to wealth, Magda believed in the maxim, "If you've got it, flaunt it," and had made a virtue of ostentation.

Her phony smile widened. "Oh, please, we go back a long way. Much too long for such formalities. You must call me Magda."

"Very well. Thank you, Magda," I answered, proceeding with the game as I made note of each luxury item. And no one could help but notice her jewelry, of which she always wore plenty. Today was diamonds day, perhaps in consideration of this visit to Rodeo Drive, where she wouldn't allow herself to be outdone by any rich or famous celebrity who might come wandering by. She wore diamond earrings, a diamond necklace, a diamond brooch, and a diamond bracelet to match her diamond wedding and cocktail rings. Most Americans would welcome a retirement funded by that bracelet alone.

Just then, a pair of old crones, also sumptuously dressed and ornamented, came by the table. One with blue hair exclaimed, "Magda, is that you?"

"Judith, dear, how wonderful to see you!"

The silver-haired woman chimed in, "We thought it was you, but we weren't sure when we saw you sitting with this handsome young man."

Magda responded with the appropriate look of flustered surprise, tossing her hands in the air and waving her diamond bracelet and rings for emphasis. "Well, this has turned out to be a day of coincidences. First, I run across an old friend of my daughter's, whom we've known since they were in college but haven't seen in years, and now, here you are. *Gehivays!*"

I stood up and offered my "How-do-you-dos" to both ladies with a slight bow.

"Judith, Rhoda, this is Michael, one of Rachael's dearest old college friends. I just happened to run into him and persuaded him to have a quick drink, so we could catch up on all his accomplishments since college. Rachael will be so jealous when I tell her."

"I'm sure," Judith said with a suspicious stare as she looked me over with her own plastic smile.

"In what field are your accomplishments, Michael?" Rhoda asked, also suspicious.

"Michael is a broker. You know, those people down the street here," Magda replied before I could answer. "Imagine, all the times the three of us have been here shopping or for lunch, and I've never run into him before, even though his office is just down the street. I took it as a sign from above and insisted he have a drink with me."

Judith turned toward me. "And you recognized each other after all those years?"

I quickly interjected, "It was easy. Magda hasn't changed a bit," and the ladies laughed.

"Well, we'll let you two get back to your... catching up." Rhoda winked as she elbowed Judith away.

I took note of the sly wink. "So, you were out shopping?" I asked, returning to matters before the interruption.

"I needed to pick up a few things. Not for me, of course. These are gifts for friends. I'm *schlepping* these bags only because I needed to establish a reason for being in this area."

I raised an eyebrow, wondering about the subterfuge. "Of course. So, how have you been?"

"I've been well. Keeping busy with the grandchildren. I see them almost every day. Our charities and political commitments have kept us very busy, also. Of course, temple, and, since Richard is Catholic, we've become involved with some of his Catholic charities, as well." Despite her distaste for publicity, Magda assumed everyone was aware of her family's social standing and accomplishments—things she worked hard for and worked even harder to appear nonchalant about.

The waiter brought her drink and asked if she would like to order anything to eat.

"Give us a minute," she answered.

She lifted her glass, and I raised mine.

"*L'chaim.*" She took two large drinks. Back in college, Magda and Aron's Yiddish idioms had been a great source of laughter for Rachael and me.

"And how is Rachael?" I asked, unable to delay getting to the point any longer.

"Not yet," she replied, retaining command as she took another sip. "We'd better order a nosh." She began to look over the menu then glanced up. "Go ahead, order whatever you like. I'm buying."

I wanted to object but knew it was futile and would just make her angry. I also knew, the more she avoided getting to the point of this meeting, the more serious the matter had to be.

The plush French armchair was suddenly very uncomfortable, and I squirmed like an impatient child. She decided on what she wanted and looked to the waiter, who came over immediately. We gave him our orders, including another double gin and tonic for her. Then she began to talk mindlessly about inconsequential matters, and I had to admire her strength and composure.

I had known immediately upon meeting Magda all those years ago that she was the rock and brains of her clan. Magda and Aron Ginsberg's grandparents died in the concentration camps, as had many of their other relatives. Magda's experience as the daughter of Holocaust victims had made her tough as nails and just as sharp. She was also more conniving and devious than anyone I'd ever known. She'd have been right at home amid the palace intrigues of the royal houses of Europe during the Middle Ages, and she'd have come out on top—the intelligence and power behind the throne.

Aron Ginsberg, her husband and Rachael's father, though tall and handsome with a commanding presence, was no match for her. And he knew this, too. Although he was the front man, because the international business world still required a man to play the leading role, he was smart enough never to do anything important without first consulting her and obtaining her advice and consent.

Rachael also understood who wore the pants and wielded power in the family. But she was smart enough to play "Daddy's little girl" when she wanted something that went against Mommy's wishes. Rachael had been born fifteen years after the youngest of her two older brothers and had always been and always would be the family's precious baby girl. Aron Ginsberg could deny Rachael nothing, and Rachael's maneuverings to pit Daddy against Mommy were the only times Aron ever went against Magda's will. Magda knew this and considered her husband's ardent devotion to his daughter a weakness. One of many weaknesses she found in him and criticized him for—often in public.

From what little I'd been able to gather about Rick Marino, Rachael's husband, I doubted he understood or accepted Magda's dominance. As the only child of doting parents, he was raised to believe he was special, not only deserving but entitled to all the best the world had to offer. There was no denying he was handsome and smart. There was also no denying he had a monumental ego that was too large even for Mount Rushmore and a shameless self-confidence that some people, especially women, found appealing. He was too narcissistic to believe he wasn't always the smartest person in the room—any room, anywhere—and therefore certain to clash with Magda sooner or later. Epic disaster seemed as inevitable as the Trojan War three-thousand years ago.

As we finished our snack, Magda ordered another double, swilled it down, and sighed. "Walk me to my car," she said, with the calm assurance of one used to giving orders that would never be disobeyed. "I have to get back to the bank."

As soon as we were out of the restaurant, she reached into her handbag for a cigarette and turned to me to light it. I also lit one of my own. As we walked, Magda began, "You know, I always liked you."

"You had a funny way of showing it."

"Of all the boys she dated, you were the only one with any integrity. It was obvious. You wore your integrity on your sleeve. Still do. I guess the FBI is the perfect place for a Boy Scout like you." She smirked. She didn't mean this as a compliment.

"I didn't realize integrity was a bad thing."

"It can be for a mother. A mother with big plans for her daughter."

I already knew this.

"And you have brains. Even back then, you had that gleam in your eyes that only people with any brains have. I also liked you because you were the only boy who seemed to like Rachael for who she was and not just for her money. Was I wrong about that?"

"Perhaps not... But I would've liked her a lot more if she'd had the strength of character to get away from her overbearing parents."

"*Feh*! That's why I was also scared of you. Rachael liked you too much. I was sure she would do something foolish and run off with you. Maybe even have your child. That would have ruined her."

That got me angry. "It may have ruined *your* plans for her, but it wouldn't have ruined *her*."

"Same thing. No difference there," Magda retorted with a violent elitism that reminded me of the many reasons why I disliked her.

I shot back, "Well, you had nothing to worry about, unfortunately. You did too good a job raising her to be what *you* wanted her to be. By the time we parted ways, she was already lost. Caught up in your world of ostentatious garden parties, charity events, and political fundraising—all very shallow, superficial, and pretentious. The tiny spark of humanity left in her was completely snuffed out by Marino and his own avaricious character."

Magda Ginsberg shot me a look of hatred that would qualify as cruel and unusual punishment but said nothing. She hesitated a moment then said, "*Genug*! Now that we've gotten that out of the way, we can move on to why you're here."

I only nodded, again impressed by the woman's command.

We had reached her car, a brand-new white Cadillac that still bore dealer plates. "Get in," she said. "So we can talk."

Once we were inside, she opened her window a crack and continued, "Before I tell you what I have to tell you, you must promise you will never tell anyone what I'm about to tell you or that it came from me. Never, under any circumstances. Do you understand?"

"Yes."

"Then say it. I want you to say it out loud."

Knowing Magda's secret must be monumental and concern Rachael for her to go through all this, I had to agree. I looked her in the eyes and said, "I promise I will never tell anyone that what you are about to tell me came from you, under any circumstances."

"Okay, Boy Scout, I guess we'll see if that integrity is for real." She hesitated a moment, took a deep breath to steel herself, and then got straight to the point. "Rachael and the children were kidnapped last week. Monday morning, when she was taking them to school."

Magda instantly lost her facade of total and unyielding self-control. I was shocked and lost my composure, also. "Are— Are they all right?"

"The children are. I don't know about Rachael. We expected her to be released earlier today, after the last ransom payment, but she wasn't..." Magda went on to explain all that had happened in the last week—everything she'd been told by Aron and Richard, everything she'd observed and heard, and everything she'd surmised. Everything except the fact that the three cars parked behind the bank were full of explosives.

"So, the children are safe?"

"Yes. We've kept them at our house. We have armed guards there twenty-four hours a day now."

"Why are you telling me this now? Leaving aside the fact that you should've gone to the FBI immediately, why are you telling me this now?"

"Aron, Richard, and I agreed to do as the kidnappers demanded, because we believe they are who they say they are and seem to be as capable of carrying out their threats as they claim. Since you're not Jewish, you couldn't possibly understand the hatred Palestinians have for us. I'm coming to you now only because something doesn't seem right. My sixth sense tells me Rachael is in great danger and might not be released, if we don't do something."

I couldn't help fidgeting nervously in my seat, sliding around on the slippery new-car leather like a helpless swimmer adrift in a raging sea. "What is it that doesn't seem right?"

"I don't know. It just doesn't feel right. And there's just something about the way Richard has been acting that's so... So not in keeping with his usual way..."

"Do you think he's in league with the kidnappers?"

She took a drag off her cigarette, considering. "I don't know. He's put himself in danger every time he's gone to make the payments. Maybe he's just as wrung out as Aron and I are. After all, he did offer to trade places with Rachael." She stared off into space and shook her head. "I just don't know."

"What does your... sixth sense tell you, then?" I had to ask, because I knew she was too smart not to have definite reasons for coming to me now.

"Well, first of all, we only have Richard's story for how this whole thing started. And we only have his story of what's happened each time he's gone to make the payments. Maybe his offer to trade places with Rachael was just a ploy. And he's been insistent about doing everything exactly as the kidnappers want things done." She shifted toward me slightly, animated in her description of the past days' events.

"Aron and I talked about bringing in our lawyers or security consultants to handle the negotiations with the kidnappers. Richard wouldn't even consider it or any possible deviation from the kidnapper's demands. Of course, Aron, being the doting father, agreed with Richard about not doing anything that might anger the kidnappers and put Rachael in more danger. I wanted them to ask for proof Rachael wasn't being harmed—a photograph, *something*. But Richard wouldn't even agree to ask." She put her palms up and shook her head, frustrated.

"And then there was this. The kidnappers first said they had to be out of the country last week. It was all very rush-rush, but then they just changed their minds and agreed to stay longer, after Aron offered them more money... Also, there's this thing with the cell phone the kidnappers first gave Richard and wanted left in the car... We expected Rachael to be in my Cadillac when Richard delivered the money, like before, but she wasn't. It's like they're tying up all the loose ends before making their escape." She took a deep breath. "I'm afraid they won't let Rachael go, if they think she might be able to identify them. Or maybe they're just going to keep holding her and asking for more money... I don't know... I know I'm rambling, but there're too many things that just don't feel right to me..."

For the first time since I'd known her, Magda looked utterly frightened and lost, and I had to agree—those things did raise concerns. It suddenly hit me, how much effort it must be taking her to maintain her composure and not burst into tears. I swallowed dryly and opened my window. We had both been smoking one cigarette after another, and the car's interior was dense with smoke. I took a couple of long breaths as I stared out the window at nothing in particular. "Did you talk to Aron or Richard about any of this?"

"Yes, of course. We just end up yelling and angry at each other— *meshugaas!*" She scowled, shaking her head. "Things got worse from the very beginning, when we found out how heavily in debt Richard was. His financial structure is a house of cards. Everything he has is mortgaged or leveraged to the hilt. He was counting on his latest projects to make him solvent—the downtown development project and the one in Las Vegas. He's had very little money to contribute to the ransom demands, and now his financial situation is a total mess.

"Rachael spoke with Aron behind my back and convinced him to contribute a larger share of the initial expenses on her husband's downtown project, much more than I had agreed to. But, apparently, the only way Richard could convince the other banks to fund his project was with Aron's pledge of our bank's backing. Then, Aron gave Richard a ten-million-dollar line of credit on top of that."

"It sounds like Richard will lose everything because of this kidnapping... How could he be so heavily in debt? The newspapers made it seem like he was rolling in money. The downtown project was just going to make him richer, a multi-billionaire."

"That's what we all thought, because he's always played the big *macher*. But he got in over his head on the Las Vegas project. He's always had several projects going at once—nothing unusual about that for a businessman like Richard. He's been working on that casino, hotel, and resort project off the Vegas Strip for a couple of years now and gone up there several times a month, this year. He mortgaged or leveraged everything he had, because he wanted to be *balabos*—the big man and sole owner of that project. But apparently, that project is shaky also, and he may lose everything he's put into it. Even if he doesn't lose it, he'll have to bring in other investors now and share control of it."

I shook my head. "Well, what do you want me to do?"

"I want you to go talk to Aron and Richard at the bank," she said, pointing a manicured and bejeweled finger at me for emphasis and making it a command. "Tell them the FBI got an anonymous tip about a kidnapping and you're there to find out if it's true. Rachael should have been released after Richard dropped off the ten million dollars. I can't wait any longer to do something, and I don't want anything to go wrong. I want to be sure she's returned safely."

"I'll need the cell phone numbers. And a forensic team will need to get into the cars parked at the bank."

Magda shook her head. "You'll have to get the phone numbers from Aron and Richard. And you have to wait until Rachael is released before you go into the cars."

"Don't you have the phone numbers?"

"What, am I an idiot? Of course, I do. But if you show up with the numbers already, everyone will know where you got them from. Since the kidnappers and I are the only other people besides Aron and Richard who have the numbers, they'll all know it was me who gave them to you."

"No one will know for sure—"

"I can't take that chance. There's more going on here than you know or need to know. No one must ever know I called you and brought in the FBI."

"Then tell me everything that's going on. You can't keep me in the dark and expect me to come to the rescue."

"You'll have to get the rest from Aron and Richard."

I shook my head again, unable to understand Magda's motivations, but knowing the subject of phone numbers was closed. Moving on, I asked, "Why don't you want a forensic team to get into the cars?"

"They can get in, but not yet. Just talk to Aron and Richard first. And when you get to work on the kidnapping, just stick to the kidnapping. Don't get sidetracked into anything else."

I turned to look out the window again, to think for a second. I inhaled a deep breath of parking-garage carbon monoxide, and the odd thought that came to mind was how the new-car smell wouldn't last very long in this car, the way Magda smoked. "You're obviously not telling me everything. You're making this very difficult. More difficult than it needs to be. And your delay coming forward has made it more dangerous for Rachael. I don't understand why you would do this with your daughter's life at stake."

"What, you think I don't know what's at stake? Like I said, there's more going on here than you could ever imagine. Things that could be dangerous for all of us. Things you and nobody else need to know. Just go talk to Aron and Richard already!"

"Well, I can't go to them directly, myself. I'll have to report this to the people who handle kidnapping cases now. I've changed jobs, and I don't work kidnapping cases anymore. I'm sure they'll let me go along with the agent to speak with Aron and Richard, but I can't just show up at the bank on my own."

"You promised you wouldn't tell anyone about me," Magda reminded me.

"I'll keep my promise. I won't tell anyone who provided the information, but I'll have to report the facts of the alleged kidnappings. I'll say the information came from an anonymous source who called me. That should keep you out of it."

Magda nodded her assent. After a moment of reflection, I asked, "Why did you call me? You could've contacted the FBI anonymously yourself."

"I wanted you involved in this. Someone I could trust to have Rachael's safety and best interests at heart, above everything else. Someone who would do as I say, stick to the kidnapping, and ignore anything else that might sidetrack the investigation. I didn't want this to be just another case to the FBI."

"What makes you think I'd want to get involved? I haven't seen you in years. How could you be sure I'd even come to meet with you today?"

"So, what's wrong with you? Why not you, *eh*?" She shrugged, raising her palms in that gesture Rachael had frequently imitated just to make me laugh. Then the corners of her mouth lifted into a wicked half-smile. "The problem with you honest people is you're very bad liars and no good at deception... About six months ago, Rachael and Richard were having problems—again, for the twentieth time. *Oy vey.* Richard was flying to Vegas every week and spending several nights there at a time. He claimed he was working on his project, but Rachael suspected he was having an affair, which he was, of course. After all, Vegas was made for *khamer-eyzls* and their *shiksas.*

"I told Aron to have a man-to-man talk with Richard and remind him of his priorities. With those two, it was more of a *pisher*-to-*pisher* talk, but it worked to keep Richard at home most nights—for a while. But then he started up again, and Rachael kicked him out of the house and was going to file for divorce. I decided to have a talk with Richard myself. I told him the bank would pull out of his downtown L.A. project and end his credit line, if he didn't end his affair and cut back on his trips to Vegas. He knew I meant it and that a divorce would ruin him. So, he agreed to end the affair and be a good little boy. But, when things were still up in the air, and before he talked to Rachael to patch things up, Rachael began behaving like a *khamer*, herself.

"About four months ago, when I went to see the children one evening, Rachael was getting ready to go out—just a girl's night out with her girlfriends, she said. But she was acting strangely and *oysgeputst*—all dressed up like a tart. She had arranged for a sitter to spend the night with the children and called for a taxi, because she said she and her friends would be drinking and she didn't want to drive. *Ha!* Like I'm a *schnook* and didn't know what she was up to. I knew something was going on, so I decided to stay with the children myself that night. I was there the next morning when she returned, wearing the same clothes she'd gone out in the night before—all wrinkled, of course. And I saw who brought her home. I saw how that man kissed her and how she looked at him after he kissed her. It was the same man who had scared me all those years before. And I knew I had to get her away from him again."

I looked at Magda without trying to hide my contempt but said nothing.

"I made two phone calls that morning. I called my travel agent and had him book a flight and hotel room in Acapulco for Rachael and Richard. First-class seats and the honeymoon suite. Then I called Richard and told him he and Rachael had better be in that hotel room that night or he was finished."

We stared at each other in thick silence for a few moments, then Magda continued sharply, "The way you kissed her and looked at her that morning is why I know you'll do everything possible to get her back safely."

So, the old bird knew about Rachael and me. I wondered what else she knew about us.

"Just tell me one thing," she demanded. "You are a handsome young man, as my nosey friend said earlier. With your looks and brains, I imagine you could have just about any woman you wanted. So why has my Rachael been so important to you all these years?"

I was filled with too many emotions to answer such a question, but Magda pressed me. "She's my daughter, and I love her, but even I have to admit there's nothing particularly exceptional about her. There are a lot of other pretty little rich girls around for you to play with. Why did you have to keep coming back to my Rachael? What is it about her you find so compelling?"

"You wouldn't understand."

"You'd be surprised at what I can understand. Try me," Magda insisted.

I looked at her and turned away. I wanted to give her an answer I was sure she wouldn't understand. "Every time she looks at me… It makes me feel like my pants are too tight."

Magda giggled like a twelve-year-old girl, and I *was* surprised. I didn't think she had that kind of giggle in her—ever.

"I think it's sad her own mother doesn't see anything exceptional in her. I've always thought *everything* about her was exceptional."

"*Oh, my,*" Magda responded.

Chapter 5

Rachael and Me

As I drove back to the office, I continued to wonder how much Magda Ginsberg knew about Rachael and me. Did she know I'd fallen hopelessly in love with her the moment I first saw her?

I remember it as if it had happened this morning. I'd survived the war, physically anyway, and had my scholarship reinstated. It was between classes, early in the fall semester. I was a junior, walking alone to my next class, and she was a frosh, walking with two of her friends. I know most guys would've thought her two friends were better looking than Rachael, but, for some reason, she just stood out from the crowd for me—she always did.

I was pretty bold back then when it came to meeting girls, and I just went up to her and started talking. Some writer who had also experienced battle said that, once you've charged into machine-gun fire, nothing is ever the same again. I knew what he meant, so the possibility of being shot down in public by an eighteen-year-old co-ed was nothing to be scared of. Rachael did ask me later why I'd chosen her, when most guys always wanted to talk to the other girls. I walked with them to their class and spoke only to her, ignoring her friends. I asked to meet her for lunch, and she accepted.

After that, I saw her as often as she'd let me. She was reluctant at first. She didn't want to talk much about herself. It wasn't until later that she told me she came from a very wealthy family and was afraid guys were interested in her only because she was rich. I didn't connect her name with the affluent Ginsbergs who donated so much money to the university and were involved with many alumni functions. It took me a long time to convince her I thought she was the most beautiful woman I'd ever seen and the most wonderful person I'd ever known.

We did a lot together, but never anything I couldn't afford to pay for: movies, take-out Chinese or pizza, the beach, or hiking in the local mountains. We did become lovers, but she didn't want us to get serious. We also became good friends. We talked about anything and everything for hours. She told me about her parents and grandparents, whom she admired as well as loved, and all they'd had to overcome to achieve the American Dream and their place in society. She always had me rolling on the floor with laughter when she imitated the Yiddish of her parents or other relatives. She often said their little idioms were just affectations or a show they put on because it was good for business, but she also believed they had an honest desire to honor their heritage and preserve "the old ways." I made her laugh when I thickened my Mexican accent and told her how the other half lived. I loved just being with her. I was never happier than when I could get her to forget about her family obligations, and we'd talk about a possible future together. Sometimes, we even made elaborate plans for a life that was just about us.

The first time I went to her house—the Ginsberg estate in Holmby Hills—was when I was invited for a fancy luncheon, along with a few dozen other scholarship students. Rachael introduced me to her parents, and I could tell Magda wasn't happy with the way Rachael acted during that introduction. I think she knew there was something more than friendship between us. Magda was even less happy when I returned, a few months later, for an awards reception the Ginsbergs hosted and was very unhappy on the several occasions Rachael brought me home for no apparent reason at all. I didn't enjoy being where I knew I wasn't wanted; I knew I didn't fit in and went only because Rachael wanted me there.

I went to law school only because I didn't know what else to do with myself and because I thought it might improve my chances with Rachael, if I became an attorney. I would've preferred grad school in philosophy or literature, but there was no possibility of a future with her, if I went the academic route. Going to USC School of Law also kept me close to her. I did enjoy law school, but one summer's clerking at a big firm was enough for me to realize I could never be a big-money corporate lawyer. I quickly learned that a license to practice law was a license to suborn perjury and fraud for those seeking fame and fortune. Devoting one's energy to accumulating wealth and achieving social status seemed like a waste of life to me. I didn't fight my way out of the barrio by way of Afghanistan just to drive a Porsche and dress in Pierre Cardin.

I hadn't at that point figured out why I'd fought my way out of the barrio, but I knew there had to be more to life than that. Nevertheless, I like to finish what I start, so I graduated law school and passed the bar exam, even though I never really envisioned myself practicing law. I signed up with the FBI when I couldn't think of anything else to do with myself.

Despite our differences, I knew from that first meeting that Rachael was the one for me. She often said she loved me, too, but was always honest and told me not to get serious about her. She said she could never marry me: her parents would never allow it, and she wouldn't go against their wishes. They had sacrificed so much and devoted their entire lives to providing the best for their children, and they had grand plans for her that didn't include her marrying the son of wetbacks from some south-of-the-tracks barrio. She was their princess, and they would see to it she married a prince, at the very least. We'd seen *The Great Gatsby* together, and as she reminded me a few times after that, "Rich girls don't marry poor boys." She knew me well and added, "Especially poor boys who are more interested in ideas than money and who think they can change the world."

After I started law school, we didn't see each other as often. Sure, there were other women in my life, but none had that magic I always felt with Rachael. I knew I was special to her, too, despite her inability to defy her parents and make her own choices. Over the next few years, we stayed in touch and got together when she wanted to. I could never refuse her call.

After she graduated, when I heard she'd gotten engaged, I was heartbroken. It was difficult to imagine her married to anyone but me. I was disappointed in her unwillingness to disobey her parents and forge her own life. Her fiancé, Richard Marino, was twelve years older than her, already a billionaire, and likely to make more. We got together a few times after her engagement. Of course, I hoped our time together would cause her to wake up and break it off. But I knew it was difficult for any woman not to be impressed by someone like Marino, someone who could fulfill her parents' dreams for her, if not her own.

The Ginsberg-Marino wedding was such a lavish event that the *Times* devoted an entire page to it. The newspaper listed the most notable of the hundreds of relatives, celebrities, and other guests who attended, detailing their occupations, positions, ranks, titles, awards, and film credits—making it clear this wasn't merely a high-society union, but a lucrative merger and acquisition both families would benefit from. One of the more cynical guests, who didn't wish to be identified, remarked that there hadn't been such a potentially profitable marriage since the Hapsburgs went out of business.

After the wedding, I made it a point to avoid anything or any place where I might run into her. She had made her choice, and I didn't want to do anything that might cause a problem for her, especially since she was already a mother. I cared enough for her to give her space and the best chance for happiness—her idea of happiness—even though I thought it shallow.

Two years into the marriage, we did meet again. One look, and it was clear our feelings were still there. Marino had already started running around with other women, and she was hurting. Her parents wanted more grandchildren, and she was anxious to please them, but Marino's behavior didn't bode well for another child.

I was too weak or maybe too selfish to be just a friend and offer her only a shoulder to cry on. I knew it was wrong to get involved with a married woman, but sometimes you just can't do the right thing. We continued seeing each other whenever she needed me. I just couldn't get over her. Don't bother asking me why. Yes, she had all the qualities that any man would find desirable, and to such a degree that overlooking any shortcomings was easy. But as anyone who's ever been desperately in love understands, none of that really matters. Whether the beloved is a cover girl or carnival freak, when Cupid's arrow strikes, all reason is lost, and the reasons for the attraction are irrelevant. My nights were filled with dreams of Rachael, and my days preoccupied with thoughts of her. Like the song says, "Comes love, nothing can be done."

Chapter 6

Rachael Ginsberg-Marino – Deceased II

I really did love you, Mig. I just couldn't give you what you wanted. I couldn't be your wife. And you could never understand what it's like to be the daughter of people like my parents. I was their princess, and they had such great hopes and plans for me.

I know you think what they wanted for me was frivolous and superficial, but I really believed they wanted what was best for me. They had been through so much and had given me so much—I couldn't disappoint them. I felt I had to do what I could to live up to their hopes and expectations. My brothers were already so successful in their own careers, and they each had plans to do even more with their lives. They were really good to me growing up, so I wanted to do whatever I could for them, too. And it wasn't just my parents and brothers, but my whole extended family. My aunts and uncles and cousins and nieces and nephews and close family friends—they all seemed to expect so much from me. I know it sounds silly, but I felt like I was a princess in feudal times and had to do what they wanted for the good of the kingdom and everyone in it.

When Rick came around, it was hard not to be impressed and thrilled. He was already so successful, and everyone admired him. My parents were especially excited and gratified by his interest in me, even though he wasn't Jewish. He introduced me to all his business and society friends, and he and my parents talked about doing business together. You have to remember, I was just out of college, and here was this charming billionaire who seemed to be enraptured by me—just little me—for no reason I could understand. Other women, beautiful and sophisticated, threw themselves at him, but he chose me. It really was like something out of a fairy tale.

My parents encouraged him and me. The fact that my parents did so, even though he wasn't Jewish, meant a lot. And, he could be very endearing, even overwhelming, when he wanted to be. We flew up to North Beach in San Francisco in his private jet just for pizza one day. He took me to New York to see a Broadway play, and we stayed at the Ritz-Carlton across from Central Park. We went on a whim, and I didn't have the right clothes, so he bought me everything I wanted at Saks Fifth Avenue. Then he took me to Tiffany's. It's hard for a girl not to be impressed by all that, not to feel extremely special.

But I really did love you, Mig. You were the only real love of my life. And you were my friend—the only person I could really talk to about anything. It was all so crazy—life!

Chapter 7

The Official Investigation Begins

As I got back to the federal building, I thought about what Magda Ginsberg had told me and what I needed to do with that information. I went to my desk for a few minutes to establish my presence in the office and come up with the story I'd have to tell to get a kidnapping investigation started. I decided the simplest way was the best. I'd call my former partner, Bart Keyes, and tell him I had received an anonymous call about a kidnapping. Since I was now on a Russian counterintelligence squad, I couldn't work kidnapping cases anymore and would have to let the Major Crimes squad handle it. This was okay with me, since Bart was also my best friend and the best agent in the Bureau, as far as I was concerned, and I knew he'd handle the kidnapping and let me remain involved in the investigation.

I had worked with Bart for most of my time in the Bureau. He was, in real life, everything John Wayne portrayed in the movies: dedicated and fearless; the personification of honor and integrity. Tall and brawny with a palpable ferocity, Bart was a guy few men would dare challenge one-on-one. Like the Duke, he wasn't the most handsome of men, but he had a magnetic attraction that drew women to him, and there was always one coming by his desk just to chat.

He'd already been in the Bureau nearly twenty years when I came in and was known and respected throughout the FBI. He was always among the first agents called to handle a difficult or dangerous assignment. And he was affectionately and perhaps appropriately called "Black Bart," because of his often gruff and sometimes violent temperament. Like the legendary outlaw, Bart didn't take crap from anyone and wouldn't hesitate to get in someone's face, even if they were holding a gun. What I liked best about Bart was, despite his impeccable sense of integrity, he was practical and down-to-earth in his work, never allowing formalities or politeness to stand in the way of getting the job done.

Fortunately for me, Bart and I got along from the day we met. In time, I came to see he deserved his formidable reputation, but he never put on airs, just went about his work with humility and a lot of humor. Although he was looked to for leadership, he never acted like anyone's boss, except when the situation required him to take command. Perhaps most telling, he had a self-effacing sense of humor and didn't mind being made the butt of an occasional joke.

I'd been on a bank fraud squad since arriving in Los Angeles out of New Agent's Training at the FBI Academy in Quantico, Virginia. Management thought my law school background would be an asset to fraud investigations. The work was challenging but didn't provide much action for a young, first-office agent and combat veteran. I was surprised to be offered a transfer to the Major Crimes squad shortly after arriving in L.A., but it came about because of what had happened on a couple of cases I'd helped out with—cases with moments that induced the same mind-racing terror as combat.

Anxious for some action, I had volunteered to help out on an extortion case. My glamorous assignment was to provide cover from inside a dumpster in an alley where the payment drop was to be made. Things didn't go as planned—they rarely do. When it was over, although I didn't do anything that any other agent wouldn't have done, it was said I had saved Bart's life and made an arrest in the process.

A few weeks later, I volunteered to help on another case, a child kidnapping this time. There was an exchange of gunfire, and Bart and I each shot a suspect and wounded another. Although I didn't see it that way, Bart said I had put myself in danger by drawing fire and giving him the chance to grab the child and run for cover. Although, again, I didn't do anything any other agent wouldn't have done, it was said I'd saved Bart's life a second time, along with the kidnapped child's.

Shortly after that, Bart took me to meet his supervisor, Jim Nulty, an old-timer and highly respected Bureau veteran himself. Nulty was an intimidating presence at six foot, six inches and built like an NFL middle linebacker. At fifty-five, he still sported his Marine Corps crew cut. His office was filled with plaques, trophies, and citations commemorating his achievements, and no one doubted his blood was red, white, and blue.

I still remember that initial conversation.

*****

"Bart says you have potential and have shown good judgment in those cases you've helped us out on," Nulty began. "It couldn't have anything to do with your college or law school background, although Bart says you're quite the scholar. He thinks it has more to do with your military experience. But he says you never talk about what you did in the Army, except to say you were in Afghanistan. I'd like to know a little more about it, before I offer you a job."

"I was just another grunt," I answered.

"I don't think so. Your Bureau file has a summary of your military record from your background investigation. It says you saw combat and were awarded a Purple Heart with Oak Leaf Clusters and a Bronze Star. They don't just give those away at the PX. I've seen those burn scars on your arms, even though you try to hide them with long sleeves, and that scar by your left eye. Did you get those in combat?"

"I don't remember. The long sleeves just cut down on the stares and the questions."

"Well, I know some guys don't like to talk about it, so I won't press you on it. Bart says I wouldn't get very far if I tried."

"Thanks."

"What really bothers me is your file also says you had a double major in college, philosophy and psychology. Why would anyone do that?"

"I was hoping to find out what the smart people had to say about things."

"What did you find out?" Nulty asked.

"Not much. I still know nothing about anything. I just got more confused."

"I doubt it. It's obvious you're smart and well-educated."

Bart turned to me and chimed in. "Yeah, we expect your kind to be hard-working and brave. You know, mowing lawns and picking grapes fifteen hours a day and throwing yourselves on hand grenades to save the rest of the troops in the foxhole." He then said to Nulty, "But this one's got a brain, too. He can be a pain in the ass, with all those big words and quotations he's always throwing around."

"Well, I won't hold it against you, as long as you do your job," Nulty said.

"I try not to let my education get in the way. I can still speak plain English when I have to."

"Good… Anyway, I decide who gets on the Major Crimes squad. That was the deal I made with the boss when I agreed to take over the squad. I got rid of the deadwood, kept who I wanted, and brought in a few more of the best agents in the Division. I'm not ashamed to say I live and breathe for the Bureau, and Major Crimes is *my* baby. All the agents on Major Crimes had at least ten years in the Bureau before coming on the squad, so I take it for granted that agents on this squad know what they're doing, and I don't try to tell them how to do their job. But I do expect one-hundred percent from every agent every day, and that's twenty-four seven. Do you have a problem with that?"

"No, sir."

"Right, then… Well, Bart says you're not afraid to fight above your weight class and can lick anybody twice your size. Since he's getting slow on his feet after twenty years in the Bureau—"

"Now wait a minute. I resemble that remark," Bart interjected.

"…But he's still the best investigator I've ever known. So, how'd you like to transfer onto the squad? He can teach you what he knows, and you can keep an eye on him."

*****

The opportunity to work major crimes and work with Bart was too good to pass up, and I jumped at the chance. You don't need a degree in psychology to suspect, as an only child of a single mother, I was in need of a father figure or big brother, but that doesn't explain everything. Over the years, Bart and I worked together almost every day and became close friends. We came to know each other well—well enough to know when to back off and give each other space, even when it meant letting the other do something stupid. I learned a lot from him and had seen him put his life in danger to protect victims and witnesses many times. His dedication and bravery were inspiring. If a grown man is allowed to have a hero, Bart was mine. Over the years, I also came to see that the transfer to the Major Crimes squad so early in my career and having Bart as a mentor had another significant advantage: it spared me from the usual demeaning assignments that most Latino and Black agents are required to suffer through just to be allowed a place at the Bureau table. I was rarely relegated to door guard, note-taker, translator, or go-fer, thanks to Bart.

At the time of the Ginsberg-Marino kidnapping, Bart was already eligible to retire and had made it known he would do so soon. He'd reach mandatory retirement age in just over a year, but our new squad supervisor was difficult to tolerate, and we'd both decided to leave as soon as possible.

In the past, the Bureau had been wise enough to appoint an experienced field agent to supervise the Major Crimes squad. But this time, the Bureau had appointed someone whose only qualification was his ability to kiss up to the right mentor at Headquarters. Nelson Rolfe was a relatively young field supervisor, fresh out of Headquarters, who saw himself on the fast track up the Bureau hierarchy. He was a by-the-book manager, a stickler for protocol, and, since he was on his way up the Bureau ladder, wouldn't risk his next promotion on any deviation from Bureau policy or procedure. In addition to his ambition and egomania, he was particularly unlikable because he was one of those supervisors who pretended to be just one of the guys when he was actually a snake looking for anything to use against an agent. He was the reason for Bart's desire to retire and my desire for a transfer. Like most agents, Bart and I were disgusted by the Bureau's dysfunctional management and promotion system, which had nothing to do with merit.

A rare opening came up on the Russian counterintelligence squad, and I decided to take that opportunity. I wanted a change, and since Bart was leaving soon anyway, I put in for that transfer and the chance to work something completely different. I got the transfer, had a week to settle in and learn the basic procedures, and then went back to Quantico for the month-long Introduction to Foreign Counterintelligence course that all agents working counterintelligence are required to take when they begin working FCI. I received the call from Magda Ginsberg my first week back.

*****

Having decided to pass the information along to Bart, I tried calling him at his desk and then his cell phone and struck out both times. I called Edith Leeds, the squad secretary, and asked if she knew where I could reach him. Edith said Bart was in Rolfe's office, taking care of his file review and a new case that had just come up. I hesitated a moment. I was reluctant to go to Bart and talk about the kidnapping with Rolfe around, but a kidnapping is a kidnapping, and if Rachael's life was in danger, I had to get the investigation going as quickly as possible. I worked out the story I'd tell and went to see Rolfe and Bart.

I stood in the doorway of Rolfe's office and asked, "Is this a private party, or can I come in?"

Bart was standing behind Rolfe, who was seated at his desk, and they were both staring intently at the computer screen on Rolfe's desk. "Mig, come in," Rolfe answered. "You're just the man I wanted to see. I'm short-handed this week and was gonna call your supervisor to ask if I could borrow you for a few hours. I'm hoping to get you to help Bart out on a possible kidnapping that just came up. If the information we got is accurate, I'd like to have you two make the initial contact with the victim's family. The *alleged* victim, I should say, since we don't know if there's anything to this, yet."

"It looks like you already have the best agent in the Bureau working on it, but I'm ready to help. Did you get a kidnapping call, too?" I asked, genuinely surprised.

"Yeah, why? What do you mean, *too*? Have you got something?" Bart was always quick to pick up on the slightest things.

"Yeah, I just got a call about a possible kidnapping. That's why I came down here."

"Who called you?" Bart asked.

"It was an anonymous caller who wouldn't give his name."

"Who's your victim?" Rolfe asked.

"I was told it was Rachael Marino, the wife of Richard Marino, the big real estate developer, and their two kids. The caller said the two kids had been returned after ransoms were paid, but the wife is still being held. What do you have?"

"All we got was that a woman named Ginsberg had been kidnapped. The call came in to the duty desk. The caller said she's the daughter of some rich banker," Rolfe said. "Bart called the bank examiner's office to find out if there's a Ginsberg who owns or runs a bank in the L.A. area, and we're waiting for them to get back to us. Bart and I were just going over what we could pull out of the computer on anybody named Ginsberg and hoping to get lucky."

"That sounds right," I said. "Rachael Marino is actually Rachael Ginsberg-Marino, and her father owns and runs the First International Bank of L.A. What else did your source say?"

"How do you know so much about these people?" Rolfe asked.

"I knew Rachael Marino when she was Rachael Ginsberg, an undergrad at USC, where I went to school. They're a very wealthy family who've donated millions to the school and other charities. Anybody familiar with the real estate business in L.A. knows about Richard Marino."

"What did your caller sound like?" Rolfe asked.

"Couldn't tell much—he was covering the mouthpiece, I think... Maybe white, male, no accent, could've been anywhere between twenty and sixty. Does it sound like your caller?"

"No," Bart answered. "The duty agent said it was a white female, no accent. And she sounded scared. She just said a woman named Ginsberg had been kidnapped, and if we checked on the name, we'd know who she was. The duty agent tried to get more information, but the caller hung up. Why do you think your guy called you?"

"I asked him the same thing. He said he knew from some old newspaper article that I worked kidnapping cases. I guess he didn't know I went over to the Dark Side and work counterintelligence now."

"What do you think?" Rolfe asked Bart.

"Let's go to the bank." Then Bart asked me, "Do you know who the father is?"

"Yeah. Aron Ginsberg is his name, if I recall correctly. The bank's not far from here, over on Olympic, just past Century City."

"And where's Marino's office?" Bart asked.

"According to the papers, he bought a building downtown a few years ago and renovated it. His office is the penthouse suite in the building."

"Let's try the bank first and then the office, if we don't get anywhere at the bank," Bart suggested.

"You're the boss," I said with a nod.

"No. He's just the case agent. I'm the boss, and I'll be calling the shots," Rolfe corrected, adding, "Give me a call as soon as you know if there's anything to this alleged kidnapping, and let me know if you need any help. I'll call in the rest of the squad and ask for volunteers, if we need more people."

Chapter 8

Girl Talk

"Don't you need to go to the ladies' room and pee before we drive out to the bank, old man?" I asked Bart.

"No, but maybe you need to be taken out behind the woodshed for a good ass-whooping." Bart climbed into his car and buckled up. "I guess a month at Quantico, learning about the sophisticated world of international espionage, didn't polish off those rough edges."

"I spent too many years working with you to ever be a gentleman."

"Don't blame me. You were a smartass when I met you. Now, fill me in on Ginsberg." We began our drive to the bank. It was already late afternoon.

"If I recall correctly, that whole family is very well connected to all the right people in L.A.'s financial and political circles, if there's any difference between the two. The father, Aron Ginsberg, started the bank years ago and is the CEO and chairman of the board. Two sons went to USC undergrad and law schools. The older son started out as a deputy DA and has been a state superior court judge for years. He may even be an appellate court judge now, I'm not sure. Wait, he is an appellate court judge now. He's been under consideration for the California Supreme Court.

"The second son went into the U.S. Attorney's Office and is a federal court judge. He has political ambitions. Or maybe it's the other way around. Anyway, the daughter, Rachael, the alleged kidnap victim, is much younger and is married to Richard Marino, who's been involved in some big real estate deals in L.A. in one way or another. They say you can't get elected to anything or appointed to any government commission anywhere in L.A. County without the Ginsberg family's backing. Or at least their approval."

"How is it you know so much about them, again?" Bart asked.

"You don't go to USC without hearing about the Ginsbergs. I actually met Rachael Ginsberg and was invited to a couple of school-related events they hosted at their house... *House* is an understatement. It would easily qualify as an estate. It's in Holmby Hills. Not quite Buckingham Palace, but pretty close, I'd say. And they have an even bigger place up in Santa Barbara, but that's just for them and their rich friends. They never allow any plebeians up there."

"I've never heard of them," Bart admitted.

"Apparently, they're the kind who're so rich, they don't have to brag about it. They have a morbid fear of bad publicity and like to keep a low profile, except when it comes to the good stuff, like their charity events, which make it into all the society pages of the newspapers. They keep their financial and political power low-key, except when they want to flex their muscle. When they want something done in L.A., they just put the word out, and somebody gets nominated, appointed, or fired. And if you don't want to offend the local Jewish community or want their support, you run your plans by the Ginsbergs first."

"They don't sound like the kind of people you'd want to make enemies of by kidnapping their daughter and grandkids."

"That's what I'm thinking. If this kidnapping story is true, whoever did it is either really powerful themselves or really stupid."

"Did you know the daughter very well?"

"She was quite a dish, I can tell you that."

"Good looking, huh?"

"Cute as lace pants," I answered.

"Did the Latin Lover ever get into those pants?

I couldn't lie to Bart, but I also had to avoid a direct answer. I grinned. "Are you kidding? There was no way the Ginsbergs would ever allow a spic from the barrio to get near their princess. They must've had a hundred cops, guards, and servants keeping an eye on the riffraff during those charity events. They wouldn't want any of us lowlifes overcome by temptation and sneaking off with any of the silverware, or their princess."

"Well, after we find out if anyone has run off with their princess, I'll cut you loose, and you can get back to chasing spies, or whatever it is you're doing now. I'm not sure I want you working on another kidnapping, especially this one."

"What's that supposed to mean?"

"You always get way too emotionally involved in kidnapping cases. I'm not sure I want you on one involving somebody you know."

Now I had to lie, to stay on the case. "I hardly knew her," I said. This was the first time I had ever lied to Bart, and I didn't like the way that made me feel.

"For someone like you, that's still too much. Let me tell you something. All modesty aside, *I am* a great investigator, and you know why I'm a great investigator? Because I never get emotionally involved in a case. That's something you haven't learned yet, even after all these years. I don't think you ever will."

I knew he was right, but I didn't like hearing it. I needed to change the subject. "Well, if there's been a kidnapping, I'd like stay involved and help out all I can."

"Okay, but I'll handle this interview. If there's been a kidnapping and they haven't reported it, there's something fishy going on. This one will take some finesse, I think."

"Are you saying I don't have finesse, cowboy? You can't even spell finesse."

"I know enough about finesse to know that you don't have any."

"Well, whatever it is, I have more than you. Anyway, I'm there for you, if you need help."

Bart nodded. "How'd you like Rolfe's comment about me being just an agent and him being the boss and running the case?"

"What a piece of work! I'm glad I'm off the squad."

"I wish you'd stayed on," Bart said. "With me leaving soon, it would've been good to have someone on the squad who knows what he's doing, even if he does get too emotionally involved in the work."

"I'd have gotten fired for kicking his ass, if I'd stayed on. Besides, you heard him. He's the boss, so with him running things, it doesn't matter who the agents are."

"Yeah, right. Another moron from Headquarters who thinks you can work a case from behind a desk. Good Lord, help us!"

Chapter 9

Round About the Cauldron Go

We arrived at the bank after five, and it was already closed to the public. Bart showed his credential to the guard at the front door, and we were allowed in. The guard called Ginsberg's secretary, and she told him she'd be down to escort us up to Ginsberg's office.

When Margaret Milstein met us at the elevator, she looked worried. She introduced herself and then said, in a lowered voice, "I'm glad you're here. There's something terrible going on."

I instantly recognized the gray-hair-in-a-bun Milstein as one of those old women who had been destined to be spinsters from early childhood. She wore a dark and shapeless, long-sleeved dress with a gaudy brooch. I'd lay odds the brooch had belonged to her mother, if not her grandmother, and that she'd never worn a sleeveless dress or one that didn't fall below the knee. I was even more certain Magda had selected the dowdy Milstein to be Aron Ginsberg's personal secretary, to avoid any possibility of his mind ever being distracted from business.

"What is it that's worrying you?" Bart asked.

"Well, I'm not exactly sure," she replied in a hushed tone as she led us down the hall, not looking at us directly. "I just know something terrible has been going on since last week. They've tried to act like everything is fine and it's business as usual, but I've been here thirty years, and I know something is wrong. They're keeping it a secret and won't say anything about it to anyone. Please find out and help them. Aron Ginsberg is a very fine man, and I'm worried about his daughter and the children."

She knocked on Ginsberg's door, opened it, and walked in with us following behind her. "These are two agents from the FBI to see you, sir," she said and immediately walked back out.

Aron Ginsberg was seated behind his extravagant desk, which again I was certain Magda had selected for him—no man except Napoleon would choose such an ornate monstrosity for himself. He was looking every bit the successful banker with his perfectly trimmed, graying blond hair, dark-gray pin stripes, cardinal-and-black-striped tie, suspenders, and a starched white collar. With him were Magda, seated to his right and still in her diamond finery—she must've driven straight to the bank immediately after our meeting. Marino, also impeccably tailored, sat to his left. They had apparently been engaged in an intense discussion before we interrupted.

Aron and Marino appeared surprised to see us, although Marino's surprise was tempered by the palpable arrogance and condescension that accompanied all his emotions. His proud chin jutted upward, as always, and begged for a fistful of knuckles. Magda's expression was blank.

As introductions were made, Aron couldn't help staring at me then said, "You look familiar, for some reason."

Magda spoke up. "Weren't you one of the USC scholarship boys who came to some of the events at our house? Or was it an alumni event?"

"Yes, ma'am," I said. "It's been a few years. You have an excellent memory."

Trying to sound blasé, Magda responded with a practiced casual wave of her diamonds. "Oh, no, no. There're too many functions and too many people who come to visit. It would be impossible to remember them all, dear. It's just that some faces seem to stick in one's memory, that's all."

"Well, now that that little mystery is out of the way, let's move on to the next one. Why don't you gentlemen tell us why you're here," Aron asked, also trying to appear unconcerned.

Bart answered, "The FBI received information concerning a kidnapping involving your family. We're here to find out if any of that information is true and why it wasn't reported to the authorities."

Aron had a deer-in-the-headlights look, while Marino maintained his look of haughty superiority. Magda remained silent, her expression blank.

After a moment of awkward silence, Aron spoke up. "What information, specifically, do you have?"

Bart responded quickly in his usual no-nonsense way. "We're not here to provide information. We're here to *get* information. And we're not gonna play games. If there's been a kidnapping, you'd better tell us about it, and I mean *now!*"

The three stared at one another, as though Aron and Marino were wondering what to do next, and Magda wondered which of the two would break first and speak up. Finally, Aron asked Marino, "What do you think?" then looked at Magda, who remained expressionless. Then he asked Bart, "Could you give us a moment to speak privately? If you would wait outside for just a minute, we need to clear up some things between us before speaking to you. Please…"

"Just *one* minute," Bart said firmly, staring hard at each of the three in turn, his physical size and menacing demeanor leaving no doubt in each that he meant business. "If there's a life at stake, we're not gonna be kept waiting."

We went out of the room, and Bart closed the door behind us.

*****

"Someone did call the FBI, just like the kidnapper said," Marino said with a mixture of anger and anguish as we waited outside.

"Neither of *us* did," Magda responded. Aron nodded in agreement. "It could've been anyone from the bank or your office. There's been so much going on out of the ordinary, someone may have caught on and called them."

Marino stood up and began to pace. "The kidnappers found out, and that's why they haven't released her. Who knows what they've done? Maybe they've already…" He didn't finish his sentence.

"We don't know that," Aron said, turning to Magda. "What should we do?"

She also stood, put her hands on Aron's desk, and leaned in toward him. "Enough with all the secrecy already. This has gone on too long. And the FBI now knows something is going on, so we have to tell them."

Marino shook his head. "If the kidnappers do anything to Rachael, it'll be on your heads," he stated emphatically. "You know I've always wanted to do whatever the kidnappers wanted and do it their way, so we'd get Rachael and the kids back safely."

"Maybe we should call our lawyers," Aron said to his wife.

"Do you really want to bring them in?" she asked. "You know what that will mean."

Marino paused, seemed to consider the ramifications. "I think we should wait. At least another day, before we say anything to anyone."

*****

Bart and I were silent as we walked out of the outer office and along the hallway toward the west windows and the setting sun.

"There's definitely something going on," Bart said. "And they know all about it."

"That's for damn sure."

He stared at me. "You know, you and Marino look a lot alike."

"Yeah, right."

"Really. I'm serious. He's a little taller and better looking than you, but he could be your older brother."

"Yeah, and you could be my grandfather."

"And he's got that same smug look plastered on his face, so you could definitely be related."

I shook my head as I checked my watch. It was exactly six o'clock.

Just then, an explosion rocked the entire building, shattering windows, immediately followed by two smaller explosions.

The mind works in mysterious ways. Despite all the intervening years since Afghanistan, those explosions made me drop to the floor as I was flooded with memories I usually recalled only in nightmares.

Chapter 10

Let Slip the Dogs

I had finished junior college and was starting the third week of my first year as a junior at USC when 9/11 changed all our lives. I immediately left school and joined the Army. It was an entirely visceral reaction.

Although I'd always felt, as all Latinos did, that I was treated like a third-class citizen, I was still a citizen. More importantly, I also had foolishly believed the lessons of two World Wars and the Holocaust had been learned and such insanity could no longer exist. Mainly, I was angry—angry at the evil that could inflict such horrific violence on innocent people, and I felt it my personal duty to strike back and right a monstrous wrong. I had to give up a scholarship I'd worked hard to get, with no guarantee of either the scholarship or a place at USC, if I survived the war. But being young and stupid, I was hungry for action and asked to go to Afghanistan ASAP. My wish was granted, and I was in a Forward Operating Base (FOB) in the foothills of Afghanistan by late 2002.

I was first assigned to a recon platoon, whose role was to go into small villages, gather intel, and identify and locate the enemy. I then volunteered to serve on a hot squad, more commonly known as a suicide squad because of its high casualty rate. Its mission was to draw out the enemy and then call in reinforcements. In the Vietnam era, this was called "search and destroy," but in our time of political correctness, such terminology couldn't be used, even in war. Whatever euphemism one chooses, it didn't take long for me to see the reality of war. Dying and dead bodies and pieces of bodies—including women and children—at first seemed unreal, like scenes from a movie. After a few missions, however, the sight and smell of dismembered and burning bodies made it clear to me this wasn't just a movie set.

Although I was deep "in the shit" and living in the midst of death, I never felt close to death myself in any of the firefights I was involved in.

In such circumstances, my mind raced with thoughts of doing what was necessary to survive and complete the mission. You either do or don't do what you're trained to do, and the truth of your life is revealed, playing out in just a few seconds.

I felt pretty invulnerable until I went on what was supposed to be a routine patrol in a friendly village. We were just supposed to show that we were around and keeping an eye on things. The town was so friendly, according to prior intel, there wouldn't even be a gunship above to provide a bird's-eye view and air support.

Our three armored personnel carriers (APCs) drove straight into the center of the mountain village a little after 0900 so as not to wake or frighten anyone. Men and women were milling about, and children played in the street. The three APCs stopped in the center of the village, and we were about to get out to patrol on foot and speak to the people, to develop friendly relations and gather whatever intel we could. What we didn't know was the townspeople had been directed by Taliban militants to go about their normal activities and appear friendly in order to draw us in.

I was in the back of the first APC, set to be the first to go out the rear door. In a combat zone, being first to go out was usually a dangerous assignment, but on this occasion, it turned out to be a lifesaver. As I jumped out, the first APC was hit with a metal-piercing, shoulder-fired rocket. The force of the explosion threw me onto the APC behind mine, and I lay there, drifting in and out of consciousness for a few moments, my legs studded with shrapnel. Since I was motionless, the attackers must've assumed I was dead and didn't bother to finish me off with machine-gun fire.

At first, I felt paralyzed, listening to my buddies scream in the burning APC, unable to do anything about it. When I regained enough consciousness to stand up, I ran back to the first APC to carry out the wounded who were still inside the burning vehicle, but I only managed two runs back there before a rocket-propelled grenade (RPG) hit nearby and put me out for the count. Fortunately, the soldiers in the second and third APCs weren't hit with rockets and were able to hold off the attack long enough for air gunships and reinforcements to come in for the rescue.

I woke up hours later with burns, shrapnel wounds, and a concussion. I was offered a ticket home, but I chose to recuperate in Germany, so I could get back to my unit as soon as the doctors would let me. The only benefit to this downtime was it allowed me to catch up on my reading, and I read all the books the nurses could get me. I went back to my old unit for my second tour of duty with a Purple Heart and another stripe on my sleeve. Having survived my first encounter with death and still young and stupid, I was now certain I was invulnerable and believed nothing bad could happen to me. I soon learned otherwise during my second encounter with mortality.

Upon my return to the Afghan foothills, I was assigned to crew a Humvee that manned a fifty-caliber machine gun mounted on back. This patrol consisted of three APCs and three Humvees, with a lieutenant riding in a Humvee in charge of this patrol.

This time, the assignment was to inspect a town that Taliban militants had been known to have occupied. Intel warned us that the Taliban militants had just left the town. It was our job to make sure they'd actually left. After several hours of inspection, we found the town was secured and prepared to leave.

As we made our way out of the town, a man came running to the lead Humvee and spoke to our lieutenant. He told him that, in addition to the Taliban militants, the Taliban religious police had been to the town, to conduct their own inspection and determine if the townspeople had been living in compliance with strict Islamic law. Like something out of Orwell, these religious police, with the assistance of the militants, had conducted interrogations of the townspeople, forcing them to inform on their neighbors. Five women had been taken into custody for violating Islamic laws and were going to be punished in the town square, but news of our approach had compelled the religious police and militants to take the women and leave town. The man was in a panic, because two women were to be executed and three women, including his daughter, were to be beaten with rods.

Our lieutenant asked the man what laws the women had violated. He replied that one of the women was found in possession of cosmetics and an old *Glamour* magazine. Another had allowed herself to be seen without a burqa by a stranger, and she had been reported by her own husband. The man's daughter and another girl had been outside their home without a male relative as escort and had been caught reading a book. He didn't know what crime the fifth girl had committed.

The women had been taken to a farmhouse about a click out of town and would be brought back for public punishment once we left. The man described at least a dozen Taliban militants and four armed religious police, but there could be more militants at the farmhouse. He was concerned about what the Taliban were doing to his daughter and the other women and what they'd do when they returned.

Our lieutenant ordered my sarge, who was in his Humvee, and me, in mine, to take the man and go out toward the farmhouse for recon. We were to scout and report back only, avoiding any engagement. Our lieutenant wanted to get instructions and air support from our base, as the man's story smelled bad and had all the earmarks of an ambush. After all, who ever heard of a woman being executed just for wearing lipstick?

As we got close to the farmhouse, a woman in a burqa came running toward us, yelling frantically. She was barefoot, with bleeding feet and ankles, and her hands were still tied with wire. Despite her burqa and broken English, we could tell she was very young, a teenager. The man identified her as his daughter's friend and one of the women who'd been arrested by the religious police.

She told the man, who translated for us, she'd just escaped from the nearby farmhouse, where the other women were being held. She said the Taliban had somehow been informed of our approach and planned to exact their punishment at the farmhouse before we could get to them. She added the Taliban had decided to execute all the women, because the townspeople had strayed from the correct path, hadn't been fully cooperative, and had informed us of their activity and intentions. They wanted to make an example of this Sodom, so other towns and villages would know the consequences of such behavior. She said her friend had loosened the wire around her ankles so she could escape, while the Taliban and religious police were busy arguing about what to do and how to prepare for the executions.

She and the man begged us to get to the farmhouse before the Taliban carried out the executions. Sarge put her in my Humvee and radioed our lieutenant, telling him the news and informing him we couldn't wait and were going to the farmhouse.

When we got there, the girl pointed to a barn and said that was where the girls were being held. About six Taliban militants were between the farmhouse and barn, and they began to shoot at us immediately. Additional shooting then came from the farmhouse and barn, where a fire broke out, and we heard women screaming from inside. Fortunately for us, our fifty-caliber machine guns put the odds in our favor. A fifty-caliber machine gun can tear a human body in half, and it's a sight you never forget—a man's head and torso falling to the ground while his legs are still standing.

I could hear the girls shouting from inside the barn, which was now engulfed in flames. With the firefight still going, I ran inside to get the women out. One of them was so frightened, she wouldn't come with me. I had to run back into the barn a second time to rescue her, and that's when I got burned again. That's also when I got shot. One of the Taliban bullets hit me as I ran out, carrying the last woman; I took a grazing round to the head.

Back in Germany again, the doc said I was lucky. The bullet had traveled at an acute angle when it hit me. A sixteenth of an inch to the right and I would've lost an eye. Another sixteenth and I would've died. The bullet only ripped across the surface of my skull and left only a scar.

I was awarded a Bronze Star and Oak Leaf Clusters to go with my Purple Heart and also ordered to take a psych exam. I wanted to get back to my unit as soon as I was well enough to return to action, but the more I asked, the more the doctor insisted I take a psych exam. So, eventually, I did. Afterward, the doc strongly suggested I forget about a combat assignment.

I knew a quiet, safe Army job wasn't for me. There's no place duller than a military outpost in the boondocks—even the barracks cockroaches just keel over and die from boredom. But my enlistment was coming to an end, and the doctor recommended I leave the military and take PTSD counseling sessions at the VA hospital, when I got home. I didn't think I needed counseling but promised the doc I'd take a session or two, anyway.

I kept my word and tried counseling, but I found pain where I didn't think there was any. I also found the pain was too raw and the counseling sessions hurt more than they helped. Vivid memories and dreams of the stench of burned and mutilated bodies didn't seem very *dulce et decorum*, and no one could explain to me why human beings would do such terrible things to one another. I couldn't explain to myself why I had been such an eager participant in the mayhem. All idealistic justifications seemed empty—horrific death turns not only bones but ideals to dust, as well. Apparently, Afghanistan left me with scars that were more than skin deep.

I had joined the Army to escape the poverty of the barrio and do my bit for God and country—or whatever; I wasn't sure anymore. I was even less sure after leaving the Army.

Being Hispanic, poor, and coming from the barrio, I couldn't understand my own country, and I had little understanding of what was going on in the Middle East or why. My reasons for joining the Army in the first place seemed foolish. At twenty-three, I was sure I was the biggest idiot who had ever lived. I had never been much of a drinker and I had never smoked, but after leaving the Army, I quickly began to make up for that.

Chapter 11

The Initial Investigative Results

Five months after the kidnapping and the explosions at the bank, the kidnappers had still made no further contact. Rachael hadn't been released. No body had been found. Dozens of FBI agents and LAPD detectives had spent thousands of hours on an investigation premised on the belief that the kidnapping had been carried out by members of the Palestinian Hezbollah to obtain money for the intifada. The video from the Marinos' gate showed the actual kidnapping by men wearing keffiyehs and carrying guns—AK-47s and pistols. The vehicles used resembled some reported stolen, but they were never recovered. The video was shown on TV dozens of times, and the public was asked to help identify the perpetrators, but there had been no leads.

In addition to the usual home-grown suspects and informants, dozens of Middle Eastern suspects and informants had also been contacted. The Bureau's terrorism and counterintelligence squads identified potential suspects associated with the Palestinian intifada or Hezbollah, and they were also contacted—some none too gently. In fact, several Palestinians hired lawyers and filed complaints against the FBI and LAPD. Even the ACLU got in on the act and filed complaints on behalf of the Palestinians who'd been roughed up and couldn't afford their own lawyers.

Because of the notoriety of the kidnapping and the Ginsbergs' influence, every subpoena and search warrant requested by law enforcement was granted, even those with questionable justification. A hundred-thousand-dollar reward was offered for any information that led to Rachael's recovery or the kidnappers' arrest and conviction. The FBI's Legal Attaché offices in the Middle East were tasked to assist.

Also, because of the Ginsbergs' influence, the Israeli government volunteered its resources to assist in the investigation. In the end, all the Palestinians contacted, both in L.A. and the Middle East, denied that any

Palestinians were involved in the kidnapping. Some went so far as to claim the entire matter was a hoax perpetrated by the Israeli government to vilify the Palestinian people and turn American public opinion further against them.

The forensic analysis of what was left of the three vehicles didn't identify any possible suspects, but what was learned from the meticulous examination of the remains was telling in itself. The only vehicle with a timed explosive device was Magda Ginsberg's white Cadillac—the last vehicle parked at the bank. It didn't contain a sophisticated explosive device, but it had enough dynamite to blow up her car and set off the gasoline cans placed in Rachael's and Aron Ginsberg's vehicles, parked next to it. The gas cans had dynamite taped to them with short fuses and blasting caps. The explosives in Rachael and Aron's vehicles didn't have timers. It was only their proximity to Magda's car that caused the gas cans to burst, which set off the dynamite after Magda's car bomb was detonated. The dynamite in Magda's vehicle wasn't detonated by cell phone, just by a simple timer. It was clear the kidnapper's claim to having placed sophisticated explosive devices in the vehicles was a hoax to keep the Ginsbergs and Marino cooperative and quiet. The timed detonation was planned to destroy any possible evidence inside the vehicles.

The two cell phone numbers used in the kidnapping were found to be pre-paid phones and untraceable. The kidnappers had turned off their cell phone when they weren't actually calling Marino and Ginsberg, and they had made their calls from different places all around Los Angeles, so there was no way to identify the location of their hideout. It was surmised they had either taken Rachael with them when they made their calls or possibly recorded Rachael's voice and played the recording back at opportune moments, to make it appear she was with the kidnappers when the calls were made. The Ginsbergs and Marino all said there was Arabic music playing in the background during every call, possibly intended to drown out any other background sounds that might give away the kidnappers' location. They all also said the caller frequently appeared to turn to his accomplices to say something in Arabic, but since none of them spoke Arabic, they didn't know what he was saying. The caller also seemed to have been well coached about what to say and followed strict orders.

Marino's Jaguar was found where he'd left it, at the parking lot near LAX. Small explosive charges were used by the bomb techs to pop open the doors and trunk. No explosive devices or usable evidence was found inside. The Jag was eventually returned to Marino but was a total loss for insurance purposes. The vehicles used by the kidnappers were never found.

The location where Rachael and the children had been taken and held was never found. Video from the parking lots and garages used by the kidnappers proved to be of no value. Every vehicle owner whose car was in one of the parking lots near LAX or any of the other pertinent parking lots during the ransom-drop time periods was interviewed, to no avail. It was surmised the long-term parking lots were used because they were the types of locations where vehicles could be safely left for long periods without raising suspicions. Nor was there any useful information gained from any of the other parking garages known to have been used by the kidnappers.

Telephone records of all the phones belonging to the Ginsbergs, Marino, and their personal staff were reviewed. The only items of interest were five calls made from Marino's personal cell phone to a cell phone belonging to a company in Las Vegas called the Edward Hawkins and Associates Real Estate Investment and Management Company. Two calls were made shortly before the kidnapping, two during the kidnapping, and one after.

At first, Marino claimed he couldn't recall making those calls. He subsequently had a vague recollection that those calls may have been about leasing or buying a house in Las Vegas. He said he'd been spending a lot of time in Vegas and was tired of staying at the Bellagio. He had contacted a real estate management company there to look into leasing or buying a house near the Strip. He said he'd spoken to a different person at that company each time he'd called and couldn't remember the name of any of them. He didn't have any notes or records concerning those calls. He also claimed he may have even left his personal cell phone at the bank when he went to deliver the ransom payments, so anyone at the bank could've used it during that time.

David and Sarah were interviewed by experts trained in the art of interviewing children. Sarah had been too hysterical and confused to provide any information. The only information gained was from David. He told the interviewers about the kidnappers wearing the Palestinian keffiyeh headscarf, the Palestinian flag, the photo of the leader of the Palestinian people, and the Arabic music at the place where they were held, just as Rachael had told him to. He remembered his mother telling him that the day of the kidnapping was also the birthday of an important person to the kidnappers, but he couldn't remember the name of the person. He just remembered it had something to do with their religion.

He also remembered the yellow-and-green flag his mother didn't recognize but had told him to remember. He was shown the flag of the Hezbollah and recognized it as the other flag in the room where they'd been held. It seemed the kidnappers didn't try to hide the fact that they were with the Palestinian Hezbollah—just the opposite: they wanted it known.

In her interview, Magda Ginsberg mentioned I had been one of many scholarship students who'd visited her home during university-related functions. I knew she'd never acknowledge that Rachael and I ever had a relationship, believing it would ruin Rachael's reputation and diminish the Ginsberg name. Aron Ginsberg thought I'd looked familiar but couldn't recall anything about me.

A full and fair investigation requires an obsessive thoroughness, and the FBI is nothing if not thorough. When the initial premise of the investigation didn't produce any results, the investigation was expanded to include other terrorist organizations, as well as any organized crime or drug trafficking groups thought capable of carrying out the kidnapping. Thousands of hours of additional investigation into these areas failed to produce any results, as did raising the reward to a million dollars.

This left to be revisited only the two leads that brought the kidnapping to the attention of the FBI in the first place. The anonymous telephone call from the unknown woman had been traced to a payphone in a mini-mart in Mid-City L.A., which was one of the few places in that area where someone without the means for a home or cellular telephone could make a call. It wouldn't be unusual for a white female to call from that phone on a normal day. The woman couldn't be identified.

The call from the anonymous man who I'd said had called me to report the kidnapping proved much more problematic, but only for me.

Chapter 12

Attack of the Empty Suits

L ate one morning, I was called by SSA Rolfe to meet him and Bart in the office of Richard Norton, the Assistant Director in Charge (ADIC) of the L.A. Field Office, in order to go over the status of the investigation. Rolfe told me, because of the Ginsbergs' and Marino's prominence, the Director himself wanted regular briefings from the ADIC, and the ADIC wanted to go over all the latest information we had before he called the Director.

When I got to the ADIC's office, I saw I was last to arrive; in addition to Rolfe, Bart, and the ADIC, Lawrence Brunette, the Criminal Division Special Agent in Charge (SAC), was also waiting for me. The only senior management person not there was the Criminal Division Assistant Special Agent in Charge (ASAC), because he was out doing whatever it is ASACs do. I don't think anyone in the Bureau has ever figured out what that is. Ida Archer, the ADIC's secretary, was also there, with her notepad, ready to take notes on all that transpired. All of a sudden, I knew Rolfe had lied to me about the purpose of the meeting. I also knew just how the fox felt right before the hounds were released.

"Agent Dehenares, have a seat," ADIC Norton said without a greeting or a smile.

The first word that came to mind when describing Norton was "prissy." He was a short, skinny half-wit who wanted everyone to believe he was intelligent and had achieved his position on merit. That pretense was quickly discredited, and he had a hard time dealing with anyone who actually was intelligent or merited a position of authority. He always had a look on his face that suggested chronic constipation.

"There's an issue we need to clear up concerning the investigation of the Ginsberg-Marino kidnapping. An issue that came up after additional investigation by one of the analysts. SSA Rolfe will go over it, and perhaps you can shed light on the matter."

Ida was busy taking notes—the invisible yet dutiful secretary doing her job quietly in the background.

Rolfe took over the interrogation. He was young and eager, a hungry dog ready to attack anything that would help him make his way up the Bureau ladder. His usual look suggested a horny teenager with a compulsion to masturbate. "In following up on the initial sources of the information about the kidnapping, the analyst went over the telephone calls to the office. You already know about the call from the payphone in Mid-City. That lead is exhausted. But what's still unclear is the call you said you received at your desk from the anonymous male. Do you recall what you told Bart and me when you came to my office to report that call?"

I looked around the room and saw all eyes on me, and except for Bart, who was looking at his shoes, they weren't friendly eyes. They were hard eyes looking for a fool to make a mistake—a mistake that would end his career and maybe send him to jail.

"Vaguely. I don't understand what that has to do with anything," I said.

"Well, it may have everything to do with the case," Rolfe said.

"I don't see how."

"Let me lay it out for you. First, our telephone records show that the last call you received that day, before you came to my office, was a call to your desk at 1:23 p.m. Your key card shows you left the office immediately after that. Then your key card shows you returned to the office at 3:59 p.m. There were no calls to your desk or cell phone after you came back to the office and before you came to my office to report the kidnapping. Do you see what I'm getting at?"

Obviously, I had been under investigation, or at least my telephone records had been. Good work by the analyst to follow up on those calls and catch that issue. I looked around the room again. Ida was still busy taking notes. Bart still had his head down. The others were staring at me with predatory eyes. "No, I don't."

"I think that call at 1:23 was from your informant about the kidnapping, and you left the office to go talk to your informant about it. Then you came back, waited a few minutes for some reason, and then came to my office. We traced that call to a phone in the lobby of the

Bonaventure Hotel. We haven't been able to identify who made that call, but I'm certain you know who that person is. For some reason, you've been withholding information, vital information."

Ida was still taking notes. All eyes were still on me. Even Bart was staring at me, only now with pity in his eyes.

"You know who that informant is, don't you?" Rolfe asked.

"I have nothing to add to what I've already said," I answered.

ADIC Norton cut in. "Are you refusing to answer that question?"

"I did answer the question. I just didn't give you the answer you're obviously fishing for."

"Who is your informant?" Norton demanded.

"I don't have anything to add to what I've already said," I repeated.

"We're not playing games here. Let me reiterate what SSA Rolfe just said a minute ago. You're withholding information that is vital to a kidnapping investigation. Either you tell us who your informant is and everything else you know about the kidnapping, or you can kiss your career in the FBI goodbye!" Norton was shouting. "I will also personally see to it that you're charged with obstruction of justice and sent to prison."

After six months of investigation, the Bureau hadn't come up with a single suspect, and the empty suits were feeling the heat. They needed a scapegoat to pin the failure on. This issue would be their salvation, and they'd chosen me to be the fall guy.

"I've said everything I have to say on the subject."

Brunette chimed in with his two cents. I'd wondered when he would. He was the only one of the management empty suits with any brains, and he wasn't afraid to use them, usually in some sadistic and demeaning manner. "We'll see about that. I have a polygrapher standing by, and you're going to tell him everything you know or claim not to know, and then we'll know whether you're lying."

"I'm not going to submit to a polygraph," I said.

"You have to. It's part of your employment agreement," Brunette said, with a vicious grin.

"But you didn't say *please*. In any case, I'm not taking a polygraph. My word alone has been good enough in court for judge and jury." I hadn't lied to these clowns, but I knew I couldn't pass a polygraph once specific questions were asked by a trained and experienced investigator.

Norton huffed and spoke with the pretentious fervor of all high-ranking fools in government jobs. "You leave me no choice but to suspend you immediately, pending further investigation. One way or another, I'll see to it you're fired for withholding information and insubordination."

Nailing a street agent on such a high-profile case would absolve Norton of a failed investigation and guarantee his promotion to Executive Assistant Director, paving the way for a lucrative job as director of security for some Fortune 500 company. Brunette and Rolfe also seemed pleased. There was plenty of gravy to go around for nailing a street agent, once they shifted the blame to me.

Bart turned to the ADIC. "Just a second," he said then turned to me. "Mig, we've known each other a long time. I understand all about protecting an informant, but this has gone too far. You have to tell us who he is. I promise you I'll do everything possible to protect him or her." Everyone could see he was pleading with me.

"I'm sorry, Bart. This is nothing against you, but I have nothing more to say."

Now Bart got tough, as we'd all expected him to. "I owe you my life, everybody knows that. And you're the best friend I've ever had. But you know better than anybody that I'm all about the job. Right now, there's a life at stake or a body to be found and kidnappers who need to be arrested. I'm gonna find Rachael Marino, and I'm not gonna let the kidnappers get away with it. Nobody's gonna stand in the way of that. Not even you."

"Sorry, Bart. I have nothing more to say."

For the first time in all the years we'd known each other, my best pal Bart appeared to get angry at me. He stood up, looming over me, and raised his voice. "If you don't tell me who your informant is, this will tear it between us, Mig. *Forever.*"

"Sorry, Bart."

After a moment of tense silence, Norton cut in. "You are hereby officially suspended, effective immediately. You will return to your desk, gather your Bureau property, and turn it over to your supervisor." He turned to Rolfe and added, "Call the Security Officer. Tell him to escort Dehenares out of the office. And tell him to make sure Dehenares doesn't walk out with anything but his personal property, when he leaves the office." He seemed very pleased with himself.

Chapter 13

Fall Guy, Scapegoat, and Whipping Boy

I didn't like the thought of giving up a job I loved and a half-decent pension, so I swallowed my pride and made arrangements to see Magda Ginsberg secretly. I asked to be released from my promise. She refused.

"What, you expect me and my family to suffer just so you can keep your job?"

"It'll mean more than just losing my job. And I don't see how you or your family will suffer much."

Magda shook her head. "There's a lot you don't know. And since we still don't know what happened to Rachael, I don't want anyone to know I told you about the kidnapping. I don't know if the kidnappers knew it was me who called you or what, but I don't want Aron or Richard to know I called you."

"I don't see what difference it makes at this point. It's clear the kidnappers intended to detonate the explosives in your car all along, since they were set to go off by a timer. Whatever has happened to Rachael would've happened anyway," I said.

"*Feh*! It doesn't matter. You know Rachael was the most precious thing in the world to my husband. If Aron finds out I told you about the kidnapping—and then kept it from him—he'll never forgive me. Nor will the rest of my family. She was always the darling pet, everybody's favorite. And Richard still thinks Aron or I or the both of us were the ones who called the FBI. He's never stopped blaming us for whatever has happened to Rachael. He's threatened to take the children away from us. If the *gonif* finds out I called you, he'll never let me see them again."

I knew that appealing to her sympathy was futile, but I had groveled this much already, so I had to give it a try. "I'll not only lose my job, but I'll go to jail because of this."

"I won't destroy what's left of my family and risk losing my grandchildren. No. I expect you to be a mensch and keep your promise. And I think it would be better for you to forget about Rachael and the investigation. Just leave us alone and stay out of it."

Not only did she refuse to release me from my promise, but to keep up appearances, she played the role of the angry mother, when it was revealed I had information about the kidnappings that I wouldn't disclose. And she played it well, demanding I be punished for my apparent intransigence.

*****

I was served with a grand jury subpoena two days after being placed on administrative leave. It was Bart who came to serve it to me.

"And the Oscar for Best Actor in a dramatic role goes to… Bart Keyes," I said with a clap of my hands and a smile.

Bart laughed. "I was pretty damn convincing, wasn't I?"

"You sure were. You almost had me crying. I think those empty suits swallowed it completely."

"I think so, too. They never asked me about you again after that meeting. They all assumed I was too pissed at you to ever want to see you again."

He came alone, and we went over my plans to continue with the investigation after I officially resigned or was officially fired. Even before that meeting in the ADIC's office, I knew someone would question my account of the anonymous phone call. And I knew I'd have to find out what happened to Rachael no matter what, so I told Bart I might have to leave the Bureau to find out who was responsible for the kidnapping. Even though he didn't understand, Bart was the only person who wouldn't doubt or question me, the only person I could trust, and the only one I could count on for help. He tried to talk me out of it, but having made my promise to Magda and feeling as I did about Rachael, I knew I couldn't rest until I got to the bottom of things.

After handing me the subpoena, Bart asked yet again, "So, you're really gonna go through with this?"

"Yeah."

"You're gonna give up the job and go to jail?"

"Yeah."

"And you're not gonna tell me why?"

"I can't."

"Well, have fun in prison. You know you're gonna have a target on your back in there, so try not to get your dumb ass shivved." Bart shook his head and sighed. "You know where to find me if you make it out alive, you dumb idiot!"

Chapter 14

Burned by an Old Flame

Carmen Stern took a deep breath and exhaled slowly as she shook her head, unable to comprehend my motivations. "Why didn't you just tell them what they want to know? What's the big deal?" she asked.

"They didn't say *please*."

"Not funny. You know what'll happen to you. I don't understand why you're doing this."

"I'm not sure I understand why, either," I said. It bothered me that I couldn't tell her more. She deserved a full explanation and a lot more from me.

"Then, why do it? Why put yourself through this?" She brushed aside a lock of dark brown hair that perfectly matched her innocent doe eyes and then threw her hands up in frustration. They fell with a slap on her bare thighs.

"You know I couldn't answer that, even if I had a good answer."

"You don't trust me? After all this time, you think I'd betray you and run to my boss and tell him anything you've told me? I'd be in just as much trouble as you, if anyone found out I came here tonight and we'd ended up like this."

Carmen had shown up at my door late on the night before my grand jury hearing. She was one of the best lawyers in the U.S. Attorney's Office, and we'd worked together on many cases over the years. We had also been intermittent lovers for many years but had kept our relationship secret to avoid any complications with our jobs. She'd broken it off about two years ago, after giving me an ultimatum, when I couldn't make the kind of commitment she wanted. We'd remained friends, though, and were able to continue to work together when the job required it. It was difficult, however, because neither of us could deny our feelings for the other.

As fate would have it, she was one of the AUSAs assigned to work with the FBI on the Ginsberg-Marino kidnapping and had been assigned to question me in front of the grand jury. In the past, we'd enjoyed arguing obscure points of law just for fun, but I didn't think she'd come to discuss the Rule Against Perpetuities tonight. She knew the likely outcome of the grand jury hearing, if I refused to answer questions, and had come by to plead with me one last time not to ruin my life. But our emotions and chemistry overcame all else, and since she remained as desirable to me as ever, we'd ended up in bed.

"Yeah, I can see where you might be in trouble with the Bar Association. This method of cross-examination isn't exactly standard procedure," I said, gliding my fingertips slowly over the curves of her lovely body. "But it's not about trust. You know as well as I do, I just can't talk about any of it."

She continued to look at me with deepening frustration. "Everyone thinks you're trying to protect a woman, but I don't think that's it. We wouldn't be here in bed if you were serious about another woman in your life. You're not that kind of man."

We stared at each other. "You're not going to draw any answers out of me, either."

"I'm not trying to draw any answers out of you. I'm not trying to trick you. Damn it, Mig." She sat up. "Can't you see I'm just trying to understand you? You know I'm going to have to grill you and give you the third degree tomorrow."

"I know."

"You think I want to do that? You think I want to send you to jail for contempt?"

"No. I know it'll be hard for you, too," I answered, angry at myself for causing her pain.

"Then give me something. Some justification for refusing to answer. It doesn't even have to be a good justification, just something I can use to let you off for not answering."

"I can't say anything that might indicate there was someone or something I was trying to protect or hide. You might want to let me off, but your boss and the Bureau won't allow it. They'll still want to know who or what and why. I can't risk opening that can of worms."

Carmen shook her head again, still not understanding. "The only other person I know you care enough about to give up a job you love and go to jail for is Bart, and I know you're not doing this for him. He'd never let you, and I know even he doesn't understand why you're doing this."

I looked at her face and smiled. She was pretty, nice to look at but not so beautiful as to cause any trouble. It was a face you wouldn't mind waking up to on Sunday morning and spending the rest of the day with. And she was charmingly feminine — not in the girly-girl, paint her toe nails for two hours way, but unselfconsciously alluring and sweet and kind and thoughtful and compassionate — all the finer qualities that make women the better half of the species. Did I mention she had the softest lips I'd ever kissed? If it hadn't been for Rachael under my skin...

She sighed. "Well, you're breaking my heart — again."

"You know I never intended that." I sat up also and kissed her gently on the cheek, just below her ear — her weak spot.

Her eyes closed reflexively for a moment. "Yes, I know. I just don't understand why you wouldn't even give it a chance. I told you we could live together for a while, and if it didn't work out, we could just end it and say we tried. No hard feelings."

"Things don't work that way. There would've been hard feelings, and we could never have remained friends or worked together again." I couldn't tell her there was another woman who'd always come between us. A woman I hadn't been able to get out of my system and who was still the primary influence in my life, even though she was likely dead now... *As trees are by their bark embraced, love to my soul doth cling...* How well I understood the poet's line.

"Are you sure you won't change your mind about your testimony...? Or us?"

I just looked at her in silence, sorry for all I couldn't give her.

"Well then, you should know, since we're speaking of things of the heart, I wanted to see you again because... I wanted to know if... I wanted to tell you I'll probably be getting married this summer. I've been dating Bob Stevens for a while. I didn't think it was that serious, but he asked me to marry him."

Although I wasn't ready to get serious with anyone, it still hurt to know Carmen would be lost to me forever. I tried to hide my hurt. "Congratulations. He's a good AUSA and seems like a nice guy, for a lawyer. I hope you'll be very happy."

She was well aware of my low opinion of lawyers and ignored the jibe. "Thanks... I couldn't wait for you forever. I knew you'd understand that."

"There's nothing to understand. Life goes on. Unfortunately, I don't think I'll be able to attend the wedding."

"Why not?"

I reached for a cigarette and lit it. "If things go as I expect them to, I think I'll be in jail this summer."

*****

Carmen did an excellent job of grilling me the next morning. I knew she would. Because of all my "I don't remember" and "I don't recall" answers, the clear inference was that I was hiding something. She had no choice but to ask a magistrate to hold me in contempt for refusing to answer questions about the source of my information about the kidnapping. Given that the underlying case was a kidnapping and likely murder, and given the Ginsbergs' prominence and the fact that their son was a judge in the same courthouse, the magistrate had no choice but to find me in contempt and order I be held until I agreed to answer.

I was sent to the Bureau of Prisons (BOP) Metropolitan Detention Center (MDC) in downtown L.A., just two blocks from the courthouse. I was denied bail pending my appeal of the contempt charge, and my appeal was subsequently also denied. I was told I'd be held until I agreed to testify or until the grand jury term expired in eight months.

After two weeks, the BOP sent me to the Federal Correctional Institution, Lompoc. Ordinarily, a witness who refuses to testify before a grand jury is held at the MDC downtown for a couple of weeks, until he gives in and testifies or until it becomes clear he won't testify under any circumstances, and it becomes a potential due-process violation. It's extremely rare for a "recalcitrant witness," as someone in my situation is called, to be held for the entire term of a grand jury. The Bureau's vindictive malice and the Ginsbergs' and Marino's influence were the only things that could account for such unusually harsh treatment in my case.

Chapter 15

Damnatio Ad Bestias

Afterward, you realize you should've noticed something wasn't right, but afterward is always too late. The always busy and noisy corridor leading to the prison infirmary wasn't busy or noisy.

A guard always walks the inmate to the infirmary when he's coming directly from the cellblock. But Michael Sachetti was walking alone to the infirmary, several paces in front of me, when I first saw him.

I knew of this high-profile inmate, the mafia captain finishing his five-year-reduced-to-two sentence for extortion in the Lompoc minimum-security prison before being declared rehabilitated and released back to society as a reformed man. We hadn't had any contact before the day of the attack, each of us for our own reasons. I'd assumed he thought I was just another busted ex-cop and, therefore, a fool who could be of no use to him. And I, having known several mafia types, had assumed he was just another sociopath and monster who could be of no use to me.

He had been ordered to the infirmary from the cellblock for his supposedly random and routine drug test, and I had permission to leave my kitchen job to get some medication for a killer toothache to hold me until the prison dentist came the next day. Toothaches don't normally merit a trip to the infirmary, but my swollen jaw and non-stop bleeding made it clear I wasn't just faking it to get some feel-good pill.

I turned into the corridor and saw him walking about five steps in front of me, just before the turn to the corridor to the infirmary. That's when I should've noticed how eerily quiet it was.

Sachetti stopped and turned his head slightly, took a good look at me, then ignored me and took a step. As he was about to turn the corner to the infirmary, another inmate lunged toward him from the corridor and slashed at his neck. If Sachetti hadn't stopped and turned his head to see who was coming behind him, he would've received a direct thrust to his jugular.

I was there strictly by coincidence. Acting only on instinct, I ran forward and fought off the attacker before he could finish the job. I got slashed several times myself before getting the shiv away from him and then using a chokehold to render him unconscious. I applied pressure to the ragged cut along Sachetti's neck until the doctor and his assistant came out from the infirmary and stopped the bleeding.

I'd served nearly all of my eight months in that prison, but Sachetti had been transferred to the facility to finish his last three months before being released. Apparently, someone didn't want Sachetti back on the street and had put a contract out on him. Biker inmates are the hitmen of choice in prison, as they'll take on a hit job for any reason or no reason at all—the amoral black ninjas of prison society. It's nothing personal, just business. Shortly after Sachetti had arrived at the facility, on a busy visiting day when his friends weren't close enough to protect him, a biker gang enforcer who'd been given the job attacked and slashed at his throat. Sachetti's sixth sense, which had saved him many times before, made him take that fraction of a second to stop, turn, and eye me.

In the violent jungle that is prison, one must do whatever one must do to stay alive and live long enough to make it to one's release date. Crimes in federal prisons are investigated by the Bureau of Prisons and the FBI, but there was nothing to investigate in this case, because the biker and Sachetti refused to make statements. As a former law enforcement officer, I was at risk every minute I was in prison, and I didn't want to make any more enemies or get involved in anyone else's problems, so I didn't make a statement, either. Since there were no witnesses aside from Sachetti, the biker, and me, no one could be certain who attacked whom or what the motive may have been.

After we'd recovered somewhat from our wounds, Sachetti sent a messenger for me, and I had a smoke with him in the yard. I knew his type was too proud to have any sense of gratitude, so I didn't expect any thanks, nor did he offer any. We spoke only briefly, far enough away from other inmates for anyone to hear. This was the first and only time I ever felt safe in the yard, since I knew no one would dare come at me with Sachetti's people looking out for him.

"Since nobody talked, nobody knows if it was one a' my enemies or yours that ordered the hit," he said as he offered me a cigarette.

"Seems that way." I took the smoke, as it would've been rude not to.

"The only thing I know for sure is the doc said I woulda died if you didn't stop the bleeding."

"I guess that first aid training came in handy after all."

In his early fifties, Michael Sachetti was a big man, an imposing six-four and two-twenty-five, but aside from height, the gods hadn't been kind. He was one of those lumbering hulks whom you could never get a good look at, or want to. A large, stupid-looking man, he was all awkward angles and protuberances, like a damaged building after an earthquake, leaning either this way or that. Although he made an effort to keep fit, on him, muscles looked lumpy. And on a face with big bovine eyes, large lips, and a bulging nose, his expensive and perfect teeth seemed perfectly wrong. I wasn't sure if even a mother could love that face. Not at all handsome, he would appear Neanderthal even in a three-piece suit, and no one would expect anything intelligent to emanate from his wide mouth. When he did open it, he spoke with the last traces of South Philly that even twenty-five years in Southern California couldn't erase.

But anyone who relied on appearances or first impressions alone would seriously underestimate Michael Sachetti. It could be a fatal mistake, or at least expensive, in one way or another. Especially after his latest brush with the law, which taught him to curb his quick temper and think things through before acting on impulse. He also had a subtle, if malicious, sense of humor.

Sachetti was lucky to have been sentenced to only five years for extortion, skating on the murder and robbery charges also filed against him. A loan shark who worked for Sachetti and owed him money testified against him on the extortion charge, along with his ex-girlfriend, and did so only because they had no choice but to accept the government's offer of help.

I'd heard Sachetti had become enraged when the loan shark, who couldn't pay his debt, had made a lascivious remark about the girlfriend, which she foolishly took as a compliment. Sachetti had assumed they'd been having an affair and had beat them both nearly to death. They were both afraid he'd come after them again or send his underlings to finish the job. By the time the trial date arrived, witnesses to the other charges had disappeared, so those charges were dropped. The loan shark and the ex-girlfriend had testified in exchange for immunity and had subsequently disappeared, after receiving their rewards for their testimony. Whether they'd succeeded in their escape or been dealt with by the mafia was unknown. Sachetti had maintained his honor within his crime family by doing his time quietly, but apparently someone didn't want him back out on the street.

Michael Sachetti took a long drag and blew smoke. "It's better if no one knows how it went down," he said emphatically.

"I wasn't planning on talking about it."

"It wouldn't be good if it looked like I got caught with my pants down and had to be saved by an FBI agent. I told my people I got in the way of a shiv meant for you."

"No problem. But it's *ex*-FBI agent."

"If you say so… Don't worry about the biker. I'll have him taken care of."

"Don't go to any trouble on my account," I said, not wanting another death credited to my karmic account.

"No trouble at all. It's just business." He smiled.

*****

Three weeks later, fate brought us together again. We were both being released on the same day, and we walked along the long corridor to the heavy metal exit door and freedom, escorted by two guards.

Although I was glad to be getting out, I'd miss having all the reading time I'd had in prison. I'd been surprised by what I'd found in the prison library and had reread some of my college favorites. Kierkegaard and Wittgenstein began to make sense, but Heidegger remained a mystery.

But the biggest mystery remained what had happened to Rachael. Eight months of thinking about Rachael and going over every detail of the investigation many times had brought me no new insights, though now out of prison, I'd be able to continue my own investigation on my own terms. I would no longer be constrained by minor technicalities, like the Constitution, federal and state laws, or Bureau regulations. My biggest worry was whether I'd be hit with another grand jury subpoena, which would land me back in prison before I could even begin my investigation.

I was being released only because the grand jury term had expired; I could no longer be legally held in contempt of a grand jury that no longer existed. Sachetti was being released early after his lawyers had successfully argued he was a marked man in prison and couldn't be guarded well enough, so it was in everyone's best interest he be released before another attempt was made on his life.

We walked, holding our manila envelopes with our only belongings: wallet, comb, wristwatch. One envelope contained Italian leather, ivory, and Rolex; the other, pigskin, plastic, and Timex. Guess which was mine. The two guards behind us had the bored looks of functionaries who'd performed the same task thousands of times before. The younger guard whistled and hummed.

When we reached the door, the senior guard with us waved to the guard behind the glass in the control room to release the locks. Then he said with a broad smile, "I don't expect to see you back, Mig. Take care of yourself."

"Thanks, Dave. You, too."

The senior guard said to Sachetti, "Mr. Sachetti, I hope we don't see you here again, either."

Michael Sachetti spoke with calm certainty. "You won't see me in prison again. That I promise you, boys. There'll never be a witness who can testify against me ever again. Lesson learned."

The guards chuckled, knowing what he meant. The senior guard said, "I guess you learned that lesson the hard way, Mr. Sachetti."

The younger guard added, "Yeah, you're lucky to be alive, Sachetti. If Mig hadn't stopped the bleeding, you'd be worm meat."

Sachetti gave the young guard a mean look for his lack of respect, and the young guard turned his head down.

As I walked out the prison door, I tasted the air of freedom for the first time in eight months. I know it was just psychological, but I couldn't help notice the difference between the stale smell of baloney-sweat-urine-vomit that permeates the air inside prison walls and the clean air just one step on the outside.

A driver stood next to a black limo, waiting for Sachetti, ready to take him wherever he wanted to go for some R&R before getting back to work. A blonde was also waiting by the Caddy, one of *those* blondes—the kind who makes twelve-year-old altar boys forget about the seminary, start smoking, and hang out with the wrong crowd. She wore a black, low-cut, side-split, skintight something-or-other that left nothing to the imagination except lascivious thoughts. After eight months in prison, she was making me smoke just looking at her.

"I'd offer you a ride, but it wouldn't be good for me to be seen with an FBI agent. And it looks like I'm gonna be busy," Sachetti said with a lecherous grin. "I don't think she'll be able to keep her hands off me."

"What woman could? You're irresistible, Michael," I replied. "And again, it's *ex*-FBI agent."

We parted ways without a handshake or even a nod. Neither of us expected to see the other ever again.

I lit a cigarette before starting the half-mile trek to the bus stop. The blonde bounced toward Sachetti while trying to keep things from spilling out. I couldn't help thinking I liked his welcome home party much better than mine.

Chapter 16

Status Quo Ante

We had turned off our cell phones and dry cleaned for nearly an hour, conducting countersurveillance by driving around erratically to detect and evade any possible surveillance. I parked three blocks away from the Galleria Mall and continued to dry clean on foot for twenty minutes. When I got back into my car, I drove around the Galleria parking lot and continued to check for surveillance. I then drove into the Galleria garage and parked next to Bart's car. This was our first meeting since I'd been released from prison nearly two weeks prior. Parking garages and parking lots are good places to meet, because it's easy to spot surveillance there. I signaled for Bart to get into my car.

He had grown a bushy, Fu Manchu mustache while I was in prison. "I didn't think the Bureau allowed outside employment, but I see you got a side job as a porn star while I was away."

"I've been told it's darn sexy and makes me look twenty years younger," Bart answered.

"Younger than who—Charlie Chan's grandfather?"

Bart made a fist and punched me lightly on the jaw. "Eight months in the slammer didn't mellow you out at all, did it?" We laughed, and with the faux punch in lieu of a hug out of the way, he asked, "So, how was prison? Did the Latin Lover maintain his macho virginity, if you know what I mean?"

"I'm as pure and innocent as the day I went in." In a small cooler, I had brought a six-pack of Coors, Bart's favorite, and I gave him one.

We each took a sip. "That's not saying much. You weren't exactly Snow White going in," he quipped.

"I never claimed to be. How about you? Did you run off and get married again for the tenth time while I was away?"

"Are you kidding? I'm paying enough alimony already. I'll just keep playing the field until they carry my bones outta the old folks' home."

"Whose field are you playing on now?"

"Do you remember Kitty Kendall, the bank robbery squad file clerk?"

"You dirty old man. You're old enough to be her grandfather! Is she the reason you grew that brush?"

"She's very mature for her age."

"Yeah, the collection of stuffed animals she keeps at her desk will attest to that."

"You just don't see all her attributes like I do."

"What attributes are those?"

"For one thing, I like her vocabulary."

"I didn't think she had a very large vocabulary," I said.

"Exactly. Words like *no*, *don't*, and *stop* aren't in her vocabulary. If I want talk, I'll get a parrot."

"Yeah, I can see you with a parrot on your shoulder. You'll need an eyepatch to go with it."

Bart nodded, peeved. "Tell me something. Just out of curiosity, how many times a day do people tell you to go screw yourself?"

"Maybe once or twice."

"I would've guessed a lot more."

I needed a smoke. I gave Bart one and lit our cigarettes. "Speaking of getting screwed, how's the Bureau been treating you? Have you gotten screwed for not getting to the bottom of the kidnapping?"

"No, nothing I can't handle. If it really was Hezbollah behind it, we may never find out who the actual players were. Remember what the terrorism squad guys told us about how those terrorist groups operate? The kidnappers may have been killed by their own people just to clean house and cover up the trail. And the empty suits seem content to keep using you as a scapegoat. That'll be a problem for you, if they decide to go for another grand jury subpoena."

"So, the case is still open?"

"Yeah, it's still open for now, but on the back burner. I'm the only one working it."

"Has anything new come up?"

"Not a thing for months. No new leads. Not even any new crackpot calls from lunatics or psychics. The well has gone completely dry." Bart shook his head and stared at his cigarette. "You know, the only time I smoke is when I'm with you. You're a bad influence on me."

"Yeah, I hear that a lot... Are you still getting pressure from the Ginsbergs and Marino?"

"Oh yeah. An Assistant U.S. Attorney calls every month. They get pressured by the Ginsbergs' lawyers, so they call to find out if anything new has come up and what I've been doing. The boss calls me and Rolfe in every month for the same Q & A, to get them off his back."

"Do you think the empty suits have any suspicions about you and me meeting again?" I asked.

"No, none at all. I'm sure they all think I've written you off. Especially after I came back from serving you with that grand jury subpoena and told Rolfe what a dick you were. I guarantee he spread the word. But I think we still have to play it safe and meet secretly. That is if you still intend to make like Don Quixote and keep fighting windmills."

"I do intend to get to the bottom of the kidnapping, and I agree we should only meet secretly."

"So, what do you plan to do?"

"First, I have to get settled. Find a real place to live. I can't stay at that motel any longer. It's too depressing, and the women there don't understand the word *no*. I'm trying to get a PI license, but I'm not sure if they'll let me have one. I was never convicted of anything, but they may hold that contempt charge against me."

"So, what've you been doing for money? Do you need some cash to tide you over?"

"No, but thanks anyway. I'm okay for now. I started working as an unofficial assistant PI for your old buddy, Jack Spencer, thanks to you."

"How is old Jack? I haven't seen him since I talked to him about bringing you on."

"He's moving pretty slow these days, but he still gets around. He doesn't want to retire. Like you told me, he'll die on the job."

"Yeah, he'll never retire. No wife, no kids. The job's the only thing that keeps him going, and he'll keep working till he drops. Anyway, what else have you been up to?"

"Well, I just finished looking over the file I got from your other old buddy, Walt Nuff, at Pacific Mutual Insurance."

"Has Walt turned up anything new?"

"Nothing new there, although Nuff still thinks Marino looks bad for buying those ransom insurance policies a few months before the kidnapping. He said they're trying to find a way to avoid paying them off. But for now, it looks like they're on the hook for millions."

"Where does that leave you?"

"Since you don't have any new leads for me, I'll start by reinterviewing anybody who'll talk to me."

"We already talked to everybody twice, sometimes three or four times. Most of them weren't too happy the first time we came around."

"I know. But now that I'm not with the Bureau, I don't have to play nice. I'll put the screws to anybody who doesn't sound like they're talking straight."

"Be careful about the enemies you make. You may have a lot more freedom to do as you please, now that you're not an agent and don't have to play by the rules. But you won't have any agents around to back you up, either."

"Yeah, I'll have to be careful not to get this pretty face beat up."

"Getting your ass kicked may be the least of your problems. Remember, whoever was behind the kidnapping must be pretty powerful and wasn't afraid of committing murder."

"Yeah."

I pulled out two more beers and gave Bart one. I lit another cigarette and offered Bart one. He shook his head.

"There's one thing I'd like you to do for me," I said.

"What's that?"

"You remember when we wanted to expand the investigation and talk to other Arab targets, and the Foreign Counterintelligence guys wouldn't tell us who the really big shots were, because they didn't want them to know we knew who they were? The FCI guys only gave us the names of some low-level mugs and told us to leave the big guys alone."

"Yeah. I'm sure they still won't tell me who the big boys are. That spy-versus-spy shit is all high-level Top Secret. There's no way the FCI guys will let us talk to their main targets, because they don't want them to know we're following them and tapping their phones and have bugs up their asses. Not even people as powerful as the Ginsbergs and Marino have the pull to get the FCI guys to give up that information."

"Yeah, well, it's time for you to use that charm and finesse you've been claiming to possess and get me some names. I'd especially like to know who the top man for Iran is in L.A."

"Iran? Why Iran?"

"I didn't get a chance to work FCI much before the kidnapping, but from what I gathered, it's believed the Palestinian Hezbollah were trained and funded by the Iranians, either directly or through the Syrians. Which means the Palestinians wouldn't do anything big that might upset the apple cart without approval from Iran."

"Okay, that makes sense. I'll see what I can do. But don't get your hopes up." He rapped me on the shoulder with his knuckles. "Gimme another cigarette, damn it. You're gonna get me hooked again on these damn cancer sticks."

I gave him one and lit it for him. "I'm not saying the Iranians were behind the kidnapping or had anything to do with it. But if it was Hezbollah, they'd know about it. It's worth looking into."

Bart took a long, deep drag. "If you do go talk to Mr. Big Iran in L.A., be careful. I'm sure he's got protection, and the Bureau and the Agency won't be happy with you, either, if they find out you've blown a major target. You may find yourself back in the slammer just for talking to the guy."

"Yeah, I don't expect to make any new friends with my investigation."

"So, why're you doing this? With your education and brains, you could make a nice life for yourself. Hang out a shingle and just be a lawyer. This isn't your job anymore, you know. You don't have to do it."

"Yeah, I do. Let's just say it's a matter of personal pride and integrity. I intend to see justice done."

"There you go with that fanatical integrity-and-justice crap again. Didn't I tell you that'll get your ass in a ringer, if not killed quicker than anything else in this line of work? There's no such thing as justice, so forget about it."

"Yeah, you told me. But the Eumenides would be furious with me if I didn't at least try to see justice done. And I know you care more than you admit."

"There you go with the fancy words again." Bart shook his head with disdain. "I don't know what the hell you're talking about half the time, but I do know you take this shit way too seriously and way too personally. I just do my job to the best of my ability. I'm no super-patriot or crusader, like you seem to think. You should just get over it and go on with your life. You've kept your informant out of it, which is more than anybody else would've done. It's just a job, but you make it out to be some holy crusade. Where did that get you?"

"I lost my job and eight months in prison."

"Exactly. I know you read all those great books and take all those big ideas seriously, but in the real world, none of that counts for shit."

"I never said I was smart."

"And that's the smartest thing you've ever said."

Chapter 17

My Doctor's Appointment

Bart came through for me and got the name of the man believed to be the leader of the most important Iranian cell in the L.A. area.

Dr. Reza Ali Hosseini went to medical school at USC, returned to Iran for a few years, and then emigrated to the United States over thirty years ago. Since returning to the U.S., Dr. Hosseini had become a well-known and wealthy cardiologist, serving the elite of Southern California from his private medical offices in Beverly Hills; he also taught at USC. He kept a low profile, for the most part, but was known to have funded scholarships for Iranian-Americans and given generously to charitable organizations that served the Iranian-American community. He was also known to have strong anti-American government sentiments because of the government's pro-Israel and anti-Iran policies.

I didn't think he'd agree to meet a former FBI agent willingly, which meant I'd have to use a ruse to get in to speak with the doctor, so I obtained a referral to see him as a patient.

Dr. Hosseini strode into his office, medical chart in hand, and looked me in the eye. "Good morning, Mr. Dehenares," he said, extending his hand to give me a forceful handshake. He was sixty-four, five foot seven, about one-sixty, with a full head of salt-and-pepper hair. He exuded intelligence, confidence, experience, and the utmost professional competence. It was easy to see how any patient would take his diagnosis as gospel and accept his prognosis as a given.

He sat behind his desk and looked over my chart again, as if to be sure. "I really can't see anything wrong with you, Mr. Dehenares. Your EKG, echocardiogram, blood work, and vitals all look normal. In fact, I'd say you're the healthiest person I've seen in this office in a long time. I don't see any reason why your primary care physician would send you to me. Exactly what is the concern that brought you here?"

I sized up the doctor as he spoke.

"I'll be perfectly honest with you, Dr. Hosseini," I said. "I'm here under false pretenses."

The doctor stared at me but didn't say anything, waiting for me to continue.

"I needed to see you on a matter that is personal and very important to me, and I didn't think you'd agree to see me any other way."

The doctor remained silent, his questioning gaze now burning into me.

"I'm sure you heard about the kidnapping of Rachael Ginsberg-Marino and her two children last year. As you may know, the case was never solved. I was one of the FBI agents who worked that case, and I was forced to resign and sent to prison for contempt when I refused to testify before a grand jury. I got out of prison a short time ago, and I intend to find out what really happened."

The doctor's look turned to anger. "What does any of that have to do with me?"

"As a former FBI agent, I'm aware of your standing and influence in the Iranian community. I have reason to believe you may have information about the kidnapping, that you may know who was involved."

The doctor's face reddened, and I could see him calculating his response. "In the first place, I don't know anything about the kidnapping. More importantly, I, like every other person of Iranian descent, am tired of the American government assuming that Iranians are behind every crime with even the slightest Middle Eastern element. If you're who you say you are, then you must know many people from the Middle East have had to hire lawyers to keep your government agents from harassing them... Now then, I have patients to see, and you're wasting my time. I will thank you to get out of my office."

"I apologize for the subterfuge, but I need your help."

"I don't know what you think you know about me, but you and your government are all wrong. I'm a respected doctor and only involved with Iranian charitable and educational organizations in this country. I resent your implication that I'm involved in anything else."

I remained seated calmly in front of the doctor, hoping my sincerity would get through to him. "Aside from the deception to get in to see you, doctor, I haven't insulted you. Please don't insult me. Although I'm no longer a government agent, we both know the truth. I need your help, and I know you can help me."

"Why should I believe you? Why should I help you get your job back? Even if I knew anything, why should I care what happened to those Jews or to you?"

"I'm not doing this to get my job back. I'll never go back to the FBI. That bridge has been burned. You should help me because it's to no one's benefit for people to think that Arabs were behind the murder of a young mother and the kidnapping of two children."

The doctor shook his head with contempt and tapped his fingertips on his desk while continuing to stare at me. "In the first place, Iranians are Persian, not Arab, although we all look alike to you racist Americans. Second, I don't believe anything you've said. I think you're still working for the FBI and are here to get whatever information you can. Well, that's not going to work. Now get out before I call my lawyer and the police."

"I told you, I'm not working for the FBI and never will again. Just think about what I've said. If no one from the Middle East was involved in the kidnapping, wouldn't you want people to know that? I'll leave you my card. Please think about it and call me." The doctor didn't take my card or even bother to look at it. I put it on his desk.

"If you aren't working for the FBI and don't want your job back, why do you care about the kidnapping? Who are you working for?"

"I'm working for myself. I've been working as a private investigator since I was released from prison. I want to clear my name of any wrongdoing, and I have a personal interest in finding out what happened to Rachael Marino."

"What is that personal interest?"

I couldn't reveal my personal interest, but I had to let the doctor know that nothing was going to stop me. "I don't care to discuss that. But I *will* get to the bottom of this case, and I'll do whatever it takes to do it."

I could tell from his angry stare that the doctor wasn't impressed by me one bit and had already made up his mind against me. I got up to leave, thinking I'd screwed up this meeting as much as it could have been screwed up and would never hear from the doctor again.

As I was about to open the door to leave his office, the doctor spoke. "If you are truly no longer with the FBI and I am who you think I am and associated with the people you believe me to be, it would be very dangerous for you to attempt to contact me again. Perhaps fatal."

We stared at each other for a long moment and the doctor continued. "I trust I've made myself clear."

Chapter 18

The Glamorous Private Detective

Although I was determined to get to the bottom of the kidnapping and find Rachael, I had to spend much of my time playing private dick to keep up appearances and pay the rent. I hoped to live up to the professional standards of Sam Spade and Philip Marlowe and have at least half the fun they were said to have had.

Jack Spencer, the retired agent Bart had introduced me to, had been kind enough to let me work under the auspices of his PI license and out of his three-room office in downtown L.A. Located in the old Meadson Building on Danton Street, it had a reception area, Jack's own large but spartan office, and a conference-file-kitchen-storage room, where I set up shop. Centrally located downtown between the financial and civic centers, most of Jack's clientele was just a short walk away. He complained he'd wanted an office in the historic nearby Bradbury Building, but that landmark was too expensive and had been made the home of too many third-rate fictional detectives by too many fourth-rate writers. Having an office address, telephone, and access to the restricted information database a PI license confers gave me some credibility and made life easier for me.

I had applied for a PI license as soon as I'd gotten out of prison, but it hadn't yet been approved, for some unknown reason. I had also applied for a license to carry a concealed weapon, but that hadn't been approved yet, either, for some unknown reason. And I had applied to reactivate my license to practice law, but that had not yet been approved, also for some unknown reason. It was clear someone wanted to keep me in limbo and was holding things up, but I hit a brick wall every time I tried to find out who that was.

Jack had been around a long time, was well-known, and had a good reputation. He'd been an investigator with the Bureau and then the L.A.

District Attorney's Office, and despite having two pensions, he'd opened his own PI office at the ripe age of sixty-eight. Small-company fraud, missing persons, and divorce cases were his bread and butter. With neatly trimmed, white hair and a rosy complexion, he was one of those lovable old bachelors who sported a rakish glint in his eye that bespoke a full life well-lived and a thousand stories worth telling.

When I met him, he was too old to do much of anything himself, but getting to the office was his only reason to get out of bed in the morning and the only thing keeping him alive. It quickly became apparent he was just too old to handle the work and just too ornery and cantankerous to give up the job. He still enjoyed playing the office front man, but his days and nights in the field were over. He was also "Old Bureau," and happy hour began at lunchtime, which meant his workday—on those one or two days a week when he did make it to the office—ended early, also. His office location gave him easy access to many of the city's finer watering holes. His years of experience with the darker side of L.A.'s politics and mean streets, along with his raconteur's ability to tell a good story, guaranteed him all the free drinks he could handle.

Jack also loved playing the ponies so, depending on the season, spent his non-office days at Santa Anita or Hollywood Park; sometimes, he would even venture south to Del Mar. Since the heads of security at all the tracks were former agents, he could always get in free and be assured a clubhouse table overlooking the track.

Jack had a very young secretary, Maria García, who came in a few hours a week to do the typing and filing. Unfortunately, Maria couldn't type or file. It wasn't because she didn't know the alphabet. She knew all the letters, but she had trouble getting them in the right order, and she spelled words phonetically when she typed. She was, however, very pretty, with long hair and big round eyes, both as black and shiny as polished onyx, along with other very obvious attributes.

After introducing us, Jack told me in all seriousness, "Borrowing a line from the movies, 'Anybody can type,' and as you see, she has huge… potential."

Born and raised in the barrio of Boyle Heights, Maria was what would be called a *chola*, but with Jack's help, she was working hard to eradicate that appearance. She was a high school dropout but, because of Jack's prodding, had obtained her GED and begun taking classes at East Los Angeles College. Apparently, she was majoring in the psychology of the rich husband—a mandatory prerequisite to her goal of landing one for herself. Fortunately, Jack was a good judge of character, and I came to see that Maria was loyal and devoted and as conscientious as she could be. She was also full of personality and, being well aware of her limitations, had a self-effacing sense of humor. Despite any shortcomings in intellect or sophistication, she charmed every client, and they loved her instantly.

Jack told me he had found Maria last Christmas, when he went to buy coffee for the office at a nearby Starbucks. It was her first day working there, and she'd only been a short-term hire for the holidays. But even at Starbucks, she was in way over her head. He may have been her very first customer.

When he asked her for a bag of coffee, she replied, "Do you want it, like, grounded, man, or in the beans?" He couldn't help laughing. Then she laughed at herself, and he immediately offered her a job for when her holiday job was over.

On those days when Jack got too happy at happy hour, Maria would drive him home to his condo in Venice. There, she'd met and bonded with Jack's cat, Eddie. The responsibility of feeding and cleaning up after Eddie was the only other thing that kept Jack going. He'd occasionally bring Eddie to the office on his way to or from the vet's or just because he felt like it. Jack told Maria the cat was named Oedipus Rex, but he usually just called him Oedipus. Not understanding the reference, Maria assumed the name was Eddie Puss, so she called him Eddie for short. The three of them seemed happier with the name Eddie, each for their own reasons, so it stuck.

Jack's reputation and connections brought prospective clients to the door, and after he and Maria persuaded a client that Johnathan M. Spencer & Associates could handle anything, I did all the actual work. Maria saw to it none of the clients ever saw Jack after happy hour. More important, she saw to it that clients never bothered me when I didn't want to be bothered, which was always.

In addition to being poor, Latina, and the usual half-literate product of a barrio public school, Maria's biggest problem was her family. Her father had been a Boyle Heights gangbanger since his youth. He was currently serving his third term in state prison. Her mother was also a barrio *chola*, now stocking shelves at a local department store and hoping her knees would hold up until she could file for Social Security.

Worse for Maria was her eldest brother, Angel, who went by the nickname "Oso," because of his heavy, six-foot-six frame. He, too, was a Boyle Heights gangbanger, following in his father's footsteps to join the same gang. His body, face, and neck were covered with tattoos. He'd already done his first prison hitch, after a couple in county jail, and was very proud of his criminal record. Even with a degree in psychology, I couldn't understand why these low-lifes were as proud of their prison terms as combat veterans are of their tours of duty.

Maria had another brother, Sammy, who was inaptly nicknamed "Chuco" by his father. He was neither big, tough, nor street smart, and try though he might, he just couldn't fit into the barrio gangbanger mold, much to the dismay of big brother, Oso. He was, however, the brains of the family and had a mind to which computer technology came easily. He was self-taught and had apparently taught himself a lot, becoming the barrio "go-to guy" for anything computer-related. After meeting Sammy, Jack encouraged him to continue his education and paid his college tuition, as he had done for Maria.

Like all gangster firstborn males, Oso thought of himself as the defender of the family honor, while his father was away in prison. To this end, he thought it his duty to visit me one afternoon with a couple of his crew and lay down the law as to his sister and brother—he didn't like that I had put ideas into their heads.

Following Jack's lead, I had encouraged both Maria and Sammy to continue with their education and make the effort to escape the barrio. Oso thought it more important for them to follow his example and conform to the barrio lifestyle. He talked like a third-rate actor in an old B movie, and I couldn't help laughing at his threats. He got angry, pointed his gun at me, and made more threats. He left only after his homies convinced him that an office building wasn't the place to pop a cap, and he could burn me some other time in a less public place.

*****

Occasionally, I generated a case of my own, although my cases were more like shaggy-dog stories and rarely paid off—in cash or laughs. Such was the case when two old enemies, Robert and David Dillard, came to the office one dark and stormy afternoon.

Robert and David Dillard were twins and low-life thugs. I first met them when they were in their mid-twenties and had already been small-time crooks and drug dealers in L.A. for years, with lengthy rap sheets and a jail term under their belts. Because they were large and mean-looking, they also hired out as muscle and gun support on a deal-by-deal basis. They were career criminals, neither ever having held a legitimate job, and were looking to make their first big score, something to move them out of their small-time deals and get them noticed by the big operators. I knew this was unlikely to happen because, despite their willingness to commit any crime, they didn't have the IQ of a trained monkey between them.

A convoluted series of events had resulted in the Dillards acting as middlemen in what was supposed to be the first deal of a proposed ongoing drug trafficking operation. I learned of this from one of my informants and was assigned to be the case agent. This deal involved a Mexican cocaine exporter and a group of drug dealers from Helena, Montana, who were looking to control the cocaine market in their part of the world. The Helena group had come to L.A. looking for a regular supplier of large amounts of cocaine.

During one part of the set-up for this first transaction, the Mexican exporter provided a small sample of cocaine to a man named Juan Mendoza, who was to give it to the Dillards, who would then give it to the Helena people for testing. This use of middlemen for the initial transaction was common for seasoned and cautious drug traffickers, who were wary of undercover law enforcement agents.

The Mexican exporter was actually an undercover FBI agent who'd been introduced into the operation by an acquaintance of Mendoza's, whom he'd met in prison after his most recent conviction. Mendoza's acquaintance was my informant. The transfer of the cocaine sample took place in a restaurant—a restaurant in which Mendoza's twin daughters, Lily and Marlene, worked as waitresses. Being the fifty-five-year-old, three-time loser that he was, Mendoza used half of the cocaine sample himself in the restaurant men's room. Nevertheless, this meeting wasn't a total loss, because when the Dillards met the Mendoza twins, it was love at first sight. A lack of mental capacity was the primary quality the four had in common.

Except for the transfer of the cocaine sample, everything that could go wrong with the proposed deal did go wrong. Telephone calls were contentious, meetings were missed or canceled at the last minute, and suspicions were raised. No one trusted anyone. Three weeks after the initial meeting between the Helena group and the Mexican exporter, nothing had been accomplished. Fortunately, the Dillards' interest in the Mendoza twins and their desire to make a big score were enough to keep the Dillards interested in completing the drug deal, so they continued pushing for it.

When the deal finally went down, the Helena people were arrested and their money seized. The Dillards and Mendoza were also arrested, but Mendoza agreed to testify against the others to avoid a possible life prison term. The Helena people and the Dillards, all of whom had prior convictions, pleaded guilty and received the mandatory minimum prison terms. Both prosecutors and defense counsel referred to the Dillards as the "Dullards," because their obvious lack of brain power escaped no one. Like many of the criminals I'd sent to prison, the Helena people and the Dullards all vowed to come after me when they got out.

Ordinarily, Mendoza would've been killed for introducing the undercover agent and then agreeing to testify for the government, but the Dullards accepted all responsibility for the debacle. After serving a two-year prison term, Mendoza was released, and he and his wife and daughters moved out of California.

I was alone in the office when the Dullards walked in. I recognized them immediately and remembered their threats. My first instinct was to reach for the gun on my hip, but I remembered I no longer carried a gun on my hip so instead asked, "Has it been ten years already?"

"They let us out after six," Robert answered.

"For good time," David said.

"Yeah, for good behavior," Robert clarified.

"Good for you," I said.

"We went looking for you and heard you got fired," David said.

"Yeah, they said you got fired and sent to prison," Robert added.

"I don't know who you heard that from, but that's not what happened," I answered.

"We went looking for you at your old office," Robert said.

"The FBI office," David said.

"That's where they told us you got fired and sent to prison," Robert said, and David nodded in agreement.

"Well, you were misinformed or you misunderstood what they told you. Why were you looking for me? Come to get your revenge?"

"No. We want you to help us," David said.

"We want you to help us find Lily and Marlene," Robert said.

I couldn't hide my surprise and motioned with my hand. "Have a seat." They sat down, angling their chairs so as to be able to see each other as they spoke. I remembered reading as an undergrad psych student that twins have a need to look at their sibling for validation and support, and the Dullards needed all they could get.

"We wrote to them in prison," David said.

"But they never wrote back," Robert added. "We don't know why."

"They must've had a good reason for not writing," David said, looking at Robert.

"Yeah, a good reason." Robert nodded.

"Women always have good reasons for tearing a man's heart apart…" I studied them both. "Why do you want to find them? So you can get to their father through them and get your revenge on him?"

"No," Robert said.

"No. We want to marry them," David said.

I couldn't hold back a laugh. "You've got to be kidding. You just got out of one prison, and you want to jump into another one?"

The Dullards didn't share my sense of humor and just gave me vacant stares.

"You don't expect me to believe you still have a thing for them after all these years?" I asked.

"Why not?" David asked.

"What's so funny about that?" Robert asked. They looked at each other with confused expressions.

"Well, for one thing, their father provided evidence against you that got you a ten-year prison sentence. And you and the other people all said you'd kill the father and me when you got out of prison."

"We didn't mean that," David said, shaking his head.

"Yeah, we didn't mean that," Robert agreed, shaking his head also.

"Well, that's what I remember. Why should I believe you now?"

"We just want you to find them so we can talk to them," Robert said.

"Yeah, we just wanna talk to them," David said. "We tried looking for them by ourselves, but we couldn't find them."

"We asked around everywhere, but we couldn't find them or anybody who knew where they were," Robert said.

"We'll pay you to find them for us," David said.

"Yeah, we'll even pay you," Robert said, joining in the lie and nodding in agreement.

"How long have you been out?" I asked.

"About a week," Robert said.

"Five days," David said.

"And you've been looking for them since you got out?"

"Yeah. After we got back home and checked in with our parole officer," David said.

"Yeah. Right after we checked in with our P-O, we started looking for them," Robert said.

"So, have you both found jobs yet?" I asked just for grins, and they both scoffed. Anyone who thought either of these two career criminals would ever have a regular job was living in fantasy land. Be that as it may, who was I to stand in the way of love?

"I'll tell you what I'll do. I'll find them and ask them if they want to see you again. If they don't want to see you again, you have to promise me you'll leave them alone. If you can't make that promise, I won't even try to find them. If they do agree to see you, you have to promise you'll meet them wherever they want to meet, someplace that's safe for them. Is that a deal?"

"Yeah! Deal," they both said, and their vacant stares turned into big smiles.

Again, just for grins, I said, "I want your word of honor and I want it official. Raise your right hands and say, 'I promise.'"

They each raised a hand and solemnly said, "I promise."

"Your other hand, Robert."

Robert looked confused for a moment then answered, "But I'm left-handed."

"Well, okay, then… I guess, if six years in prison doesn't prepare a man for marriage, nothing will."

"Huh?" Robert asked.

"What?" David asked.

"You'll figure it out. As Socrates said, marriage makes philosophers of all men."

"Who?" David asked.

"What?" Robert asked.

*****

I located Lily and Marlene Mendoza the next day. It wasn't hard. A third-grader with an Internet connection could have found them in a couple of hours.

Contrary to what the movies and TV would have you believe, it's difficult *not* to be found, if someone is looking for you. The only way to really get lost is to change your identity and permanently sever all ties with everyone you've ever known—no phone calls, no mail, no nothing, never ever. But the Mendozas hadn't even made any effort to hide. They just moved to Phoenix. The Mendoza twins, being no smarter than the Dullards, agreed to a meeting, and a week later, they were married in Vegas.

Did I say this was a shaggy-dog story? The Dullards didn't pay me, but I was invited to the wedding.

Chapter 19

The Doctor Needs Help

Given his anger and belligerence at our first meeting, I hadn't expected to hear from Doctor Hosseini ever again. But the universe works in mysterious ways, and a week after our first meeting, he called and, sounding very troubled and apologetic, asked me to come to his home that night at midnight. From the street noise on his end of the line, I could tell he was calling from a payphone. Yes, there are still a few payphones around Los Angeles for the poor or paranoid, but I would recommend keeping plenty of sanitizing wipes on hand for this purpose. The doctor didn't give me his address and assumed I either already knew it or would find it. He told me to make sure I wasn't being followed before going to his residence. Clearly, he was very concerned about physical and electronic surveillance, perhaps with good reason.

At midnight on the dot, I arrived at his home in Beverly Hills, which was not quite a palace but still a few dozen tax brackets out of my league. No lights were on, and it looked like everyone had already gone to bed. Thinking that's what the doctor wanted it to look like, I went ahead and rang the doorbell. I was ushered inside by the doctor's daughter, a beauty in her mid to late twenties. She wore a silk hijab in jade green that was outshined by her sparkling green eyes. Her headscarf was so thin as to be almost transparent, and although it covered much of her face, it couldn't hide her fine, delicate features and perfect skin. She was stunning, and I was appropriately stunned, so much so that it took a moment for me to gather my wits, smile like an idiot, and introduce myself.

"Hello. I know who you are and why you're here. I'm Nousha. My father asked me to take you to his study when you arrived," she said with a dazzling smile that came easy to her. I could tell she was a woman who liked to smile—a smile like that would make life a lot easier. A lock of dark-blonde hair had escaped the confines of her damned scarf and left me wanting to see more.

"Thank you," I replied as I stared at her. "Nousha—what a beautiful name. I could get used to saying that name." Her eyes lit up, and she rewarded me with another glorious smile. "I didn't know the hijab was required to be worn in the home," I added, eager to talk to her for any reason, just to have an excuse to look at her.

"My father is very traditional and strict. We knew you were coming, so propriety requires I wear it on this occasion."

"I see," I said, still staring at her with an idiot's grin.

"My brother will be coming down to join you. I'll let him know you're here after I take you to my father."

I only nodded as she knocked and then opened the door to her father's study and led me in. As I walked behind, I admired her perfect figure.

"Father, this is the gentleman you were expecting, Mr. Dehenares."

Dr. Hosseini didn't bother to stand up from behind his large, antique desk. "Thank you, Nousha. I'll need five minutes with Mr. Dehenares and then tell your brother to come down." He turned toward me and gestured to the leather chair in front of his desk, clearly noticing the smiles Nousha and I exchanged before she took her leave. "Please sit down."

As I sat down he said, "My beautiful daughter is completing her residency at USC Medical Center. When she finishes next year, she will return to Iran. My eldest brother has arranged for her to marry a very promising young lawyer in the Ministry of Justice. They will be the toast of Tehran, as you Americans would say. More importantly, they will serve as an example of how a young couple should live in obedience and service to Allah and Iran."

Perhaps assuming more than I should have, I said, "I'd think it would be difficult for a young person who's lived all their life in America to return to Iran and enter an arranged marriage."

"Nousha has always been an obedient daughter. She understands her duty to Allah and her country."

"You must be very proud of her."

"Yes, Allah has blessed me with one obedient child. Which brings me to the reason for your visit. First, I thank you for coming at such a late hour, but it was necessary to avoid certain possible difficulties. Given your former employment, I'm sure you can understand my concern for physical and electronic surveillance by your government and others. Nevertheless,

I find myself in a situation that is both delicate and dangerous, and I have no choice but to ask for your help."

"What can I do for you, Doctor?" I wondered what curve ball the chaotic universe had thrown him. I tried not to be too obvious in my curiosity as I looked around his office and saw that, despite his apparent loathing of all things American, the room was, with all its antique furniture, bookcases, paintings, and bric-a-brac, what any wealthy American of great means and little taste would've appreciated. The only thing missing was a wet bar, which was a shame, since I could've used a drink.

The doctor didn't answer my question but instead said, "I've done some checking of my own, and it appears you are considered to be a man of honor and integrity, as well as a courageous and highly competent investigator. More important, you are said to be a man who is not afraid of doing that which must be done."

"I like to think I have my priorities in order," I answered, wondering from whom the doctor had gotten his information.

"I hope so, because I find myself in need of someone with your talents. Given our history, I refuse to go begging to the police or FBI for assistance, and I can't go to the people I would normally go to for help, for reasons that will become apparent." With a worried look, he continued, "I trust everything said here tonight will remain strictly confidential. I'm not being overly dramatic when I say this is a matter of life and death." The doctor was serious, his hands folded on his desk as if in prayer.

"Of course," I said. "No one will ever know I was here."

The doctor unlocked a drawer, removed a large manila envelope, and handed it to me. It bore the doctor's name followed by *"Personal and Confidential – To be opened by Dr. Hosseini only,"* scrawled in large, childlike handwriting. I opened it and saw several nude photographs of a boy—clearly the doctor's teenage son—with another young man, blond-haired and blue-eyed, smiling, hugging, kissing… and doing more, much more. The other boy, though small-framed and slender, was generously endowed. *Very* generously.

I looked up for a moment. The doctor's head was bowed as he breathed heavily, his expression angry and disgusted.

"I gather someone wants money to keep this quiet?" I asked.

With a look of resignation, the doctor nodded.

"How did you get these pictures? And how did they contact you for the money?"

"It began eight months ago. The envelope was left at my office, and then I received a telephone call from a man who threatened to make the pictures public on social media, if he didn't get money. It was an older man's voice, an American." The doctor spat out the word *American* like it was slime. "He was very cocky and sure of himself. He wanted a payment of one thousand dollars a month to keep quiet."

"You agreed to that?" I asked, incredulous.

"I had no choice. I couldn't go to my own people, for obvious reasons. But if you're not familiar with Islamic culture, this deviant behavior is considered an abomination to Allah and a crime. If this had become public, it would have ruined my family, and in Iran, my son would be imprisoned, if not executed. I agreed to pay the man if he agreed to keep the other boy away from my son. I had hoped to keep this quiet until Nousha completed her residency and we could all return to Iran next year. My son knows about the pictures now, but he doesn't know I've been paying to keep the other boy away from him."

"Something must've happened for you to call me."

"Yes," the doctor said, nodding slowly. "A few days ago, the man called again and demanded one hundred thousand dollars."

"Why would he do that? What made him change the agreement?"

"He wouldn't say. He only said that he needed the money immediately, but he would give me all the photographs he had, and it would all be over."

"Well, what exactly do you want me to do?"

"Find out who is behind this and what their intentions are. I will pay, if that is the best way to put this behind us, but I can only pay once. I don't want them thinking they can hold this over us and come back for more whenever they please. And I need to keep this quiet until we leave for Iran in a few months."

"You've never met with the man or the other boy?"

"No. I have no desire to meet such people."

"How did you get the money to him in the past?"

"He told me to mail it in cash to a post office box at the main L.A. post office on the first of each month. That's what I've been doing."

"And when and how are you supposed to get the hundred thousand to him?"

"He gave me until this Friday to get the money together and said he would call then with instructions."

The door to the office opened, and a long-haired young man of no more than twenty walked in. As in the photographs, his features made it obvious he was the doctor's son, but, like his sister, those features were finer and more delicate. He was shorter than his father, had an effeminate aura, and walked with a dancer's grace. I instantly sensed his anger and resentment.

With a tone of disappointment, Dr. Hosseini said, "This is my son, Babak Muhammad. Once the source of all my joy, and now the cause of all my pain."

The boy looked toward me with a scowl, and I nodded at him.

"Sit over here," the doctor commanded, pointing to a chair by his desk. "My son has chosen to bring shame upon his family and put himself in great danger, as well."

"I haven't chosen anything. It isn't a choice," the boy said, provoked and rebellious. "It's who I am."

"You're too young and foolish to know who you are," the doctor replied with equal fury.

"I know who I am. It's you who can't accept me for who I am."

"Stop! *Enough*! We've been through all this before. You are going to live with your uncle in Tehran, and there you will learn who you are and what is expected of you."

"I'm not going," the boy insisted and then sat, pouting, with his arms crossed.

"You are going! We've been through this, and it's settled. I should have sent you back years ago, away from this sick country and its permissive culture."

Father and son looked fiercely at each other, then both looked down and shook their heads in anger, each for his own reasons.

"I guess you know about the pictures. Who is the other boy?" I asked Babak.

"A friend," he replied.

"He is not a friend," the doctor interjected. "He wants one hundred thousand dollars. That is not a friend."

"He doesn't want money. He wouldn't do this. It must be somebody else who's doing this or making him do it." Babak looked at me directly for the first time.

"He is an abomination. This entire matter is an abomination," the doctor muttered.

I wanted the boy to understand what was going on here. "This is a very serious matter," I said to his father. "This is clearly extortion. You could go to the police or the FBI."

The doctor also made things clear for the boy. "No. I refuse to beg the police or FBI for help. If this became public, under Islamic law, my son could go to prison or even be executed, when we return to Iran. In any case, my family would be shamed forever. We would be ruined. I want this handled quietly, and once this is behind us, I can send him to live with my brother in Tehran, where he will learn what it is to be a good man and a servant of Allah."

"I'm not going," the boy repeated.

"You are going!" the doctor shouted, rising from his chair quickly and then slowly sitting back down.

"I'm not ashamed of who I am. I don't care if this gets out. I'm glad it finally came out. I've been hiding it all my life and living a lie just to please *you!*"

"You don't know what you're saying," the doctor said, his reasoned calm returning. "In a year, you will be ashamed of this and wondering how you ever came to be involved with these evil people."

After a moment of silence, I asked the doctor, "Do you want me to make the payment or scare him off?"

"I don't care about the money. I just want this handled quickly. Once my son is safely in Iran, my brother can arrange a suitable marriage for him to a girl from a good family, and this foolish phase will be over. Satan is not allowed to roam freely and infect the minds of the young in our country."

I couldn't help wondering if Satan was also responsible for making minds intolerant and bigoted, but I stayed with the matter at hand and turned to Babak. "Who's the other boy? What's his name?"

His face brightened for the first time when he answered. "Billie Carson. He's actually a really good person. And he's not involved. I'm sure of that. Someone else must've gotten ahold of the photos."

"He's a criminal and an abomination," the doctor spat. His son grew sullen again immediately and sank deeper into his chair.

It was clear there was more going on here, but I couldn't speak with Babak in front of his father. I handed the boy my card and asked him to call me first thing tomorrow morning, when he'd had a chance to get Carson's last known phone number and address.

"What will you do?" the doctor asked, followed immediately by the son asking, "What're you gonna do to him?"

"I'll meet with him and find out what he knows. Then I'll find out who's behind this and what their intentions are. I'll call you, and you can decide how you want it handled from there," I told the doctor.

"You won't hurt him, will you?" Babak asked.

"Of course not. But you must call me first thing tomorrow, okay?"

The boy stared at my card and nodded.

I got up to leave, hoping Nousha was still around to walk me out, but no such luck.

Chapter 20

The Baby

Babak called early, but only to say he wouldn't give me any information about Billie Carson unless I agreed to meet with him in person, away from his father, so he could give me his side of the story. This was exactly what I was hoping for, since I knew there was more to it than Dr. Hosseini had told me. This would give me the chance to get more of the story from him.

Babak gave me the name of a well-known LGBTQ restaurant and bar in West Hollywood, a trendy place with overpriced food and expensive parking often frequented by out-of-towners from Peoria and the like who stop in just to have something astonishing to talk about with their incredulous friends and neighbors, once they got back to America's heartland. Of course, the perversity that goes on in America's heartland is no less astonishing, but the video just doesn't make the evening news.

I met Babak there for an early lunch at 11:30, after assuring him homophobia wasn't one of my problems. Since Daddy wouldn't be around, Babak had no reason to hide his true nature, so he let it all out in the friendly surroundings. He wore tight-fitting jeans, white sneakers, and a T-shirt emblazoned with a rainbow flag and the word *Pride* scripted across the front. His walk and mannerisms were unrestrained, also. He ordered a white wine spritzer from the waiter, Chad, who called Babak, "Baby."

"Are you old enough to drink?" I asked.

"I will be, in a year and a half. Anyway, the people here know me and don't ask for ID."

Even his speech was different, with no attempt to hide a slight and telling intonation. How he managed to conceal all this from his parents was both impressive and sad. We both ordered the house special: grilled mushroom-and-onion burger with fries. I guessed it was special only because this house charged twice as much as it would cost anywhere else. The décor couldn't explain the high prices, either. The interior was filled with the same phony film and sports memorabilia as any other chain burger joint.

"So, tell me about Billie."

His story began with a heartfelt sigh. "I met him about a year ago, in a bar in Long Beach. There was instant chemistry between us. I didn't think things like that really happened, but it did. I mean, you hear about it and read about it and see it in movies, but you don't really believe it can happen to you. It was magical."

He spoke with that goofy, faraway look of naïve young people who think they're in love. I wanted to slap him repeatedly.

"It got hot and heavy between us right away. We couldn't keep our hands off each other. I mean it. I know it sounds silly, but it's true. It really is."

"So, what happened?"

"I'm not sure, really. I mean, I don't know why he was attracted to me in the first place. He's super-pretty. And fem. I mean, he really is a woman. At first, we didn't think we'd get along, because I'm more on the fem side, too, but there was just something special between us. There really was a connection that was more than just about sex. We were soulmates, really. And he's two years older than me and so much more mature and sophisticated than me. He said he fell in love with me because I was so innocent."

I wasn't interested in his teenage soap opera, and it was getting harder to stop myself from reaching across the table and slapping the kid, but Babak seemed determined to tell his story his way. "Okay, go on," I said.

"Anyway, after we'd been seeing each other for a while, he decided he wanted to go for it and transition. That's when he said we weren't really right for each other. I still wanted to be friends, but I guess he didn't. Or I think Troy didn't want him to be friends with me anymore. I think Troy was jealous of me because he knew how much Billie cared about me. I called Billie a few times after that, but he never picked up or returned my calls."

Our burgers and fries came, and we both dug in. "Who's Troy?" I asked.

"Troy is his only boyfriend now. They live together. He's a bouncer at L&L in Long Beach. The Leather & Lace Club. It's really cool. They have theme nights there for whatever you're into. Troy was the one who wanted him to transition, I think. He's a real dom—a dominant alpha male, I mean. He's big and tough. He rides a Harley. When we first met him at the L&L, we were afraid of him. Everybody was, because he can be mean and violent. He's gotten into trouble with the police, too, because he's so rough with people at the club whenever he throws them out. He said he was a professional wrestler for a while. He's even been in jail for something. He brags about that."

"Do you think Troy could be the one trying to get money from your father?"

"I think so. I know Billie would never do anything like this. Really."

"Why do you think Troy is behind it?"

"Well, for one thing, Billie's been living with Troy for a while now. They have a really nice condo in Santa Monica. I don't know how they can afford it. I visited Billie there a couple of times before Troy got jealous. Troy could've found the pictures and done all this without Billie even knowing about it."

"Aside from having access to the photos, do you think Troy is the kind of person who'd do something like this?"

"Oh yeah. He's really mean, like I said. He's been in prison, and he likes to scare and hurt people. I've seen it. And like I said, I don't know how they can afford to live where they do. Billie's never worked, and Troy is just a bouncer, so how much could he make? Billie said Troy always has some kind of scam going, too. He scams people, and then he scares them so they won't go to the police. He always has drugs, too, so he's probably dealing. He gets away with it because he's so big and mean. I mean, who's gonna tell on him?"

Chad came by again, filled our water glasses, and asked, "Another spritzer, Baby?"

"I better not. I have class this afternoon," Babak answered, and Chad nodded and sauntered off.

"Why does Billy put up with Troy, if he's so mean and violent?"

Babak gave this some thought. "I think Billie thinks he needs to have someone big and tough to protect him. And Troy gives him a place to live and takes care of him. Plus, he's really ready to transition—that takes some support, too, you know."

"Where exactly do Troy and Billie live?"

Babak hesitated, staring at his glass of wine. "What're you gonna do to Billie?"

"I'm not going to do anything to him. I just want to talk to him and find out what he knows about this."

"You're not gonna hurt him, are you?"

"I tremble at the thought of violence," I said, instantly realizing only Marlowe could use that line without sounding cheesy. "I don't see any reason why I'd want to hurt him. Do you think they're home right now?"

"Billie's probably home. He comes and goes during the day. Troy is usually gone during the day. I know he goes to the gym and works out every day—that's why he's so buff. And who knows what else he's up to, like I said. He usually comes home sometime in the late afternoon, before going to work at the club." As though still having doubts about me, he said again, "I'm worried for Billie. I won't give you his address or telephone number, but I'll take you to him. I'd like to see him again, and I want to be there when you talk to him."

Not a bad idea to have a friendly face with me the first time I approach Billie, so I agreed to follow Babak to Troy and Billie's condo.

Chapter 21

The Boy

I followed Babak to a ritzy townhouse and condominium neighborhood in Santa Monica that had lots of expensive landscaping surrounding the enclave. In addition to underground parking beneath each building, there was private assigned parking for each unit, the spots filled with late-model sports cars and foreign SUVs. It was the kind of neighborhood favored by hipsters with lots of money they hadn't earned and a sense of entitlement to a lifestyle they weren't entitled to. I doubted I'd like anyone who could live in such a neighborhood.

Babak walked me to the Vista Del Rey condominiums, a high-rise building that was well beyond my means. We took the elevator up to the sixth floor, which was certain to provide an expensive and impressive view of the Pacific. Billie's doorbell was one of those pretentious and annoying long jobs that always make me want to kick the door down just to get it over with. *Dong dong dong ding, dong ding ding dong, ding ding ding dong, dong dong dong ding*—you get the picture.

When the door finally opened, Billie Carson first looked surprised upon seeing Babak and then scared. Then he looked more scared when he saw me standing behind him.

Billie composed himself quickly and flashed a giant smile before screaming, "Baby, it's you!" and threw his arms up, moving forward to give Babak a big hug.

Babak returned the hug, and Billie spoke while eyeing me up and down over Babak's shoulder. "It's been so long. Where've you been, Baby? I've missed you!" When they disengaged from their hug, he continued, "What've you been up to? You have to tell me everything!"

Billie spoke with a husky yet high-pitched falsetto. His light-blond hair was now longer than in the photos and cut in an unmistakable female style—*bob cut*, I believe it's called—although I'm no expert on women's hairstyles. He wore a scoop-necked Breton shirt with blue stripes, white short-shorts, and blue canvas slip-ons. His limbs were feminine and slender, sexy in a cheap sort of way. Although Babak had said Billie was two years older than he, with his well-applied makeup, the kid looked the same age.

"Can we come in, Billie?" Babak asked, still standing beside me in the hallway. "There's something I need to talk to you about."

"Of course. Where're my manners? Keeping you standing there. Come in, please," Billie responded, trying to sound more sophisticated than he'd ever be. "Who's your handsome friend?" He flashed me a phony, lascivious smile.

"This is Mig Dehenares. He's a private investigator. He used to be an FBI agent. My father hired him to look into something that involves all of us."

"Oh, my. That sounds positively thrilling," Billie said, ushering us toward the living room as he continued to look me over with suspicion. "But how could I possibly be involved? I haven't even seen you in months, Baby, and you know my life is such a bore... And you're such a meanie for not staying in touch." As he eased Babak onto a white sofa and pointed to a white recliner for me, he seemed to be making a point of blaming their lack of contact on Babak, even though the kid had told me it was Billie who'd ended the relationship and wasn't returning Babak's calls.

There were fresh-cut roses of various colors in a crystal vase on a small glass coffee table and tasteful white rugs in front of the sofa and recliner.

Billie sat down next to Babak and gently touched his thigh. "Now tell me, what's this all about, Baby?"

Babak was clearly still infatuated with Billie and couldn't keep an adoring, stupid smile off his face. "Well, it's all so crazy. I know you're not gonna believe it."

"Well, just tell me, Baby," Billie purred, leaning a bit closer.

I wondered if "Baby" was just Billie's pet name for Babak or the name he went by in the LGBTQ milieu. "Maybe I should spell it out, just to save time," I said. "To put it simply, someone is trying to extort thousands of dollars from Babak's father. This someone sent his father copies of photographs showing you and Babak engaged in sexual activity. As you know, Babak's family is Muslim and extremely conservative. Photographs like this would ruin his family's reputation and standing in the Islamic community and could be dangerous for Babak."

"Oh, my gawd!" Billie cried, feigning wide-mouthed surprise. He pressed his right hand limply over his heart while looking back and forth from me to Babak.

Babak bought the show. "I know you couldn't have anything to do with it."

"Of course not, Baby. How could I? You know I'll always love you." Billie snuggled closer to Babak and put his arms around him. "You know I'd never do anything to hurt you or your family."

"I know, I know." Babak put his head on Billie's shoulder and began to whimper.

"Do you have any idea how anyone could've gotten hold of those photos?" I asked Billie.

"I don't know. Baby and I took dozens, hundreds of pictures with our iPhones. We were crazy about each other, weren't we, Baby?"

Babak smiled and nodded.

"Who has access to your phone, Billie?"

"Anybody. Everybody. I leave it lying around all the time. I'm such a ditzy space cadet. I've lost three phones in just the last year. You remember the time I lost one in the sand at Crystal Cove, when you couldn't keep your hands off me?"

Babak stopped whimpering and giggled.

"I don't know who could've taken my phone and gone through my pictures. It makes me mad just thinking about it."

"You keep your phone locked with a password, don't you?" I asked.

"Not always. Anybody could've gotten into it."

"I thought maybe Troy might have gotten into it and done this," Babak said, looking up at Billie. "You know he can be mean sometimes."

"Sure, he can be mean sometimes, but he'd never do anything like this. The most he'd do is get mad at me for keeping the pictures and make me delete them."

"Where's Troy now?" I asked.

"He said he'd be out running errands all day after his workout. He never really tells me where he's going or what he's doing," Billie confided with a shrug.

Babak seemed to accept Billie's explanation. "I knew you couldn't be involved in this."

"Of course not, Baby, you silly." To reassure him, he stroked Babak's hair then said to me, "I'm sorry. I just can't help you, I guess."

Babak said, "I knew it wasn't you. I just wanted him to hear it from you, so he could tell my father. You know how he is. I'm sorry we had to bother you with something like this. I feel so bad about it."

"Don't be silly. At least it was a reason for you to come see me again." Billie flashed a big smile that drew another adoring look from Babak. "Now that that's over with, can I get you a drink or something?"

"No, thanks. I can't stay. I have a class at three," Babak said but didn't make any move to leave. "You know how traffic is around USC. But it was good to see you again, Billie." He looked up at the boy with those puppy-dog eyes that were making me want to slap him yet again. "Maybe we can get together again sometime?"

"Still at USC?" Billie asked, feigning interest to avoid the question. "What class are you taking?"

"Yeah, still a Trojan. It's an art history class. On the male nude throughout history and what the changing depictions of the male nude say about the society they were created in," Babak answered, impressively yet obviously regurgitating the course catalog description. "It's very interesting. I think you'd like it."

"Oh, no. It sounds way too complicated for me, Baby. I'm just a silly bimbo." He ran his fingers through Babak's hair, giving him just what he wanted. "You're the one with all the brains."

I stood and waved Babak toward the door. "You go ahead. I just have a couple more questions to follow up on. I'll talk to you and your father later, okay?"

Babak nodded, having seen what a light touch I was and now been assured I wouldn't be rough with his friend. And in front of Babak, Billie couldn't object to a couple more questions, if he didn't have anything to hide.

Billie walked Babak to the door, cooing, "I'll call you, okay? We'll have lunch or something. I don't want to go another six months without seeing you, Baby. You mean too much to me." He kissed him on the lips, knowing just how to play him.

Billie came back and sat down on the white sofa, making a show of crossing his slender legs before staring at me seductively. I stared back. And continued to stare back, my face becoming hard, no longer congenial.

He lit a cigarette nervously. His face also lost its phony congeniality—he seemed to age ten years in an instant. He gulped and took a drag.

"Do you have any idea what happens to someone like you in prison?" I asked. "Within one hour of arrival, some prison gang will make you their bitch. It might be the Aryan Brotherhood, the Mexican Mafia. Maybe one of the biker gangs or the Crips or Bloods. One of them will claim you, and you'll be their fuck hole for as long as you're inside. And when the gang that owns you isn't using you, they'll rent you out."

Billie couldn't look at me. His hand began to shake, and ashes fell from his cigarette onto the white rug between the sofa and chair.

"You'll be raped every day so often, your hole will become so loose you'll need a diaper to keep from shitting on yourself. And since the kind of people who go to prison aren't the cleanest people in the world, you'll be infected with every sexually transmitted disease there is. Even with medication, you'll be infected so often, your insides will begin to rot, and you'll be pissing through a tube into a bag. They'll beat you regularly just to keep you in line, so you can forget about that pretty face of yours. If you survive, by the time you get out, you'll be old and sick way before your time."

Billie remained silent. A tear ran down his cheek.

"But I don't think you'll survive. We both know you're not tough enough. That's why you hooked up with Troy. You need someone like him for protection. But it doesn't work that way in prison. In prison, you don't belong to just one bull. You'll be used by everybody, even the guards. I'd give you two months before you slit your wrists."

He was crying audibly now, his head down and his whole body shaking. I almost felt sorry for him.

I wanted to give him a moment to let reality sink in, so I stood to look out the picture windows to the west onto the pier and boats and the blue Pacific beyond. I decided to take a shot in the dark. "What a beautiful view. You won't see anything like this from a prison cell, which is where you'll be soon. I know Troy has been pimping you out and then blackmailing the suckers to keep quiet... Did I say *suckers*...? That's the only way you two could afford to live in a place like this and drive that nice set of wheels you have outside."

"What do you want?" Billie asked, delicately wiping tears from his cheek with a finger.

"The problem is, and it's not your fault because you couldn't have known, you picked the wrong mark this time. Babak's father isn't what he seems. He was willing to pay a few thousand just to keep you away from his kid and keep things quiet, but you and Troy got greedy. Babak's father is very well connected, because he does some very important work for very powerful people. He's not just some doctor for rich, old moneybags with bad tickers. He's got a lot of pull with the right people, and he's protected. He can pick up the telephone and, with just one call, make people disappear, and there's nothing the police or the FBI can do about it. Babak doesn't know about any of this, and he doesn't know I'm not *just* a former FBI agent who became a private investigator."

"What do you want?" Billie asked again. "I'll do anything."

"What made you go after Babak's father?"

He lit another cigarette. "Troy didn't know Babak's father was a doctor until I let it slip a few months ago. He wants me to have implants and start hormones, so we were talking about how much it costs and finding the right doctor. I joked that maybe Babak's father could do it for free or at least gimme a discount. That's how it slipped out. I wish it hadn't, but we were getting high, and it just slipped out.

"I didn't want to get Babak involved in this. You have to believe that. But Troy got violent like he always does when he doesn't get his way and made me tell him all I knew about Babak and his family. Then he did some checking on his own. He has a friend, an Arab guy he gets his drugs from, and he found out all about Babak's father. He told Troy that Babak's father was a big shot doctor who lived in a Beverly Hills mansion worth millions. He said, because they were Muslims or Moslems or whatever they're called, his father would pay just to keep it quiet, to protect Babak and avoid a scandal. That's what the Arab guy told him."

"Well, he's not going to pay any more," I said. "Not another penny. At this point, it's cheaper just to get rid of you. But he doesn't want to do that unless he has to, because he knows how much Babak cares about you. That's lucky for you. Their relationship was already strained, and now, he's afraid it would turn his son away from him completely if you were hurt. The bottom line for you and Troy, though, is you have very few choices. You give up the photos and get out of California, or he'll make you disappear. If you don't give up the photos, at a minimum, you'll go to prison. You know what that means for you."

Billie blew smoke. "You're gonna kill me anyway, aren't you? Even if I give you the photos?"

"Not necessarily. And it won't be me. The people they have who do that sort of thing are experts at it. They have poisons, drugs, guns with silencers. They can make it look like suicide or an accident. They know how and where to get rid of a body so it'll never be found. My job is just to get to the bottom of things, so Babak's father can decide what to do with you."

"So, what do you want from me?"

"Right now, I want any camera or phone with photos of Babak. I want any hard copies of photos of Babak. I want any computer or media that has any photos of Babak."

"You can have my phone, and the computer's in the other room. There're some photos in the desk drawer."

"Are those the only places with photos of Babak?"

"Troy copied the photos to the computer. He always copies the photos to the computer."

"I'll take your phone and the computer hard drive now. Are you sure Troy doesn't keep any photos on *his* phone?"

"I'm sure he doesn't. He's into dealing drugs, so he's too worried about his phone being tapped or confiscated by the cops or the feds. He doesn't want anything incriminating on his phone."

I didn't believe him. I'd have to come back for Troy's phone. "When Troy gets home, I want you to use his phone to call me. I'll come for it tonight and have a talk with him."

"Troy will never let you have it. He'll kill you first. He's big, a lot bigger than you. And he's tough. I've seen him beat up three guys who jumped him all at once."

"I'll handle Troy," I said, trying to appear confident so Billie wouldn't change his mind about rolling over, but having my own doubts. "I've done my homework and know all about him… Are there any other places where there might be photos of Babak?"

He shook his head unconvincingly.

"You understand, if even one photo shows up, you're dead?"

"There may be some on some memory cards. Troy put a camera in the bedroom that he uses when I bring a John here. It uses a memory card, too. He usually transfers the video to the computer, so there'll be room on the card for more."

"Let's get them," I said.

Billie was reluctant to move, so I grabbed him by the arm and pulled him up forcefully, to make sure he understood I meant business, then pushed him toward the bedroom, saying, "Move it!"

"Ow! Owie!" Billie howled, cringing as if he were going to start crying again.

I had Billie get me his phone, the photos, and memory cards, and also remove the computer's hard drive. I didn't want my fingerprints on anything in the place. As he worked, I continued to question him, and it became clear he was very knowledgeable about computers and technology, in general, and had been a willing participant in the whole mess that was his and Troy's life. He denied knowing much about the Johns, though, claiming they were just guys he'd met at nightclubs or Troy had found for him.

"That doesn't explain how you can afford this condo or the Beemer," I said.

"I have a regular, a sugar daddy. He pays for the condo. I see him every week."

"What do you know about him?" I asked.

"Nothing, except he must be really rich. He's just another old guy who can't even get it up half the time. I think he's in love with me. He likes me to call him Daddy."

"You must know more about him."

"No, really, I don't. He's just another John Troy found, and then he found out from Adam that he was really rich."

"Who's Adam, and how'd Troy find out he was rich?"

"Adam? That's the Arab guy he gets his dope from. But I don't think that's his real name. It's just the name he goes by here. He's from the Middle East somewhere. Anyway, it was by accident, another accident. They were here getting high, and Troy was showing him the pictures of all the Johns and me. He kinda gets off on that. Then he was gonna show him the pictures of me and Babak. That was when he first wanted to ask Adam about Babak's father. When Adam saw the picture of the old guy, he told Troy that he was really, really rich, and Troy should hit him up for a lot more than he was getting. That's when Troy got him to pay for the condo."

"So why didn't you just get your sugar daddy to pay for the surgery and hormones, instead of going after Babak's father?"

"He likes me the way I am, and Troy was afraid the old guy wouldn't want me anymore, if I transitioned. Troy said he's seen it before. Guys have a thing for someone like me and lose interest if I go too fem. You know, too much like a woman, with breasts and everything."

"Yeah," I said, recalling that everyone has their own kink, as my psych professor used to say.

It became clear that, although Billie may have been reluctant initially, he'd gone along with the scheme to extort money from the doctor because it was the quickest way to come up with big money all at once to pay for his implants and hormones—which he wanted—and because Troy promised him he wouldn't pimp him out anymore.

As he talked, he caressed his arm where I'd grabbed him. His delicate skin was still red.

"Sorry about your arm," I said. "I didn't mean to hurt you."

"Everybody hurts me, sooner or later," Billie whimpered.

Chapter 22

The Big Sleep

It was six o'clock when my cell phone rang, the time when bombs exploded. I had been waiting for Billie to call, but it was Babak, not Billie, and he had a bombshell of his own for me.

Babak was crying and sounded frantic. "Mig, something happened. I don't know what to do."

"What happened?" He just cried and cried. "What happened? *Where are you*?" I shouted into the phone.

"I'm at Billie's. I came here after my class. I had to see him again," he said, still crying. It sounded like he had marbles in his mouth and it was hard for him to speak.

"*What happened*?"

"Billie's dead, I think. I'm pretty sure he's dead. Troy killed him."

I let that sink in. "Were you there when it happened?"

"Yeah. It happened right in front of me. I can't believe it. It was awful. *Awful*."

"What exactly happened?"

"I came to see Billie, like I said. We were just talking. He told me everything that happened after I left, how he told you about how Troy made him give him the pictures and how Troy was behind everything... He said he didn't know Troy had sent my father the pictures and wanted money. I knew it wasn't Billie's idea. I knew he couldn't do anything like that."

"So, what happened to Billie?"

"When Troy came home, he was drunk or high or both. He was already angry about something. When he saw me, he got really mad and asked Billie what I was doing there. He thought Billie and me had been having sex and called Billie a faggot slut. Then he slapped him, and I thought he was gonna hit me. But he grabbed Billie and started shaking him and slapping him harder.

"Then Billie told him about you, that I came with you, and how you said they'd go to jail, if he didn't give you the pictures and the computer stuff. Billie tried to tell Troy he was only trying to protect him, but Troy went crazy and started beating Billie up. I tried to stop him, but he hit me, too. Then he knocked Billie down and started to choke him. I jumped on top of him, but he slugged me with his elbow and knocked me out. That's all I can remember... Billie's face was already bloody and red. When Troy started choking him, he turned blue, and his tongue was sticking out. It was terrible."

"Can you drive or walk?" I asked.

"I don't think so. My jaw hurts really bad, and I have a bad headache. I feel dizzy."

"Are you sure Troy has left?"

"Yeah. It's really quiet here now."

"Do you know how long ago all that happened?"

"No, but it couldn't have been too long ago. Maybe just ten or fifteen minutes, at most."

"Okay, just stay there. Don't touch anything. Don't call anybody. Don't answer the door except for me. I'll be there in twenty minutes, okay?"

"Okay."

*****

I took my ratty old raincoat with me and a new one I'd just bought—if I was going to play Spade and Marlowe, I'd figured I'd need a snazzy new trench coat like they were always seen wearing, rain or shine. I also brought along two ball caps, several rags, and some large, plastic trash bags.

When I got there, I checked Billie, just to be sure. The sad life of Billie Carson was indeed over—he'd never be hurt by anyone again. His body lay in an uncomfortable heap—you never find a murder victim lying comfortably; the pangs of violent death always leave a grotesque corpse in an awkward pose. A very fine but sometimes excessively romantic novelist wrote that there's dignity in every death, but as Billie lay there with hideous black-and-blue strangulation imprints on his throat, a battered face, tongue hanging limply out of the corner of his mouth, and open eyes rolled back, I failed to see any dignity at all.

I wiped things down as best as I could and put Babak's soda bottle and cigarette butts in a plastic bag. I cleaned and flushed the toilet several times after Babak had vomited in it twice. Fortunately, he hadn't bled much, mostly on himself and on the small, white rug in front of the sofa.

"Your jaw looks pretty bad," I told him. "It may be broken. I'm not sure about your nose. I'll take you to the emergency room. You can tell them you fell down some stairs and hit your jaw on the handrail or stairs." Thinking it might be a good idea to have some help at the hospital, I asked, "Do you and your sister get along well?"

"Yeah, why? We're very close. We understand each other. She's the only one in the family I was out to. We trust each other with everything."

"Where is she now?"

"Probably still at the hospital. She does evening rounds about this time, I think."

"Good. We'll call her and tell her to meet us in the ER. She can get you taken care of quickly and help you, herself, if there's any problem with the hospital people." *Good, indeed,* I thought to myself, happy about the prospect of seeing the beauty again. Nousha could also help keep her father calm when I broke the news to him.

"What're you gonna do about Billie? We can't just leave him there like that."

"I'll make an anonymous phone call to the police, after we get you taken care of. I'll report the sounds of a struggle and screaming. They'll think I'm another tenant in the building. That'll be enough for the cops to come in and find what's here."

I had Babak put on my new raincoat, a ball cap, and his sunglasses. "Keep your head down, and don't look at anyone directly," I told him. No one would be able to make a positive ID of him, at least none that would stand up in court.

I rolled up the blood-stained white rug, put a plastic bag over each end, and stuffed it inside my old raincoat. I put on my sunglasses and cap then walked out with the bagged carpet inside the coat slung over my shoulder. I carried the plastic bags with the other incriminating items while helping Babak walk, and hoped no one would ever know we'd been there.

It was overcast outside and looked like rain, so we didn't appear too suspicious with our raincoats as we walked out of the building to my car. I hoped there'd be no forensic trace of us in the condo, but I knew from my own experience that the horrific sights and sounds of Billie's murder would remain forever burned in Babak's mind.

Chapter 23

Post Mortem

I used Babak's cell phone to call his sister as soon as we arrived at the hospital. Nousha took charge of the situation as I'd hoped she would and began to help him immediately.

X-rays confirmed a broken nose and a severely bruised jawbone. Nousha and the attending emergency room physician did what was needed with no questions asked, thanks to her presence. Babak would spend the night in the hospital, just to be on the safe side.

After Babak had changed into a hospital gown, I told Nousha I'd have to take his clothing with me and that she'd have to get new clothes for him from home, for when he was released.

The hospital had quarters for interns and residents when necessary for them to stay the night. Nousha said she'd spend the night there, so she could check in on Babak from time to time. Her devotion to him was apparent, and she seemed pleased with my concern for him.

Although a hospital isn't the optimal setting for romance, the circumstances provided an opportunity to exchange a few words, and I wasn't about to let that opportunity go to waste. "Now that you have Babak taken care of, perhaps you can take a look at me, Doctor," I said to Nousha when we were finally alone in Babak's room. Thanks to modern medicine, the lights went out for Babak; he'd fallen into a comfortable, drug-induced sleep before having to explain anything to anyone that night.

We were standing next to Babak's bed, and I moved in closer to her.

"Is there something wrong with you?" she asked.

"Nothing you couldn't fix."

"My specialty is cardiology, like my father's. You don't look like someone who needs a cardiologist."

"Appearances can be deceiving. I'm having troubles of the heart and in desperate need of tender, loving care." I slid my hand over next to hers on the bed rail.

"I don't think I can help you with that, Mr. Dehenares."

"Please call me Mig." We both turned to face each other. "I disagree. I seem to come alive when you're around. I think you're exactly the person to help me."

"You had better calm yourself down," she said, smiling, "or you may work yourself into an arrhythmia."

I looked deeply into her eyes. "That's okay with me, if that's what it takes to get your attention."

She returned my gaze. "My father is the best cardiologist in the area. And given your prior consultation with him, I'd have to refer you back to him."

I moved in still closer and said softly, "He couldn't provide the treatment I'm hoping for."

We heard Dr. Hosseini in the hallway ask a nurse for his son's room, and Nousha said, "You're in luck. Here he is now. So, if you truly need a doctor…"

"I'm getting over the idea. Bad luck for me. Maybe for the both of us," I replied as I stepped back.

The doctor came into the room, followed by his wife, Morvarid, who wore a traditional hijab. I was curious about her but didn't want to seem impertinent or raise questions by interjecting myself in what was normally a family matter. Nousha explained to them how Babak had fallen down stairs while visiting a college friend, and then she provided the medical diagnosis and prognosis with clinical detachment. She then warmly reassured her mom and dad, calming their concerns. She was especially good at easing Morvarid's anxiety, as it was clear from her motherly behavior and questions that Babak was still her baby, despite his age.

Morvarid appeared highly educated, with an elegant manner indicating she came from a family with money and status. She was also at least ten years younger than the doctor. I could see where their children had gotten such good looks.

Fortunately, the explanation that Babak had fallen down stairs satisfied them both, for the time being, thanks again to Nousha's persuasiveness. Before I left them, Dr. Hosseini asked me to come to his home later that night.

*****

I had a few things to do before seeing the doctor, like toss the plastic garbage bags with Babak's soda bottle, cigarette butts, clothes, and the rags in a dumpster behind a strip mall. I'd have to bleach the bloodstains out of the carpet and cut it to pieces before dumping it, also.

I wanted to wipe and destroy all the data on the phone, memory cards, and hard drive before getting rid of them. A year ago, I wouldn't have thought it possible I'd be destroying evidence from a crime scene. A lot had changed in a year.

I took an Uber to a restaurant in Santa Monica, found a payphone, and made an anonymous 911 call to report the screaming in Troy and Billie's condo. I walked from there to Babak's car, so I could drive it to the Hosseini home when I went to see Dr. Hosseini. After our meeting, I'd walk a few blocks before calling Lyft to take me home. It had begun to rain again lightly, which continued off and on all evening. I was glad I still had my old raincoat.

The good doctor wasn't in a good mood when I went to see him. His bad mood got worse when I told him about the murder. In his eyes, I had screwed things up as much as humanly possible. He yelled and waved his arms in anger. He wasn't pleased I had met with Babak alone and then taken him to see Billie, thereby creating an opportunity for them to rekindle their relationship. If I hadn't done that, Babak wouldn't have gone back to see Billie again and wouldn't have been present at the time of the murder or gotten hurt.

He pounded his fists on his desk and yelled, "How could you do that? *How could you do that?*" It was as if I had been the one responsible for his son's injuries.

The doctor got up from behind his desk and began to pace around his study. While I remained seated, he continued ranting and waving his arms. He was thankful—to Allah—I had had the minimal level of competence to clean up the crime scene and hopefully keep the Hosseini family name out of the sordid affair. In his tone and diction, the doctor made clear he was used to being in command, giving orders, and rendering discipline. I hadn't had a dressing-down like that since leaving the Army.

"Unfortunately," I had to say, "I don't think you're out of the woods yet."

"What do you mean?" The doctor stopped his pacing and turned to face me. "If you did your work correctly, there's nothing to tie my son or me with what happened," the doctor reasoned. "Surely that other animal will want to leave us alone now and get as far away from here as possible, and as quickly as possible."

"Yes, but it will take the police a few weeks to complete the forensics on everything in the condo. I wouldn't relax until they finish their investigation. And Troy will certainly want to get away, but he'll be desperate for money to make his escape. I can guarantee you'll be hearing from him very soon, and he'll demand money immediately."

The doctor shook his head in frustration. "What should I do?"

"Tell him you'll pay him, but tell him you can't come up with all the money he wants. Offer him five thousand. He'll settle for that. It's enough for him to get away, and that's all he's concerned about now. Also, tell him you want his cell phone, to be sure he doesn't have any pictures on it. Tell him I'll be the one to make the exchange of the money for the cell phone, wherever and whenever he wants, just to make him feel comfortable. And tell him, if he ever contacts you again, your son will provide eye-witness testimony to murder, regardless of any other consequences. That should be enough to get him to leave you alone."

The doctor nodded.

"Call me as soon as you hear from him," I said and handed him Babak's car keys.

Chapter 24

Muchas Gracias, Señor

I got home that night tired after a very long and eventful day. I knew I'd be out as soon as my head hit the pillow and was looking forward to a good night's sleep.

I still felt a chill from the damp weather and poured myself two fingers of Scotch. I figured I'd earned it. I tuned in KUSC, sadly the only classical music station in Southern California and USC's greatest contribution to the world, and sat down on my recliner to listen to some relaxing Chopin. Taking a sip, I smiled at the memory of the reaming the good doctor had given me. Maybe we all need a good dressing-down once in a while, whether deserved or not, just to keep us on our toes. Then I remembered Nousha and our banter earlier that evening. Although her words had expressed disinterest, her expression had been coy.

The doorbell rang, and, much to my surprise, Nousha was standing there, wearing my new raincoat, the one I gave Babak on our way out of Billie's condo.

"Well, this is a surprise," I said, trying hard to keep the idiot grin off my face.

"I wanted to return your raincoat and thank you for all you did for my brother and my family," she said. She wasn't wearing her hijab, and her radiant beauty was in full view: the lustrous, dark-blonde hair, luminous green eyes, and dazzling smile. I couldn't think of a woman I'd seen in the last year she didn't outshine.

"Please come in," I said, and she did.

She looked around and was clearly not impressed. "So, this is how private detectives live."

Since I hadn't known how long I'd be in prison, I had arranged to sell my condo and most of my possessions, once I was incarcerated. At this point, I had few furnishings and several unpacked boxes scattered around the place. Some books lay on an end table by my recliner and reading lamp.

"Be it ever so humble. Are you disappointed?" I asked, realizing how shabby my small apartment must look to anyone with a little money and taste. My only attempt to decorate, if it can be called that, was an old photo of my mother and me in an antique silver frame, taken when I was a child, that I'd placed on my bedroom dresser. It was the only photo that had survived the fire.

"No. I wasn't sure what to expect."

"Well, keep in mind, I've only been out of prison a few weeks. This place is only temporary, and I haven't had much time to do anything with it."

"I heard about that. It seemed unfair to me. That you would go to prison for something like that, I mean."

"Story of my life. Would you like something to drink?" I asked.

"What are you having?"

"Scotch."

"*Hmm*… I'll take a rain check on the alcohol. I have to get back to the hospital. I will have some juice, if you have any."

I nodded, noting the Hosseini children didn't follow the strict, Islamic "no alcohol" rule of their parents.

"Please have a seat," I said as I went to get her a drink. She was still standing, holding a book and looking over the other two books on the end table, when I returned with her glass of orange juice.

"*Ada* by Nabokov, the *Collected Stories* of Saul Bellow, and *Ontological Relativity and Other Essays* by Quine," she said with a questioning look.

"I like a little light reading and music before bed." I handed her the juice, and she put Quine back down on the table. "What shall we drink to?" I asked.

"To surprises," she said.

"I'll drink to that." We tapped glasses, and each of us took a sip. "Why don't you peel off the raincoat and have a seat?"

She smiled mischievously, put down her glass, and unbuttoned the raincoat, staring at me intently as she did so. She wasn't wearing anything underneath, and she was fantastic—there was nothing I would've added or changed; there simply wasn't anything to improve upon. I remembered reading somewhere that that was how some artist or poet had defined beauty.

"The Hosseinis are full of surprises," I said.

"You must think me very immodest."

"I'm thinking of only one thing right now, and it has nothing to do with modesty."

"I wonder what you could be thinking."

"I wonder if you wonder."

*****

She didn't seem to mind the small bedroom with the small bed and sheets that hadn't been changed in a week. The messy bathroom didn't bother her, either. If she enjoyed our tumble half as much as I did, I'd say she also had a very good time. In any case, she had a smile on her face when she left, still wearing my raincoat and leaving me to wonder where her scrubs were. She promised to call and let me know how Babak was doing, when she got back to the hospital.

"By the way, how did you know where I lived?" I asked as she opened the door to leave.

"My father is a very careful man. He did his due diligence and had you investigated before he hired you. I peeked into the file and read all about you. I expected you to be taller."

"That's how you knew I'd been in prison and why."

She nodded. "Was I a naughty girl for peeking into your file?"

"Very. But that's okay. I like naughty girls."

I sighed as she drove away. You hear about things like this happening and read about it and see it in movies, but you don't really believe it can happen to you. It was magical. Yeah. Really.

Chapter 25

Billie Carson – Deceased

I have to say something because I don't want you to hate me.

You see, I always felt like I was all alone. It was just me and my mom and my little brother, Timmy, and little sister, Betsy. My father wasn't around much, which was a good thing, because it was better when he wasn't around. When he was around, he was always drunk and mean and violent. He used to hit Mom and me. Even when he wasn't hitting us or pushing us around, he'd say awful things to us, just to make us feel like shit.

The only help we ever had was from my Uncle Dwight. He was my mom's big brother, but he wasn't like what Mom thought he was. She loved him and looked up to him, because he'd come around and help sometimes and give Mom money. He was big and tough and had been in the Marines. When he was there, Dad wouldn't do anything to us, because Dad was afraid of him. The last time Dad beat up on Mom, Uncle Dwight and his friend got him and beat him up real bad and told him never to come around again. That's why Mom was always so grateful to him, but, like I said, Uncle Dwight wasn't what Mom thought he was.

I was nine the first time Uncle Dwight started touching me. Then he raped me. It hurt really bad the first time. I was gonna tell Mom, but I was scared, and he said it would be bad for me, if I told anybody. Mom wouldn't believe me anyway, he said. He was right, I think, because Mom looked up to him and was always saying how much we needed his help. Uncle Dwight would bring groceries and give Mom money for food and clothes and stuff. So, there was no point in trying. And I didn't want him to do anything to Timmy and Betsy, even though I don't think he liked girls. So, I just kept my mouth shut and didn't say anything to anybody.

At first, he'd do it whenever he could get me alone. I tried to never be alone with him, but sometimes Mom would be gone or tell me to go to the store or someplace with him. He'd take me to his trailer whenever he could and make me do things.

Then, when I was about twelve, he started bringing his friend around and wanted me to do things for him, too. First, it was just the one friend, but then he brought more. Sometimes, there were four of them together. Then his friend told him how he could make money on the Internet. At first, he'd just take pictures and videos and sell them on the Internet. Uncle Dwight would gimme some money, but not much. He kept most of it. He said, if I didn't do it, Mom and Timmy and Betsy would starve, or maybe he'd have to start using Timmy and Betsy. He knew I was afraid of that and that I wanted to protect them. I was the big brother. I was supposed to protect them.

Then Uncle Dwight's friend told him how he could make even more money. He'd bring strangers from all over who'd pay him so they could be with me in a motel room. Uncle Dwight said, if anybody found out about people coming across state lines, I'd be sent to prison or to an institution. They might even put me in a straightjacket, he said. That scared me more than anything. I was so stupid, I believed everything he said.

Then one day, I heard Uncle Dwight's friend talk about what he could do with me to make a lot more money. They made plans about what they'd do with me, and I knew I couldn't take it anymore. I ran away and came to California. Life on the streets wasn't easy, but at least I was free of them. I could keep the money I made and live how I wanted and have friends. It wasn't great, but at least it was better than anything else I ever had.

Once in a while, I met someone who took me in. That's how I met Troy. At first, I was scared of Troy, but I liked him, and he promised to help me and said he'd always protect me. Sure, he could be mean and violent, but with him, I knew he was the only one I had to be afraid of. He'd always protect me from everybody else, as long as I kept him happy and didn't do anything that got him mad. And we lived in a nice place, nicer than any place I'd ever lived in before. It was like a dream come true, except for when Troy got mad. I learned not to think about the other stuff.

I didn't know anything about Baby's father, except that he was a doctor and rich. Baby never talked about his family, except to say his parents were really old-fashioned and strict. He said the only person in his family who knew he was gay was his older sister. I don't remember her name or if Baby even told me her name. He said they got along great, though, and he could count on her for anything. I wish I'd had somebody who cared about me like that, but I never did. He said his father might kill him, if he found out he was gay. Or at least disown him and kick him out. He said his religion was really strict, and, back in Iran, a person could be sent to jail or even killed just for being gay.

When I told Troy about Baby's father being a rich doctor and strict about his religion, he came up with the idea to get money from him. Troy said we could take him for a lot more money than any of the others. He said it was the big break we needed, and we'd be on Easy Street after that.

I'm really sorry for Baby. I really did like him and didn't want to hurt him. But Troy said I wouldn't be hurting Baby, because his rich father had the money and wouldn't even miss it.

I really am sorry.

Chapter 26

Pro Bono Publico

It was shortly after ten the next morning when I got the expected call from Dr. Hosseini, again from a payphone. Troy had called and demanded his money immediately. Apparently, he wasn't happy about having to settle for a measly five grand, but in his position, he had to take whatever he could get.

The doctor instructed me to come to his home before the meeting to get the money, and he insisted I return afterward and report. He was still concerned about his phone being tapped and wanted my report in person. How little he knew about the extent of electronic surveillance, I thought, but that was another matter.

I was to meet Troy in a dark alley at midnight, of course. The location was in an old industrial area by the L.A. River, between two rows of commercial buildings. I was to park on the street, walk around back then halfway down the alley, and wait.

I picked up the money, drove to the drop site, and waited. The alley was indeed dark. Unusually dark, it seemed, even for a moonless and foggy night. Someone had taken care of the street lights and building lights with a pellet gun earlier in the evening. I waited. And I waited some more. I watered a weed that had sprouted beside a dumpster. And I kept waiting. I desperately wanted a cigarette, even though I knew it would give away my position, ruin my night vision, and give me an instant case of stage-four cancer.

Time goes by slowly when you're waiting in a dark alley for a pimp, murderer, and extortionist. At about 12:30, I heard the unmistakable sound of a Harley drive up from the other end of the alley; its intentionally loud and distinctive engine roared and its headlamp was blinding in the darkness. I covered my eyes with my hand as the bike drew close. Troy parked ten yards away and walked toward me.

"You Dehenares?" he asked. His voice was deep and angry.

"That's right."

"You got my money?"

"Do you have the cell phone?" I asked.

"Yeah, but like I told the doctor, there's nothing on it. You already got everything there was, thanks to that sissy faggot."

"Let's see the phone."

He pulled a cell phone out of his jacket and held it up for me to see. "Let's see the money."

I removed an envelope with the money from my coat. He walked toward me, and I could clearly see he was a large man who spent hours in a gym every day. His shaved head and broad, muscled frame made him an intimidating presence. Anyone would guess him to be a bouncer or professional wrestler, someone used to physical confrontation. He didn't look scared or even slightly nervous. I was hoping he was thinking the same about me.

"You know, the doc is gettin' off easy," he said. "I shoulda got a lot more. I never catch a break."

"Your kind never does."

"What's that supposed to mean? I got a raw deal here, man!"

"What kind of a deal did Billie get? The way I see it, you're getting off easy. You've got a murder rap hanging over you now, and if you don't get out of the country fast, you'll be spending the rest of your life in prison, where you belong."

"Fucking asshole." He held out the cell phone with one hand and his other hand with its palm open.

"I've been called worse and by better people than you," I said and held out the envelope. Before we could make the exchange, though, a car drove into the alley fast, its headlights and high beams blinding both of us.

"*God damn you*! I told you to come alone, you bastard!" Troy shouted as he grabbed the envelope and put it in his jacket pocket along with his cell phone, all while shielding his eyes from the bright lights.

I went for the cell phone, but he grabbed hold of me.

"You bastard!" he shouted again, taking me by surprise as I was still blinded by the headlights. He forced me to the ground, his hands around my neck, and he choked me and banged my head against the pavement, shouting more obscenities at me.

Then, his other hand still at my throat, he reached into his jacket again and pulled out a gun. I tried to fight him off as he struck my forehead with the butt of the gun, but I felt I was about to pass out.

I heard two puffs and the sound of brass casings hitting the pavement. Troy went limp and fell on top of me, his dead weight knocking the wind out of me.

For a split second, I was strangely intrigued by something that didn't smell right. As I tried to push him off me, a revelation was trying to form in my mind, but I was already too far on my way to never-never land. I blacked out with Troy on top of me before I could complete the thought.

*****

I couldn't have been out for more than a few minutes before I regained consciousness. Troy was no longer on top of me. His body lay faceup on the ground next to me—someone had rolled him off me and turned him over, firing one more round into his forehead just to be sure.

I remembered the sounds of those two puffs then the casings hitting the pavement—the unmistakable sounds of a pistol with a silencer doing its job. Troy had two small bullet holes in the top of his head, .380 caliber, I'd guess, about four inches apart. He had another shot in his forehead, with significant powder burns, indicating this one had been fired at extremely close range. This was the work of a nervous or inexperienced shooter, but one who wanted Troy very dead. He died almost instantly, so there wasn't much blood.

The three bullet casings were gone. I patted myself to check for damage and then took the envelope with the money and Troy's cell phone out of his jacket pockets.

A lot of questions went through my mind, but this wasn't the time to sit and ponder. I was sure of only one thing. *Okay, tough guy. Time to get your ass up and get the hell out of here, fast!*

*****

I knew I had to report to the doctor, but I wasn't looking forward to another ass-ripping. Not without a drink first.

Since I couldn't count on the doctor having any liquor, even for medicinal purposes, I stopped on the way to his house at a gritty bar that looked like the kind of place where the management and clientele didn't ask questions or bother with formalities. Just off the freeway near Skid Row, the Club Mallard was a drinking man's bar—small, dark, quiet; just what I was looking for.

I made my way past the drug dealers and streetwalkers and walked in. Despite the dark interior, my disheveled appearance and the bloody lump on my forehead caused the bartender and several patrons to look me over good. I walked straight to the bar and sat down.

The bartender came over and asked, "What'll it be?"

This was neither the time nor the place for polite drinking. "A shot of Old Forester."

The bartender nodded and came back with a shot glass and a bottle. He poured me a full glass, and I downed it quickly as I continued to think about what to tell the doctor.

"Rough night, slugger?" the bartender asked as he filled my glass again.

"I've had better."

"What does the other guy look like?" He smiled.

"I didn't stick around to find out."

"You might wanna get rid of that shirt, friend," he said.

I looked down at my shirt and saw the dark-red stains. "Good idea. Thanks." I downed the second shot quickly, paid, and left.

Chapter 27

Follow-Up with the Doctor

I had hoped to see Nousha again, but the doctor himself answered the door after several rings of the doorbell. He'd been sleeping in his office's easy chair and returned to it before demanding a report. He wore red silk pajamas, a paisley robe, and slippers, and he looked very small, very old, and very tired.

I turned one of the chairs in front of his desk to face him and sat down. After I told him what had happened, he looked even older and more tired. He sat quietly for a few moments, tapping his fingertips on the red leather armrest.

After thinking things through, he said, "Assuming there were no witnesses or forensic evidence left at the scene, there should be nothing to tie my family or you to the death of that animal. This may have worked out for the best for all of us."

"That's a valid assumption, but I'd still like to know who the shooter was and how he knew where to come looking for Troy," I said. "You were the only other person who knew where and when the meet-up was taking place."

The doctor understood my implication. "I told you from the beginning I couldn't use any of my usual sources of assistance. That hasn't changed. And, for all I know, it was you who shot that animal and are just making up this third person to cover your own ineptitude. With him dead, there's no one to tie you into any of this sordid mess. Nothing to say you were involved as an accessory after the fact or in the withholding or destroying of evidence."

Even old and tired, the doctor was one cool cookie. If Islam allowed gambling, he'd have made a hell of a poker player. "I didn't knock myself in the head for the sake of appearances." I placed two items on his desk. "Here's the cell phone and your money."

"Take them with you. Destroy the phone. You can keep the money as your fee for your services, though those services have been of questionable value." The doctor was always on the attack.

I put the phone back in my pocket. "No thanks on the money. It's tainted in more ways than one. But I'd like to know how your son is doing."

The doctor's face brightened. "Babak is doing well. He should be coming home tomorrow, or this morning, I should say. His sister is staying with him again tonight. She is devoted to him and will not leave his side."

"Thanks. I'm glad to hear that." I got up to leave, and the doctor stood, also.

He seemed pleased with my concern for Babak and threw me a bone. "I don't want you to think me completely ungrateful, so I will tell you something that may be of value to you. I can tell you with complete certainty that no one associated with the Palestinian intifada was involved in the kidnapping of the Jewess and her children. I can also tell you that you should focus your attention on people closer to home, if you truly wish to find out who was responsible for the kidnapping."

"How can you be so sure?"

"If any Palestinian element had been involved, I would have known about it in advance. And I would have put a stop to it. It would have been counterproductive, as its consequences have shown it to be. The Israelis couldn't have done a better job of turning public opinion against the Palestinians if they had tried."

I nodded. "Thanks for the information."

The doctor walked me to the front door, but, before opening it, he offered me a last bit of advice. "Let me also give you a word of warning, young man. If you truly intend to find out who was responsible for this kidnapping, be very careful. If you are as good an investigator as you are said to be, you will be shocked by what you discover, and you will make some very dangerous enemies in the process. Your life will be in danger, so trust no one. Nothing is as it seems."

I nodded again. "Thanks."

"Now you must go, and you must never attempt to contact me again."

Chapter 28

Troy McBain – Deceased

I woulda had it made and been on Easy Street with that hunderd grand. If only that sissy faggot hadn't got scared and folded... I woulda taken care a' him, like I said. I'm a man a' my word. I'd a' gotten him his tits and hormones and let him take it easy for a while. I coulda made a lot more money off a' him with tits... It woulda been sweet...

My one chance to hit the jackpot, and that sissy faggot blew it for me... I never catch a break. Never hook up with anybody that can take me all the way...

Man, he really pissed me off this time. I couldn't help it. What else could I do? I couldn't help it...

Chapter 29

A Lover's Secret

Her perfume intrigued me, but I couldn't quite put my finger on why. "Is that sandalwood perfume?" I asked Nousha as we cuddled in my bed afterward, staring into each other's eyes. I'd made sure the sheets were fresh this time.

"This is where you're supposed to look deeply into my eyes and tell me I'm the most beautiful woman you've ever known," she said. "Not ask about my perfume."

"Sorry about that… I really could stare into your eyes for hours, and you really are incredibly beautiful. You're one of the most beautiful women I've ever known."

"That's better."

"I just couldn't help noticing the scent. It's very unusual."

"Yes. Do you like it? It's a special formula—sandalwood with just a hint of citrus. It's made only in Iran. I pick up several bottles to bring back every time I go."

"I love it. It's very distinctive, just like you."

"You're distinctive in many ways, yourself… Mig Quixote, the gallant knight who gave up his career and went to prison to protect his lady's honor."

"What makes you think it was a woman? Or that she was mine or had any honor?"

She laughed dismissively.

"I'm going to miss you," I said, admiring her enchanting smile.

"Why? Are you going away?"

"Not me. You. Your father told me you were going to Tehran to get married when you finish your residency."

"Those plans have been changed, although my father doesn't know yet. Please don't tell him, if you see him again."

"Sure, but I doubt I ever will. He was very adamant about me never contacting him again, and about his plans for you and your brother."

Nousha's mood turned serious, and she propped herself up on an elbow. "Even he has to take orders, and even he doesn't know everything that's going on." She gazed at me intently, as though there was much more she wanted to tell me.

I looked up at her. "Would you care to enlighten me?"

"My father doesn't know that I know about his actual role for the government of Iran, aside from his medical practice. I found out by accident about four years ago. Since then, I've come to know his superiors and colleagues in that aspect of his life, all without his knowledge. I've gone to Iran several times between semesters and on holidays, for training. Family visits and that courtship with a lawyer in the Ministry of Justice made a convenient cover for those trips. Even my father doesn't know the engagement is just a cover.

"It has been decided, when I complete my residency, I'll begin to work at my father's medical offices and learn the business side of medicine. Although he wants us all to return to Tehran as soon as possible, his medical practice has proven to be too valuable a resource to just abandon. The doctor-patient confidentiality privilege in the American legal system and the money that flows through a lucrative medical practice are too useful to throw away. After a year or so, my father and mother will return to Tehran, but I'll remain here, to take over his medical office and some of his other duties. My brother will also be allowed to remain. That was part of the deal."

"Deal?"

"The deal I made with my handlers. I'll remain and continue my father's work here. My brother will be allowed to remain also and will be left alone."

This was a lot to take in. I sat up, reached over for the pack of cigarettes on the night table, and lit one. "Why are you telling me this?"

"Because I want you to know the truth. I want you to know because I do care for you. It's also good to have a friend with connections, someone who's capable of doing difficult things that must be done."

I stared at her. I'd been played but too stupid to know it. Served me right for getting involved with the daughter of a known enemy agent. I felt like an idiot. Again.

Nousha sat up and leaned back against the headboard beside me. "You look like a sad puppy... Look, I know a long-term or committed relationship between us is out of the question. It was never possible. But I don't want there to be any unnecessary secrets between us. I really do care for you, and I want our relationship to continue. I want us to be friends and allies."

"Okay. But you should know, even though I left the FBI under rotten circumstances and was sent to prison, I'm still an American, and I'll never do anything that might harm the Bureau or my country."

"I know. I would never ask you to do any such thing. And I would never try to trick you into doing any such thing. I know what kind of man you are, and I think too highly of you and care about you too much for that. I'd like for us to remain friends no matter what, and I think we might be able to help each other, when it's to our mutual benefit."

"Like how?" I asked.

"Like encouraging you to finish your investigation of the kidnapping of the Ginsberg woman."

"How would that help you? Help Iran, I mean?"

"To get to the truth, your investigation will lead to the discovery of things that are very damaging to the State of Israel and the American government, but they will serve to make America better, in the long run. You see, I also care very much for America. I've lived here almost my entire life, and I plan to remain here for a very long time, maybe forever." Nousha nodded slowly as she spoke, emphasizing her sincerity. "I want relations to improve between Iran and America. If they don't, well, it wouldn't be good for either side. As for the Ginsberg thing, when you reveal the truth, it will clear Iran and the Palestinians of any involvement in the kidnapping. I don't want Americans to think of Iranians or Arabs as kidnappers and murderers."

"Do you know who was responsible for the kidnapping?"

"No, not specifically. But you'll find out."

"How?"

"As has been said before, 'follow the money.'"

"Can you be more specific?"

Nousha reached for the glass of wine on her nightstand and took a sip. "No. But I think you'd find it worthwhile to stop thinking of the Ginsbergs and Marino only as victims. An investigation of the Ginsbergs and their bank, along with Marino and his business ventures, will raise many interesting questions. The answer to those questions will lead you to what you're looking for."

I nodded. "Like I said before, the Hosseinis are full of surprises."

She granted me another of her enchanting smiles and leaned forward to kiss me. I caught her scent again and suddenly realized why her perfume intrigued me so. "Did that training in Iran include firearms training?" I asked.

She stiffened and lifted her chin. "Some. Not much. Why do you ask?"

"You'd do anything to protect your family, wouldn't you?"

"Wouldn't you?" she asked.

"Did you make this deal with your handlers because of your family?"

Nousha knew what I was getting at. "My brother wouldn't have a chance in Iran, and my parents would be humiliated and ostracized. I had to do whatever I could for them."

I nodded slowly and put my arm around her. "You've given me advice. Let me return the favor and give you some, too. Don't wear such a distinctive perfume when you go out on a mission. It leaves an impression, even on a man about to pass out."

She looked away and held her glass with both hands. "It couldn't be helped. When you're the resident on duty, you can't leave the hospital for very long, even when someone is covering for you. I didn't have time to shower or change."

Chapter 30

Girl Talk II

Dry cleaning meant driving around L.A. to be sure I wasn't being followed. Then I did more on foot. It was time-consuming and tiring but necessary, especially after taking Nousha's advice to look into the backgrounds of the Ginsbergs and Marino, with a little physical surveillance of my own on them just to be thorough.

I began to get the feeling I was being followed, although I could never spot any one person or vehicle tailing me for an extended period. If I was being followed, they were very good at it. I also began to wonder about my phones, wonder about my computers, and wonder about my sanity.

"Did you get anywhere with any of those Iranians?" Bart asked when we finally met in the student parking lot at Cal State LA. Night classes were in session, and the library was still open, so there were many students coming and going.

I handed him a can of Coors and offered him a cigarette. "Nothing definite, but what was intimated was interesting."

"What was that?"

We opened our beers, and I lit our smokes. "I don't know if it's just their animosity and paranoia, but the feeling I got from the Iranians I talked to was that there's more to the Ginsbergs and Marino than meets the eye. I know we looked into them just in case it was an inside job, but I'd like to go deeper, especially into their financial backgrounds."

Bart took a sip. "That would be tough for me to do. Impossible, probably, at this point. Norton and the U.S. Attorney's Office wouldn't let us go deep, remember, out of fear of offending them. I'd need subpoenas and search warrants to get into their financial records and tax returns, and, without something solid to justify it, I don't think I could find an Assistant U.S. Attorney who has the balls and would be willing to risk his career to go after them."

"Yeah, you're probably right about that. But what about an independent forensic financial investigation? Didn't you say you had a friend at that big private PI firm that does all the financial investigations for the big law firms on those billion-dollar lawsuits?"

"Yeah. Jason Clarke. He's still with Kemper & Associates. He was a CPA before the Bureau and then got smart and realized he could make three times the money working for them. You can't afford him."

"I wasn't planning on paying him. Arrange a meeting for us, and we'll use our charm on him. If the Iranians' suspicions are right, he wouldn't want to miss out on the most challenging case of his life," I said.

"What do you think was going on?"

"I have no idea. But I'm told it's big. Really big."

"I'll invite him to dinner. Someplace nice. It's about time I got more than a can of beer and a smoke out of you. And you'll have to be the one to pour on the charm and convince him. This is your show, remember?"

"I'll pay for the drinks and pour on the alcohol. We'll get him liquored up and persuade him to agree to help before he knows any better."

"You're paying for everything. This is all your game now."

"Okay, okay. By the way, what's his story? Why'd he leave the Bureau? Was it just the money?"

"No. He got in a jam with the Bureau, kinda like you did. That should be an incentive to make him wanna help you, so play that up."

"What kind of jam?"

"Well, first, you have to understand, Jason is an oddball, to put it nicely. He's about forty-five now but still has a pudgy baby face. I've always called him 'Big Boy,' just to yank his chain. He's as sharp as there is when it comes to digging up the business and financial dirt, but you gotta keep an eye on him to keep him on track or he'll go rogue on you... Like I said, he's a CPA, so, right outta Quantico, the Bureau put him to work on major frauds. After about ten years of that, he got tired of it and wanted to do something different. So, he put in for bomb school. Now, anybody who knew Jason knew it would be a big mistake to let him anywhere near explosives, but the Bureau, in its infinitesimal wisdom, granted his wish and sent him to Redstone to become a bomb tech.

"He's back from Redstone less than two weeks when there's a bomb incident where an IED didn't go off. It turns out there were two dudes making bombs to blow up the front of ATMs, so they could reach in and grab the cash. Not very sophisticated, but the big problem was that they didn't know what they were doing. They were experimenting with their IEDs, and some of the bombs they made blew the ATMs to shit, money and all. One time, they blew the entire wall off a bank. They hit banks in out-of-the-way places and at night, so nobody ever got hurt.

"Well, when Jason gets back from bomb school, there's another bomb attempt, only this time, the bomb doesn't go off at all, so there's an unexploded bomb at a bank ATM when the bank employees show up for work in the morning. They call the cops, and the cops call their bomb squad. The bomb squad calls the sheriff's bomb squad and the Bureau bomb techs, because this one is different than anything they've ever seen before, and they don't know what to do with it."

Bart was enjoying telling this story. He took a long drag, chugged his beer, and continued with a smile. "Jason goes out with our bomb techs to get some real-life, on-the-job training. After looking things over, all the bomb guys and brass get together with the bank management to decide how to handle the situation. As you know, Bureau regulations say Bureau bomb techs can only give advice and aren't allowed to defuse bombs. But while they're all arguing about how to handle this unexploded IED, Jason goes back out to the ATM and defuses it. Then he goes walking back into the room with all the bomb techs, law-enforcement brass, and bank management, holding the damn thing.

"As you can imagine, everybody went apeshit. The cops and sheriff's bomb guys and the bank management all wanted Jason fired. Bureau management was pissed because he violated regulations and the standard protocol with the cops and banks.

"He didn't get fired, but the Bureau put him on leave without pay for a month and took him out of the bomb-tech program. Like I said, Jason is an oddball, so he didn't think he'd done anything wrong or even understand why he was punished. He thinks he should've been hailed as a hero, so he wrote a personal letter to the Director, complaining about the treatment he was given. This pisses off Bureau management again, because he didn't go through the chain of command with his complaint, and it makes them look bad.

"Then, management takes away all his cases and assigns him to review all the expense and accounting records for the Field Office. And they take away his Bureau car and overtime pay allowance. So, Jason has to drive his own car to work and spend eight hours a day in a basement office with no windows and no overtime pay. That lasted about a month before he resigned and went to work at Kemper for three times what he was making as an agent."

"I like a guy who marches to his own drummer," I said as I took out another cigarette and gave Bart one. We took a moment to admire a pair of attractive young co-eds walking by my car.

"Yeah, I thought you would. You'll also like his wife, Mary, another brilliant oddball. She's the typical little soccer mom, except she's an astrophysicist at Caltech and works on projects for NASA. She rides a Kawasaki Ninja, the biggest and fastest one they make. When she's working out a problem in her head, she'll jump out of bed at two in the morning and go riding for two or three hours to think about it. She was stopped by the CHP a few times before they finally got her to wear a helmet and something over her pajamas. Apparently, there was something about a tiny woman going tear-ass on the Interstate in her pajamas at three a.m. that freaked some people out."

"They are my kind of people," I said. "By the way, can you find out if the Bureau has me under surveillance? I've had the feeling for a couple of weeks now that I'm being followed."

"I haven't heard anything, but I'll check. What've you noticed?"

"I can't say I've noticed anything in particular. That's what's been giving me the willies. If I am being followed, they're definitely pros."

"I'll look into it," Bart said and then sighed, "*Ahh*," as he looked out the window at another young beauty. "The scenery here makes me wish I was twenty years younger."

"*Twenty*? If you were twenty years younger, you'd still be old enough to be their father."

"One of these days, I'm gonna kick your ass."

Chapter 31

The Poet Warrior

A few days later, Bart and I met with Jason Clarke. From what Bart had told me, I had a pretty good idea of what to expect. Jason was a large man, broad-shouldered and big-boned, with lots of shaggy blond hair, blue eyes, and a demeanor that always left you wondering if he was being serious or pulling your leg. I could see why Bart called him Big Boy, as he was a fair-haired version of the Big Boy statue you used to see in front of the Bob's Big Boy restaurants, which, sadly, no longer exist. He also ate and drank faster than anyone I'd ever known. After guzzling several vodka martinis, scarfing down prime rib, salad, and baked potato, and hearing the full story, he couldn't resist the challenge.

He was understandably reluctant at first. Looking into the Ginsbergs and Marino was risky. He'd have to do his work without anyone else in his firm knowing about it. If anyone did find out, he'd make powerful enemies and likely lose his job, and he could be sued for invasion of privacy, at the very least. Given the Ginsbergs' and Marino's power and influence, the worst case for him could be the ultimate worst.

But the one thing all good investigators have in common is an insatiable curiosity. Once the unanswered questions began piling up, there was enough of the former FBI agent left in him to make it absolutely necessary for him to get to the bottom of things. Out of fairness, I reiterated the possible danger and told him I wouldn't hold it against him, if he didn't want to get involved.

"Are you sure you want to be in on this?" I asked him.

Jason looked me in the eye and replied, "Of course I will. There's nothing I hate more than the stench of lies."

I wasn't sure if he was joking or just plain crazy and looked to Bart for an answer, but he only smiled and kept eating.

Jason continued with studied seriousness, "I've been wanting to do something worthwhile since leaving the Bureau. Something that wasn't just about making money for one fat cat at the expense of some other fat cat. 'All I could think about was getting back into the jungle. I sit in my comfortable little office and think, every minute I stay here, I get weaker, and every minute Charlie squats in the bush, he's getting stronger. Each time I look around, the walls move in a little tighter…'"

We all laughed, and Bart said, "I forgot to mention, Jason is a movie nut. He'll watch a movie he likes twenty times. Then he'll drive everybody crazy by parroting the lines every chance he gets." Jason smiled, and Bart asked him, "What is it, *Deer Hunter* this time?"

Jason scoffed and turned to me. "'Everybody gets what they really want. I wanted a mission, and for my sins, you brought me one. Brought it to me like room service.'"

"Well, as long as you understand the risk involved," I said.

"'One look at you, and I know it's gonna be hot…,'" Jason said. "From what Bart told me about you, I thought you'd be taller. But that's okay. Fuck… 'You never get the chance to know what the fuck you are, working in some factory in Ohio.'"

"Glad you feel that way about it. You also understand you'll never be able to tell anyone about this?"

"'I understand, Captain, this mission does not exist nor will it ever exist.'"

"Bart said you were a good man."

"I like to think of myself as 'a poet warrior, in the classical sense.'"

"So, can you get me the financial backgrounds on the Ginsbergs and Marino, to start?" I asked.

"Definitely. I'll start by surfing the Web and go from there. 'Charlie don't surf,' but I do. There's a lot more information on the Internet than most people realize, if you know where to look." He pulled out his air guitar and began to sing, "'Let's go surfing now, everybody's learning how…'" He looked at me with a lunatic's grin. "You're probably beginning to think I'm 'wrapped too tight for Nam.'"

"You're wrapped too tight for Earth," Bart answered before I could say anything.

Chapter 32

PBR Street Gang

We told Jason we needed to meet clandestinely and after extensive dry cleaning. We couldn't risk being seen together. After just a week of digging, Jason felt he had something to report. We dry cleaned and met for dinner at a tiny diner in the Valley none of us had ever been to before. The prime rib and pricey drinks at our last meeting had run up my credit card, so I had to find a less expensive place for us this time.

"A diner? In the Valley?" Jason asked, disappointed. "I was hoping for some excitement... 'Shit, I'm still only in Saigon...' I mean, L.A. 'Every time I think I'm gonna wake up back in the jungle—'"

"Jason, stick with the program," Bart commanded, and we ordered our dinners: pork chops, fried potatoes, and beer this time.

"Sorry it took me so long to get back to you guys. I had to be careful, so I wouldn't get caught," Jason said, head bobbing as he looked at both Bart and me. "We have a new managing partner who's strict about shit like this. But what the hell does he know? He's 'from goddamned New Jersey!'" Bart sighed and shook his head. Jason then switched characters and continued. "'Part of me was afraid of what I might find, of what I might do... It's pretty hairy in there now. I felt like a snail crawling on the edge of a straight razor.'"

"Enough of that. Just the facts, ma'am," Bart ordered.

"Oh, all right... Since I don't have a badge or subpoena power, I couldn't get into any legally protected records, but there were plenty of public records and required filings with various government agencies to keep me busy. What I found is pretty interesting and mysterious."

"Just spill it, Lucy," Bart said.

"Let me start by giving you the big picture first, or should I say, the big question first. You'd think, after having to cough up forty-four million dollars in cash to kidnappers, these people might be a little light in the wallet. But, much to my surprise, the kidnapping didn't seem to affect them financially at all. In fact, they're doing better now than ever before. They had big projects going before the kidnapping, projects that required major cash up front just to get going. You'd think the loss of that kind of cash would've stopped those projects cold, but no. They didn't skip a beat."

"Tell me about those projects again, just so I know what we're talking about," Bart asked.

"The Ginsbergs' bank was backing Marino's downtown L.A. development project and was also expanding its own loan portfolio, meaning it needed to have cash or highly liquid assets on hand to meet federal bank requirements for solvency. Marino had the downtown development project and the Las Vegas resort project, both major cash guzzlers just to get off the ground. Despite the loss of cash and credit due to the kidnapping, they were able to keep those projects going, and they're making money back on them already.

"Not only were they able to keep those projects going with their own assets, but they also brought in new investors who dropped millions into them. The new money came in so fast, the bank examiners couldn't fault the Ginsbergs when they looked into how they took cash from the bank to pay the ransoms without going through the usual channels. It appears— and I say *appears* because I haven't personally seen the documents—the Ginsbergs were able to take the money based on their promissory notes, which were backed by the new investors. New money came in from the investors immediately, so the bank had more than enough cash to meet federal requirements."

"Who were the new investors?" Bart asked.

"This is where it gets interesting. The new investors were venture capital partnerships made up of corporate entities with long genealogies that eventually go back to foreign corporations and partnerships. It was impossible for me to find out exactly who owns those foreign entities without legal process. But the interesting thing is, and I found this out by going back to the initial start of the Ginsbergs' bank—which was called the Bikkurim Bank of Los Angeles then, by the way—the bank started with funding from similarly mysterious sources and has received cash infusions from those sources throughout its history. Even more interesting is the fact that those mysterious sources have withdrawn little of their capital investments, and they've reinvested much of their profits back into the bank."

"Is that unusual?" Bart asked.

"Very. Venture capitalists generally take their profits and invest in the next big moneymaker. They don't let their money sit and draw ordinary single-digit profits."

We looked at each other, nodding. Clearly, the situation Jason had described meant something fishy was going on. Our meals arrived, and we ordered more beer.

"What did you find out about Marino?" Bart asked.

"Another interesting character. His story is more public than the Ginsbergs'. He likes the limelight and brags about his rags-to-riches life. Only it wasn't quite a rags beginning. He grew up in an upper-middle-class home in L.A., went to USC, then went to work for a big real estate company for a couple of years. After learning the ropes, he left that company and started his own real estate development company.

"He hit the real estate market when it was hot and became a billionaire in just a few years. What sets him apart is his brains and business model. He comes up with a great idea and puts in the seed money to get the project started, then sells pieces of the project to investors. So, he's able to get these billion-dollar projects going with just a few million of his own to start with. And, he's one of those people with the golden touch. Every project he's started has made millions, and investors are lined up to get in on his projects. That includes the downtown L.A. development and the Las Vegas resort. The L.A. project was too big for him to handle on his own, so he had to get several major banks to provide funding, which they did, once the Ginsbergs' bank provided the initial funding and a ten-million-dollar credit line. He wanted to keep the Vegas project to himself, but eventually, maybe because of the kidnapping, he had to let in an outside investor. Another venture capital partnership with mysterious origins stepped in and provided millions for the resort project."

"So," Bart said, taking a swig of beer, "it sounds like we need to find out whose money is behind the Ginsbergs and Marino."

Jason shook his head. "That's Cambodia to me. That'll be your job, boys. I've gone as far upriver as I can go."

Bart turned to me. "You heard the man. You know I can't help you with that, either. You're on your own."

"What else is new? By the way, did you ever find out if the Bureau is tailing me?" I asked Bart.

He cut into his meat and began to chew. "Yeah, I checked… Damn good chop. You may not know squat about how to work a case, but you sure know how to pick a restaurant. I'll give you that."

Offended, I stared at Bart for a moment then turned to Jason for support. He just nodded then shrugged and continued his own contented chewing.

Bart continued, "I asked my boss and Jeremy Stiles, who's the surveillance coordinator now, about the possibility of having you under physical surveillance for a while, just to see what you're up to, now that you're out and on the loose again. I told them I thought you might get in contact with that source you were trying to protect. Rolfe thought it was a good idea but didn't think Stiles would go for it. He was right. Stiles said the FISUR squads are too busy to start a FISUR just on a hunch, and I'd need to come up with more to justify expending that kind of manpower. So, based on that, I'd say the Bureau isn't interested in you right now, unless the FCI side of the house has something going on you that they don't want me to know about. Do you still think somebody is following you?"

"Yeah, there's definitely someone tailing me. If it isn't the Bureau, the question then is, who?"

Jason added his two cents, again drawing from his favorite movie. "'Aren't you curious about that? I'm very curious. Are you curious? There's something happening out there, man. You know something, man? I know something you don't know. That's right, Jack.'"

Chapter 33

Strange Encounters of the Violent Kind

I had to agree with Jason, there was something happening out there. When I was out on the street, I continued to have that uneasy feeling and was certain I was being watched, but I just couldn't catch anyone at it. The skin at the back of my neck was itchy, and my sixth sense was working overtime. I never saw anything, I just felt it—that queasy feeling you get in the pit of your stomach when you know something just isn't right.

It started after I'd begun my surveillance of the Ginsbergs. Perhaps their security people had spotted me and alerted them—I never was any good at physical surveillance; I just couldn't keep a low profile. Everyone always said I had the kind of face that people remembered, maybe not in a good way. Even when I wasn't working on one of the Ginsberg clan, I felt someone on my tail, like when I was on one of the divorce or missing person cases Jack had tossed me.

It was while on one of those dirty divorce cases, where one spouse wants evidence of the other's infidelity to enforce a punitive prenuptial agreement, that my suspicions were verified. The client was a wealthy businessman who'd been referred to Jack by a divorce lawyer who sent him a lot of business. The man was in his late forties and had married a bimbo twenty years younger whom he'd met at a strip joint. He'd been on the rebound from a nasty divorce from a wife who'd cheated on him with a younger man and had figured a glittering pole dancer would mend his broken heart and bruised self-esteem. What better way to show up the ex-wife than to parade around with a young, new wife whose bra cup was the deepest thing about her? Being foolish but no fool, his prenup specified there'd be limited alimony if infidelity could be proven beyond a reasonable doubt. He gave Jack a five-thousand-dollar retainer to get that proof.

Suspecting his young wife of infidelity, or just having gotten tired of her, the client arranged a week-long business trip, during which time I was to follow her in hopes of catching her delicto-ing in flagrante. It didn't take long.

Late on the client's first night away, I followed the blonde from the client's fancy digs in Brentwood south on Crenshaw, much farther south on Crenshaw than any blonde had reason to go—unless she was meeting someone she knew. She parked behind a nightclub where she'd be the only blonde in the place, and where I couldn't go in to see who she was meeting because I wasn't the right color either, and my presence would stick out like a Nilla Wafer in a bag of Oreos.

I parked across the street in an alley where I could see her leave, see who she left with, and follow them in whichever direction they went, to wherever their love shack was located. After forty-five minutes of cigarettes, cold coffee, Nilla Wafers, and Oreos, I got out of my car to stretch my legs and water the area behind a trash bin. It occurred to me I spent a lot of time in alleys and behind trash bins, and I wondered what that said about my life.

As I took care of my business, I went through in my mind the list of my favorite philosophers and psychologists but couldn't recall any who had anything to say about dark alleys and trash bins. Apparently, the substance of my life didn't give rise to much philosophizing or psychologizing.

My deep thoughts were interrupted when a car that had been parked at the far end of the alley behind me began to drive forward. Not feeling safe in this part of town, I hurried to finish my business and get back in my car before the other vehicle came close. I made it back into my car, but a third car came into the alley and stopped directly in front of me. The one coming up from the far end stopped right behind me. Two men got out of the car in front, and a man and a woman got out of the car behind mine, all four being white meat as out of place in this neighborhood as I was. I looked the surly four over, and the only words that came to mind were, *Fucked is me.*

The three stooges were in their thirties, dressed casually in slacks and polos, with light jackets to conceal the guns on their belts. The woman was also in her thirties and wore a gray pantsuit that matched her cold, gray eyes. Her dark hair was long but pulled back tightly and knotted in back, so as not to be a problem if things got physical. She moved with the fearless confidence of General Patton and looked just as tough.

The Fearless Female was the apparent leader of the pack and the only one who spoke. "Get out of the car, Dehenares. I want to talk to you."

Boxed in, I had no choice. Besides, if they'd wanted to kill me, they could've done it already. I got out of my car.

"Okay, talk," I said, trying to sound as tough and confident as I could. "Start by telling me who you are and why you've been following me."

Up close, Fearless Female had the woeful eyes of a child and reminded me of a sad Holly Golightly. I couldn't help wondering what may have been the cause of that sadness.

The two men from the front car came around to either side of me and grabbed me by the wrists and elbows, twisting my arms with expert pressure that rendered me immobile—I knew, if I struggled, I'd pop a ligament. They also each had a foot inside of mine, spreading my feet wide apart. They knew what they were doing and were good at it.

Fearless Female looked me over and said with disappointment, "*Hmph.* You're not very tall, are you?" She then nodded to the fourth man, who was built like a gorilla and had a perpetual snarling expression that would frighten away all other gorillas.

He came forward and launched a hard right hook to my stomach. My knees buckled, and I puked my dinner. I could've said I popped my cookies, but that would be too literal, and I hate clichés.

After I regained some composure, I said, "You have a funny way of talking. But you're very convincing."

"I'm here to deliver a message," Fearless Female said.

"I think I got the message."

The woman nodded again, and the hitter landed another right hook, this time a little lower, to the intestines. I thought I was going to die.

"The message is, you're done with the Ginsbergs."

I was in no condition to disagree. I would've agreed to anything. "Yeah, I'm done with the Ginsbergs. I got it." I could barely stand or get the words out.

The woman gestured to the two men holding me. "Hold him up. Hold his head up." And then she gave the gorilla another nod.

The hitter came forward with a right cross to my left cheek. He was wearing weighted leather gloves, the kind with tiny steel pellets at the back of the knuckles—perfect for this kind of "conversation." It's funny what you notice when you're getting the shit beat out of you.

"This is just a friendly warning, because we know you have no idea what you're getting into. But it's your only warning. Forget about the Ginsbergs or you're dead. If following cheating bimbos isn't enough to keep you busy, try investigating Marino. He's the one you should be looking at, anyway."

"Thanks for the advice," I said, barely able to keep my head up. I was standing only because my two friends were still holding me up.

The woman repeated her command to hold my head up and told the hitter, "Put him out."

"Don't go to any more trouble on my account," I said.

The gorilla came forward and gave me a roundhouse shot to the jaw, right where the mandible meets the skull, and I felt my head explode. I even saw fireworks. I like fireworks. I hadn't seen any fireworks in a while. I'd missed the fireworks on the last Fourth of July. They don't have fireworks shows in federal prison.

*****

I woke up the next morning at first light in the back seat of my car, where my new friends had been kind enough to deposit me after our conversation. They'd even been nice enough to leave a window open a crack to let some air in.

I dragged myself into the driver's seat and turned the rearview mirror to check the damage. Then I wished I hadn't—it wasn't a pretty sight. My left eye was swollen shut and most of the left side of my face was black and blue. My jaw hurt like hell. It didn't feel like my nose or jaw was broken, but I'd bled a lot, a whole lot, from my nose and eye and mouth. I grabbed a water bottle and handkerchief and washed my face before heading home.

I tried to avoid thinking about how much I hurt by going over the kidnapping and investigation in my mind, and particularly about the three stooges and their fearless female leader who'd done such a number on me. They were professionals, no doubt about that. I knew they weren't there to kill me or even do me permanent damage.

But wanting me to leave the Ginsbergs alone meant the Ginsbergs had something to hide, and they didn't want me to find out what that was. Suggesting I investigate Marino meant he was hiding something, too, and they *did* want me to find out what that was. Would the answers to these questions lead me to the kidnappers? Not necessarily. I still couldn't believe the Ginsbergs had anything to do with kidnapping their daughter and grandchildren. I could believe Marino might set up the kidnapping of his wife, but not his children. But so far, there was nothing to establish any of that.

Just over a year had gone by since the kidnapping. I had been to prison, gotten shanked, been knocked out and beaten up, and two people had been murdered. Yet, I was no closer to identifying the kidnappers or finding out what had happened to Rachael than I was a year ago. Some people had told me where to look, and some had told me where to stop looking, but no one had given me any specific information that would lead to any answers. So far, my investigation had just raised more questions.

It was time I started to demand answers. I'd begin at the beginning again, right where I had gotten involved in this mess—with Magda Ginsberg. She owed me some answers, especially after last night. I didn't think the Ginsbergs had sent the crew, but these four were clearly trying to protect them and the bank, and I was pretty sure they were Jewish. I had spent several weeks of R&R in Israel when on leave from Afghanistan, and I recognized Fearless Female's accent as a sabra's.

But first, I'd have to get myself checked out, just to be sure I was fit for duty. My condition would've been a good excuse to see Nousha again, but I'd decided not to see her unless it was absolutely necessary. It would do me no good to be seen with the daughter of a known enemy agent, who was an agent herself. And given the fact I was being followed by people of unknown loyalties, it wouldn't do her any good, either. I'd have to settle for whatever doctor I could get in to see.

Then, professional ethics would require me to get the goods on the blonde bimbo and earn that retainer. It's what Sam Spade would've done.

Chapter 34

Girl Talk III

A fter another hours-long dry cleaning to evade surveillance, Bart and I met up for a drink at one of the nicer watering holes that line Colorado Boulevard in Pasadena. The evening was pleasantly cool, so we sat in the vine-covered patio smoking area. We ordered our drinks, and Bart reluctantly accepted a cigarette. For our safety and security, I thought it best to compartmentalize my investigation as much as possible, and I wanted to ask Bart about something I didn't need to bring Jason in on yet—one of those new questions that had arisen while trying to find answers to an old one. I still had a shiner and significant black and blue around the jaw.

"You look like somebody mistook your head for a piñata, amigo," Bart said. "What did you do to the other guy?"

"He may have some bruised knuckles from the beating I gave them."

"Is that all?"

"I think I hurt his feelings when I didn't go down right away," I said.

"Was it worth it?"

"The jury's still out on that. But I've met some interesting people on this case."

"Like who?"

"Probably better for you if I don't tell you just yet. You can't be held accountable for what you don't know. Look at what's happened to me. After I get this kidnapping figured out and you're safely retired, I'll tell you everything. But there's one person I wanted to ask you more about. Who was it who told you about the Iranian doctor?"

"It may be better if you didn't know that. Who knows what could happen next, the way you see things."

"What's that supposed to mean?"

"You have an inflexible, and therefore dangerous, sense of morality, my friend. Everything is either black or white, right or wrong with you. You already lost your job and went to prison because of your sense of integrity. I don't want anything else to happen to you because you don't know when to bend and go with the flow. And I don't want you going after somebody I name, because you think they're somehow responsible for what happened to you."

"That won't happen. I just need to connect the dots, and I can't do that unless I know who or what the dots are. I don't see how knowing who told you about the doctor could be a problem. Did you make any promises to your source?"

"No, I didn't make any promises. I didn't have to. But I don't think my source would be happy if it came out that he gave me a name."

"There's no way that information would ever come out. But things have been happening that make me wonder who's pulling the strings behind the scenes."

"You're getting paranoid…" Bart considered his Scotch. "Are you sure nobody will ever need to know who gave me the doc's name?"

"Positive. It's just to help me figure out where to go next."

"Okay… Do you know Sol Abrams?"

"I know he works FCI. I wasn't on the Dark Side long enough to get to know anybody or what they worked."

"Sol's been around as long as I have and has been supervisor of the Iranian squad for years. We were in New Agent's class at the Academy about the same time. He's been on the Iranian squad since day one in the Bureau. He's probably the Bureau's best authority on Iranian matters. He was the one I talked to when you asked me about getting a lead on an Iranian who might know about any Palestinian involvement in the kidnapping."

"What did he have to say?"

"You know how those FCI guys are with their secret-squirrel shit. They play it close to the vest. Even if something isn't really a big secret, they don't talk about it, if for no other reason than to not get in a jam about disclosing classified information. You know as well as I do that they have to take a polygraph every year."

"So, how'd you get Abrams to tell you about the doctor?"

"I made it a point to run into Sol outside the office. We shot the breeze for a while, and I complained about how the FCI guys had been unwilling to help point us in the right direction. At first, he followed the party line and said their primary targets were too important to risk losing, even on a kidnapping investigation. They couldn't let them know we knew who they were. Better to let them go about their business and just keep tabs on them until war breaks out and we really need to put the screws to them. That's all he'd say, at first."

The fact that Abrams would violate a sacred rule by offering up the doctor's name was interesting and worth looking into, I thought. I had to ask, "So, why'd he give you the name?"

"Like I said, he didn't, at first. We ran into each other again a few days later in the garage and walked back to the office together. We were just shooting the breeze again, and he asked me how I've been feeling. I told him I was fine, and he said if I ever needed to see a cardiologist, he knew a good one. I told him again that I was fine, and he said, if I needed a doctor, he recommended Doctor Reza Hosseini, because he was the top Iranian, the top Iranian doctor. Then he smiled and said it again. 'Yeah, Doctor Reza Hosseini, Beverly Hills, the top Iranian, the top Iranian doctor.' I got the message and nodded, and we just went on shooting the breeze. That's the name I gave you. He couldn't get hurt on the annual polygraph with that. I gather you got something out of it."

I thought about the Hosseinis, and especially about Nousha, and smiled. "Yeah, I got something out of it. Why do you think Abrams gave up the doctor's name?"

"Beats the hell out of me. You're the only one who's got all the pieces. Put them together, and you tell me."

"I'm still missing too many pieces to make any sense of things. What else can you tell me about Abrams?"

"You don't think he's involved in some conspiracy, do you? Now you're really starting to sound paranoid."

"There's just too many unusual and weird things going on in this case to rule anything out yet. What kind of guy is Abrams?" I ordered another round and pulled out two more cigarettes.

"He's the salt of the earth, my friend. Makes the rest of us look like evil sinners. I'd trust him with anything. Like I said, he's been working Iranian FCI his entire career. He's had plenty of chances to move up the ladder and go to Headquarters, but he wants to stay in the field, where he can make a difference. He'll keep working it till mandatory retirement and then stay on as a consultant. He's that kind of guy—totally dedicated. And he's Jewish, so you can't blame him. The Iranians are committed to wiping out Israel. You hear it on the news every day." Bart blew smoke. "I'm gonna end up a cancer-riddled alcoholic, if I keep hanging out with you."

"Yeah, right. Blame me. What about his family? Any connections to the Ginsbergs?"

"Nothing came up in our investigation. He's never mentioned any. I think he would have, though, because he knew we were working the kidnapping."

"What about a wife? Is he married?"

"Yeah. His wife is a partner in a big law firm in town. Her father was a founding partner, and she joined the firm after law school. He told me about it a long time ago. Mentioned she was still working there when we were shooting the breeze... Let me think... Levinson... Levinson... Levinson, Rabinowitz & Taubman. Yeah, that's it. Her father was the original Levinson."

"Levinson, Rabinowitz & Taubman. Sounds like the kind of law firm that closes on the High Holy Days. The kind the Ginsbergs and their bank would do business with."

"Now you're starting to scare me. Maybe you should take a few days off to clear your head. Always a good idea to get a fresh perspective on a big case. Or maybe you need a steady girlfriend. How's your love life been going?"

"My love life is fine, but you may be right. I could use a few days off. Give this face a chance to heal, so I stop scaring dogs and children. But there's something else I need to talk to you about."

"You're worse than a blue-flaming Bureau supervisor looking for his next promotion. What do you want now?"

"Is Rolfe still riding your ass? Haven't you done enough to get him his next promotion yet?"

"That son of a bitch won't be happy until he can retire at fifty as an Assistant Director. He spends half his day on the phone with his friends at Headquarters, kissing ass. But I can handle him. What do you want?"

"I'd like you to dig up all the Bureau has on Rick Marino. See if the Organized Crime squad has come up with anything new on him since the kidnapping."

"First, you're paranoid. Now, you're prejudiced. Not every Italian is in the mafia, my friend."

"Yeah, yeah, I know. I just want to find out if he has any connections to any known players. I'd especially like to know if any telephone records show any connections."

"Your wish is my command. Just do me a favor. Try to keep that big head of yours from running into any more fists. You're already too ugly to look at, and you'll never find a girl to polish your knob with a face like a worn-out catcher's mitt."

Chapter 35

The Thin Woman II

I knew Magda Ginsberg was sick of me a long time ago and would've been happy never to see me again. But I needed answers that only she had.

She wouldn't answer my phone calls, so I went to the Ginsberg estate, where I was met by an armed guard at the gate. He called the house to find out if I should be granted permission to enter. The guard told me Mrs. Ginsberg wouldn't see me, and the police were to be called if I didn't leave immediately.

I never thought she'd see me on the estate, but I had to do something to get her attention. She called me that afternoon from another hotel phone, and I told her about the events on South Crenshaw with the four thugs who were obviously trying to protect her. I said I was sick of being told to stay in the dark.

She reluctantly agreed to meet. I advised her to drive around downtown L.A. erratically for at least thirty minutes, watching for surveillance. If she was certain she wasn't being followed, she'd meet me at the Bird of Paradise Motel, a fleabag joint just off the Interstate in Monterey Park.

*****

"I'm *schlepping* all over town for an hour to come here? Is this the kind of place FBI agents usually meet people?" she said with contempt.

"Sometimes. I thought this would be safe and appropriate under the circumstances," I replied.

Magda was right, though—this dump reeked of unspeakably nasty odors. The permeating stale cigarette smoke was the cleanest smell in the place. But unless Magda was being closely followed, no one would ever expect her to come to a motel like this for any reason, particularly as she was attired in her usual couture clothing and lavish jewelry. Today was ruby day, and she was garishly decked-out with the red stones.

"Can you at least turn on the air conditioning, if there is any? I'm *shvitzing* already... So, what's so important that you had to threaten me and drag me out to this *shreklekh* dump? And get to the point. I don't want to spend a second more here than I have to. Already I feel the fleas crawling around my ankles." She remained standing, clutching her purse tightly and scanning for vermin.

"Have a seat. This is going to take a while."

"*Ha*! I'm not putting my *tuchus* on any filthy chair here."

I sat down and pushed the other chair at the table toward her with my foot.

She scowled and perched reluctantly on the edge of the seat. "I can see you've had a rough time. I hope you don't think I or Aron had anything to do with that."

It had been more than a week since my conversation with the weighted gloves on South Crenshaw, but I still sported a hell of a shiner and a large bruise on my jaw.

"That possibility occurred to me. What do you know about who did this to me and why?"

"What? Didn't I already tell you, the day we met about the kidnapping, things were going on that were bigger than you could ever imagine? I told you that's why I couldn't tell you any more than I did. And that you had to leave alone anything that didn't have to do directly with the kidnapping. But no, you had to be a *khamer* and couldn't leave it alone. You started nosing around and put us all in danger."

"Yeah, and now I believe you. But that's not how investigations or investigators work. We have to follow leads wherever they take us. Unanswered questions have to be answered, and unexplained occurrences have to be explained. That's just the nature of the beast."

"Even if snooping where you have no need to snoop can get you and others killed? Who needs it?"

"I need it. That's where the answers are."

She sighed and shook her head in resignation. "I told you before, just leave it alone already. As much as I want to know what happened to my daughter, I think it's best for everyone if you just left it alone."

I shook my head slowly. "I can't. I owe it to Rachael to find out who was behind the kidnapping and see them brought to justice."

With a jerk of her chin, Magda scoffed. "Justice—*feh*! There's no such thing. I told you before, your stupid idealism was one of the things about you that scared me. That youthful idealism you had in college was just the sort of thing that foolish girls like Rachael found appealing. She was too much taken by you. I told you I couldn't let that relationship continue then, and I can't let your foolishness continue now. When idealism becomes fanaticism, you lose all common sense. Look in the mirror, and see where it's gotten you. You're going to get yourself killed, jousting with windmills, Mr. Quixote. And get others killed, too." She paused her tirade, leaned forward and, in a hushed voice, asked rhetorically, "My grandchildren may have lost their mother already. Do you want them to lose their *bubbe*, too?"

I sat back. "If that's how it's gotta be, then that's how it's gotta be, because you're not leaving here until you tell me everything. If you don't, I'll continue to make trouble for you. Where will that leave you?"

She leaned back, too, and looked me in the eye. "You can make trouble for me, but I'll survive. You won't. I can guarantee you will disappear. Maybe not tonight, but definitely before you can cause any real trouble."

We stared at each other for a few seconds. "Well, our bets are down, and we've drawn our last cards," I said. "Either you get up and walk out or you start talking."

Magda toyed with her ruby necklace, continuing to stare at me. Then she shook her head. "*Oy vey*. It's a long *shpiel*. Don't say I didn't warn you. First, see if you can find some clean glasses." She reached into her purse embossed with the *LV* initials and pulled out a large, leather-covered silver flask similarly embellished with the designer's *LV*, sparing fashionable lushes the embarrassment of placing their liquor in a mismatched bag.

I rinsed out a couple of glasses in the bathroom. She poured, and I lit our cigarettes.

"How much do you know about me and my family?" she asked.

"Just what's publicly known and what Rachael told me, which wasn't much."

"Well, I'm surprised. Given how she felt about you, I'd have thought she told you everything. I'm glad she had enough discretion not to air our family laundry."

"Once again, I have to tell you, Rachael was— *is* a much better person than you give her credit for." Apparently, the Ginsbergs not only avoided publicity to hide their secrets from the public but also had hidden secrets from one another.

"Let's not go *there* again. Enough with the *schmaltz* already. Anyway, so you'll understand and not think too badly of the Ginsbergs, I have to begin a hundred years ago. What happened then, long before Aron and I were born, is important to what's happening now. You see, our great-grandparents were friends and business partners in Germany. They saw what was happening and what was coming. It had happened in Russia and the Balkans, and they knew Europe wasn't safe for Jews.

"They scraped together what they could and sent their eldest children to America, to make a new life here. And to make enough money to bring the rest of their families over. But what happened next happened too fast. There wasn't enough time or money to bring over all the families, before they were sent to the ghettos and then the camps. Only a few got out. What you and most Americans don't know, or choose not to remember, is that there was a lot of rabid antisemitism in America before the war, and there were restrictions on Jews coming to the States.

"But when our parents did get here, they eventually did well. They made their way to Southern California, to Chino, if you know where that is, and started a chicken ranch. It seemed like a good way to make money, a lot of money, because there was a big demand for eggs and poultry back then. They hired mostly your people, and it didn't matter to our parents if they were here legally or not. You should be pleased about that."

"My people worked seven days a week for pennies just to put beans on the table, while other people got rich," I replied.

Magda shot me a dirty look. "*Kvetch*—there's gratitude for you." She shook her head. "Anyway, our parents didn't start making money until it was too late to bring their families over, which hurt them more than we realized, growing up. But once they started making money, they made a lot of money, and life was good for a while. My parents and Aron's even had enough to hire people to search Europe for their parents and other family members. But few of them had survived the war or could be found. So, our parents went on with life, until life brought them down again."

Magda sighed and stared into her glass, rolling it between her hands, her ruby bracelet and ring glinting brightly along with her diamond wedding ring in the low light of the smelly motel room. "*Der mensch tracht, und Gott lacht*—man plans and God laughs, as the saying goes. Have you ever heard of Newcastle disease?"

"No. Never."

"Neither had our parents, until it was too late. It's a disease that infects chickens and spreads quickly. If it's not identified immediately and quarantined, it will destroy an entire ranch. And it can spread from ranch to ranch. It can even infect some unlucky people. When the disease begins to spread, the government comes in and orders the entire ranch destroyed. The chickens, the coops, the feed—everything is burned. The smell is terrible, I can tell you.

"Anyway, that's what happened to our parents. They lost everything. Their ranch, their homes, even their cars. Everything was mortgaged or tied up in liens, and there was no money to pay for anything. My father survived and went to work at a dairy farm in the area as a common laborer, but he was never the same man.

"Aron's father wasn't so lucky. He just sat in his chair and stared out the window. Not being able to save his parents and then losing everything was too much for him. He believed *HaShem* had punished him for not working harder and getting his family out in time. Nearly two years of staring at nothing before he finally had a stroke and died. Do you have any idea what bankruptcy can do to a man? To his family?"

"No. My people were too poor to have anything to lose in bankruptcy."

"*Feh*! Maybe it's better that way. It saves you from a lot of pain. Maybe not. You have to be Jewish to understand what bankruptcy means to a Jew, especially if you live in a very tight-knit community, as we did. It's a shameful humiliation, worse than death."

I recalled Rachael telling me about her parents' and grandparents' upbringing in a very insular Jewish community and how that explained much of their outlook. Magda poured more gin, and I lit new cigarettes. "Go on."

"Anyway, from that time, Aron and I decided we would make something of ourselves and for our children, and never be in a position where we could lose everything. You see, Aron and I knew ever since we were children that we were a team. Without even knowing it, we were business partners since childhood—marriage was just an afterthought. Knowing that at an early age made life simple for the both of us. We had the same goals and helped each other reach our goals. Our main goal was to never be poor again and never let our children know what it was to be poor.

"We both got scholarships to USC and majored in finance. We both went to work at banks. Aron moved up quickly, but it wasn't as easy for a woman to move up the corporate ladder back then, even though I was smarter. Still, I made it to corporate operations manager before I left the bank because of the children. Back then, you couldn't just leave, have children, and then come back to your old job. But that was okay. I enjoyed my children."

Magda stared at me hard and, as if assuming I doubted her maternal devotion, repeated, "I did. I really did enjoy raising my children. I knew I could prepare them to be what they have become. And I continued to help Aron get ahead. He never would have made it without me, and he knows it. He can be such a *shlemiel*. *Oy,* such a *shlemiel*, at times. I have a better head for business. And what's more important, I can read and handle people better than he can."

"That's all very interesting, but what does it have to do with what's going on now?" I asked.

Magda lifted her hands off the table and held her palms out wide. "I told you it was a big *megillah*. Just listen… After learning the business, Aron and I decided it was time to start our own bank. That was our plan all along. You see, banks never lose. They always have the money or the property as collateral or both. The Rothschilds learned this centuries ago. They made fortunes and were hated for it, because they were Jews. But we learned from their mistakes, and with our political and charitable donations and our scholarships and gifts to schools, we made people love us. Or at least pretend to love us and give us the respect we deserve."

"Again, very interesting, but it still doesn't answer any questions," I said, impatiently. I knew better than to interrupt a witness who was on a roll with her story, but the funky room and Magda's rambling were starting to get to me. I would've accused her of verbose self-pity but, thanks to *Der Führer*, it'll be at least another two-hundred years before anyone can accuse a Jew of self-pity.

Magda lifted her arms and shook her hands at me, highly animated. "What is it with men? You always want to get straight to the point. Women know the road is never straight. Just listen, *chaver*… When we wanted to start our bank, we had many small investors but still not enough capital. Then, our lawyers told us about a group of very wealthy

Jews who would lend us the money to get started. The lawyers said they were a secret partnership, very Orthodox and conservative. They wanted to remain secret, so the bank had to avoid all scandal or negative publicity of any type. They wouldn't tolerate *schande far di goyim*—not even a hint of impropriety. This meant Aron and I also had to avoid any scandal. We had to agree to this. The legal papers even had a morals clause, so, if there ever was any hint of scandal, Aron could be removed as head of the bank and both of us would be removed from the board of directors. They could also take back every penny they'd invested immediately.

"This investor group put up all the money we needed to get the bank started, even more than enough. We were immediately able to invest in big projects, which began an income stream that would carry us for years. At first, they left their initial investment and all their profits in the bank, which gave us more working capital. All they asked in return was for the bank to handle transactions between the United States and Israel and to help with various charitable organizations serving Jewish needs, in Israel and other countries around the world. This was to our advantage, and we had no problem doing this.

"So, that's how the Bikkurim Bank of Los Angeles began. We were profitable immediately. Our investors were happy and never interfered. We never even knew who they were. They communicated through their lawyers to our lawyers. To make a long story just a little shorter, we never had a problem with our secret investors until they found out about Aron's problem."

Like most people, Magda hesitated when it came down to spelling out the distasteful nitty-gritty. I poured us each another drink and lit new cigarettes. "What problem is that?"

Magda looked down at her glass, took a long drag, and blew it out slowly before answering. "Aron has a problem, and his problem has some peculiar elements, apparently. Don't ask me what, because I don't know, and I don't want to know. I was more surprised than anybody, because he's never been very interested in sex. Never been very good at it, anyway. But every once in a while, he finds some *shiksa* who'll indulge his particular kink, whatever it is. Although our secret investors left us alone to run the bank without interference, they kept a close eye on the business and on us. They somehow found out about Aron's peculiarities when one of his freako *shiksas* tried to blackmail him."

Magda looked up at me. "I don't know how they found out, but they did, and when Aron got desperate and wanted to go to the police or FBI for help, the investors, through their lawyers, wouldn't let him. They didn't want any negative publicity or the police or FBI involved. But the lawyers said *they* had people who would handle it. Again, I don't know what they did or how they did it, but we never heard from the *shiksa* again. That was years ago, and there have been other problems since then that they've taken care of in the same way."

I recalled the look of suspicion Magda's friend gave her when we'd met at the restaurant and Magda had introduced me as a friend of Rachael's. Although I had a hard time imagining Magda as a cougar seducing young men, perhaps it was only my dislike of her as a person that blinded me to her feminine appeal. I couldn't help asking, "I gather Aron wasn't the only one who had a problem with fidelity?"

Magda gave me her Gorgon's look again, and I felt a chill run down my spine.

"I'm not the one with the problem, but life is what it is, and we all have to make the best of it. *Az me ken nit vi me vil, muz men vellen vi me ken*—if you can't do what you like, you must like what you can do, as the saying goes. Perhaps you'll be less judgmental if you know that the night Rachael was conceived was the last time Aron touched me, and *that* was a surprise. It had been a long time before that… I'm only human, and the Talmud teaches that we must enjoy life and to refuse a blessing is ingratitude. But nothing I've ever done has jeopardized the bank or our family's name."

"I'm not judging. I'm just trying to understand. So, if I understand you correctly, you and Aron were afraid, if the FBI looked too deeply into your bank and family, the indiscretions would be discovered and possibly become public. Your secret investors would pull their money out, and you'd lose control of the bank."

"Yes."

"So, the people who told me to leave you and the bank alone work for your secret investors or their lawyers?"

"That's likely, but I can't say for sure. You have to understand, they don't work for the Ginsbergs. Our interests and theirs are not entirely or always the same. We don't know who they are or what they do, and we have no control over them. What little I do know comes from their lawyers to our lawyers.

"The bottom line is, I can't do anything to help you, and I have to think of my own family. Ezra, my eldest, has a chance to be nominated to the Supreme Court. My younger son, Daniel, wants to be mayor of Los Angeles. We have to avoid any scandal. And I'm caring for Rachael's children now, so please, don't ever call me again. Our lawyers have told us we're dealing with people who believe the best way to solve a problem is to get rid of the people causing the problem. I don't want to be seen as the source of a problem."

"Doesn't Marino have custody of the children?"

"He has legal custody, but I keep them with me. He sees them once or twice a month, when he's not busy *shtupping* his *nafkas*."

Chapter 36

PBR Street Gang II

B art came through for me again, quickly this time.

Just a few days after our last meeting, we got together with Jason. After my talk with Magda Ginsberg, I had called Jason and asked him to find out if there was any connection between the Ginsbergs and the law firm of Levinson, Rabinowitz & Taubman. I also wanted to know what firm represented the Israeli Consulate in Los Angeles. This time it cost me steak and lobster dinners at an upscale Mexican restaurant in San Pedro, after the usual dry cleaning.

Jason insisted we start with top-shelf margaritas and tried to impress the attractive Latina waitress by attempting to roll his r's and sway his head like Ricardo Montalban. *"Trace Marrr-garrr-ritas, poor fa-voor,"* he said with a silly grin. As the waitress walked away to fill our orders he added, "Something about her reminds me of Raquel Welch. And mangoes. Giant, jungle mangoes."

"Calm down there, Big Boy." Bart grinned and shook his head then began his report. "I checked with Bill Nelson, the Organized Crime squad supervisor, and told him I wanted to follow up on the kidnapping. I asked him if anything new had come up from any sources, wiretaps or telephone records that might indicate any OC connection with the Ginsbergs or Marino. He had one of his analysts run everything and report to me on what she found."

"Don't turn this into a documentary," I said. "Just tell me what you got."

"Patience, my boy. Your paranoia may have paid off. Do you remember those calls made from Marino's cell phone to that Las Vegas company that we couldn't figure out?" Bart asked.

"Yeah. Those were the calls that bothered us the most." I filled in Jason. "Phone records showed Marino made those calls from his personal cell phone to a company in Vegas. We hit Marino hard about those calls, but he claimed he didn't remember anything about them, at first. He even tried to put Aron Ginsberg on the hot seat by claiming he may have left his cell phone at the bank, so it could've been Ginsberg or someone else at the bank who made those calls. But Ginsberg claimed he never used Marino's cell phone and never even saw it at the bank.

"We found out those calls were made to a cell phone belonging to a company in Vegas called the Edward Hawkins and Associates Real Estate Investment and Management Company. Vegas Division looked into the company and tried to identify the user of that phone but came up with nothing. We thought it was a dead end."

Bart finished his drink, pushed his glass away, and looked at Jason. "Why did I let you talk me into this girly crap? I take my tequila straight with a chaser."

"'Who's in command here, soldier?'" Jason answered with mock ferocity and then called the waitress over to order three shots of Añejo with Corona chasers. With another silly grin and bobbling head, he ordered, "*Trace a-knee-hos ee con trace sir-vay-sa Car-o-na.*"

I dropped my head and covered my face with my hands in shame. Then I peeked through my fingers at the cute Latina waitress, who seemed confused by Jason's attempt at the Spanish language. I repeated the order for her.

"Oh! *Sí.*" She laughed and went to get our drinks.

"That's more like it," Bart said and continued. "Well, anyway, that dead end came to life, at least a little, maybe. The analyst ran the phone number that received the calls again, and it turns out that number was very busy, but only for about four weeks around the time of the kidnapping. Some of the numbers called were identified as belonging to known or suspected mafia types. Vegas also checked with IRS and DEA, and they suspect that Edward Hawkins is a mafia front company. Nothing can be proven, but some of the so-called Associates are known mafiosos. It looks like the company is just a front to launder money and provide phony jobs, so the mafia types can claim a legitimate source of income to keep the IRS off their backs."

"Could Vegas put the phone in any one particular person's hands?" I asked.

"No," Bart answered. "Vegas said the people at the company weren't very cooperative. All they'd say was that they have thirty cell phones that any employee can use at any time. Very convenient for them, don't you think? Vegas also said they switch out the cell phones every month or two."

"Typical for mafia and drug dealers," Jason said.

"Absolutely right, Big Boy," Bart said. "But nobody's been able to establish any definite connection between the company and the mafia. It looks like it'll take an informant on the inside to give us that. All the smart guys, like Jason here, who can figure out that shit have left the Bureau to make their own millions."

"Right. Blame me," Jason said. "I should've stayed in the Bureau and worked for an asshole whose only interest is his next promotion. I would've had an ulcer and a heart attack by now, if I'd stayed in the Bureau."

Bart gave him a little nudge on the shoulder. "I'm just busting your balls. You know that."

"Yeah, I know. It just burns me up, the way things are in the Bureau. Like the man said, 'you need wings to stay above the bullshit.'" Jason added, "But you know I love the Bureau. Not a day goes by that I don't wish I could still be an agent."

"Yeah," Bart said. "I know."

Our meals arrived, and we all attacked as soon as the plates hit the table. But Jason got worked up and into character. "'I had to get off the boat. Split from the whole fucking program or go nuts, man.'" He feigned wild eyes as he swung his arms like a crazy man.

"Calm down, Jason. Just tell us what you came up with for show-and-tell," I said.

"Sorry. I got carried away. It must be the fancy steak and lobster. My usual R&R is squatting in the bush with 'cold rice and a little rat meat.'"

"Stick with the program, Jason," Bart said.

"Oh, all right." Slowly nodding, he dropped his head like a chastised child.

Our second round of drinks came, and I toasted, "*Salud*," as we lifted our shots of tequila.

Jason continued. "I think you'll find this interesting. I don't know how you came up with Levinson, Rabinowitz & Taubman, but you're right. They're the Ginsbergs' lawyers, both for the bank and them personally. And they've also represented the Israeli Consulate on several matters. The Consulate uses another firm, too, Epstein & Shep, but not as much."

"How big are they?" I asked.

"Big enough," Jason replied. "They have twenty lawyers here in L.A., another twenty in New York, about ten in D.C., and an office in Tel Aviv with at least a dozen lawyers. Their clientele are definitely major-league and big bucks."

"What does that tell you?" Bart asked me.

"I don't know yet. There're too many pieces to this puzzle, and I haven't figured out where they fit. But some connections are starting to show up."

"Like what?"

"Nothing I can tell you about yet... Can you see if you can come up with anything on Edward Hawkins, Jason?"

He took a swig of beer and looked at me gravely. "'My orders say I'm not supposed to know where I'm going with this boat, so I don't! But we'll go together... on the boat, okay? We came this far, so we go together. All the way! I'll take you up there, I'll go with you... but on the boat!'"

Bart asked Jason, "What did you say about going nuts?"

Chapter 37

Twilight Zone Time

The second-floor window of an office building in downtown L.A. is a great place for people-watching. You could spend all day looking out at the flotsam and jetsam moving below you in all directions and wonder what motivations keep that sea of humanity ebbing and flowing. You could spend all day watching, but watching wouldn't pay the rent on your perch.

I wasn't just wasting time, staring out the window. My undergrad psychology studies taught that staring out windows reduced stress, increased creativity, and heightened problem-solving ability. Today, it allowed me to think about the puzzle and all the pieces still missing. The pieces that somehow connected the Palestinian intifada, a dead transsexual kid, Jewish bankers and lawyers, an Iranian doctor, an L.A. development project, and a Las Vegas resort. Or maybe chaos theory ruled the universe, and there was no direct connection between any of these people or things—it was all just a matter of subatomic particles randomly bouncing around and occasionally into one another. A quantum physicist might be able to make sense of this tangled web, but it was beyond my understanding at this point.

It was while doing this deep thinking that I noticed a woman looking up at my office window. Actually, it was Jack's office window, but he encouraged me to use his office whenever I wanted, especially when meeting clients. The reflective glass made it impossible for her to see me, but there was no doubt she was looking directly at me, or at least at the window to my office.

She was in her mid to late thirties, poorly dressed in a faded plaid blouse, jeans, and sneakers. Caucasian, with messy, dishwater-blonde hair, about five-four, overweight. She held a purse tight against her chest the way a hungry man hangs on to his lunch pail. She was too far away for me to make out the color of her eyes but not too far away for me to see the world had taken its toll on her, leaving her old and weary before her time.

I'd first noticed her several days ago and had seen her a couple of times since then. Sometimes, she'd walk back and forth along the street; other times, she'd stand directly across from my office, but always she'd be looking up at my window.

I asked Maria to come into my office, take a look at the woman, and tell me if she knew anything about her. Maria said she'd seen her in the hallway just outside our office a few days ago. As Maria had approached our door, the woman had appeared to get scared and then ran off. Maria had thought it strange at the time but had forgotten about it until just now, when I asked her about the woman.

I didn't think the woman could be involved with any of the people following me. She was much too obvious and world-worn for that. Could she be a throwaway surveillance agent, someone intended to be seen to make me drop my guard and miss spotting the actual people following me? The answer was still no.

With nothing better to do, I decided to get to the bottom of this little mystery. I went out the back of the building, circled around the next block, and came up behind her. I watched her for a few minutes in the busy street, just to see what her body language might tell me about her. She didn't look homeless, but she was clearly only one welfare check away from being so. She was nervous and fragile, like a scared little bird. And she had that lost look I'd seen in many of the former soldiers I'd met at the VA hospital counseling sessions for PTSD patients. I wondered if I looked that way to people, at times.

I walked up behind her and said, "Wouldn't you prefer to come up to my office and talk about it? I promise I won't bite."

Her face exploded with fear. She clutched her purse tighter and took a step back. I was afraid she'd scream and run away.

When she didn't scream, I said, "Honestly, don't you think it's better to get whatever it is off your chest? I can offer you a cup of coffee or tea, if you like."

She didn't answer but calmed down a little, although she was still frightened and breathing rapidly. She nodded her assent. We walked to the corner and waited for the light to change then crossed the street, went into the building, took the elevator up to my office, and went in—all without saying a single word. As we passed through reception to Jack's office, Maria had a look of surprise and curiosity but didn't say a word, either.

"Please, sit down. Can I get you a cup of coffee or tea? Water?" I asked.

"No. Thank you," she said nervously and then shook her head. Surprisingly, despite her appearance, she had the voice of a young girl.

"Okay. Well, my name is Mig Dehenares. What's your name?"

"Gwen. Gwendolyn James."

"Pleased to meet you, Gwen. I couldn't help noticing you the last few days. Looking toward my office. Is there something you think a private investigator can do for you?"

"No," she said emphatically then shook her head rapidly and remained silent.

This wasn't going to be easy. Like trying to get change out of a vending machine after it ate your dollar. "Okay. Then why such an interest in my office?"

She hesitated. "I know something."

"What do you know?"

"Something about Rachael."

Now it was my turn for stunned silence. I could feel the color drain from my face. It took a moment to regain my composure. "Do you know Rachael?"

"No... I mean yes... Maybe."

"How do you know Rachael?"

"She came to me."

"Where did she come to you? To your house?"

"No."

"Where, then?"

"She just came to me. Like the others."

"The others?"

"All the others... that have... gone on."

"Gone where?"

"Gone over. To the other side."

"What other side? You mean death? Rachael's dead?"

Gwen nodded. "It's the in-between place, I think. I don't know."

Great. A nut case. When will I ever learn? Maybe she's a plant to throw me off the track or lead me on a wild goose chase. Let's see where this goes.

"So, Rachael is dead, and she came to you. Like the others. How does that happen?"

"They just come to me. I see them. It's like when you're at the airport. All these people from everywhere, just walking around, talking. So many of them. I can hear them all talking. Even the foreigners, I can understand them... Sometimes, one of them will look straight at me and say something. Sometimes, one of them will come up to me and say things they want me to tell someone." She stopped for a moment then slowly added, "Sometimes... they make me see things."

"Did Rachael say something to you that she wanted you to tell me?"

Gwen nodded.

Throughout this time, even as she spoke, Gwen never stopped fidgeting and squirming, like a junkie in desperate need of a fix. She was uncomfortable in her chair, uncomfortable in her skin, uncomfortable in her life. "What did she want you to tell me?"

"She's not happy where she is. She wants you to come for her and take her someplace else."

The expression on Gwen's face hadn't changed since she began. I got the feeling she could pass a polygraph test, if she were asked whether everything she'd said was true. "Where is she? Why isn't she happy there?"

"She doesn't belong there. There's another woman there. An old woman. She's nice, but she doesn't want Rachael there, either."

"Where is this place? What does it look like?"

"I don't know... It's nice... There's grass and trees. I can see mountains... Rachael doesn't belong there."

"Why doesn't Rachael belong there? What's wrong with it?"

Gwen just shook her head.

"Did Rachael say anything else?"

Gwen nodded and then smiled. "Rachael knows how much you love her. That makes her happy. She wants you to know she's okay and doesn't want you to worry about her. Everything is okay now. She just wants you to come for her and take her someplace else."

I felt myself beginning to shake on the inside. That little motor within that keeps us all going was starting to go haywire. I couldn't think straight. All I could get out was, "What... else?"

"She loves you, too. Always has. She wanted you to know that."

When someone believes something deeply, they can make you believe it, too, even without trying to convince you. The force of their belief makes you believe, despite any evidence to the contrary... But I couldn't take it anymore. I had to stop before I went down this rabbit hole any deeper. "Who are you, Gwen?"

She shook her head. "Nobody."

"Why did you come here?"

"Rachael wanted me to."

"Who told you about me?"

"Rachael."

"Rachael told you where to find me?"

She nodded then shook her head. "I don't know. I just came here. I knew this was where to find you."

"Why? How?"

"I don't know." Then, with a nervous smile, she added, "I thought you'd be taller."

"What do you know about me?"

"I guess you're a private investigator."

"Is that all you know about me?"

"That's what it says on the door. You said so just now."

"Where do you live?"

"I have a place."

"Where do you work?"

She shook her head slowly. "I can't work."

"Why not?'

Gwen's face contorted in anger, and she shouted, "Because they won't let me! It's too much. I can't do anything, because they won't leave me alone... Why can't they just leave me alone? I don't want this. Don't I deserve to have a life, too? A life of my own?"

She had that wild, vacant look of the insane. And she knew it. And she knew that's what I was thinking. She clutched her purse tightly, got up, and ran out the door as I stood and shouted, "*Wait*! I want to talk to you!"

She didn't stop. After a moment of stunned silence, I realized I was trembling and sat down. I reached down and opened the big drawer where Jack kept his bottle of Bushmills. I got a glass out and poured, spilling more than I filled. I knocked it down all at once.

Maria came in and looked at me. She became frightened—frightened for me, frightened the way a mother looks when she sees her baby with a temperature of 102°. I poured another, again spilling, and knocked that one down, too.

"Are— Are you okay?" she asked.

I didn't answer. I felt like a piece of gum that had been chewed and chewed and chewed until all the flavor had been sucked out of it. I was all used up, and the only thing left was to be spit out.

I got up and left without saying a word, not knowing where I was going.

Chapter 38

Mortal Sin

After I ran out of the office like a scared cat, I jumped into my car and drove, not knowing or caring where.

After about an hour, I found myself at the beach—Crystal Cove in Laguna—that Billie Carson had mentioned. Why I wound up there, I don't know. But I needed time to clear my head of all the psychic nonsense. I changed into the workout clothes I always keep in my gym bag in the back of my car—a habit I continued from my days as an agent. After a hard run along the water's edge, I went back downtown to my gym, showered, changed, and returned to the office for some unknown reason—just a pigeon returning to the coop out of habit. Thankfully, Maria had cleaned up the mess I'd left.

It was 6:30, and I found myself staring out the window again. It was already dark. Few people milled about outside, and I felt both loneliness and dread. There's something strange about an office building at night that magnifies both the loneliness and dread. Other people were going home to family or out to meet friends. But being alone in a big city office building at night was like being marooned on the moon. The dread was that I'd never escape the loneliness.

I knew I had to find Gwendolyn James and talk to her again. I didn't want to, but I knew I had to. But not tonight. I was still too wound up from our meeting this afternoon. What I needed now was a drink. And companionship. Female companionship. Bart was right: I did need a woman in my life. Maybe it was time to start looking for one. There were plenty of fern bars, oak rooms, and semi-dark lounges where the young hipsters in downtown L.A. played the mating game. I decided to join them tonight to forget my troubles, at least for a little while.

The Blue Parrot was close by. It was always a target-rich environment for grouse hunting and served a nice Tom Collins. The free hors d'œuvres weren't bad, either, and sufficient to substitute as dinner for a man on a tight budget. Tonight, the Blue Parrot was just right: crowded enough to be lively, but not so crowded as to bump elbows every time you turned around.

I sat at the bar to take in the scene and watch the river flow before launching my attack. This was a city where small-town beauty pageant winners arrived by the busload every day, hoping to be the next Hollywood "It Girl." But even they had to compete in the evening rituals against aggressive female executives and sexy secretaries. So, there were plenty of young and not-so-young beauties being attended to by an equal number of young, not-so-young, and just plain-old Romeos.

About twenty minutes after my arrival, there was a noticeable stir in this den of iniquity. Mortal Sin had walked in. Sin had taken the form of an incredibly gorgeous redhead in a crimson silk blouse and black skirt. She sat down at a table in the center of the room. She was petite and voluptuous at the same time, and her luminescent emerald eyes and iridescent cascading mane made her the center of attention immediately. Although she was only in her mid to late twenties, she had the aura of sophistication of an older soul.

She knew she was being watched and examined closely by both men and women, but she didn't appear to mind the scrutiny—she knew she'd always be desired and envied. She also knew the more she was checked out, the sooner desire would turn to lust and envy to admiration.

It was just a matter of seconds before the first of several suitors came to call on her. The first two arrived almost simultaneously and fought for the privilege of lighting her cigarette. Both were spurned with disdain. The next fifteen minutes saw five more Romeos give it their best shot and fail miserably.

After the seventh loser walked away with his tail between his legs, I couldn't help chuckling, then I smiled in the direction of the stunning beauty myself. It had been an entertaining yet brutal show, and I'd enjoyed it—even a philosophy-slash-psychology major isn't above a little schadenfreude now and then.

Much to my surprise, she looked at me and smiled back. Then she crossed her legs, and the slit in her skirt fell open, revealing more of her magnificent legs. I noticed a honey of a green-jeweled anklet on her left ankle. Years ago, on Bart's advice, I'd taken to wearing a snub-nosed revolver on my ankle as a back-up weapon. But that mesmerizing anklet was much more dangerous. It was for me, anyway. Mortal Sin smiled at me again.

I never claimed to understand women, but this much I did understand. Instantly and willingly, I committed to break every commandment Mortal Sin would have me break. That's how smart I was.

I walked over to her table. "There should be paramedics stationed nearby for all the wounded who leave your table with their egos crushed. Especially when it's done so brutally and publicly."

"Aren't you afraid of having your ego crushed?" she asked. "Or isn't yours so fragile?"

I was beguiled by her sultry voice. "No, my ego is as hard as my head. Are you waiting for someone? Or do you prefer to sit alone this evening?"

"I'm waiting for something interesting."

"What a coincidence. I've been waiting for something challenging."

"You begin to interest me, vaguely."

"I take that as a challenge."

She flashed her million-dollar smile, a smile that would stop the expansion of the universe. "Aren't you going to offer to buy me a drink?" she asked.

"Aren't you going to ask me to sit down?"

She sat up straight and leaned forward. "Would you care to sit down?"

"I'd love to. Would you care for another drink?"

I sat down and called the waiter over.

"Have you come to save me from all the wolves?"

"I came to light your cigarette," I answered.

"You look familiar. Haven't I seen you somewhere before?" she asked.

"I doubt it. I've never been there."

"Do you come here often?"

"Only when I'm looking for trouble."

"Do I look like trouble to you?"

"You look like Pandora's box."

"Do you intend to open my box?"

We had fun trading barbs. Alison Grayle had a great sense of humor, which is to say she laughed at all my jokes. Well, most of them. When she didn't find my attempt at humor funny, she adroitly turned a lame joke into something funny herself, usually at my expense. I didn't mind. As long as I had all her attention, she could make fun of me all she wanted.

Her own sense of humor was wicked and full of double entendres—the sexual references were unmistakable. After our second round of drinks, she said, "I'm hungry, and I don't like talking about... whatever we were talking about... on an empty stomach. Take me to dinner."

"I can't have you on empty. I shall do my best to fill you up. What does the lovely señorita desire for dinner tonight?"

"I hope your best will be enough... Know any good Italian places nearby?"

"I was hoping you'd be interested in something Mexican."

"Maybe for dessert. I'm in the mood for pasta."

"I've heard the Cappello Marrone isn't bad. Do you like Chianti?"

*****

I was clearly underdressed, but I knew a woman like Alison would be welcome anywhere, even if she brought along a scruffy escort to light her cigarettes.

We began dinner sitting across from each other in the elegant ristorante. It had a five-star reputation and was well out of my price range, but for some inexplicable reason, I felt the need to impress this woman. The lasagna was excellent, and the Bruno Barolo Alison ordered to go with it was also excellent. No cheap Chianti in a straw-covered bottle for her. A Mt. Holyoke fine arts degree and Stanford MBA had prepared the young finance executive for a life of luxury.

She was intelligent, educated, sophisticated, and well-traveled—clearly out of my league in more ways than one. Nevertheless, I was determined to enjoy the evening, even if I had to chase philandering Casanovas and bimbos for the next three months to pay for it. Why was I always attracted to women who were beyond my reach?

The romantic Italian music in the background was punctuated by an occasional aria or duet performed by the waiters—in la-la land, the waiters are all out-of-work actors or singers. The amorous ambiance brought me around to sit next to Alison. She didn't deny me a kiss as I sat down next to her.

"Do you always kiss on your first date, immediately after dinner?" she asked.

"Only if the food was good."

"And how was it?"

"It was nice. It left me wanting more."

"I'd like more, too, but only if you have it in you to impress me."

"Having it… is exactly what concerns me, so I shall do my best to impress you."

"Just how do you propose to impress me?" she asked.

"I could invite you to my penthouse by the Marina to see my art collection, but I wouldn't want you to think I was only trying to get you alone to take advantage of you."

"Where would you like to take advantage of me?"

"The Ritz Paris is nice, so I hear. Unfortunately, I live in a rundown Spanish bungalow in Echo Park, and the only art on the walls are the ersatz Rorschach tests left by the peeling paint."

"I've stayed at the Ritz Paris several times, and it's very nice, indeed. But I'd like to know what you make of those ersatz Rorschach tests on your walls. It would be very revealing."

"Revealing, perhaps, but not very interesting."

"I doubt that. In case you don't know it, you've done all right… so far."

Alison followed me to the Barcelona Bungalows in her bright-red Mercedes GT coupe. Apparently, she'd found it necessary to obey the rule that requires all gorgeous redheads to drive an expensive foreign convertible—this was not only their due but their obligation, as well.

The Spanish-style apartments may have merited their pretentious name sixty years ago, but time and lack of upkeep had rendered the once-snobbish address to the pitiful state of an aged actress without the benefit of makeup artist and hairstylist. It wasn't the kind of place one brings a woman like Alison, but she was a trooper and maintained her good humor, despite the shabbiness.

She walked around, looking things over. "I gather the maid comes in tomorrow?" she asked.

"Right after the exterminators. Would you care for something to drink?"

She shook her head then went over to the dinette table, where there was a chess game in progress and a nearly finished *Times* crossword.

"You do the *Times* crossword every day?"

"I try. I can never finish."

"Who's your chess opponent?" she asked, looking the board over.

"The managers here are an older couple. Francis and Frances Francis. It can be confusing, but they're good people. Former aspiring actors who gave up on the dream but occasionally still get parts as extras in crowd scenes. She sends him here to get him out of her hair, and he comes to drink my Scotch and beat me at chess."

"Is he beating you now?"

"He says he'll checkmate in three moves—knight moves. He had to go fix something and left the game as it is, to give me a chance to figure it out."

"Have you figured it out?"

"What I'd really like to figure out is what it was about me that interested you."

"Your shoes."

"These old things? They're just casual knock-arounds."

"I was referring to the size."

*****

Aspiring to be a gentleman, all I can report is that Alison Grayle's honey of an anklet is actually jade, and she's a natural redhead... And she's spectacular. Spectacular with a capital "S." In fact, spectacular in all caps: SPECTACULAR.

SPEC—TAC—U—LAR!

*****

"I don't suppose you provide breakfast as part of the service?" she asked in the morning, looking the way redheads look best—in bed, naked, with hair disheveled. Cabanel's *Venus* came instantly to mind.

"What does the lovely señorita desire for breakfast?"

"Pancakes!"

"The Larchmont isn't far and puts out a nice spread. Throw on your duds, Toots, and let's go."

"I'll just need to powder my nose."

"Your nose is fine."

She crinkled her nose at me and went to the bathroom to freshen her makeup. She came out freshly made-up fifteen minutes later. "You must think me a vain woman."

"Is there any other kind of woman?"

She gave me a look of feigned irritation—or maybe it wasn't feigned—and commanded, "Let's go."

We went. In her car. She drove. With the top down. She tuned in Erroll Garner. It was one of those gloriously perfect Southern California mornings you have to experience to believe: sunny, crisp, fragrant, with fluffy clouds, birds chirping—everything that makes you happy just to be alive. We were silent as we drove, taking in the beauty of the day. I wondered if this is what Sophocles really meant when he said silence gives the proper grace to a woman.

I just stared at her the entire way. She turned and blew me a kiss. This was heaven.

*****

She drove me back to the Barcelona Bungalows, and we exchanged phone numbers. "Put me on speed dial," she said and added with a wink, "As you know, when you press my button, I come right away."

We kissed goodbye. It was one of those kisses Shakespeare must've had in mind when he wrote about the sweet sorrow of parting.

We went our separate ways, and I couldn't help thinking what a fantastic time I'd had with Alison and hoped she felt the same. It was like one of those things you hear about and read about and see in movies, but you don't really believe it can happen to you. It was magical…

No, I'm not *that* stupid. Charming and witty though I may be, I knew something was going on, but I didn't know what yet. Having the right shoe size didn't explain it, either. A woman like Alison—if that was even her real name—doesn't just drop down from Olympus for no apparent reason. But I had to play along to figure out what was going on—and that was okay with me. Sometimes life seems very much like a ride at Disneyland: You know it's completely and totally phony, but you enjoy it all the same, just as if it were real.

Chapter 39

Strangers on a Train

I had reinterviewed everyone the FBI and police had previously interviewed about the kidnapping and followed up on any leads that came from that effort. Some of those interviews hadn't gone smoothly, and I'd had to get tough with a few people and do things that would've gotten me fired, if I were still an agent.

A few of my new enemies threatened to get even with me, if they ever caught me alone in a dark alley. Some of them had filed complaints with the FBI and LAPD, and I'd been visited by detectives and agents who told me to cool it, lay off, fuck off, and remember I wasn't in law enforcement anymore, and they said I'd be arrested for assault, if there were any more complaints. Bart called to inform me I'd officially been awarded the vaunted "Gold Penis with Oak Leaf Clusters" medal by the law enforcement community of Los Angeles County for being the biggest dick around. He also said ADIC Norton was particularly angry with me for committing the one unpardonable sin any agent—or former agent—could commit: embarrassing the Bureau in the eyes of the public and other law enforcement agencies. Yet, despite the hundreds of hours and all the new enemies I made in my efforts, I still hadn't made any progress on the kidnapping.

One Sunday afternoon, I was getting my mind off my troubles, which now included wondering if I'd ever see Alison Grayle again, with a cup of coffee at the French Café and a new book I'd just bought at Skylight Books down the street. It was another bestselling "mystery-detective thriller" from an author content to pander to an adoring and moronic public with two-hundred pages of tried-and-true tropes, clichés, and an entirely predictable ending—the twelfth installment in the series, I think.

A long shadow fell across my table like the shadow of a giant Redwood falling in a forest. The large-framed man came up behind me and said in a husky voice, "I guess they even allow ex-cons in here."

Although it had been several months since we had been released from prison on the same day, I instantly recognized the mafia boss Michael Sachetti's voice. "Technically, I'm not an ex-con. Just a defrocked agent. Have a seat."

Sachetti sat down opposite me and took a sip of his coffee as we looked each other over. He was dressed very casual yet imperious, in Versace slacks and polo and Gucci loafers. The gold bling around his neck and on his fingers was solid and twenty-four karat. Apparently, we shared an affinity for Florentine gold. He went with Versace for his cologne, as well, and used plenty of it. Hey, just because I can't afford any of it doesn't mean I don't recognize the good stuff.

"What're you reading?" Sachetti asked.

"Just another silly mystery from a bestselling author. I wouldn't recommend it. It's not very mysterious or any good."

"Then why waste your time reading it?"

"I'm trying to figure out why people buy this crap. This guy sells ten million copies of every book he puts out."

"Why people do what they do is always a mystery. You'll go crazy trying to figure it out," Sachetti said with surprising acumen. "It's best just to deal with what is and forget about the why."

Perhaps Sachetti was an adherent of Nietzsche's perspectivism, but I didn't think he came to discuss philosophy. I asked, "Could someone go crazy, trying to figure out why a busy man in your line of work would come all the way out here for a cup of coffee?"

"I don't know what you're talking about. Right now, I'm actually spending the afternoon with my *comare* in her condo in Marina Del Rey. I'm kicking back, looking out at the ocean. It's beautiful. I'm sure I don't have to tell you what she's busy doing."

"Okay." I grinned and nodded.

Sachetti smiled. "I hear you're still investigating that kidnapping from last year."

"Now it's me who doesn't know what you're talking about," I answered.

"My sources tell me you're still investigating the Ginsberg snatch."

Who are Sachetti's sources, and why would he care? I wondered. "Maybe," I replied.

"Nobody's been able to figure out what really happened, cuz everybody's been lookin' in all the wrong places."

"I still don't know what you're talking about." *Why would he take the time to come all this way to talk to me about this?*

"Let's take a walk. If you can tear yourself away from that book."

We grabbed our coffee, and Sachetti led the way to the parking lot in back. We passed a bright-red Mustang convertible, and he said, "This is mine."

"I'm surprised. This doesn't seem like your kind of car. I imagine you in an Alfa Romeo or a Maserati."

"You got that right. I've got both and many more. I leased this one for my *comare*. She picked it out. I hardly ever drive it."

"That would explain it."

"The car, the condo, the clothes, the shoes… This girl is driving me to the poor house."

"You're breaking my heart."

"She's twenty-four, a part-time model, and wants to be an actress. What can I say?"

"That says it all. At least you're spending your money on a worthy cause."

"Yeah, well, I don't mean to be rude, but I gotta get back to the Marina before anybody knows I've been gone, so let's get in your car and go for a drive."

"Okay," I said. When we got into my Highlander, he pushed the seat back as far as it would go, but it still seemed too cramped for the big man. We both lit up, and I began to drive.

"I heard you did time because you wouldn't identify your snitch on that kidnapping. Is that true?" Sachetti asked.

"I can't answer that."

"It's okay. You can tell me. I admire a man who's got a sense of honor. *Omertà*, we call it. And you should know I'd never give any cop the time a' day, so you can trust me to keep quiet."

"What I mean is, I can't admit that I even had a source. To anyone," I replied.

"You made a promise, and you were willing to go to jail to keep that promise?"

I looked at Sachetti but didn't answer.

"Would you be willing to make that kinda promise again?" he asked.

"I can't even admit I ever made that kind of promise."

"But if you could get information that would put you on the right track on that kidnapping, would you make that kinda promise?"

I thought for a moment. "If someone had information about that kidnapping and were willing to provide me with that information, I could promise that person I would never disclose to anyone under any circumstances that I'd received information about that kidnapping from that person."

"Make me that promise," Sachetti demanded.

I hesitated for a second, remembering the price I'd had to pay the last time I made such a promise, but I had no choice—my investigation was going nowhere. I was in the middle of the ocean and as dead in the water as a sailboat on a windless day. "I promise I will never disclose to anyone under any circumstances any information you provide about that kidnapping or that it was you who provided the information."

"Your word of honor?"

"My word of honor."

Sachetti nodded. "You guys got it all wrong. You were chasing the wrong fox in the wrong field and up the wrong tree. It wasn't no A-rab behind the kidnapping. It was my people. Not my crew, but another crew under another captain."

I was stunned. "But it was definitely an Arab who made the calls," I said.

"He's a Turk, actually. One a' our guys in the horse business. We use him to work the opium imports. He grew up in Turkey and Iraq and speaks Turk and A-rab, so he helps with settin' up the deals and bringin' in the shipments. It helps to have somebody who knows the culture and the language, so there're no misunderstandin'. And the guys on the other end feel more comfortable, dealing with one a' their own kind. He started out working with his own people at the other end, but he got burned over there, so he came here. He came in through New York, cuz he was workin' with the Family there, so he belongs to them."

"What do you mean, *belongs to them*?"

"One a' the New York Families owns him. He's their boy. They sent him here for his own protection. The boss here agreed to keep him outta trouble as a favor to New York and so we could get a taste a' the action and use him when we need to. But we gotta get permission when we use him and pay them tribute, in addition to paying him for his work."

"That's a complicated arrangement."

"You're tellin' me. He gets twenty-five Gs and a key a' pure shit for every shipment he helps bring in. He was hired special for the kidnap job cuz a' his accent, just to say he was Palestinian and play up the Jew-hater angle to throw you guys off the trail. Apparently, he did a good job." Sachetti chuckled. "You guys were tossing A-rabs left and right for no reason. I heard there were even some lawsuits filed against the FBI for harassment and false arrest. Shame on you boys for violatin' people's constitutional rights like that."

"Yeah, I always felt really bad about that," I said, wanting to move on and get all the information I could out of Sachetti. "I guess everybody's outsourcing these days, even you guys."

"You got that right. And it's gettin' worse. We gotta work with bosses and crews outside the Family every day now. I don't mind the heebs. We been workin' with them since the old days, and we know what they're about. I don't even mind the spics and niggers so much. But the Columbians and Cossacks, *fuck*! You gotta take an army every time you meet with them. It ain't like the old days." Sachetti shook his head.

"That's true," I answered. "But why bother hiring someone outside the local Family just to make the phone calls with an Arab accent? Your people could've pulled off the kidnapping without it, and bringing in someone outside the Family just complicates things, doesn't it?"

"It had to look like the kidnappers were going after the Ginsbergs just cuz they were Jews. Jews that supported Israel. What's that word for Jew-haters?"

"Anti-Semites. But why play that angle?" I asked, not understanding why Sachetti was telling me anything and definitely not convinced he wasn't sending me down a dead end.

"We had to protect the guy who came up with the idea for the snatch in the first place. He was an insider, and he could be a big earner for us in the future. The Family needed to protect him, and we needed to protect ourselves. The Ginsbergs are too well connected to fuck with."

That made sense. I nodded.

"We knew you'd follow every lead, leave no stone unturned, as the saying goes, to catch whoever would go after the Ginsbergs. And there aren't many people who could pull off a caper like this one and get away with it. We knew you'd suspect us, so we had to make it look like it wasn't us and point you in a different direction—one you'd believe. After 9/11, everybody has it in for the A-rabs, so that's what we gave you. You morons went for it hook, line, and sinker."

I took a sip of coffee and stared at Sachetti, still not grasping what was going on here. I had been driving south on Vermont, circling around a couple of times in countersurveillance mode, and was now on Highway 101. I hadn't noticed any tail. "So, who was it the Family wanted to protect?" I asked.

Sachetti took a sip of coffee also. "I can't talk about that. All I can tell you is the caller was the Turk. You're a smart guy and supposed to be a good investigator. It's up to you to take it from there."

I gave a half-hearted smile. "So, why're you telling me this?"

"Maybe I feel I owe you. You didn't have to jump in when that asshole shivved me. You took a few cuts yourself. And you stopped the bleeding before the doc got there. They said I woulda died, if you hadn't done that."

"You don't owe me anything. I was just reacting," I said honestly.

"Well, maybe I'm just reactin'. I heard you've been bustin' balls and pissin' people off all over L.A., tryin' a' figure out what happened with that kidnapping, so you can get your job back. That's if you aren't still with the FBI now, workin' undercover."

"No, I'm not undercover. And I'll never go back to the FBI."

"So, why stir up all the shit? You've made a lotta enemies. Every punk with a kitchen knife is lookin' to stick it to you. You're lucky to be alive, and you may not live long, if you keep goin' with this."

I wondered how Sachetti knew all this. "I have my reasons," I answered, continuing to look at him skeptically.

"You don't believe me?"

"Your reason for giving me this information is very nice and gives me a warm feeling in the pancreas, as David Hume would say, but I find it hard to believe that's all there is to it. Someone in your position doesn't talk unless there's a damn good reason, or unless it's all bullshit to throw me off the right track."

"Who the fuck is David Hume?"

"An eighteenth-century philosopher who would've enjoyed talking to you. I think you might have changed his entire philosophy."

"Yeah, whatever, college boy. But it's no bullshit... Here's the deal. The big boss here in L.A. is retiring soon. He just turned seventy and wants to spend the rest of his time at his place in the Virgin Islands, hittin' golf balls and bangin' the native girls when he can get it up. One a' the L.A. captains will replace him, unless the boys back East wanna send out one a' their own. They put up the money to get things started out here seventy years ago, and they still back some a' our deals, so they got a lotta say and get a taste a' just about everything that goes on out here. Right now, it looks like another L.A. captain will take over, a *facia bruta* asshole named Eddie Canino. That kidnap was his caper, and all that cash put him at the head a' the line. That kinda cash is pure skim, big money like they used to bring in from Vegas before you guys cracked down. It's all untraceable, tax-free, and can be used for anything.

"The problem is, Canino and I don't get along. Never did. He's from New York and thinks anybody not from there doesn't know shit. If he takes over, he'll find a way to squeeze me out or have me whacked. My sources tell me he was the A-hole that had me shivved in the joint, cuz I'm his only competition for the top job. And I wanna be the boss. My problem is, I didn't have the chance to earn big and kick up cuz I was in the joint. My crews still made money, but nothin' big, nothin' like that kidnapping caper. The only chance I have a' gettin' the top job is to get rid a' Canino. But that's not somethin' I can do myself. At least, not directly. You're gonna do it for me."

"*What?*" Again, I was stunned. There wasn't a shred of hard evidence to prove anything Sachetti had told me, but it made sense. The pieces of the puzzle were coming together, and the big "who done it" question was finally answered. But the price tag for this information was to do the bidding of one mafia captain and get rid of another one for him. "Just how do you expect me to get rid of Canino for you?"

"I don't want you to get rid a' him yourself. You just gotta finger him as the brains behind the kidnapping. And you gotta do it without him knowin' you're on his ass. How you do that, I leave up to you. Like I said, you're a smart guy. I have every confidence in the world you'll find a way."

I understood Sachetti's point. The challenge now was to build a case against Canino without him knowing he was under investigation, otherwise the consequences would be fatal. "If I go after Canino, won't he come after me?" I asked, looking for help.

"It doesn't work that way. First, it's like I said, some people think that maybe you're still with the FBI, workin' undercover, so you got some protection with that. Second, once it gets out that you got somethin' on the Turk, Canino will have to do somethin', cuz the Turk can tie him to the kidnapping. He's the only one who can. And since the body a' the woman was never found, it'll be assumed she was killed, right?"

My mouth suddenly went dry, and I nodded, trying not to show any emotion, though Sachetti had just implicitly confirmed that Rachael was dead.

"Kidnapping plus murder equals twenty to life, so the Turk will have to roll to save his own ass. Canino knows that, so he'll have him whacked. Besides, the Turk's been tryin' a' shake down Canino for more a' the dough from the kidnapping. He was only paid his usual twenty-five grand and a bonus cuz it took longer than expected. But he cried about it, cuz he knows he brought in a lot more. He's been bugging Canino for a bigger share. That would piss off anybody, so he's already on Canino's shit list. Once Canino hears that the Turk is on the hot seat, he'll have the excuse he needs to get rid a' him, so his New York owners can't complain. That's one more murder to pin on Canino, if you do your job. But like I said, you gotta be smart and do it right or Canino will have you whacked in a New York minute."

Sachetti and I stared at each other for several seconds. We both lit up again and sipped our coffee. He seemed to be reading my thoughts when he said, "Even if you broke your promise to me, which I know you won't, you can't use anything I've said against me. My crew wasn't in on it, and I was in the joint when the snatch went down. Just remember, the Turk and Canino are your targets. You won't live very long if you go after anybody else, so forget about it." He then put on his best goombah imitation and said, laughing and shaking his raised hands, "*Fuh-ged-daboud-it!*"

I got the message, again. "It would help if you gave me something to start with. I can't just show up at the Turk's or Canino's door emptyhanded and say, 'trick or treat'."

"Just do what you guys always do. Start with the little fish and work your way up. Put the screws to the Turk and get what you need from him before Canino has him whacked."

"So, who is the Turk? And how do I put the screws to him?"

"You want it on a silver platter?"

"How fast do you want Canino out of the way?"

Sachetti pursed his big lips and nodded. "The Turk's real name is Ahmet Ozan. He goes by Adam. He's in his mid to late forties. He's too lazy and stupid to work more than a couple shipments for us every year, so he lives like a jamook in Long Beach with his fat little American wife and two kids. He thinks he's hot shit and in like Flint just cuz he's connected to New York. He's always tryin' a' hang out with our people here, but nobody can stand him cuz he's just another stinkin' camel jockey and always complainin' about somethin'."

"Good to know, but how do I *get* to him?"

"Like I said, he gets twenty-five Gs and a key a' pure shit for every shipment he helps bring in. My guess is, if you paid him a visit, you'd find some shit and cash he couldn't explain to the DEA and IRS. If you're really not with the FBI anymore, you don't have to play by the rules, do you? You don't need a warrant, and you don't have to ask nice. He's already wanted for trafficking back in Turkey, so I'm thinkin' he'd prefer an American jail, if he can't get a pass. Is that enough? Or do you want me to slap the cuffs on him, too?"

"I'll take it from here," I said, as I began to think about this Adam. "By the way, how'd you know where to find me?"

"You're too easy to track and keep tabs on. You should change your routine once in a while. I thought they taught you that in the FBI."

"Good to know," I acknowledged.

"Now, drive me back to my car. I gotta go say goodbye to my *goomah* and get home to the wife and kids for Sunday dinner before anybody knows I've been gone. I'm a family man in more ways than one. If people in my business are unaccounted for for too long, the old guys start to wonder if we've been meetin' with the FBI, and we end up dead. They're all crazy paranoid."

"I guess life in a mafia family can be tough."

"It is what it is," Sachetti said with a shrug and a sigh.

"There hasn't been a family dynamic like that since the House of Atreus."

"Atreus? Never heard a' them. Who're they?"

"Ancient Greeks. Not important."

Sachetti gave me a look of irritation and shook his head. "Tell me something, college boy. Does all that smarty-pants talk ever get you laid?"

"No."

"I didn't think so. Instead a' havin' your nose stuck in a book all those years, you coulda been takin' care a' business, makin' money, havin' fun. All you got outta it is some fancy-pants shit to show off with in front a' people who couldn't give a damn. What a waste."

Maybe Sachetti was right. Socrates would disagree, but look what happened to him.

I drove back to the parking lot behind the French Café and stopped in the lane behind Sachetti's Mustang. I knew a man like Sachetti tells only half of what he knows, and half of what he tells is only partially true. I'd have to get him to tell me more.

"How do I get in touch with you, if I need to talk to you again?" I asked.

"You don't, so fuh-ged-daboud-it. If I need you, I'll get in touch with you."

As he spoke, a biker on a Harley pulled up and stopped directly in front of me. I didn't think anything of it until the biker pulled a pistol from under his jacket and pointed it at us with one hand.

Out of sheer instinct, I grabbed Sachetti from the back of his head and pulled him down, pressing my body over his. The biker emptied his magazine through the windshield and sped off.

We were both covered in shards of glass, but neither of us was hit. Sachetti pushed himself up and brushed off the broken glass.

"*What the fuck!*" he shouted.

"Somebody doesn't like you, or me, or both of us," I said.

"I can't be seen here." He jumped out of my car, ran across the lane to his car, and took off with tires screeching, burning rubber. In the chaos of the moment, several other people went running and screaming and sped off also.

The parking lot turned into a circus once the LAPD arrived. I just wanted to have my car towed to a garage, but the cops wouldn't let me go. When the detectives arrived and found out who I was, they insisted— as only big-city cops can insist—that I accompany them to Central Detectives to answer questions.

Chapter 40

To Protect and Serve

Even after two hours in the interrogation room, the four LAPD detectives who took turns questioning me found it hard to believe I had no idea who shot at me or why. As a Latino child and teen from the wrong side of town, I'd had run-ins with cops before, but this was my first experience as an adult on the receiving end of a hard interrogation. It felt strange—and aggravating and demeaning.

Despite their repeated questioning, I never mentioned that Sachetti had been with me. What was most surprising and baffling was how they seemed to think the shooting had something to do with the kidnapping. I told them I couldn't see any possible connection, and they didn't explain why they thought there must be one. Like most cops, they applied Occam's razor to their work, and although they'd probably never heard of that philosophical principle, they looked for the easiest answer and quickest solution to a crime, even if it meant an innocent person was sent to prison.

Since they weren't getting anywhere with me, they decided to bring in Detective Bernie Hernandez, with whom I'd worked on several joint investigations in the past, and a few LAPD cases he hadn't gotten anywhere on and needed help with on the q.t. The four detectives had moved on from playing the "good cop-bad cop" hand and were now down to playing their last card, hoping a friendly fellow Latino cop could get the truth out of me.

I liked Hernandez, who'd made his way from the barrio also, and I respected him for his competence as a detective. I remained cautious, however, since he was, after all, an LAPD detective looking for promotion. Even a good apple gets tainted with a little mold in a barrel full of rotten and half-rotten ones, and the internal politics of a police department are even worse than what goes on in the FBI. The insular, small-town nature of a police department—even a large one like the LAPD, where every street cop straight out of the academy knows the secrets of everyone from the Chief down to mail clerk—makes the jockeying for position akin to gladiatorial combat.

Captain Daryl Gregory, in charge of the Detective Bureau, came into the room with Hernandez for a moment, just to say a quick hello. His shirt sleeves were rolled up over his formidable and very hairy forearms, and he held a sheaf of papers in one hand and a half-chewed cigar in the other. Husky and crusty, Gregory was nothing more than a bully with a badge. His father had been a tough LAPD street cop and named his son after his hero, the hard-nosed former LAPD Chief Daryl Gates.

Gregory hated the FBI, and his antagonism was palpable. As Chief of the Detective Bureau, he thought of himself as on the same level as a Special Agent in Charge of an FBI Field Office—at least—and resented having to deal with mere FBI supervisors. The only thing he had in common with SACs, however, was the mistaken belief that he'd achieved his position on merit. Nevertheless, I thought it a good thing he was in management, as he was the type of cop who would've been pushing people around just to prove his masculinity, if he were still out on the street. When he was compelled to speak with lowly FBI street agents by the necessities of the job, his attitude was nothing less than insulting.

"You've been giving my detectives a hard time," Gregory said with a mean look, already angry with me.

"They could use a lesson in common courtesy. They never once asked nicely or said *please*."

Gregory wasn't amused. "You'd better start talking, Dee-hen-nar-rees, or you'll be in lock-up until I get this sorted out."

"I'd be in lock-up till Ragnarök, if I had to wait for you to sort anything out. You couldn't find your office if it didn't have your nameplate on the door. I'll give your detectives another ten minutes, and then I'm walking out or calling my lawyer. How'd you like another lawsuit for false arrest in your personnel file?"

"Raga *what*?" Hernandez asked.

"Forget it!" Gregory shouted at Hernandez and turned to me, his eyes boring into mine. "He's just showing off again... I never liked you, Dee-hen-nar-rees. Always the overrated agent and smartass. You got in a jam on that kidnapping last year, and now this. I always knew you'd wind up in jail for something or other. Unlike your federal boys, who couldn't handle that kidnapping or your part in it, I've got you now, and I'm gonna get to the bottom of whatever it is you've been up to. If your federal boys had stayed out of it, we'd have had the kidnapping wrapped up in a week. The feds should stick to mail fraud and leave real police work to us."

I leaned back in my chair, barely able to contain a laugh. "*Ha!* Your idea of police work is beating confessions out of street punks. When it comes to anything more complicated than that, you just sit around, scratching your ass, if you can't pin it on the obvious suspect, like the spouse or business partner of the victim."

Gregory's face contorted grotesquely, and he leaned into me. Like all arrogant egomaniacs, he was thin-skinned, and it didn't take much to get him going. Red-faced now, he responded rapidly and loudly. "You've been causing trouble all over L.A. since you got out of prison. I don't know what kind of payoff you've been trying to extort or from who, but L.A. is *my* city, and I'm not gonna let some third-rate former fed playing private dick go around causing trouble here. You got that?"

"Are you accusing me of extortion?"

"Strike a nerve, did I? Yeah, extortion, Dee-hen-nar-rees." He charged on without breathing. "Try this on for size. You weren't even supposed to be working kidnappings anymore, but you stuck your nose into it anyway. You somehow managed to figure out who was behind it. Probably just a lucky guess. Then you made a deal with one of the dirtbags involved, to squeeze some of the ransom out of the big boys behind the kidnapping. It was early retirement for a third-rate agent and a lot more than you'd get even after twenty years in the Bureau.

"You didn't want anybody to find out who was behind the kidnapping or about your deal with them, and that's why you refused to testify in front of the grand jury. But you got sent to jail before you could collect, or maybe your accomplice got away with your cut. Now you're out, tear-assing all over the city, trying to collect. But you pissed off the wrong people, and they sent somebody to shut you up—permanently. How's that fit you?" Spittle leaked out of the corner of his mouth as he raged.

I jumped out of my chair and lunged at Gregory, but Hernandez grabbed me before I could get at him. "You've made a career of sending street punks to prison for crimes they didn't commit," I shot back, "but you're not going to fit me in *that* frame!"

Gregory came at me, and another detective had to hold him back, too. "I'll teach you what happens to punks like you in my city! I'll make it my business to put you behind bars, smartass!"

"You don't have the brains for that line of business," I said, pulling away from Hernandez.

"Yeah, well, if you're so smart, maybe you can explain why the feds haven't issued another subpoena and hauled your ass in front of another grand jury," Gregory asked, pushing away the detective holding him back. "Who're they trying to protect? Or what're they trying to hide?" He wiped away the spittle with the back of his hand.

I'd been wondering the same thing ever since I'd gotten out of prison and didn't have an answer. I just stared at him. "Unless being shot at by a stranger is a crime, I'm done here."

"Let me talk to him, boss," Hernandez said, and the second detective walked Gregory out of the interrogation room in a huff.

I no longer had to wonder why the detectives had questioned me about any possible connection between the kidnapping and the shooting. It seems I'd been under LAPD investigation and surveillance, as well.

"Must be that time of the month," I said to Hernandez. "I've never seen Gregory so emotional."

"You know what he thinks of the FBI and FBI agents," Hernandez said.

"Yeah, the same thing every other cop whose application to be an agent was turned down by the Bureau. He's too resentful to see it's his own temperament that kept him out of the FBI."

"Take it easy, hotshot. Remember where you're at and who you're talking to… It's been a tough day for us. We've been working a homicide of a VIP downtown since last night, and everybody's worn out." Hernandez pulled up a chair. "That's in addition to the usual drive-by shootings in Watts and East L.A. and the drunk husbands shooting their cheating wives. Gregory's had the entire Detective Bureau working non-stop since yesterday."

"Who's the big shot who got killed?"

"Some professor who was a former advisor to the president. Apparently, the prez still called him from time to time for advice. The only lead is a name that a couple of witnesses said they heard the professor say just before he died."

"What was the name?"

"Neal something. Nisay, Neal Nishi… something like that. Gregory has us tracking down every Neal Nisay or Nishi or Neely or anything similar. We've been going down the list of every similar-sounding name in every phone book and database we can get our hands on, but so far, nothing."

"How'd it go down?" I asked, knowing Bernie was looking for help.

"The professor and his wife were walking back to their car after a concert last night at the Disney Concert Hall, and they were attacked and robbed. Other people saw what was happening and started screaming. The robber must've gotten scared and shot the professor then ran off. As he was dying, the professor tried to talk. The wife was upset and crying, but a couple of bystanders thought he said something like 'Neal Nisay' or something like that. Anyway, it's the only lead we have, and Gregory's had us going after it since yesterday."

I nodded. "Go on."

"If it wasn't for the name, this would be just another street mugging gone wrong. Gregory thinks there's more to it, 'cause the professor was a VIP and must've known the killer. He thinks the professor was trying to say the killer's name as he was dying, or maybe the name was some other kind of clue. Cracking this one will have everybody thinking he's the great detective and get him one door closer to the chief's office. And, he wants this one wrapped up fast, before the prez calls in your old outfit to take over the case."

"Bringing in the FBI would really fry Gregory's balls," I said.

"You guys always hog all the glory."

"That's management. The agents doing the actual work couldn't care less who gets the glory."

"Try telling that to Gregory… On second thought, don't try telling that to Gregory. Just stay away from him. He's hard enough to work for without you pissing him off."

"Don't worry, he's not one of my favorite people… Neal Nisay, huh?" I asked with a smirk.

"Yeah."

"Come on, walk me out. We're done here, and you know it," I said to Hernandez.

"Yeah, we're done, and too busy to bother with your ass anymore."

"What else do you know about the professor? Do you know what he taught?" I asked as we walked.

"Humanities, whatever that is, at the Claremont Graduate University. Some Ph.D. program for eggheads. He and his wife drove in from Claremont for the concert. Why?"

"Humanities is what good colleges and universities taught before they became nothing more than the glorified trade schools we have now. The good ones still have a humanities program. A professor of humanities would be familiar with Latin."

"Yeah, so? What's that got to do with anything?"

"It means I'm all for following up on every lead, but I'd be very surprised if there was anyone named *Neal* involved in the murder. If there was, it would be purely coincidental."

"Why's that?"

"I don't think the professor was saying anyone's name. He was repeating a Latin phrase, *De mortuis nil nisi bonum*, which means speak only good of the dead. The witnesses must've heard the *nil nisi* part and mistook it for a name. The professor knew he was dying and was only repeating a common phrase, asking that he be well spoken of after he died."

Hernandez chuckled, shaking his head. "Gregory wouldn't be happy to hear that. Not after all the overtime and wasting about two thousand man-hours chasing every *Neal* in the book."

"Are you going to tell him?"

"Yeah, right… I get paid the same if I'm getting shot at, sitting behind a desk, or chasing down Neals that don't exist. But I don't make lieutenant by embarrassing Gregory in front of the entire Detective Bureau. Especially on advice from you."

"Well, for what it's worth, my advice is to forget about chasing down Neals and instead hit on your usual street-punk informants. Find out who's been lying low since last night or left town in a hurry last night. That'll be your man."

"I'm on it," Hernandez said as we reached the front door of the station. He opened it and stood against it, allowing me to pass through.

"Your buddies kept me here so long, it's dinner time. Care to join me?"

"No, thanks. I gotta keep going on this murder, now that I know where to start looking. And I don't think it would be good for my career to be seen hanging out with you. But what was that *Raganot* thing that got Gregory pissed off?"

"It's nothing, but Gregory was right, for once. I *was* just trying to piss him off."

"Well, mission accomplished. You did that, all right. So let me give *you* some advice. Watch your step. Gregory's had you on his shit list, and now he's got you on his radar. He's pissed and will arrest your ass as soon as he's got anything solid on you. His chonies get wet just thinking about throwing your ass in jail."

Chapter 41

The Visitation

Late Monday morning, I was finishing a report on a missing, loser husband whose wife wanted him back for some reason I couldn't fathom, when Maria knocked on the door to Jack's office and came in with a big Cheshire-cat grin on her face.

"Hey, man, there's, like, a woman here that wants to see you."

"So, shoo her in."

She cocked her head to the side and gave me a questioning look.

"What's the big deal? Who is she?"

"That's, like, what I wanna know, man. I mean, she's gorgeous. She's like the most beautiful woman I've ever seen in person. She makes Marilyn Monroe look like nothing, man."

"Didn't Jack ask you to stop saying *man* and *like*?"

"Oh, yeah."

"And not to say *yeah* except when you're talking to friends?"

"Yes."

"Shoo her in."

Maria opened the door and, very professionally, said, "Mr. Dehenares will see you now."

Alison Grayle walked through the doorway and, as much in acknowledgment of Maria's admiring gaze as for her holding the door open, said, "Thank you." She was wearing a knee-length, emerald-green dress, black belt and shoes, and held a small, black D&G handbag. Jade earrings, necklace, rings, and that jade anklet completed the ensemble— as if that face and figure required any adornment. And Maria was right: Alison did make Marilyn look common.

Maria remained standing at attention at the door, admiring eyes still fixed on Alison. I said, "You can close the door on your way out, Maria."

"You must find your secretary very… entertaining," Alison said with a wry smile after Maria left.

I gestured to one of the chairs, and Alison sat down. "She's not my secretary. The boss hired her before I started working here. I think she's his Eliza Doolittle project."

"Really?"

"He's seventy-something and well beyond any evil intention, so it's an entirely platonic project. I can tell she's quite in awe of you."

"I'm sure," Alison said casually as she looked around carefully. "So, this is your office. I gather the maid comes in tomorrow?" she asked, repeating the question she had asked at my apartment.

"Right after the exterminators," I answered again.

"Well, it's a little nicer than the way private detectives' offices are portrayed in old movies—those dark, dingy little rooms with old, worn-out furniture, where greasy little gnomes put their feet up when they're not lurking around hotel lobbies."

"This is actually the boss's office. I only use it when he's not here. My usual place is the kitchen table, between the fridge and sink in the other room. To what do I owe the honor of your visit?"

"I just happened to be in the neighborhood and thought I'd surprise you and let you take me to lunch."

"Lucky me. Where would the lovely señorita like to go, keeping in mind I only have the resources of a greasy little gnome?"

"Doesn't the private detective business provide well?"

"Not if you're honest."

"Are you one of those who believes affluence requires corruption?"

"I think it's difficult for an honest man to attain wealth in a corrupt society without becoming a little corrupt himself. The cards are stacked against uncompromising integrity."

"And you've never compromised your integrity for profit or anything else?"

"I've never been important enough for anyone to tempt me."

"Do you avoid temptation so you can be known as the only honest private detective in L.A.?"

"I don't avoid temptation. But the system itself is corrupt, so I'd be satisfied to be known as the least dishonest private detective in L.A."

Alison gave me that look of irritation that speaks volumes. "We'd better get going. I don't want to discuss economic and social theory on an empty stomach."

I stood up. "It's not just theory. Remember what Balzac said. 'Behind every great fortune lies a great crime.'"

She crinkled her nose at me and got up also. "Let's go."

We went. As we walked through the outer room, Alison asked, "Aren't you going to introduce me to your lovely secretary. I should be very jealous to think of you with such a beautiful, young woman right outside your door."

"But of course. Where are my manners?" With the appropriate bow and hand gestures, I said, *"Señorita Alison Grayle, te presento la señorita Maria García."*

"Hello," Maria said with an adoring smile.

"Pleased to meet you. You have such a beautiful complexion. If you don't mind me saying so, you don't need such a bright lipstick color with that vibrant skin. A shade or two darker would be perfect for you."

Maria beamed in gratitude for the compliments and advice. I knew she'd be stopping at a makeup counter on her way home tonight.

"Does this other door lead to your actual office?" Alison asked as she made her way to the conference-kitchen-storage room where I worked when Jack was here. She opened the door and looked in. "Not quite as nice as the other room."

"I told you, didn't I?" I knew she'd come to check things out.

*****

Sandwiches, chips, and Cokes made for a pleasant lunch at the hole-in-the-wall down the street. It was okay with me. Bread and water anywhere with Alison Grayle would be okay with me. As we ate, her subtle way of interrogating me consisted of her telling me a little about herself or what she wanted me to believe about her, and then she asked about me.

Alison said she worked as an investment counselor for WTC Financial, located in the nearby U.S. Bank Tower. She had clients all over the world and traveled frequently. Most of her clients were partnerships, but she did have a few individuals as clients. She had a condominium in the Metropolis but was getting tired of condo living in downtown L.A. and was thinking of buying a house in an older, residential area for a homier feeling. She invited me to visit her at her office or condo any time I wanted.

She asked me about my background and work, and I told her about my status as a defrocked agent and former inmate of the federal prison system. She didn't seem to mind either and even offered to help me in my work as a private investigator. She said she had access to just about anyone's financial background and credit report. I told her I'd keep her offer in mind. She wanted to know if I had any interesting cases at the moment. I told her I didn't.

"Oh, come on. Movie theaters and bookstores are full of stories about the murder and mayhem you private eyes are always getting yourselves involved with. You must have something juicy going on."

I knew what she wanted, so I told her. "I don't know how interesting it is to anyone other than me, but the most important case I'm working on is the kidnapping case that got me bounced out of the Bureau. There's no money in it for me, and I'm not doing it to get my job back, but I intend to find out who was behind the kidnapping and see to it that justice is done."

"Don Quixote, knight errant—I knew it!" she said with glee.

"I wouldn't put it that way."

"Then how would you put it? There's no financial incentive and no legal obligation."

"I just think the victim deserves to see justice done on her behalf, and her family also deserves to have some justice, if only to bring closure."

"Taking on evildoers for no other reason than to see justice done. If that isn't Don Quixote jousting with windmills, I don't know what is."

"Call it what you want and make fun of me all you want. I'm going to see it through."

"Of course you are. That's what knights errant do... You used the word *victim*. Do you think the woman is dead? Murdered?"

"Yes."

"How can you be so sure? There hasn't been anything reported to indicate she's dead or any body found."

I couldn't tell her what Sachetti had told me. At least, not yet. Not until I found out who she was working for.

"I think she's dead for two reasons. First, there hasn't been a kidnapping where the victim has been sequestered for so long without the kidnappers maintaining contact with the victim's family. If she was still alive, the kidnappers would still be in contact with the victim's family to get a ransom payoff. The Getty kidnapping was the longest modern kidnapping on record, and that lasted only five months. Second, a psychic came to me and told me Rachael Ginsberg was dead."

"A psychic? Are you serious?" Alison couldn't help laughing. I didn't mind her laughing at me. Her laugh was a joy to see and hear. No man and few women look good in the convulsion of a hearty laugh, but when Alison laughed, she was even more beautiful, and all I could do was smile in appreciation.

"Why not? There are more things in heaven and Earth than are dreamt of in your philosophy, Ms. Grayle."

"I can't imagine quoting Shakespeare helped you much in your career with the FBI," she replied.

"It may be what got me canned."

"But, you're serious about the psychic. I never would've thought you one to go in for that sort of thing. Who is this psychic? What did they tell you that made you believe him? Or her? It was a her, wasn't it?"

"I don't know who she is. A crazy old woman I saw on the street said she could see dead people. She said she knew who I was and that she'd seen Rachael Ginsberg in one of her visions. She wanted me to know she was dead. Then the old woman ran off before I could get any more out of her."

"That's it? That's all? Why would you believe her?"

I just shrugged. "Some things you just find believable, despite the lack of supporting evidence."

"So, how close are you to solving the case? Didn't the papers report that the police and FBI thought it was some Palestinian military group who kidnapped the woman because she was Jewish?"

"It may have looked that way at first. Now, I'm not so sure."

"Why? Did you find out something?"

"I'm sorry, but I can't talk about anything I may have learned as an FBI agent. You have to understand, even though I'm not working for the FBI anymore and never will again, I'm still bound by the confidentiality agreement I signed when I first became an agent. There're people in the FBI who'd love to send me back to prison just for violating that agreement."

"You don't trust me? You don't think I can be discrete or keep a confidence?"

"It's not a matter of trust. I just wouldn't want to put you or anyone else in the position of having to be discrete or keep quiet about anything I say. Life is easier that way."

She seemed hurt. She looked down, and her eyelids fluttered sadly for just a moment. She was good. "I'm sorry you don't trust me. I hope someday you will."

"If ever there was a woman I wanted to trust and wanted to believe in me, it's you." It was a good line. It worked. She seemed mollified.

Then she looked me straight in the eye. "Well, like I said, if there's ever anything I can help you with, just ask. I'd do anything for you. I want you to know that."

It was a good line. It worked.

Chapter 42

The Turk

It would've been nice to have some help, but I knew I couldn't bring Bart in on my meeting with Ahmet Ozan. His dedication and sense of duty would've required him to get the Bureau officially involved, or at least to take things in hand himself, and I didn't want that—yet.

I did ask Bart to check with his friends on the Organized Crime squad and get me the big picture on the L.A. mafia: who the major players were, and what was known about them. He, of course, wanted to know the reason for my sudden interest, but I could only tell him I was working on another possible piece to the puzzle. I also asked him to see if the Bureau had anything on Alison Grayle and to have Jason look into her and WTC Financial for me.

It was easy to identify and locate the Turk with the information Sachetti had given me. But, unlike Spade and Marlowe, who cut to the chase immediately and got their hands on their suspects as soon as they knew their names, real detective work requires methodical preparation. An FBI agent learns fast the importance of knowing as much as possible about a suspect or witness before making contact. Finding out about someone's criminal, employment, financial, credit, and personal history takes time, sometimes weeks or even months. A few days of physical surveillance is also a good idea when working on an important suspect. All this to prepare for an interview, so you'll know the suspect better than he knows himself.

After a few days of conducting the usual background checks and surveillance, it was easy to establish the Turk's routine. The hard part would be not killing him with my bare hands the moment I confronted him.

Ahmet Ozan kept a low profile and was living the good life in a nice, two-story house in an upper-middle-class residential neighborhood in

Long Beach. His fat, little, American, Green-Card-enabling wife was a nurse's aide at a local hospital. She worked the day shift, leaving for work at 6:30 every morning. On those rare occasions when he didn't get home late, Ozan saw their two kids off to school before leaving for the gym or to run errands at 11:00. He had lunch at one of several Middle Eastern or Greek restaurants in the area before getting home in time to meet the kids returning from school at 3:00, unless his business or extra-curricular activities kept him away. As one would expect, he had a special young lady friend he met on a regular basis at her condo overlooking the water in the pricey Naples area of Long Beach. Dinner with the family, then off again to meet with his business associates, friends, or to have fun at a restaurant or bar. Less often than not, he was home by 1:00 a.m. I wondered what he told his wife he did for a living. Like most wives, she probably didn't care, as long as he brought in some money, took out the trash, and spent a few nights at home, taking care of mama.

This background work was uneventful until, one night, I saw Ozan meet with Maria's gangster brother, Oso. I had followed Ozan to a bar in East L.A. and then saw him exit the bar with Oso and another Hispanic male. They each went to their cars, and then Oso and his partner went to Ozan's car. An envelope was exchanged for a bag, and they each went their separate ways.

I wasn't concerned about the drug deal that had just gone down until Oso drove by and recognized me. I knew this would cause me trouble somewhere down the line.

*****

I decided to get into the Turk's house, to look for any incriminating evidence and telephone and travel records, before confronting him.

I parked one block down and two blocks away from Ozan's home. Getting into the house was easy enough. My only concern was Ozan's dog, who started barking when I entered the back yard. It was a small, Pekingese-type that wouldn't have been a problem if its barking hadn't attracted the attention of a neighbor's dog. The neighbor's dog must've been much larger, as it barked loudly while I picked the lock on the back door.

Residential burglary would be another crime I'd have to add to my unofficial rap sheet of crimes I'd never thought I'd be committing a year ago. The line between me and "the bad guys" was diminishing, but like everyone else who'd ever been issued a badge and a gun, I believed I was on the side of the angels and that my minor transgressions would be forgiven. Weren't all the philosophers in agreement that a good intention excused a bad act?

Experience had taught me to go straight to the master bedroom closet. There, I found two fireproof strong boxes, also easy to get into for anyone experienced with the right set of lock picks.

One box held a half kilo of opium, several thousand dollars in cash, and a pistol with its serial number filed away. The other was full of cash and another pistol. I left the strong boxes open on the bed, as I planned to confront Ozan with their contents when he returned. I took photos of this evidence with my cell phone.

I'd make Ozan an offer he couldn't refuse: he'd either have to cooperate with me and provide enough information to get Canino, or he'd have to face Canino and the FBI on his own.

The only other item of interest was a bag of marijuana and a pipe in a dresser drawer, things that no longer had to be kept hidden in California, after common sense had prevailed over the politicians.

I was on my way downstairs to look for telephone bills when I saw and heard two Long Beach Police patrol cars come to a screeching halt in front of the house. A neighbor must've heard the barking dogs, seen me breaking into the house, and called the police.

I immediately ran out the back and jumped the fence, where I was confronted by a dog—a very big dog. A very big, mean, loud, barking dog. It was a rottweiler, and it wasn't looking to make friends. I ran to a side fence and jumped over just in time to avoid getting bitten.

Okay, I did get bitten. That damn mutt got a piece of my ass before I made it over the fence. You can understand my reluctance to report this fact. When did anyone ever hear of Spade or Marlowe getting their ass chewed by a mutt?

*****

The next day, the *Times* reported the arrest of Ahmet Ozan for possession of opium and an illegal weapon found in his residence. The police had entered his home to conduct a welfare and safety check, following a neighbor's report of a man breaking in through the back door. A man was seen running out the back door when the police arrived.

The police had found the opium and weapon in plain view, plus a large amount of cash and a second weapon, which were all confiscated pending further investigation.

It was surmised the burglar had been preparing to steal the contraband items when the police arrived and ran out before he was caught. It wasn't known if the burglar had targeted the residence or if it was simply a target of opportunity.

Ozan was being held pending his arraignment and bail hearing later that day. As is always the case, the neighbors were surprised and shocked by Adam Ozan's arrest, having believed the Ozans to be very nice people.

*****

The LBPD reports revealed that the neighbors knew Ozan's wife, Tonya, worked at a local hospital. The police found her and brought her home. She denied any knowledge of the contraband items. Threatened with possession, being an accessory, and losing custody of her children, she agreed to call Ozan and get him to come home immediately without telling him why. The police vehicles were moved away from the Ozan residence so as not to spook him, and he was arrested upon arrival.

Ozan immediately invoked his rights and refused to make a statement until he could speak with an attorney. As is standard practice these days, Ozan was videotaped while being questioned, arrested, and processed, and during his very short intake interview at the LBPD. He was held in custody pending his arraignment and bail hearing the next day.

He made his allotted phone call, and a high-priced attorney appeared at his hearing to represent him. A five-hundred-thousand-dollar bail bond was posted on his behalf, through his attorney, and he was released. The attorney wouldn't reveal who was actually paying him or who put up the money for bail. Ozan made arrangements to meet with the attorney the following morning.

The next morning, after getting his wife off to work and his kids off to school, Ozan left home as usual. He never made it to his attorney's office that morning. His attorney had no idea why Ozan didn't show up at his office. Ozan's wife and children had no idea what happened to him or where he might have gone. Ozan was never seen or heard from again.

Chapter 43

The Turk – Deceased

God damn fucking thief!
God damn fucking neighbor!
God damn fucking cops!
God damn fucking mafia!

Chapter 44

PBR Street Gang III

I had arranged for a quick early lunch with Bart and Jason, this time in South Central L.A., where it was unlikely we would run into anyone who might know us. The best barbeque in the city was in South Central, which made it worth the drive.

Jason got happy as soon as we walked into the Whistl'n Pig BBQ, an unpretentious little restaurant with a cement slab floor, rickety wooden tables, and a giant smoker in back. Who needs roses on linen when the food is the main attraction?

"'You smell that? Do you smell that?'" Jason said, already in character, standing tall with his fists on his hips like an Army colonel. "That's real barbeque, son. 'Nothing else in the world smells like that.' I love the smell of barbeque in the morning."

"What happened to Charlie Chan?" I asked the clean-shaven Bart as we approached the counter and studied the menu board.

"Had to get rid of it. Turns out Kitty Kendall's little kitty is ticklish. And I mean *really* ticklish. It's tough to get the job done when she's laughing like a hyena in heat."

"Sorry I asked," I said. "That's more information than I ever wanted to know."

Jason grabbed me by the shoulder, got in my face, and again taking from his favorite movie, said in all seriousness, "'Captain, I don't know how you feel about this, but if you eat it, you'll never have to prove your courage in any other way…'"

With lunch ordered and the preliminaries out of the way, Bart filled us in on the latest information Bill Nelson, supervisor of the Organized Crime squad, had on the L.A. mafia. "The top boss is Vincenzo Florian, a seventy-year-old veteran mafioso who came to L.A. from Chicago as a young man. He rose through the ranks from bottom-level street hood to capo and has been boss in L.A. for about twelve years. Informants consistently reported that Florian was chosen by the New York and Chicago Families to be boss here because he wasn't greedy, paid tribute when he was supposed to, shared his manpower and informants, and was always willing to negotiate and compromise to keep the peace. He also keeps a very low profile and avoids anything that might bring media attention. He delegates the work as much as possible and only steps in when necessary to keep things moving or keep the peace."

Jason sipped his Coke and said, "Sounds like a smart guy... I guess you have to be, to stay in power that long."

Bart nodded. "Right again, Big Boy... Next down on the hierarchy is a scumbag named Eddie Canino. It's rumored that Canino will be the next boss in L.A., once Florian decides to retire or is moved out by Canino, whichever comes first. According to Nelson, Canino is ambitious and ruthless, a real heavy hitter. He has four crews working under him, and he's into everything—murder, protection, extortion, gambling, drugs, prostitution, bust-outs, you name it. Never touches anything dirty himself and has his crews do all the dirty work for him. Nelson said they can never get anything on him because he eliminates any possible witnesses against him, meaning he has them killed. They suspect he's personally ordered hits on at least twenty people, but that's just the tip of the iceberg, according to Nelson."

Our rib-and-potato-salad plates came, and we knew the food was going to be great even before taking our first bite—the meat was slathered in sauce and so tender, it was already falling off the bone. "I know you've got a package on him for me, right?" I asked Bart.

"Wrong. All I could get you for now is a copy of an old New York driver's license with a photo. Apparently, Canino is from New York and has the backing of the bosses there. The address on the license was just a mail drop known to be used by the Big Apple mafia. Nelson's intel says he moves around a lot, mostly between L.A. and Vegas now. He said he'd get me a Nevada DL photo and a surveillance photo of Canino from Vegas Division for me, and I'll give you a copy.

"Nelson said Canino likes to think of himself as a businessman. Like all the smart mafia bosses, he launders his money and puts it into legitimate businesses. Now get this... Remember that Edward Hawkins and Associates company that came up on those phone calls from Richard Marino's cell phone? Well, Canino is listed as an associate in that company. It may be time for me to pay Marino another visit and ask him about Canino."

I had to stop Bart. "I'd like you to hold off on that for just a little while. Let's think about how that fits in and get more on Marino and Canino first. If you or I go to Marino now, he'll just deny knowing Canino, anyway, and we couldn't prove otherwise. What else do you have for me?"

"Gimme, gimme, gimme. That's all I ever hear from you these days. What've *you* done for me lately?" Bart teased, biting into a rib dripping with sauce. "Now that you're a big-time private dick, you should be passing me information to make *me* look good."

"Chasing after cheating husbands and bimbos isn't what I'd call big time. What if I pay for lunch?"

"'Did you know that *if* is the middle word in *life*?'" Jason asked with all the sincerity he could muster. "I mean, 'I'm a little man.' Just a little man—"

Bart stopped him from going too far off the tracks. "Yeah, now getting back to Planet Earth… Nelson said there're four other captains in Southern California, all with three or four crews of their own. The only major player among them is a dirtbag named Michael Sachetti. He was in line for capo also, but he got busted and was in the can for two years, which put him out of the picture. If you're not earning and kicking up cash to the big bosses, you don't count."

I got up to refill our soda cups and grab another handful of paper napkins. Jason had a swig of Coke and shook his head. "Too bad this place doesn't have a liquor license. This would be great with a cold one… So, how'd this Sachetti mope get busted?"

I didn't want anyone to know I knew Sachetti or anything about him, so I kept my mouth shut and let Bart answer.

"The story I heard was that Sachetti thought his girlfriend and a loan shark who worked for him were getting it on behind his back. Sachetti looks like an orangutan that got hit in the face with a hot frying pan, and he's the jealous type. But, because he's a mafia captain, he can buy any bimbo he wants. The loan shark was a young, good-looking dude, so when Sachetti heard his hot little babe was spending time with the pretty boy, he got jealous and beat the both of them to a pulp.

"This happened in a restaurant in County territory, and somebody in the restaurant must've called the Sheriffs. Since the Sheriffs are a third-rate agency and their dirty deputies are also third-rate, they couldn't keep it out of the news, and word got out. The girl and boy were afraid Sachetti would finish the job, so they came to the FBI and turned him in on an extortion charge. The pretty-boy loan shark owed Sachetti big time and couldn't pay, so Sachetti had threatened to whack him.

"The Bureau and U.S. Attorney's Office put together a case against Sachetti with everything they could get on him, including murder and robbery charges. But when it came time to go to trial, all the other witnesses either recanted or disappeared. The ex-loan shark and ex-girlfriend were the only witnesses, and that meant only one count of extortion. Sachetti copped a plea, and by the time all was said and done, he was out in two years."

"Two years in prison for losing your temper and beating up a cheating bimbo in a public place," Jason said while finishing a mouthful. "Not what you'd expect from a mafia captain. He must've been really pissed."

"Not as pissed as Sachetti's wife must've been," Bart responded, grinning. "Can you imagine what that conversation must've been like?"

The restaurant had been steadily filling, and now every seat was taken. There was a long line for take-out orders, and the little place was very noisy. "Did either of you come up with anything on Alison Grayle?" I asked.

Bart answered first. "The Bureau has nothing on her. Absolutely nothing. Nothing in Indices, nothing in NCIC. Not so much as a speeding ticket on record."

Jason added, "All I could come up with was that she's a licensed securities dealer. She's too young to have made a reputation for herself yet, so there's no word on the street about her. She was just another market analyst at Fidelity until last year, and then she somehow made the jump to WTC Financial as a client advisor. WTC is a major international player that manages billions. They can take their pick from all the top graduates from the best business schools and steal the top talent from other financial firms. If WTC grabbed her out of Fidelity, she must be pretty sharp or must've had some pretty good connections and recommendations."

"Why're you interested in her?" Bart asked.

"I'm only interested in her because she's interested in me." I told them about how Alison and I had met and her curiosity about my work. "Imagine the ten most beautiful women you can think of, and I guarantee you, if you saw Alison Grayle, you'd think she was more beautiful than any nine of them, at least. Even other women drool over her. I can't help feeling there's more to her interest in me than just my good looks and charm."

"It sure couldn't be because of your pecker or your brains," Bart said, wiping sauce from his mouth.

"Since I'm not as familiar with your endowments as Bart apparently is and couldn't know if she'd be impressed by the immensity of your... intellect... maybe she's just slumming," Jason suggested.

"Thanks for the votes of confidence, guys, but no. My gut tells me there's something more going on here. I'd like to find out more about her."

"When it comes to women, does any man really want to know everything about a woman's past?" Jason asked. "Take it from a happily married man. You don't."

"Jason's right," Bart added. "You're better off not knowing too much about some women. And from what you've told us about this one, I suggest you believe everything she tells you and just enjoy the ride."

"I wish I could, but I can't help feeling she's another piece of the kidnapping puzzle. This hasn't been like any ordinary investigation. Information has come in unusual ways, sometimes from people who wanted to get in the way of the investigation. So, keep your eyes and ears open for anything about her." I wiped sauce from my mouth and fingers. "And any ideas on how I can meet up with Canino without getting whacked?"

"Good luck with that. If you can figure that out, you'll have done better than the entire Bureau. I know you've already run into some bad dudes on this case, but none like this Canino. If he thinks you can tie him to the kidnapping, you're dead. Period. End of story," Bart said. "If you do come up with information that connects him to the kidnapping, I think you should turn it over to me, and I'll get the SWAT team to make the arrest."

"I keep hearing the same thing from everybody about everybody connected with this case. But it seems the only way I'm going to figure out what really happened is by pissing off the right people and getting them to talk," I answered.

"Well, if there's anybody that can piss off people, it's you. Offending people is your greatest talent," Bart said. "I just hope you live long enough to tell me what you find out."

Jason chimed in. "Piss people off to get them to talk to you. 'My God, the genius of that! The genius! The will to do that...'"

Bart shook his head at Jason then asked me, "So, what do *you* have for show-and-tell?"

"I had a visit from a wild-eyed woman who claimed to see dead people. She said Rachael Ginsberg was dead."

"Well, this is la-la land. You were bound to run into a crazy bird sooner or later," Bart said.

Jason interrupted, animated. "'Wrong! *Wrong*! You dare to call her crazy?' 'It's not just insanity and murder. There's enough of that to go around for everybody.' 'That's dialectic physics, okay?'"

Bart replied, "Maybe *you're* crazy."

Jason changed characters, sat up stiffly, and responded in all seriousness, "'As for your charges against me, I am unconcerned. I am beyond timid, lying morality, and so I am beyond caring.'"

"Okay, just checking," Bart said and turned to me. "And while I'm on the subject of crazy, do me a favor. Let me know before you do anything crazy yourself, like confronting any mafia captains. If you go missing or your body turns up in the L.A. River, I'd like to know who to go talk to."

Chapter 45

A Woman Scorned

I returned to the office after my lunch with Bart and Jason to find Margaret Milstein, Aron Ginsberg's secretary, waiting for me. She was sitting on one of the two old, wood chairs that were bolted to the floor just outside the office door for visitors who desired to wait when there was no one inside. She rose, smiled meekly, and extended a gloved hand. As always, she looked like something out of a 1950s clothing catalogue in her long, belted, navy-blue shirt dress decorated with tiny red roses. Matching shoes, veiled pillbox hat, and pocketbook completed the vintage look.

In our earlier contacts, she'd been cooperative but dutifully protective of Ginsberg. I always had the feeling, though, like everyone else involved in this case, she was hiding something. Unlike everyone else, she had no guile in her and couldn't hide the fact that she was hiding something. After I got out of prison and went to see her again, she'd simply refused to speak with me out of loyalty to Ginsberg.

Still unable to hide her emotions at all, her nervousness made it obvious she was troubled. I escorted her into Jack's office and offered her something to drink, which she refused with a quick shake of her head. "Given how uncooperative you were the last time we met, I'm surprised to see you here," I began.

She sat, gripping her pocketbook tightly with both hands. "Yes, I know. I'm sorry for that. But some things have happened, and I feel I need to talk to someone about it. Are you still investigating the kidnapping?" she asked.

"Yes, of course."

"There are things I think the police and the FBI should know, but I'm afraid to go to them."

"Have you been threatened?"

"Well, yes and no. There wasn't a specific threat, but… I'm afraid."

"Tell me about it."

"If I tell you, will you promise not to tell anyone I told you about this?" she asked.

Again with this obsessive need for secrecy and promises. I wondered if anyone involved in this case had the courage to come forward and just tell the truth. I was tired of making promises, so I said, "I don't know if I can make that promise without hearing what you have to say first. The only thing I can say now is that I'll keep your name out of it, if I can, and for as long as I can."

She thought for a moment. "Okay, I guess that will have to do… Well, as I told you before, I had a bad feeling something was going on even before you and that other agent came to the bank the day the bombs went off in the cars. I've known the Ginsbergs and Richard Marino for years, and the way they were acting and the things they were doing were so unusual and out of character for them. And the children, when they were brought to the bank unconscious, I knew they weren't just sleeping. Plus, Rachael would never be away from her children like that. She was a good mother. Some would say overprotective, even. I knew something terrible was going on, but the Ginsbergs and Richard Marino didn't call the police or the FBI or anyone for help. I couldn't help wondering why. Then, after about a week of what was going on, I just couldn't take it anymore. So, I knew I had to call someone."

"You were the one who called the FBI that day?" I asked.

Milstein nodded and began to weep. "Is it my fault that Rachael—"

"No. Definitely not. Everything that happened would've happened anyway. It was all planned to end that way."

Milstein sighed loudly and cast her gaze upward. "*Baruch HaShem*, I wasn't responsible for her death! I've felt so guilty, ever since I heard that the kidnappers said they would kill Rachael, if anyone called the police or FBI."

"It wasn't your fault. That's a fact. What else is on your mind?"

She composed herself and went on. "Well, something else was going on. I don't even know if it has anything to do with the kidnapping. It was just unusual. And then, a few weeks ago, something else happened that seems like it might be related. I don't know." Milstein seemed unsure of what to say next.

"What was it?" I asked.

"Well, for about a year or so, Aron— Aron Ginsberg had been acting strangely. He would leave the bank in the afternoon, usually once a week, sometimes twice a week. And he acted suspicious. He wouldn't tell anyone where he was going. When I'd ask him what I should say, if anyone was looking for him, he said just to say that he was out and would be back soon. I knew he was seeing someone."

"It does happen," I said.

"Yes, I know. I guess I just didn't want to believe it," Milstein answered.

"Why didn't you want to believe it?"

"I've always thought of Aron as a *mensch*. I mean, I wanted to think of him that way. He's had affairs in the past, I think, from time to time. He would leave the bank for a few hours or leave early. But it didn't happen very often. I couldn't blame him, with Magda being the way she is."

"And how is Magda?"

"She's so cold," Milstein said and shook her head. "Aron and Magda are more like brother and sister than husband and wife. A brother and sister who don't get along. I've never seen any real affection between them. And she's always so… controlling. I don't know how he's put up with it."

"But this last time seemed different to you? Why?"

"He just acted differently. If I didn't know any better, I'd say he had fallen in love. And he went out more often than ever before."

"Did you ever find out where he went?"

She dropped her head and nodded. "Yes. I was worried about him, so, one day, I told him I had a doctor's appointment and needed to take the afternoon off. I somehow knew that was a day he would be going out in the afternoon, too. Don't ask me why—I just felt it. So, I left the bank at noon and then waited across the street for him to leave. When he did, I followed him."

"Where did he go?"

"He went to buy flowers first. A dozen roses, all different colors. Then he went to a high-rise condominium in Santa Monica. The Vista Del Rey condominiums."

I hid my surprise. At least I think I did. "Did you find out who he was visiting there?"

"No. I never did. I was too afraid to go in there. But I guess there's no doubt he was having an affair." She started to weep again.

"Delivering a dozen roses one time doesn't necessarily mean a man is having an affair," I said, looking for more.

"I followed him three more times. Always the same thing. Sometimes he had a gift-wrapped box with the roses."

"Why would you be so interested in where he went? Why were you worried about him? Or did you have feelings for him, too?"

She nodded, reluctantly. "Yes. When you see someone every day for thirty years, you can't help but have feelings. I've been to his home many times and to his estate in Santa Barbara. I know his children and grandchildren very well. I feel like they're my own, in a way. They call me Aunt Margaret. And Aron's been very kind to me. I've been his personal secretary for thirty years, but it's been more than that. At least, I thought so. And I knew he couldn't be happy in his marriage."

"Did you and he ever have an affair?"

With a pained look, she shook her head sadly. "No. We've hugged, and he's kissed me on the cheek on special occasions. But it's never gone beyond that. He's bought me expensive jewelry for my birthday. The card always said it was from him and Magda, but I knew it was from him. He picked them out, I'm sure. He knows my taste." She dried her tears and exhaled deeply and then solemnly folded her hands on her lap, took a moment to compose herself, looked directly at me, and stated emphatically, "I live with my older sister in the house we inherited from our parents after they died. We've both lived in the same house our entire lives. We'll both die there. We're pathetic old maids. It was ridiculous of me to think I could ever be anything more to Aron than his secretary."

That's exactly what I was thinking but said, "I think there must be something more to this story."

She nodded. "Yes, there is. A few weeks ago, Aron suddenly stopped going on his afternoon trips. I don't know why. I knew something had happened, something that changed him, hurt him. I could see he was worried and suffering. I tried to ask him about it, so I could console him, but he wouldn't let me. Then, shortly after that, two detectives from the Santa Monica Police Department came to see him. They spoke privately in his office for an hour. When they left, I went in to see him. He looked… crushed. Totally lost. I had never seen him so… I don't even know the word for it. *Defeated*, I guess. He hadn't looked that sad and lost even during the kidnapping."

As she spoke, Milstein looked toward me but not at me, lost in her emotions, and her head and shoulders swayed slowly, back and forth, as if she were sitting on a rocking chair. She went on without any prodding. "I was afraid for him. Worried about what he might do. I knew Magda couldn't understand—she didn't care for him the way I did. I thought it was the right time to tell him how I felt about him and let him know I would do anything for him. So, I told him I knew about his trips to the condominium in Santa Monica and asked if the police visit had anything to do with that."

"What did he say?"

"He just stared at me for the longest time, then he got angry. That was the first time he'd ever gotten angry with me. I've seen him angry with Magda and other people but never really angry with me before, not once in all those years. But that day, he called me a *meeskite* and *beheyma*. He said he was sorry if he'd ever said anything endearing to me and told me to get out of his office and never interfere in his personal life ever again."

She started to weep again.

"Then what?" I asked gently, handing her a tissue box.

"That night, a woman and a man came to my house. The woman did all the talking. She had two envelopes with letters. One was a letter of resignation for me to sign. It said I agreed to resign immediately of my own free will. I would get three months' salary in advance, as severance pay. It also had a confidentiality clause, to keep me from ever talking about anything that had ever happened in connection with my employment or my association with the Ginsbergs. The severance pay was in cash in the envelope. The other letter was a letter of recommendation for me, in case I wanted to look for another job."

"Did you agree to resign?"

"Yes. I had no choice. The woman said I would be fired if I didn't resign. She said things would be very difficult and dangerous for me and my sister, if I didn't. She said things would also be difficult and dangerous for us if I ever said anything to anyone about anything I had ever seen or heard in connection with the Ginsbergs or the bank. She repeated that things wouldn't just be difficult, they'd be *dangerous*. Very dangerous. The man had brought a box, and when he opened it, I saw my personal belongings from my desk. He looked very mean and angry. They told me I was never to go back to the bank or have any contact with the

Ginsbergs… After all those years, after everything I've done for him—*bupkes*."

She burst out crying uncontrollably. I tried to console her, but she had to have her cry and regain her composure in her own time. I went to get her a glass of water and urged her to take a sip.

When she had calmed some, I asked, "Since you must have come to me for a reason, what is it you want me to do for you?"

"I want you to finish your investigation of the kidnapping. I have to know what happened to Rachael. I need to be sure I wasn't responsible for a *meesha masheena*. I don't have a lot of money, but I'll hire you to find out. I must know the truth."

"I don't want your money. I've always intended to find out for myself, anyway. I intend to see justice done for Rachael and the children."

Milstein wiped her tears. "I'm so glad, but please be careful. I think things are much more dangerous than I ever imagined."

"That's okay. I can handle a reasonable amount of danger."

"It's just that I don't want to be responsible for another death."

"You haven't been responsible for any deaths, and you certainly won't be responsible for mine. You just leave it to me. Danger is my business. It's the only thing I'm good at." Marlowe's line didn't sound so cheesy this time. It might even have been true.

Before I sent her home, I asked her to describe the two people who'd come to her home. When she did, I was certain it was Fearless Female and her gorilla, the ones I'd run into on South Crenshaw. I had a feeling I'd have to deal with them again. Now I was sure of it.

Chapter 46

Cui Bono

With the Turk gone before I could speak with him and nothing concrete from Bart or Jason, I had nothing to use against Canino. I'd gone to the Turk's old haunts and spoken to several of the people I'd seen him with. The few who'd talk to me didn't have any idea what had happened to him. Those who indicated they were aware of his drug-dealing said they weren't aware of his involvement in anything else. Some said he was a devoted father and would never have left his children, so they'd assumed the worst. The Long Beach PD detective who'd been working the drug and firearms case also had no idea what had happened to Ozan but, like everyone else, assumed he'd been made to disappear by his criminal associates before he could rat them out. I stopped by Ozan's special lady friend's condo and found that she was a Turkish immigrant also and very concerned—concerned that, with him gone, she'd have to give up the condo, the convertible, and the credit cards.

With nowhere else to go, I knew I had to get in touch with Sachetti. I'd made a note of the license plate on Sachetti's girlfriend's Mustang. It was leased in the name of a company that was no doubt another mafia front. I couldn't risk going to that company, which wouldn't have done any good anyway, so finding the girlfriend would take some work. I hired Maria's brother, Sammy, to help out and stationed him near the parking areas of some of the ritzy condos in Marina Del Rey, to look for the red Mustang with the right license plate.

I thought Sammy still had a chance to break out of the barrio gang-bang lifestyle and wanted to do what I could for him. But first, I needed him out of the "full *cholo* homeboy" costume he usually wore to please his brother and get along in his neighborhood. I told him he needed to dress less "gang banger" and more "regular dude," so as not to get rousted by the cops in Marina Del Rey every five minutes. He looked good in a collared shirt and jeans instead of his usual white undershirt, extra-baggy hip-hop shorts, and white knee-length socks. He seemed to enjoy the change.

A few days of surveillance paid off, and I was able to ID the girl, Ilsa Lind Andersson, and her condo address. I'd wondered if Ilsa Lind was the same woman who'd been waiting for Sachetti on the day of our release from prison. She wasn't. This one was tall and slender and easy to see as a lingerie model, when she wasn't busy training with the Swedish bikini team. I guess Sachetti believed in the old adage about variety being the spice of life.

I visited Ms. Andersson, gave her my card, and told her I needed to speak with Sachetti. I told her he could find me at the same place as before. Although she was physically perfect, her open-mouthed, vacant cow-eyed stare caused me to wonder if she had the mental capacity to pass on such a complex message, so I also wrote it down on the back of my card.

I knew Sachetti would be angry with me just for contacting Ms. Andersson, but I had no choice. With the Turk gone and nothing solid on Canino, I needed more from Sachetti to move the investigation forward.

*****

The following Sunday afternoon, I again saw the shadow of a giant redwood fall across my table at the French Café. Sachetti glared at me and said only, "Let's go."

We went. In my car. I drove. It was another one of those gloriously perfect Southern California Sunday afternoons you have to experience to believe is possible—except it wasn't. Sachetti was furious, and his anger was enough to ruin even a day in paradise. Sachetti is one of those people whose anger is palpable and who can frighten even the brave, because you don't know what he's going to do, but you know he's capable of anything. I could easily understand how he got himself into prison for nearly beating a man to death out of sheer rage.

I began to drive, and after a few moments of tense silence, he said, "I oughta kick your fuckin' teeth out. Two years ago, I would've. Lucky for you, I've learned to control my temper. But if you pull shit like that again, you'll be eatin' through a straw and pissin' blood, if you live."

"I had no choice. I needed to talk to you, and I had no other way of contacting you."

"So, what's so fuckin' important that you had to scare the shit outta my *comare*?" He reached into his shirt pocket but came up empty. "Damn, gimme a cig."

I got us each one and lit both. Remembering our last meeting, I took out my cell phone and turned it off and asked Sachetti to do the same. I was still paranoid about surveillance, especially after that last meeting with Sachetti, the subsequent shooting, and LAPD interrogation.

"You worried about somethin'?" he asked.

"Just being careful."

Sachetti was reluctant but took out his cell and turned it off. "You'd better make this quick, then. I told you before, I can't be gone for too long. That includes havin' my cell phone off for long."

"This shouldn't take long. You know the Turk is gone, right?"

"Of course I know. I know all about it. You screwed that pooch. I told you Canino would whack him, if he became a problem."

"Unfortunately, Canino got to him before I did. So, now, I've got nothing on Canino. Nothing I can use against him. Nothing I can threaten him with. I don't even know where to find him."

"You fuck up and come runnin' to me? What good are you? You're as useless as a dick on a transvestite."

There was no point in discussing the psychology of transvestitism, and besides, he was right; I did screw that up. I had to let that one go and stick to business. "I'm no good to you unless you give me something to use against Canino. Something to work with. Something solid."

Sachetti pursed his lips and nodded but remained silent as he thought. He was thinking like a chess master about his next move, its results, and the likely moves after that. Bits of information were chess pieces; he had to decide what he could reveal and sacrifice without endangering the entire game, and to weigh what would be the likely counter moves of his opponents.

When he was done thinking, he said, "Okay, I'll give you a little more a' the big picture, but I'm gonna need another promise from you."

"What promise?"

"What I'm gonna tell you is gonna piss you off like nothin' has ever pissed you off before, Boy Scout. You gotta promise you won't do anything to Marino or Canino yourself. You just finger them and let nature take its course. And remember your other promise—you never tell anybody any a' this came from me."

I didn't know what he thought might enrage me so much I'd want to kill Marino or Canino myself, but I had no choice. I had to agree. "Okay, I promise."

"You can get to Canino through Marino. It was his idea."

"What was his idea?"

Sachetti shook his head. "The fucking FBI gets way too much credit. The answer has been staring you in the face, and you still don't get it. You guys still haven't figured out who came outta it way better off than he was before the snatch."

"Okay, I'm an idiot. We're all idiots. Spell it out for me."

"The kidnapping was Marino's idea, plain and simple," Sachetti answered coolly.

I stared at him. "You've got to be kidding. Marino arranged to have his own wife and children kidnapped?"

"He didn't arrange anything, but it was his idea. He was in hock up to his eyeballs on his L.A. and Vegas deals, and he was up to his ass in debt to some casinos on his gambling losses. Losses that he needed to keep hidden from everybody. I mean, he didn't want anybody to know about his gambling. Who's gonna wanna do business with a gambling junkie, right? So, the Family bought his markers. The Family wanted in on his Vegas project, and he had to cut us in in exchange for his markers, once we put the screws to him. But once the Family gets a piece a' you, we come in for all the rest. Marino was legit, had all the right contacts, knew all the right people, and could be a big earner for the Family for years.

"So, now the Family is in on both projects, but the projects are underfunded. The Family can't let the projects go under, not with all the money there is to be made from them, so they put the squeeze on Marino to do whatever he's gotta do to get more start-up capital. He needs cash up front and quick, to get the big banks and other investors to come in on the projects, so he comes up with the idea for the kidnap."

"I can't believe that's enough to make a man arrange to have his own wife and children kidnapped," I said, shaking my head. "I can understand a man might do that to a wife he's sick of and wants to get rid of, but his own children?"

"No, no, no," Sachetti said, shaking his head. "He didn't know about the children. His idea was just to have the wife snatched. He knew that would be enough to get the Ginsbergs to pay up. And he had other reasons. It was a perfect storm a' reasons, all come together. Love, hate, money, and self-preservation."

"Explain it to me. I just don't see it, and I don't buy it."

Sachetti's smile widened into a vicious smile. He enjoyed being the big man with all the information and telling the story, especially if the story exposed moral corruption and hypocrisy in people he despised. "You get the money part, right? That's easy. This wasn't about fazools and beaners. We're talking millions here. He woulda lost millions, if those projects didn't pan out. Lost face and status, too. And to a guy like him, that's just as important as money, maybe more important. And if he couldn't come through on the projects and pay back what he already owed the Family, he knew he was a dead man. He could write off his losses on his tax return, but the Family wasn't gonna let him write them off—no way. It doesn't work that way in our line a' business." Sachetti smiled, raised his arms and began to shake his hands in what was apparently his favorite gesture. "Fuh-ged-daboud-it!"

"Okay, so that's the money and self-preservation parts. What about the rest?" I asked. I had driven toward downtown and was now driving around the intersection of the 110 and 101 highways, with their many off-ramps, on-ramps, and one-way streets—a canyon of concrete, steel, and glass between the tall buildings. This area wasn't busy on a Sunday afternoon, making a tail easy to spot, if there was one. Of course, all this counter-surveillance was useless if anyone had put a bug or tracker in my car, but I still had to do what I could. One can only do so much. Then you just have to trust to luck and hope for the best.

Sachetti's vicious smile widened again. "He hated his in-laws. The poor boy felt they never thought he was good enough for their little Jew princess. They treated him like he was lucky they let him in the family. He especially hated the mother-in-law, a real ball-buster, according to him. He was really happy about taking them for all they were worth."

"What about the wife?"

"He was sick a' her," Sachetti said emphatically, still smiling. "Couldn't stand to look at her."

"I heard they had problems, but everybody the FBI talked to said they'd patched things up and were getting along. I heard they even went to Mexico for a second honeymoon, and everything was good." I wondered just how much Sachetti knew about the Ginsbergs and Marino.

"Yeah, that was all part a' the plan. Marino was told to patch things up, so it would look like everything was good and he wouldn't be a suspect. You guys always suspect the husband first, but we still needed him around after the snatch to complete the financing and get the projects off the ground. So, he had to play the loving husband for a few months. That's why they took that trip to Acapulco and went out in public together lots, holdin' hands, arm in arm, kissin'—all that romantic shit. He hated it. Said it made him sick to touch her."

I was beginning to feel sick myself.

"Then, he got tired a' waitin' for somethin' to happen, started complainin' and runnin' around with his Vegas bimbo again. He kept calling Canino to get the kidnap going. Canino had to send some a' his boys to pay him a visit to keep him in line and let him know what was at stake, if he didn't keep up the act."

"Were the life insurance and kidnap and ransom insurance policies part of the plan?"

Sachetti shook his head. "No way. The dumb bastard got greedy. He took out those policies on his own, to make some extra green for himself. He thought we wouldn't find out about it. When we did, after it was all over, the big boss went through the roof. He knew you guys would be all over Marino cuz a' those policies. They made him suspect number one all over again. And worst of all, it showed no respect—*infamita*! He put the whole fuckin' deal in trouble, and without talkin' to Canino or the boss about it first. Canino made Marino hold off on filin' any claim until the shit had settled, and the boss made Marino sign over all the money he'd get on the policies, to make up for his lack a' respect. Marino was pissed about that, but what could he do?"

I nodded, breathed deeply, and gripped the steering wheel tightly in preparation for what I was afraid would be the answer to my next question. "Did Marino know the wife would be killed?" I asked, already hating Marino and ready to kill him, if he was behind Rachael's death.

"That was part a' the deal. He insisted on it. Marino wanted outta the marriage but didn't wanna go through a divorce. As much as he hated her and her family, he knew he'd be screwed financially, finished. The mother-in-law promised him that."

I felt my stomach knot in anger but hid it from Sachetti. At least, I hope I did. "But Marino came up with the idea of a kidnapping for ransom and knew the wife would be killed eventually?" I asked, just to get the story straight.

"Yeah, but he didn't know any details. He didn't know when or how. And he didn't know the bambinos would be snatched, too, like I said. But here's the real kicker. When the snatch finally went down, and the Turk told Marino and Ginsberg that he was Palestinian, Marino called Canino, cuz he was pissed that his kids had been snatched—that wasn't part a' the deal.

"Canino told him he didn't know anything about it and said the A-rabs must really have done it. That was Canino's genius idea. And it seemed like a great idea at the time, I gotta give him that. Canino told Marino he couldn't help him and he was on his own. He even told Marino not to call him again until it was all over, in case his calls were traced, and that he still owed our people, no matter what the towelheads took him for. All that guaranteed that Marino would be surprised and scared and act the part. And it guaranteed his complete cooperation and more money. Canino got Marino to pay up twice. Once on the kidnapping and again for what he was already supposed to pay back."

"I don't understand that. Tell me again."

"Am I going too fast for you, college boy? Marino bought that it was the A-rabs, cuz before the snatch, Canino kept telling him he wanted to wait to pull off the snatch for at least six months after Marino and the wife got back together, to make the reconciliation look real. The boss insisted that the snatch go down after Christmas and New Year's, so there'd be lots a' pictures a' the family sittin' around the Christmas tree and fireplace, all lovey-dovey. But Canino wasn't sure Marino could wait that long. Marino was gettin' antsy. He couldn't stand to be around the wife or her parents, and his own financial situation was falling apart. So Canino came up with the idea to go with the snatch ahead a' schedule and blame it on the towelheads. Not only did it get more money outta Marino, it protected Canino's ass from the boss when the wife was whacked."

"You've lost me again. Why did Canino need to be protected?"

"Didn't I tell you? Marino wanted the wife wasted, and Canino agreed to it, but Canino never told the boss about that part. He knew the boss would never agree to that—he's too smart to knock off somebody big, if there's no need for it. It could backfire and cause more problems later on. The boss knew the Ginsbergs are too well-connected to piss off, so he'd only okay the snatch a' the wife, and only if she wasn't hurt, just in case anybody figured out who really done it. If it got out how one a' his crews pulled off the snatch, it wouldn't really matter, as long as she wasn't hurt. No boss is personally accountable for everything one a' his employees does, right? That's just business. The Ginsbergs coulda been satisfied by sendin' a few a' the crew to prison, the ones the boss didn't have whacked as a peace offering. But killing the wife? No way. The boss knew that upped the ante, and the Ginsbergs would want revenge and a lotta blood. Canino thought, by makin' everybody believe it was the towelheads, the boss wouldn't be pissed, even when she was whacked."

"So, Canino was taking a big chance by thinking he could keep everybody in the dark?" I asked, just to feign ignorance and get as much out of Sachetti as I could. "Tell me more about him."

"Fuh-ged-daboud-it," Sachetti said slowly for emphasis. "All you need to know is that he's the captain a' the crew that pulled off the snatch. Just work with that, and you'll live longer... Oh, but get this. Canino took the schmuck for another five mil on top a' the ransom, too."

"How'd he do that?"

"He had help from the Ginsbergs for that. On the last payment a' ten mil, the Ginsbergs demanded that Marino put up half, even if he had to sell his balls. That was the mother-in-law again. Now, there's a Jew for you!" Sachetti said with a malicious laugh, shaking his head and slapping his thigh. "Most a' the green for the ransom was coming from the Ginsbergs, and the old broad had it with that. She really put the screws to Marino... Anyway, Marino didn't have the cash or any way a' coming up with it so quick, so he called Canino again and begged him for a short-term loan. Canino agreed to give him the five mil, but the vig was another five within thirty days or Marino would really lose his balls. The bottom line is, Canino got Marino to put up the money for all a' the Family's investment in the Vegas project without Marino even knowin' it. Canino couldn't help braggin' about it, and that's how me and some a' the other wise guys found out about it. Like I said, you gotta give him credit for the way he handled Marino."

"Yeah, he's an evil genius. But I still don't get the money angle. All sources indicated Marino was a billionaire and rolling in dough," I said, again just to get all I could from Sachetti.

Sachetti rapped me on the shoulder. "Gimme another cig," he ordered. I got us each one and lit both. "Yeah, he looked good on paper, but even the dough from his other projects, like the shopping centers, the apartment complexes, and office buildings, wasn't enough to fund the downtown L.A. and Vegas projects, like he'd figured. Most a' that goes to pay the mortgages and liens and operating expenses on those properties, plus his own living expenses. He likes to live large and play the big shot to impress everybody. And, like I said, he likes to gamble, the schmuck.

"Marino knew he'd have to get funding from the big banks, and they wouldn't get on board unless he had a boatload a' cash to get started. And they wouldn't give him a dime if they found out about his gambling. He didn't know how much longer he could keep up the lovin' husband act or keep his own ship floatin'. He was so hard up for cash, he wasn't even sure he could hold on to that Porsche he loves so much. That's when Canino sent his boys to pay him a visit and convince him to keep up the act a little while longer. That was on orders from the boss. He wanted Canino to keep stringin' him along to be sure he was totally hooked and ready to do anything."

"When you say *the boss*, you mean Vincent Florian, right?"

"It's no big secret who's boss in L.A. Just don't go tossin' that name around. And you never, *ever* heard me even mention that name, understand?"

"Got it… So, it was Florian who was running the operation?" I asked.

"No." Sachetti shook his head slowly but then gestured, palms up. "I mean, he wanted in on Marino's Vegas project, and once we had him hooked on that, he went after the L.A. project, too. Don't you listen? I told you before, he wanted to retire, and his share a' the legit income from the Vegas and L.A. projects would guarantee him a comfortable retirement. I was in the joint, so he had to put Canino in charge a' goin' after and runnin' Marino. But Canino got antsy and greedy and came up with the idea a' using the Turk. With Marino gettin' those insurance policies and Canino bringin' in the Turk to get the snatch goin' ahead a' schedule and then knockin' off the bitch, all without even tellin' Florian in advance, Florian knew he was losin' control. With a few mil in clean cash to the other bosses, Canino knew he could force Florian out and take over L.A."

"So, just to be sure I have it right," I said, "Marino came up with the idea to kidnap Rachael Ginsberg, to raise the money he needed for the Vegas project. Canino took the idea to Florian, who approved it. But Florian didn't know Canino was going to kidnap the children, too, and had agreed to have Rachael Ginsberg killed. It was Canino who came up with the idea to use the Turk to make Marino and everyone else believe it was the Palestinians who'd kidnapped Ginsberg and the children. Canino thought Florian wouldn't be angry for the unauthorized kidnap of the children and the killing of Rachael Ginsberg, because Canino got a lot more money out of Marino and had everybody believing it was the Palestinians. Canino also paid off the other bosses, so he could get their support and take over L.A. Is that about it?"

"Simple as that, bright boy. What would all your big shot philosophers say about that?"

"Machiavelli would be impressed."

"Him I heard a'. He's Italian, right?"

"Right… So, Marino never knew about Florian's involvement, and they never had any contact?" I asked.

"Not exactly," Sachetti said, bobbing his head slowly from side to side. "After Marino got antsy and Canino sent his boys to calm him down, Marino demanded a meet with the boss and made a stink about it. As it turns out, the boss had a personal favor to ask Marino, so he agreed to a sit-down. Normally, Florian woulda stayed outta the caper and let the captain run it. I mean, that way, he can't be tied in to the caper, and he doesn't piss off the captain or the crew by stickin' his dick where it don't belong. A good lesson for all managers there, right?"

"Yeah. I wish the managers in the FBI were that smart. What was the favor Florian wanted?"

"Beats me," Sachetti said, shrugging and shaking his head. "But it must a' been somethin' important for Florian to break his own rule and have a sit-down with Marino to ask for it."

I lit myself another smoke and offered Sachetti one, but he shook it off. I was silent for a moment, thinking things through. "You said there was a love angle involved. What was that?"

Sachetti gave a perverse grin. "That was another beautiful part. You're gonna love this."

I knew there'd be nothing beautiful about it and I'd probably hate it.

"Early in the game, when Canino was still tryin' a' hook Marino, he and a couple other wise guys took him out for some entertainment with a few broads—pros they brought along just for fun. They take him to see the lounge act at the Tropicana, a singer in front of a combo. Much to everybody's surprise, Marino gets the hots for the singer. I mean, why should he care about some third-rate singer nobody's ever heard a', when he's already got a couple broads for the night who know how to make a livin' with their ass? Anyway, our guys arrange for him to meet the singer, and he goes totally batshit over her.

"What the schmuck doesn't know is that she belongs to us—our Atlantic City people. So, our guys tell her to string him along, play hard to get, and not give in to him too easy—make him work for it, so he thinks she's totally legit and somethin' special. At first, she was just entertainment, to keep him interested and follow through with us. But then, the schmuck goes and falls for her—all the fuckin' way.

"If you need to figure out why people do the crazy shit they do, college boy, this one will drive you nuts thinkin' about it... I don't know, maybe it's cuz she's so different from his Jew princess. I hear the wife was blonde, blue, and slender. This one has dark hair and eyes and built like a brick house. And ten years younger. Best of all, she's Italian!

"Anyway, after just a couple weeks, he's usin' his own connections to get her gigs all over the country. She's got him thinkin' she can't live or get a job without him, when it's our guys pullin' the strings to get her the gigs Marino wants for her. He liked playin' the big shot and havin' her believin' it was all him. In a way, he was right about that. She was just another third-rate lounge singer who'd never make it to the big room. Another singer-wannabe tramp before the boys found her in Atlantic City and put her on stage to drum up business for her real talent.

"Wait'll the schmuck finds out the love a' his life was turnin' tricks for two grand a pop when she was done singing—three or four a night. I heard she especially loved workin' conventions. She could turn eight tricks a day without leaving the hotel. I guess nobody likes havin' a' fight traffic to get to work, huh?"

"Yeah, I guess not... Well, that's a lot to take in. A lot of it I can't use, but the phone calls between Marino and Canino, the insurance policies, the Vegas girlfriend... By the way, what's the girl's name?"

"What difference does it make?" he asked with another shrug and questioning gesture. "She's a nobody... Fuck it, gimme a cig, and get me back to my car. This is takin' too long."

I got out two more cigarettes, lit both, then began heading back to the café. "I need to convince Marino I know everything. Knowing about the girl will help me establish that I hold all the cards."

He nodded. "Her name is Valento. Lola Valento. A real looker. I wouldn't mind a piece a' that myself."

"Okay… All that should be enough to convince Marino he's fried. Then, all I'll have to do is get Marino to give up Canino."

"That should be easy once Marino finds out Canino played him for a chump. When you tell Marino all about his tramp girlfriend and how the Turk was workin' for Canino, he'll know he was being used like a five-dollar whore. What ya' think he'll do then?"

"He'll be pissed. And once I put the screws to him, he'll be ready to go to the FBI. He'll claim he was set up by Canino and had to play along to save his wife and kids."

"Exactly. It's a story that fits the facts. Marino connects directly to Canino, and that makes Canino a liability to the Family. A captain with three counts a' kidnapping, two counts a' murder, and a RICO charge hangin' over him. The death penalty or life in prison with no possibility a' parole makes Canino a perfect candidate for the witness protection program, wouldn't ya' say? But he'll never get the chance to sing for the feds, I promise you that."

"How can you be so sure?"

"Like I said, Marino and Canino will be a liability to the Family, once you finger them. It's that simple. The Family doesn't need 'em anymore, anyway. We got all there was and all we needed from Marino. The Family is in, and the lawyers and business managers have taken over. Our involvement in the L.A. and Vegas projects is totally legit now. Besides, Marino isn't in the Family and he's pissed off everybody, so he's history already. Canino's a made guy, but that's not enough to save him. He knows enough to send twenty made guys and even a few capos to the joint for life, and they ain't gonna risk him offerin' them up to save his own ass. He's smart and had a good plan, but he's always been too devious and greedy for his own good. Everybody knows that, and that's what'll cook him."

"Okay, you get Canino out of the way, and then you get to be the big boss in L.A. after Florian retires. But what about me? What do I get?"

"You wanted to be the hero and solve the case, right? Well, you get that, for all the good that'll do you. And you get to stay alive, even after you pissed off a shitload a' people. You can thank your guardian angel for that."

"That's not enough. I want one more thing. I want Rachael Ginsberg's body."

Sachetti shook his head. "Fuhgeddaboudit."

"That has to be part of the deal."

"I don't get it. What difference does that make? What good's it gonna do you?"

"Her body will tie up all the loose ends and bring closure for her family."

"So what? Big deal. Closure shmosure. Her family will get along without it."

"I'm a Boy Scout, remember? I can't rest until all is right with the world. I'll do whatever it takes to deliver Canino, but I want Rachael Ginsberg's body."

"You don't know it, but you're askin' for a lot."

"Everything has its price."

Sachetti stared at me while he thought. He was good at it—the stare-down. His simian appearance gave him an unfair advantage, and I'd put my money on him to win any staring contest.

"Okay," he said, "but first, you deliver Canino. After he's gone, I'll tell you where to find the body."

"I want your word you'll tell me where to find the body, even if the big boys don't make you L.A. boss."

"Don't you worry about me. You deliver Canino, and I promise you the next capo of this town will tell you where to find the body. But you'd better get movin', Boy Scout. The only reason I'm tellin' you all this now is cuz I gotta feelin' Canino's gonna make his move. He's tired a' waitin' and started makin' noise. You're not workin' for the government anymore, so get off your ass."

I didn't like being ordered around like a buck private, and I stared hard at Sachetti. He returned the stare and added, "I wanna see some action, and don't fuck it up like you did with the Turk."

I nodded slowly with disdain, and Sachetti did the same. I dropped him off at his girlfriend's new car. A bright-blue Porsche Boxster convertible with dealer plates still on it. Fortunately, there was no biker or gunfire this time, although both Sachetti and I couldn't help looking around nervously.

I thought about what Sachetti had just told me and knew he'd been wise to get me to promise not to take matters into my own hands, although it also bothered me that he'd have me make that promise. It couldn't be a good thing to have a mafia capo know me so well.

The more I thought about it, the more I wanted to kill Marino with my bare hands. I wasn't sure I could keep my promise. And I knew Sachetti still hadn't told me everything. What was he holding back, and why?

Chapter 47

Something Wicked This Way Comes

I had gotten into the habit of driving to the Ginsbergs' and Marino's homes and offices whenever I had nothing better to do and just wanted to think about the case. I guess I was hoping I'd miraculously find the answers to all my questions, or at least spot some shifty-eyed character walking out of one of their doors who'd then lead me to the answers. That's the way it always worked for Spade and Marlowe, wasn't it?

As I sat in my car outside Marino's office building on Monday morning, I was fed up with waiting. I was tired of hoping for a break, and Sachetti's warning about Canino making his takeover move soon had me worried. I couldn't wait any longer for Marino and Canino to come to me, gift-wrapped in a pretty box with tissue paper and pink ribbons, so today I'd make something happen, regardless of any consequences or collateral damage.

I went up to Marino's office and told his secretary I wanted to talk to him. I had been there three times before: twice as an agent, and once after getting out of prison. Bart and I had gone there the first time to question Marino on his own turf about the facts of the case and just to take a look around and get his story straight. The second interview had been to go over the inconsistencies of the case and ended with Marino getting angry and threatening to call his lawyer, the U.S. Attorney's Office, and our boss. I also went back to see Marino after I got out of prison but was rebuffed by Susan Russo, who knew I was no longer with the Bureau, so I couldn't claim any legal authority for seeing Marino.

This time, Russo and I instantly recognized each other, and neither of us liked what we remembered. To me, she was the typically dutiful, loyal, moronic little secretary who'd do just about anything to protect her sleazeball of a boss from the prison cell he deserved. To her, I was just a hardnosed, pitiless, moronic ex-cop who'd do anything to send an innocent man to prison.

"He's in a meeting and can't be disturbed," Russo said with all the gatekeeper's authority she could muster.

I turned to go around her desk and toward Marino's office door. "He's going to be disturbed. I intend to see him now."

Sensing I meant trouble, she tried to placate me. "*Wait!* He's in a very important meeting with several bank representatives and people with the city planning commission, to go over the final plans for tomorrow's press conference on the L.A. project. It's going to be covered by all the media, and they want it to be perfect. Even the mayor and several celebrities will be there. They can't be disturbed. I'll tell him you were here, and maybe he'll agree to see you some other time."

"Tell him I'm here now, or I'll go in and tell him myself."

She saw I meant business and gave me a hateful glare. She picked up her phone, pressed the intercom button, and, when Marino answered, said, "That former FBI agent is here again, and he's demanding to see you now... I told him that, but he's very insistent and refuses to leave."

I moved closer to the door to Marino's office and shouted loud enough for Marino to hear me through both the intercom and the door, "*Marino*, you can't hide behind your secretary anymore. I want to talk to you now. I know all about you and Eddie Canino. That's right, you and mafioso Eddie Canino."

I could hear a good deal of noise behind the door. Then Marino opened it just enough to show his face. "If you don't leave immediately, I'll have you arrested and sent back to prison, where you obviously belong."

Again, I shouted, loud enough for anyone behind the door to hear, "If anyone is going to prison, *it's you*! I know all about you and Eddie Canino. I know more about the scheme you two cooked up than you do. Canino played you for a sucker, and you don't even know it. Lola Valento was used to play you, you chump. You'd better talk to me, or you might not live long enough to go to prison. Maybe you'll get to share a cell with your father-in-law. The police are still looking into two murders with motives Aron Ginsberg might be able to explain."

The blood drained out of Marino's face, and his jaws worked nervously. He struggled to think of what to say but maintained his composure, his arrogant chin still jutting upward. Finally, he said, "Susan, call building security and the police. Have him removed from the building and arrested, if he doesn't leave immediately." He slammed the door shut, and I could hear the door being locked.

Russo picked up the phone, and I said, "Don't bother. I'm leaving." I dropped my card on her desk. "Tell your boss he'd better call me, if he hopes to stay alive and have any chance of staying out of prison. And you'd better start looking for another job. This office will be closing soon."

Chapter 48

Such Stuff as Dreams are Made

I went back to the office after an early lunch and found Maria in a particularly good mood.

"Hey man, your friend Alison came over again," she informed me.

"What did she want?"

"She said she was hoping a greasy little ghost would take her to lunch."

"Greasy little gnome?"

"Yeah, that's it. So, what's a gnome, man?"

"Maria…"

"Oh, yeah. I mean, yes. What's a gnome?"

"I'm not exactly sure, myself, but I hope she meant it as a joke. Did she have anything else to say?"

"No, but look at what she got me, man." Maria showed me a posh leather cosmetic case and opened it to reveal expensive, designer-label makeup, lipsticks, and a lighted mirror.

I sat on the edge of the desk and looked over the swag. "Very nice. And expensive, no doubt."

"Yeah, man. I've seen these at, like, Nordstrom's and Macy's, man. They're, like, hundreds of dollars. And look at the makeups and lipsticks she got me, man. They're, like, eighty bucks each, at least."

"Maria…"

"I know. I'm just too excited. Nobody never got me nothing like this before."

"Gave me anything."

"What?"

"It's *no one ever gave me anything*. Not *never got me nothing*."

"Oh, okay… I don't, like, have to give it back, do I? There's, like, no rule against me getting a present from a customer, is there?"

"It's *client*, not *customer*, and she's not a client or customer, so there's no possible ethical violation."

"So, I get to keep it?"

"Of course."

"Right on, man! And you know what else? She said she'd take me to her makeup artist and hairdresser. For, like, a birthday present or something. Can you believe it?"

"Strangely enough, I can."

"She's so nice. I thought I was gonna cry, man. And she, like, gave me a hug and said I was beautiful. She said, with the right makeup and hairstyle, I could look like a movie star. Can you believe it? *She* thought *I* was beautiful."

It was like watching a lucky child on Christmas morning. I put my hand on her shoulder. "I'm very happy for you."

"Yeah… Oh, yeah. There's, like, two guys from the FBI in Jack's office, waiting for you."

"*What?*"

"Two FBI agents came looking for you. I told 'em you weren't here, but they said they'd wait in Jack's office for you and just walked in there. I didn't know what to do. Was that okay?"

"It's not always easy to know what to do."

Chapter 49

Subpoena Ad Testificandum

I opened the door and walked into Jack's office to find Bart and Don Randall, a seasoned agent who'd transferred into the Major Crimes squad after I transferred out of it.

Randall was a former Navy SEAL who wore his masculinity on his sleeve and wanted everyone to know what a tough and manly man he was. They were seated, but from the opened drawers, opened file cabinets, and papers left on the desk, it was obvious they'd been searching the office.

Bart stood up and gave me a wink. Then his outward demeanor stiffened.

"I usually have the riff-raff wait outside. I don't appreciate you muscling your way past my secretary and searching my office. To what do I owe the dishonor of this illegal intrusion?" I asked sternly.

Don Randall scoffed, and Bart said, "Well, you haven't changed much."

Randall added, "Yeah, still a smartass. I'd've thought you might've learned something, all that time in prison."

"I learned who some of your former boyfriends are. They're looking forward to hooking up with you again when they get out."

Randall stood up, angry. "Asshole."

"Funny—that's what they said they liked about you. But enough chit-chat," I said. "Say what you came to say and get out. Those of us not sucking on the government tit actually have work to do."

"In your case, it's about time you did some work," Bart said. "Especially since I had to carry your sorry ass your entire time in the Bureau. But we're not here to talk. The boss wants to see you and sent us to deliver you to him."

"Am I under arrest?" I asked.

"Not yet," Randall answered. "But from what Bart tells me, it's just a matter of time."

"I wouldn't pay too much attention to what Bart says. He's known to be wrong most of the time. And if you don't have an arrest warrant, you can kiss my ass. I'm not going, so get out."

"You're going, all right," Randall said, ready to pounce.

"Don't you know how to leave when you're told? You open the door and walk through it. Then you keep walking. And take your new boyfriend with you."

Bart didn't move. "You don't have to be an asshole all the time. Just come and hear what the boss has to say. You might learn something."

I caught Bart's message. Looking them both over, I made sure Randall saw my contempt, so he could report it to his superiors. "Learn something? Sure, I guess I could take another lesson on how to lie through my teeth without batting an eye."

*****

The drive to the Federal Building was fun. Bart and I continued our feigned animosity, trading more insults for Randall's benefit. We both wanted to make sure he saw there was no shred of friendship or loyalty left between us.

The Federal Building in Westwood hadn't changed one bit since my agent days. The concrete-and-glass block was just as cold and foreboding as always. We went up to the fifteenth floor and waited outside the ADIC's office. ADIC Norton wanted SAC Brunette and SSA Rolfe present at this meeting.

The criminal ASAC was still out doing whatever it is ASACs do. For ASACs, the safest way to move up in the Bureau is to hide somewhere until an opening comes up and then, and only then, appear and put in for promotion.

Once the others were present, Norton spoke to all of them privately, including the agents, in his office. I assumed he wanted to hear from Bart and Randall about whether I'd made any admissions and what my attitude and demeanor had been.

When he called me in, he didn't waste time on pleasantries. His secretary didn't come in, so I assumed Norton didn't want a record of what was going to be said. The last year must've been hard on Norton: he'd aged considerably since I saw him last and developed wrinkles and gray hair. Brunette and Rolfe looked weather-beaten also, and their predatory eyes were hungrier and more desperate. For excessively ambitious bureaucrats who're always seeking promotion, being stuck in the same job for more than two years was a humiliating failure and had taken its toll on all of them. In contrast to their unjustified ambition, I couldn't help thinking, in a slightly better world, where people had occupations that matched their talent, trustworthiness, and temperament, these three would be out selling magazine subscriptions door-to-door.

"Despite repeated warnings to stay out of the investigation of the Ginsberg-Marino kidnapping and leave the job to professionals, you've continued to harass the families of the victims, even though you know they were investigated and not found to have any possible connection to the kidnapping. This morning, you made some very serious allegations against Richard Marino and Aron Ginsberg. Why do you continue to harass them? And what exactly do you think you have on them?"

I was in no mood to be pushed around by an empty suit in front of other empty suits. For some reason, Jason Clarke's favorite movie came to mind, and I answered as sarcastically as possible, "I am unaware of any such activity, nor would I be disposed to discuss such activity, if it did in fact occur."

Norton's face reddened. He shot back, "Up to now, the U.S. Attorney's Office has refrained from calling you in front of a grand jury again and compelling you to testify. You do know that you'll be back in prison, if you refuse to testify again, don't you?"

"I didn't come here to be interrogated. If you have something to say, just say it and get it over with, so I can get back to work. At least I'm doing something, unlike all you empty suits."

"Fine, then," Norton said, shaking his head. "Aside from your being the right ethnicity in these times of political correctness, it's hard to understand how someone like you ever got in the FBI in the first place."

"I'd always wondered the same about you," I said, "until I heard your father was a SAC. I'll bet you were also a legacy admission to your father's college frat house."

Norton's face reddened even more, and he snarled, "Consider this your final warning. The incident at Richard Marino's office this morning, while he was in an important meeting, was the last straw. As I understand it, you accused Richard Marino of involvement with a known organized crime figure and accused Aron Ginsberg of involvement in two murders.

As I'm sure you know, Ginsberg was at that meeting, along with officers of several other banks and representatives from the mayor's office—"

"As usual, you're misinformed and mistaken," I interjected.

"Just shut up and listen!" Norton shouted. "The Ginsbergs' and Marino's lawyers called the U.S. Attorney, and he called me to say they're fed up with your harassment and accusations. He wanted me to tell you in no uncertain terms that if they or any of their employees ever see your face again, you'll be subpoenaed to testify before another grand jury. If you refuse to answer, you'll be taken into custody immediately. You'll also be charged with stalking and harassment in state court.

"The only reason you're not being served with a grand jury subpoena right now is because of the press conference tomorrow morning. They don't want you to upstage or do anything to disturb that event. They don't want to give you or your accusations any credibility in the eyes of the public. And I personally am sick of you rolling around like a loose cannon, shooting your mouth off and giving the Bureau a bad name."

It was my turn, and I went on the offensive. "Mostly, you're sick of the fact that your boot-licking go-fers haven't been able to resolve the kidnapping, so you can get your next undeserved promotion. At least I'm not afraid of doing something, and now that I'm close to cracking this case wide open, some people are starting to feel the heat. The Bureau has been sitting on its collective ass, waiting for something to happen, because the Ginsbergs and Marino and the U.S. Attorney don't want any bad publicity. You were counting on using me as a scapegoat to get you that office next to the Director, but that didn't work, did it? Now you're sweating it out here in L.A., because you know you'll never get that big six-figure salary out in the real world, if you can't do your job-hunting from behind a desk at Headquarters."

Norton looked at me with the kind of burning hate usually reserved by ex-wives for their cheating ex-husbands. *"Get out!"* was all he could manage to say.

As I got up to leave, Norton changed his mind. "Wait... I want to talk to Dehenares alone." The others got up and left quickly. After the room emptied, he said, "Sit down. All this animosity isn't getting us anywhere."

I sat and watched him take a few seconds to think through his next move, his fingers drumming on his desk. He was clearly feeling the heat for the failed kidnapping investigation and knew his career was on the line.

"I know you've applied for a PI license and a license to carry a firearm and to reactivate your law license. I pulled the strings to have those applications put on hold. I can see to it that you get those licenses immediately. And if I were an Executive Assistant Director, I might even be able to get you back in the Bureau. After all, you haven't been convicted of anything. We might be able to consider your jail time as a suspension without pay for insubordination. You would have your pension restored."

"I'm not interested in coming back to the Bureau. I don't like being used as a scapegoat by people like you."

Norton's face got red again, but he bit his lip and refrained from shooting back in anger. "What do you want, then?" he asked.

"What do you want?" I asked.

He took a few moments to think. "I want you to leave the Ginsbergs and Marino alone. That is, unless you really do have a smoking gun that ties any of them to the kidnapping... You're right, I'm not going anywhere with them on my back and blaming me for a failed investigation. And I want the Bureau to get the credit for solving the kidnapping, so I— we don't look like a bunch of idiots. I want it soon. Very soon. I should've been back at Headquarters long ago."

"I'm not doing this for the credit. I don't care who gets the credit."

"Then why not let the Bureau claim the credit for resolving the kidnapping? Do what you have to do to resolve the case, but don't do anything that might embarrass the Bureau. Just keep the Bureau out of it until you have something for me. Then stay out of the way and keep quiet when it's time for the Bureau to hold the press conference, okay?"

"I'll think about it."

I left Norton's office, and SAC Brunette's secretary stopped me and said he wanted to speak to me privately, also. She walked me to Brunette's office and closed the door behind her on her way out.

Brunette looked at me, trying to figure out where to start. "What did Norton want to talk to you about privately?"

"Ask him."

"No need. Threatening you didn't work, so he offered you a deal. I just wanted to know what he had to offer."

"What do you have to offer?" I asked.

Brunette gave a wolfish grin. "I heard Marino got pissed off because you threatened to expose him. Do you really have something on him? Or were you just blowing smoke up his ass?"

"What do you think?"

"I think I would've been sitting in the ADIC's chair a year ago, if Norton had the brains to move up the ladder and get out of my way."

"Be careful what you wish for. The ADIC's chair seems to be a *siège périlleux*. Look what it's done to Norton. He looks twenty years older."

"Siege what…? Well, it doesn't matter. We all know you're smart. But you can be too smart for your own good."

"No intelligent or well-educated person has ever said that to me."

Brunette scoffed and nodded smugly. "You're not as smart as you think you are. If you were, you'd know that you've gotta go along to get along. Like now… As ADIC of L.A., I could send a lot of PI work your way. I could even get you a job with one of the big PI firms. I know all the senior partners. You'd be making a lot more than the Bureau could ever pay you."

"And all I have to do to get along with you is what?"

"If you do break the case, let me know first. I'll call my contacts in the media and arrange the press conference."

"Norton wouldn't be happy if you took the spotlight away from him."

"He'll be okay. He'll still be the center of attention, but he won't be able to cut me out completely and hog all the limelight, if I'm the one who broke it to the press first."

"I'll think about it."

I walked out of Brunette's office and found Bart and Randall waiting for me. Bart told me Rolfe wanted to see me before I left. I wondered what he had to offer.

"I've been here over two years now," Rolfe said, immediately after ordering me to close the door to his office and pointing me to a chair. "That's too long. I know one guy my age who's already a Unit Chief. If I'm going to leave the Bureau with maximum benefits as Assistant Director on my fiftieth birthday, I need to move up now."

"That means you'll need to be appointed Assistant Director by forty-seven," I said.

"Exactly. Cracking that kidnapping should be enough to get me a Unit Chief's desk at Headquarters. Then I'll be well on my way to AD by forty-seven."

"You mean *if* you crack the kidnapping case."

Rolfe snorted. "We'll do it together. You see, I know you're right about the Bureau not getting anywhere. But you seem to have lit a fire. Bart

260 ♦ MARTIN R. REGALADO

hasn't gotten anywhere in months. At this point, he's just retired-in-place deadwood. I wanted to get rid of him months ago, when he showed up with that ridiculous mustache. Anyway, he'll be facing mandatory retirement in a couple of months, and I know he wants an extension, so he can keep working on the kidnapping. He wants to close out his career with a bang, not a failure."

"All that may be true, but why should I care about what happens to you or him?"

"Bart needs my approval to extend, or he'll have to go. I know you've gotta be pissed at him for turning his back on you when you refused to give up your informant and testify in front of the grand jury. And after you saved his life. Twice. Some friend, huh? Well, now you can return the favor and fuck him good. If you agree to work with me, I'll help you, and I'll deny his request for an extension. I'll see to it that he goes out with his tail between his legs."

Rolfe definitely has what it takes to be Assistant Director, I thought to myself. "I couldn't care less what happens to him," I said, wanting to make sure Rolfe believed Bart and I were no longer friends.

"But I can help you, too. I'll help you any way I can, all on the q.t. If you need any names, addresses, or license plates checked out or run through the computer, you just tell me, and I'll see to it. No one else has to know. All you gotta do is let me know when you have enough for an arrest, and I'll handle it from there."

"I'll think about it."

*****

After surviving Satan's three temptations, I chatted with the squad secretary, Edith Leeds, until Bart and Randall came to walk me out of the building. Bart told Randall he'd drive me back.

"Why? Make him walk home," Randall said.

"Naw. We brought him," Bart said. "I'll take him back."

"Very white of you," I said.

"Smartass," Randall replied.

On the drive back to my office, I told Bart all that had transpired in the offices of his three Bureau superiors. "Not one of them said *please*. My old psych professor would say they're perfect examples of excessively severe potty training. I don't think any one of them is ever happier than when they're taking a shit or shitting on someone."

"None of them offered you their wives or daughters? I am surprised," Bart said. "But Rolfe was right about one thing. I'll be mandatory in two months, and without his approval for an extension, I'll have to go."

"Do you really want to extend?" I asked.

"Hell no! The only reason I stayed on was to help you. Like I told you before, I wanted out as soon as Rolfe got the desk. I've had enough of the blue-flaming assholes for one lifetime. I hoped you'd stay on the squad, but you jumped ship and then got your ass in a ringer. I stayed on only to help you when you got outta prison."

"Yeah, I remember. I just wondered if you'd changed your mind."

"No way. I would've retired a year ago, if you hadn't gotten a bug up your ass about this kidnapping. I still don't understand why it means that much to you."

"I don't understand it all, either, but the more I find out about what was really going on, the more I feel the need to see justice done."

Bart scoffed and shook his head. "There you go with that justice crap again. When will you learn there ain't no such thing? And that being an agent is just a job. It's not who you are. You always take every case so personally."

"And I still don't know how you can say that. You put in a lot of unpaid hours and put your life on the line many times," I said.

"I was just doing my job to the best of my ability. That's all I owe the world. No more, no less. Besides, it's a lot more fun than selling insurance or teaching driver's ed. What other job pays you to do the shit we get to do?"

"Well, you don't have to worry about getting an extension. I have a feeling things are going to move pretty fast now. If Marino got as upset as I think he did, he probably called some of the other people involved in the kidnapping. And I don't think those other people will want Marino to have too much time to think about his options."

"So, you're sure Marino was involved? The prick had his own wife and children kidnapped?"

"As sure as ten dimes make a dollar. And they weren't kidnapped by any Palestinians, either. Your buddies on the Organized Crime squad are going to be busy, once things start to happen."

"So, *that's* why you asked for a rundown of the L.A. mafia."

"Yeah. I needed to know who the players were, so I could figure out which captain was most likely running the show and go after him."

"So, who was it?"

"Eddie Canino. Marino came up with the idea, and Canino pulled it off."

"You're sure?"

"Darn tootin', cowboy. And it wasn't even a Palestinian who made the ransom calls. It was a Turk. I'm hoping Marino or Canino or both of them will be scared enough to do something stupid. Stupid enough to break the case wide open."

"If that something stupid means a dead body will turn up, you know I'll have to get involved officially."

"I'm counting on it. Maybe that'll get you back in the good graces of Rolfe, Brunette, and Norton. I know how much that means to you."

"Smartass."

"Speaking of ass, how do you like working with Randall?"

"He's okay. You just have to ignore his macho-man bullshit."

"He's probably got a closet full of dresses and a drawer full of panties."

"You may be right about that, but he's right about you, too. You *are* a smartass."

"Yeah? Well, what was that remark about you having to carry me the entire time I was in the Bureau?"

"I knew that would get a rise outta you." Bart laughed so hard he nearly choked. "Nice line, wasn't it?"

Chapter 50

Visiting Mt. Olympus

Maria had already left by the time Bart dropped me off at my office. No messages were waiting for me, so I waited for Richard Marino to call me.

He didn't call. Maybe my threats weren't enough to scare him. Maybe they just made him mad. Maybe he and the Ginsbergs would have their friends pay me a visit. Maybe I was the one who should be scared.

I poured myself a shot, lit a cigarette, and noticed my hand shaking. I *was* scared.

I didn't like being scared. I knew the best way not to be scared was to scare the people who were scaring me. It was only late afternoon, a few minutes before five, so there was still time to shake the tree again and see what fell out—but which branch to shake this time?

I decided to call the Edward Hawkins Company in Vegas and ask to speak with Eddie Canino. It was the only way I could think of to get through to him.

The young girl who answered put me on hold, and, a moment later, an old, gruff, male voice came on the line.

"You were calling for Eddie Canino?" The man spoke slowly, confidently, enunciating every word.

"That's right. May I speak with him?"

"Who are you?"

"My name is Mig Dehenares. I'm a private investigator, and I have important business to discuss with Eddie Canino."

"What business?"

"That's between Canino and me," I said, wanting to create a little mystery and not wanting to overplay my hand by revealing more than I had to at this point.

"Why did you call here for Canino?"

"He's listed as an associate with your company, and I know he's done business out of your office."

"Has he?"

"Is he there?"

"No."

"I need to speak with him as soon as possible on an urgent matter. Do you know where I can reach him tonight?"

"No."

"Isn't he still associated with your company?"

"Why don't you leave your telephone number and address. If he calls, we'll see that he gets your message."

I gave him my information. There was no reason not to. If Edward Hawkins was a mafia front, it wouldn't take them more than an hour to trace the call and have me fully identified anyway. And I *wanted* Canino and his associates to know who I was.

Canino didn't call me back. What did I expect? A mafia captain would return the call of an unknown and unimportant private dick immediately? Even if Marino had called him and told him about me, I was sure Canino saw me as nothing more than a fly buzzing around his ass. If I became a problem for him, he'd swat me away in his usual and terminal manner.

I shuffled some papers and stared out the window for an hour. It was already cocktail hour, so I didn't feel guilty when I poured myself another, lit a cigarette, and stared out the window, hoping for enlightenment.

*****

Marino didn't call. Canino didn't call. Alison Grayle did call. I still wasn't sure whose side she was on or where she fit in, but if this was to be my last night on Earth, I couldn't think of a better way to spend it than with her.

We had dinner and then went to her ritzy condo, which turned out to be on the top floor, one of four penthouse suites. The address bespoke affluent respectability and refinement—lovely places for the rich to indulge their vices. It was the opposite of my digs in every other way, as well.

The interior was modern chic, done by a professional decorator with expensive and impeccably conventional taste. Everything was shiny and new and looked as if it had been brought in this morning to decorate a movie set. The salient features were large picture windows to the west and north that provided panoramic views of the city. If Balzac was right, this was a place that had required more than just one great crime to pay for it. And although it was beautiful and luxurious, I knew it wasn't the kind of place I could feel comfortable in for very long.

Alison turned on some music and went to fix our drinks. "Do you like Billie Holiday?" she asked.

"Of course," I answered as I continued to look around.

Alison's affinity for oriental jade went beyond her mesmerizing anklet. She had two large display cases filled with the stuff and had several pieces on her end tables and coffee table, laid out as if left casually. Some pieces appeared to be antique and must've been worth a small fortune. Or maybe a large fortune, for all I knew. Even the pieces that weren't antique were intricately carved and would've exceeded the national median annual income several times over.

Alison came away from her bar with our drinks—Scotch on the rocks for me, and a white wine for her. "Do you like jade or know much about it?" she asked as I admired her collection.

"I only know it's green, like money. These pieces must've cost a lot of it. *Santé*." I took a sip and recognized the nectar as the kind I could only buy for very special friends on very special occasions.

"*Santé*. Most of these belong to my father. He's a collector and got me interested in it. He let me borrow some of his collection when he saw how barren my place was and thought this was a safe place to keep it."

A safe way to avoid confiscation by the FBI and IRS, if my suspicions about Alison are accurate, I thought to myself. "It must be nice to have a rich daddy. I imagine it makes life a lot easier."

"Are you suggesting I couldn't make it on my own?"

"Not at all. From what little I know of you, I'm certain you would've done all right even without a rich daddy. I'd like to know more. You know the line—'Who are you really, and what were you before? What did you do and what did you think?'"

"You already know a lot about me."

This conversation was beginning to bore me. The hardest thing about being alone with a woman like Alison was overcoming the animalistic desire to throw her on the nearest bed and have my way with her. Her natural beauty and innate sexuality made talk superfluous. But I had to restrain myself, because there were things I needed to know, and there was the obligation to maintain at least a minimal level of civilized behavior.

Instead of her bed, Alison ushered me to the white, soft, L-shaped leather sofa covered in throw pillows that faced the picture windows looking out on the city lights. We sat, and Alison reached down to take off her heels. "You don't mind, do you? They're beginning to pinch."

"You're welcome to take off anything you like. And no, I don't know much about you or why you've shown such an interest in me."

"I told you I work at WTC as a personal financial advisor to a select group of clients and that I find you interesting. Much more interesting than the office drones and rich playboys I usually meet."

"I'm sure that's all true, but I think there's more to the story."

"I don't know what you mean. I think your suspicious nature and job training have gotten the better of you… Speaking of your job, how has your quest to get to the bottom of that kidnapping been going, Mr. Quixote?"

She wasn't very subtle this time, but at least I knew why I was here and where she was going now. "You seem to have an unusual interest in that particular case," I said.

"Is it wrong for a woman to take an interest in the work of the man she cares about? If it's important to you, don't you think it should be important to me, too?"

She was good. Good enough to make me want to believe her and tell her everything she wanted to know and then let her have her way with me. "The case is going great. I think I have it all worked out. I just need to figure out a way to get an admission and find some hard evidence without getting myself killed."

"You mean you know who did it?"

"Yeah. And it wasn't the Palestinians."

"Then, who?"

"The local mafia, with some help from their friends back East."

She did her best to look shocked. "So, there's still a mafia? I thought the FBI had put them out of business."

"It's changed a lot. It's not all Italian anymore. *Organized crime* is a better term for it. It's a loose association of criminal groups that help each other out as the need and opportunity arise."

"And one of these organized groups of criminals was responsible for the kidnapping?"

"Yep."

"Do you know who, specifically?"

"Yeah."

"But how? How did you find out? It's terribly interesting!"

"I just followed the directions on page forty-seven of the private investigator's manual. That's the textbook that comes with the correspondence-school course on how to be a private detective."

She wrinkled her nose at me again with that look of irritation that made me weak in the knees. "I guess there must be some people who find your sarcasm charming."

Ouch. A lot of people have accused me of being a jerk, but when Alison said it, it mattered—I wanted her to like me.

"You have a way of pissing people off, you know, and for no apparent reason."

"Yeah, I've had complaints about it, but it keeps getting worse," I said, hoping Marlow's line still had some charm in it. She continued to stare at me with disdain. I felt I had to give her something, and since everyone involved in this case was lying to me in one way or another, I thought it was time I told her some lies, too, just to see where it got me. "There's an old saying in the FBI, 'It's better to be lucky than good,' and I was very lucky. I won't bore you with the details, but I was lucky enough to come across a street punk who knew one of the people involved in the kidnapping. Then, I got ahold of that jerk and persuaded him to tell me what he knew."

Alison hadn't taken her eyes off me, only now the disdain had turned to rapt attention. I liked the feeling that gave me, so I continued. "He didn't know much, but he did know the name of the guy who pretended to be the Palestinian and made all the phone calls for the ransom money. He was a Turk who spoke fluent Arabic and was hired specifically for the job just to make everyone believe it was the Palestinians who carried out the kidnapping. I found the Turk and persuaded him to tell me all he knew, and it was a lot. He wanted me to work out a deal with the Feds for him in exchange for a full confession and protection. Unfortunately, he got busted by the cops for something else right after I talked to him, and he disappeared before I could get him to give me a videotaped confession. I think the mafia captain who ran the operation had him killed before he could squeal, to save his own neck."

"Wow! I didn't think that sort of thing happened anymore. Do you know who this mafia captain is?"

"Yeah, I've already called him, and I'll be calling him again, if he doesn't get back to me soon. I expect to be dealing with him in the next day or two."

"Who is he? Do you think he'll talk to you?"

"He'll talk. He's looking at either the death penalty or life in prison without parole. That's if his own people don't silence him first. He has no choice but to cut a deal at this point, and I can make that happen for him."

"Who is he?" she asked again, as nonchalantly as she could, taking a sip of her wine. "What kind of person could do these things?"

"It's better if you didn't know his name. For your own safety. I've probably said too much already."

"You still don't trust me to keep a secret?"

"It's not about that. I told you before, I just don't want to put you in a difficult position. It would be dangerous for you if certain people thought I'd told you what I know about the kidnapping."

"How could anyone know that?"

"I've been followed since getting out of prison. There're several different groups of people, each with their own interests, who've been following me. It's likely they know that you and I have been spending a lot of time together. They'll assume I've spilled some beans just to impress you. Pillow talk, to keep you interested in me."

Alison shook her head. "Don't you think you're being just a little paranoid? You're describing something out of a bad movie."

"I wish it was that simple, but you have to remember who's involved in this thing—the Ginsbergs, Marino, the mafia, thugs doing the dirty work for a major bank, the FBI, CIA, and LAPD. I don't know which of them is worse. I've found out the millions in ransom that was paid was just the tip of the iceberg. There's hundreds of millions of dollars and many more lives at stake here."

"That's a lot to take in. If I heard that story from anyone else, I'd send for the men in the white uniforms."

"I know it sounds crazy, but it's true."

She snuggled up closer to me. "I can see you're worried. Why don't you let me help you relax?"

"Well, okay. If you insist."

Alison then checked her watch and feigned concern, trying to look as if something had just popped into her mind. "I have clients in Mumbai whom I promised to call this evening about an investment opportunity I've been researching for them. It's already tomorrow morning there, and I should've called them an hour ago. Why don't you fix yourself another drink and relax while I make the call? I promise it won't take more than five minutes. I'll slip into something more comfortable and be right back."

I wondered who she was really calling. The answer to that question could resolve a lot of issues. I tried to think of all the people she might call and what that would mean for my investigation and me. I really tried to think of all that, but in truth, all I could think about was Alison coming out of her bedroom in something comfortable.

She took six minutes, but the wait was worth it, as I was well-rewarded for my patience. Alison walked out of her bedroom wearing long jade earrings, that jade anklet, and jade marabou slippers... and nothing else. She walked with neither pride nor timidity, the way the Venus de Milo would walk—in knowing perfection.

I sat in silent admiration and wondered if this might be what Santayana was talking about when he defined beauty as pleasure objectified.

Chapter 51

Res Gestae, Res Judicata

A lison insisted I spend the night at her place. She didn't have to insist very hard. When she came out of her bedroom as she did, Seal Team Six and the Hostage Rescue Team combined couldn't have taken me out of there. The next morning, I enjoyed waking up next to her. It gave me feelings I'd like to have every morning for the rest of my life. I guess she must have enjoyed it, also—it took us a while to get out of bed...

When I finally did get going, I went to my apartment and found my door open and the interior searched none too gently. Nothing had been taken, not even my TV or stereo, so it wasn't the work of common criminals. Whoever did this was looking for something in particular. I cleaned myself and the apartment up a bit, picked up a breakfast to go, and went to the office. I wanted to see if it had also been ransacked and be there in case anyone called.

The office had been given the same treatment. Every drawer and file cabinet had been opened and upended, every seat cushion cut open, and the refrigerator door was left open. Even if Canino or Marino didn't call, I'd have plenty of cleaning up to keep me busy. But first things first.

I stepped around the mess and made my way to Jack's desk, where I read the paper as I had my breakfast and thought about my next move. I knew Marino would be busy this morning with his press conference scheduled for ten. It was supposed to provide the general public with an update on the progress of the downtown L.A. project. There had been a good deal of controversy generated by the traffic congestion already created by the large-scale construction and concerns about the tax incentives granted by the city and state for a project that would seem to benefit primarily the well-to-do. The media event was intended to quell the negative publicity and generate positive interest in the finished product.

Since Marino would be inaccessible this morning, there was no point in trying to shake him up a little more. Nothing would stop him from attending the media event. He'd be rubbing elbows with all the local politicians and financial bigwigs involved with it, and even a few celebrities from the entertainment industry would be there to lend a little glamour to the festivities. After all, the project included a major hotel, expensive condos for rich yuppies, ritzy retail shops, five-star restaurants, and an entertainment complex with an auditorium and theaters. It was billed as a luxury city within the city—for those with the cash to enjoy it.

The press conference was carried live by all the local TV stations. I watched and listened as I cleaned up the office. Unfortunately, the press conference held no surprises and presented nothing relevant to the kidnapping. Marino and the Ginsbergs, like everyone else on camera, maintained big plastic smiles throughout the event, while they each praised the project and assured the public it was worth the traffic congestion and cost.

I went out for lunch and returned to the office immediately after. My cell phone rang as soon as I came through the door. No caller ID appeared on the phone. "Yes," I answered, hoping it was either Marino or Canino.

"I'm calling from a cold phone." I recognized Bart's voice on a Bureau phone that couldn't be traced.

"What's up?"

"Have you been watching the news?" he asked.

"You mean the L.A. project press conference this morning?"

"No, you moron. Get your head outta your ass and turn on the local news. A body was found in a car early this morning in the parking lot of one of the card clubs in Commerce. It was just identified a few minutes ago as Eddie Canino. Two bullets through the mouth to the back of the head. Looks like it happened last night."

"Damn!" I said, thinking there goes the full confession I was hoping for and all the hard evidence that would've come with it. Was I callous for having no compassion for the death of a cold-blooded murderer? "Any leads on the killers?"

"Not yet. There probably won't be. It looks like a professional hit. The car was stolen a couple of days ago. He was shot somewhere else, and the body was left in the parking lot on purpose, so it would be found. Somebody wanted to send a message that he was a snitch and made sure it would go public. Do you have any ideas on the subject?"

"Like you said, it sounds like a professional hit. The question is who ordered it and why now."

"You tell me," Bart said. "You stirred up the pot pretty good with the scene at Marino's office. Did you piss off anybody else who might think it was time to get rid of Canino?"

I told Bart about my call to Edward Hawkins yesterday.

"That must've been the straw that broke the camel's back," he said. "You'd better watch your step. They might come after you now."

"The question is, which *they*. I'm an easy target, and there're several different groups involved in this thing. Any one of them could've had me whacked already."

"So, who woulda wanted Canino whacked now?"

"It would've been Florian or one of the other captains or even one of the capos outside L.A... Anyone Canino could've offered up to save his own neck."

"That's what you were going for, wasn't it?"

"I was hoping to talk to Canino first and get a confession. Someone must've known that's what I was going for with the scene at Marino's office and the call to Edward Hawkins. They got to him before I could."

"So, who was it? Which group?" Bart asked. "If you're right about it being a mafia hit, who could've passed the word on to Florian or one of the other captains or capos?"

"I don't know. There were a lot of people who could've done it. Anyone at Edward Hawkins. Maybe Marino got through to Florian himself. Anyone at Marino's office. There were a lot of people at Marino's office, and any of them could've talked about it when they got back to their own offices. I'm sure the Ginsbergs relayed what I said to other people besides their lawyers. And then there're all the lawyers involved in this thing, including those at the U.S. Attorney's Office. I wouldn't be surprised if there was a snitch at the USA's office passing information to the mafia."

"I'd be surprised if there wasn't," Bart said.

"Yeah. Then there're your friends, Norton, Brunette, and Rolfe. Even if one of them isn't compromised, they're dumb enough to let something slip."

"That's for damn sure. Not half a brain between 'em... Well, think about it, and let me know if you come up with a likely suspect. And watch out for your own dumb ass. You've managed to piss off people enough to commit murder."

"Yeah, right… I guess the Organized Crime squad is all over this."

"Like flies on shit," he said and ended the call.

Chapter 52

Eddie Canino – Deceased

What the fuck?
How could they do this to me?
TO ME!

It woulda been great. Once I got the old man outta the way, L.A. woulda been just like Vegas in the old days.

Those fucking bastards.
FUCK!

Chapter 53

In Propria Persona

Canino's murder was on every TV station. It swiftly supplanted the media's interest in the downtown project press conference. The smiling politicians who'd been talking nonsense about the L.A. project now looked serious and responded with more nonsense to questions about crime in the city.

I watched the news on several stations to see what each had to contribute to the story. It wasn't every day that an "alleged" mafia figure was murdered so publicly. As is the usual case, when no hard facts are available, the media resorts to wild speculation. Every law enforcement official and local politician hungry for attention was given their two minutes of fame and asked to add to the speculation. And when the story had been exhausted, the media resorted to its old trick of reporters interviewing reporters, to get the last possible drop of speculation. All involved seemed happiest when speculating as to whether Canino's murder was the start of another mafia turf war. I imagined the media executives were salivating at the thought of all the advertising revenue a mafia turf war would generate for their newspapers and TV news shows. Pardon my cynicism.

I continued to clean up the office as I tried to figure out who'd carried out the hit on Canino and why last night. The office was quiet and would remain so, as Maria had classes today, and it was already too late in the day for Jack to make an appearance.

After stacking up case files before returning them to their file cabinets, I took a break to look over some of Jack's old cases, as a few might be worth following up on. There were several old insurance, theft, and missing persons cases that not only offered financial rewards but looked interesting as well. "Which way did he go?" and "what did he take with him?" were grist for any keen investigator's mill. I made notes to the files, listing the investigative steps to be taken on each, and decided to go out for coffee just to get some air.

It was already late afternoon when I returned to the office. There was no one waiting for me, nothing on the answering machine, no messages slipped under the door. I was beginning to think Spade and Marlowe were liars—no leads were falling from out of the blue into this private dick's lap.

I couldn't bring myself to continue with the clean-up, so I stared out the window and began to feel lonely and sorry for myself. I thought about Alison and how much I wanted to see her. I hadn't mentioned her to Bart as a possible passer of information, even though she certainly was a possibility. What I wanted to believe about her was overcoming my objectivity and common sense.

Don't be a chump, I thought to myself. *This one's out of your league, too.* I had played the fool for one woman already, waiting for her for years and years, and after the last time I saw her and listened to her tell me I was her one true love, she ran off to Mexico with her husband the next day. Now I'm trying to solve her kidnapping and murder.

All that's gotten me is fired from a job I loved, eight months in prison, beaten up and knocked out, and it's now put me at the top of the list of people likely to be murdered in the next twenty-four hours. Not exactly the "happily ever after" fairy tales tell us love is supposed to bring.

I was jolted out of my reverie by the sound of someone pounding on the outer door of the office. I got up to see who it was and found myself staring at Rick Marino. He was holding a snub-nosed revolver in his right hand, and he seemed both angry and scared. I wasn't sure which emotion was in control, but neither was good, when coupled with a man pointing a gun at you.

"Is that the same gun you used on Canino?" I asked, noting it was nickel-plated with pearl grips—the perfect gun for the ostentatious egomaniac holding it.

"It wasn't me. I wish it had been. He deserved it," Marino answered.

"So do you."

That got him angrier. He pushed his way in and closed and locked the door behind him while keeping his gun pointed at me. "Let's go to your office. You have some explaining to do."

I led him into Jack's office, navigating our way around the mess of files and other debris remaining on the floor, and he ordered me to sit on one of the chairs in front of Jack's desk. He went around and sat down in the chair behind it. He was a man used to being in charge, making himself at home, and always having the place of honor. "The king is always at home," they used to say in feudal times, meaning wherever the king was *was his home*.

I couldn't allow that here—I had to get Marino off balance and make him uncomfortable.

"If you didn't kill him, then it must've been one of his own people," I said with a grin. "That means they'll be coming after you, too, if they haven't already."

"Why would they come after me?" he asked, trying to appear unconcerned by that possibility but obviously digging for information.

"Because you're the only other person who can testify as to who really was behind the kidnapping of your wife and children. Vincent Florian and the other capos aren't going to allow that. They won't even take that chance."

Marino pointed his gun at me again. "What exactly do you think you know about the kidnapping?"

"No need to threaten me with your toy. I'll be happy to explain it all to you, and when I'm done, you'll see what a chump Canino played you for and why you need me to arrange a deal with the FBI, so Florian won't be able to get to you."

He rested his hand and the gun on the desktop. "I'm listening," he said.

"According to the Turk and Canino, the kidnapping was your idea," I said before Marino cut me off.

"Who's the Turk?"

"Who *was* the Turk is a better question. I'll get to him. Don't be impatient." I went on to relate most of what Michael Sachetti had told me, while keeping Sachetti's name out of it. Marino didn't interrupt, although he became visibly agitated and then morose when I went over the part about Lola Valento. When I was done, I said, "There's a bottle of Bushmills in the bottom right drawer. You look like you could use a shot. I know I could."

Marino thought about it for a moment then transferred the gun to his left hand and brought out the bottle and two glasses. He filled his glass and then looked at me. He wasn't the kind of man who'd enjoy pouring another man's drink, and he had to think about it. He poured a small amount of whiskey into the other glass and pushed it toward me with the muzzle of his revolver.

I reached for the drink, and we stared at each other for a few seconds as we each thought about our next questions and moves. I broke the silence.

"The Turk was arrested by the police on drug and weapons charges before I could record his statement on video. He made the mistake of thinking Canino was his friend and would help him with the police. Instead, Canino made him disappear—permanently. You can check on that with the Long Beach PD or read the story in the *Times*.

"Even without a statement on video, the Turk gave me enough to approach you and Canino. With the Turk dead, I knew I'd need either you or Canino to testify and give up Florian. I tried to reach Canino through Edward Hawkins in Vegas first, but he didn't get back to me as fast as I thought he should've, so then I went to your office. I know you and the Ginsbergs or your lawyers contacted the U.S. Attorney after that, because the FBI told me so when they threatened to arrest me for harassing you and the Ginsbergs. I'll bet my last dime you also tried to get ahold of Canino and Florian."

Marino breathed heavily, took a drink, and poured himself more whiskey. He didn't offer me any.

"Thanks for that, by the way," I said. "Because it turned the screws on Canino even more. There was no way Florian could give Canino a chance to talk, any more than Canino could've given the Turk a chance to talk. If it wasn't you who put a bullet in Canino's head, and I don't think it was, then it must've been Florian who ordered it. Which means Florian will be coming after you. You're the only person left who knows the full story and can finger him. Given your showing up here with a gun in your hand and your raggedy-ass appearance, I'd say you know that already."

Marino stared at me with undisguised hatred. "You bastard… You're all bastards," was all he had to say.

"You offered up your wife for kidnapping and murder, and we're the bastards? I don't think so. That's not how a jury would see it. That's not how Florian sees it, I'm sure of that."

Marino finished his whiskey and sparked up. "There's still a way out. I'll talk to Florian myself. We're businessmen. And he owes me a favor. We'll work something out. There'll be no bullet to the back of *my* head. You're the only one who might talk, and you're easy enough to get rid of."

"No, it's past that. I've taken steps to ensure the story will get out even if I'm dead. People know that. That's why they ransacked my apartment and this office last night. Florian will certainly know that and won't take any chances. He'll make sure the evidence of the kidnapping stops with you and Canino as the fall guys, which means you'll have to be killed so you won't talk. Once you're gone, there'll be no reason for him to risk the fallout that would come from murdering a former FBI agent who everybody knows was working on the case and had nothing but unsubstantiated hearsay to offer. Some people even think I'm still with the FBI, which will make Florian think twice about doing anything to me."

Marino thought some more. "All right, so I'll go away for a while until things cool off. I'll go to Mexico or South America or Asia. I have money stashed away everywhere, and I can make money from anywhere. I know how."

"As long as you're alive, you'll be a threat to Florian. He can't allow that. He won't risk that when all it would take is another little bullet to have peace of mind and not have to worry about the FBI breaking down his door."

"We'll see about that," Marino said as he got up. He made his way around the desk, still pointing his gun at me. "Don't worry, I'm not going to kill you. I'll let Florian take care of you." As he reached the door, he looked at me with mean disdain and got in his parting shot. "I heard Rachael knew you in college. No wonder she never gave you the time of day. It must've been obvious even to her that you're a loser and would end up in a dump like this."

Sachetti had been right: Marino's pride and need to maintain his sense of superiority were just as important to him as money. Despite the many things I could've said in response, I let it slide and instead asked, "Just tell me one thing. I think you owe me at least one answer. What was the favor Florian asked you for?"

Marino scoffed derisively. "He needed my help to get one of his bimbos a job. His kind of money and power doesn't work everywhere, but I have connections. She was just a dime-a-dozen market analyst sitting in a cubicle ten hours a day and wasn't going anywhere. I got her a job as a client advisor at one of the biggest financial firms in the country, with just one phone call."

"Why was that so important to him?"

"Why is any woman important to a man?" Marino asked as he backed out the door.

Chapter 54

Hell is Empty

After Marino left, I went around the desk, sat down, poured myself another, and lit a cigarette. Before I had a chance to take a sip, though, the office door was opened again. I wondered if Marino had changed his mind and come back to take care of me himself. Even if he had, there was no point in wasting good whiskey. I took a sip and waited.

"Was that Richard Marino who just tore out of here like a bat out of hell?" asked Tom Curtis, a crime reporter for the *Times*, as he entered Jack's office.

"I don't know what you're talking about," I answered. Our paths had crossed many times over the years, but Curtis and I weren't friends. In fact, I didn't like him. Like most newspapermen, he'd sell his granny just to get his name on a front-page story. He probably didn't like me, either, but that didn't stop him from coming around from time to time like a vulture scavenging for carrion.

"Aren't you gonna offer me a drink?" he asked with an irritating smile that never left his face. He was about my size and age, with short, blond hair, blue eyes, and wire rimmed glasses. Clearly intelligent and educated, with the talent to sniff out a good story that most others would miss. He might otherwise pass for an ordinary guy, but there was something in his manner that would compel rental agents and lap dancers to ask to see cash up front and everyone else to think about washing their hands after shaking his.

I pushed the bottle over to the empty glass Marino had left on the desk.

Curtis poured himself a big one. "Now, what would a big-time wheeler-dealer like Richard Marino be doing in your lowly digs? No offense."

"Your mere presence is offensive, Curtis."

"I don't understand what you have against journalists. This country would be another Nazi Germany if it weren't for the Fourth Estate. I would think someone with your education should understand that."

"I understand that your idea of journalism is more about selling newspapers than the public interest. Newspapers with your byline on the front page."

"You have to sell papers to inform the public. And what's wrong if I get a little juice out of it? That's what America is all about—a little piece of the pie for everybody."

"Save that crap for your brainless readers. Finish your drink and get out. I have work to do."

"*Hmph.*" He shook his head. "No wonder they kicked you out of the FBI. Agents are supposed to build rapport and get along with everybody. You've always been an antagonistic smartass. I'm surprised you lasted as long as you did in the Bureau."

He may have been right about that, but I didn't need to hear it from him. "What do you want, Curtis?"

"You don't have to be a hardass all the time, do you? Lighten up. We've known each other for ten years, for Christ's sake. You can at least call me Tom."

I stared hard and blew smoke at him.

"Okay, hardass… After Eddie Canino got clipped, I checked with my sources and found out you paid Richard Marino a visit yesterday and claimed he was involved with Canino. Then our research department went to work and found out that the said recently departed Eddie Canino was associated with a company in Vegas called the Edward Hawkins and Associates Real Estate Investment and Management Company, and that Marino has that big resort project going in Vegas. That's what I came to talk to you about. Imagine my surprise now, when I just happened to find the said Richard Marino tearing out of your office as if his ass was on fire. What's the connection? Does it have anything to do with the kidnapping a year ago?"

"You've been drinking the special Kool-Aid too long. You should be writing for the *National Enquirer*."

As I responded to Curtis, the office door opened again, and three stereotypes from central casting walked in. A tall one in his mid to late thirties, followed by two heavy-set ones in their late twenties, all wearing expensive and shiny three-piece Italian suits and ties, expensive and shiny black shoes, expensive salon-cut slicked-back black hair, and expensive tanned Sicilian complexions. They couldn't have been more obvious if they had name labels with *MAFIA* on their lapels.

The tall one looked us over. Mr. Mafia was confident and cocky and exuded a viciousness that would instill fear even without his two muscle men standing behind him. His feral eyes expressed an unmistakable affinity for violence and cruelty—the kind of man who would've enjoyed boxing more if the rules required it to be a fight to the death. He also looked like he needed a shave, but he was one of those men who would always look like he needed a shave.

"You must be Dehenares," he said.

"No, I'm Doghouse Reilly. Who're you?"

He glared at me and ignored my question. "Who's this jamook?" He pointed his chin at Curtis.

"He can speak for himself, if he wants to."

Mr. Mafia gave me another dirty look and turned his head to Curtis. His gaze demanded an answer.

"I— I'm Tom Curtis. I'm a reporter for the *Times*."

Mr. Mafia wasn't impressed and turned his attention back to me. "Where's Richard Marino?" he asked.

"How should I know?"

"Don't get smart with me, dickhead. I'll paint the walls with your ass. Now, where's Marino?"

Mr. Mafia was a mafia crew sergeant looking to make lieutenant. He reminded me of all those Bureau supervisors hungry for promotion— ready, willing, and eager to follow any order and do whatever it takes to climb up the ladder.

I answered, "I don't know where he is. I wouldn't tell you even if I did. I need to talk to him myself before you get to him. And I don't think your boss would like it if you whacked me just yet. I don't intend to expose your boss, but if anything happens to me, it'll all come out. I've already made arrangements for that." I was getting good at lying. The lies were rolling off my tongue now with hardly any thought.

Mr. Mafia was thinking through his next move when the office door opened again. The twenty-somethings drew their pistols, and Mr. Mafia turned casually to the door. In walked the three stooges from South Crenshaw with Fearless Female Leader behind them. The stooges drew their weapons as soon as they saw the mafiosos with their guns out.

"Great. Just what I needed," I said, to no one's amusement.

"Shut the fuck up," Mr. Mafia said then turned to Fearless Female. "Who the fuck are you?"

Fearless Female looked Mr. Mafia up and down with intentional disdain. Ignoring his question, she turned to me and asked, "Where did Marino go?"

Offended, Mr. Mafia was quick to respond, "I don't know who you think you are, bitch, but you and your boys better back out now, while you still can."

"In case you can't count," Fearless Female answered, "you're outnumbered as well as out of your league. Put your guns away. After I get the information I want from Dehenares, he's all yours."

"He's mine now, and you're not getting anything until I'm done with him," Mr. Mafia replied.

I felt left out of the conversation and needed to interject my opinion. "It's nice to be wanted, and I hate to break up your pissing contest, but I'd appreciate it if all of you got the hell out of my office!"

Fearless Female ignored me and said to Mr. Mafia, "Maybe you and I should speak privately in the outer office. Everyone else can wait in here."

Mr. Mafia thought for a second and then nodded. "Okay, we'll talk." He turned to his men and said, "Nobody goes anywhere," and they nodded in response.

Fearless Female repeated the same instruction to her stooges.

The two went out of Jack's office and closed the door behind them. Indistinct conversation could be heard, as well as cell phone calls being made. After a long five minutes, the two returned to Jack's office, an accord having been reached. They told their men to holster their weapons and move me to one of the chairs in front of Jack's desk. Mr. Mafia, having the same arrogance as Marino, sat down behind Jack's desk. Fearless Female sat on the edge of the desk, directly in front of me.

Fearless said, "You were told to stay out of it, but you didn't listen."

"You didn't say *please*."

"Well, your guardian angel must be looking out for you. You just might live to see another sunrise, if you cooperate. What have you told your reporter friend here?"

"He's not my friend, and I didn't tell him anything. But now that you're all here, I'll tell you all what I have to say to each and every one of you. It'll save me time. Kiss my ass and get out."

The gorilla came up behind me, put both hands on top of my shoulders, and pushed me down hard on the chair. I tried but couldn't stifle a grunt. He dug his fingers into me. I was beginning to hate him.

Fearless continued, "You already know what we can do to you, and you know you're going to talk, eventually. Is it worth another beating just to prove to your friend what a tough guy you are?"

I scoffed. "I told you, he's not my friend. As far as I'm concerned, reporters are only one step above thugs like you. He's just an unlucky bastard who came here looking for information, just like you. I wouldn't have given him the time of day even if you hadn't shown up."

Curtis was shaking and his pale complexion now a shade of white only the Inuit have a word for. He gulped and said to me, "Remember what I said about not being a hardass all the time?" He turned to Fearless. "It's true, I got here just before you all did. We didn't have time to talk about anything. He didn't tell me anything."

Fearless turned to Mr. Mafia. "We can decide what to do with the reporter after we're done with Dehenares." Mr. Mafia nodded in agreement. She told one of her other stooges to take Curtis to the outer office and hold him there. She then asked me, "Tell me what you and Marino talked about when he came here just now."

"Mostly about the Dodgers. We both were hoping Kershaw would be pitching better this year."

Fearless stared at me with a contempt that ripped me apart.

I answered her stare. "I don't like being pushed around by a bunch of low-life thugs, especially in my own office."

The gorilla squeezed my shoulders, and one of the twenty-somethings came around and slugged me in the jaw. I wondered if I'd lose a tooth or two. Maybe not. They're working miracles in dentistry these days. I spat blood at Fearless Female's feet. "Get out of my office." I could feel my jaw beginning to swell already.

Mr. Mafia told his other twenty-something, "Put your silencer on and stick it in the reporter's ear. Maybe then this smartass will know we mean business."

I looked at Mr. Mafia and Fearless. I could see neither was bluffing. Just one look and it was clear they'd each done terrible things to people, so one more killing wouldn't mean anything to either of them. There was no point in holding out now.

I said, "Marino came here wanting to know what I knew about the kidnapping, because I went to his office yesterday and told him I knew all about it and Eddie Canino and Lola Valento. I knew that would get his attention and make him come to me. But I'm sure you know that already. That's why you're here. Well, he came, with a gun, and pointed it at me, just like you idiots. So many guns and so few brains. There must be a magnetic attraction between idiots and guns."

"What did you tell him?" Fearless asked.

"I told him all I'd learned from the Turk about the kidnapping, which, as your new friend Mr. Mafia here knows, is enough to put him and everyone else involved in the kidnapping in prison. More important, it was enough to get him totally pissed at Canino for making a chump out of him and enough to get him scared for his own life. I told him everything I knew would be released to the public, if anything happened to me, so even if he wasn't killed, he'd still be ruined. I also told him I could make arrangements for him with the FBI for protection, if he agreed to cooperate with me."

"What did he say to that?" she asked.

"Being the arrogant bastard that he is, he said he'd make his own deal, and if he couldn't get a deal he liked, he'd take off and disappear. He claimed to have money hidden all over the world and said he could make money from anywhere."

"What else?" she asked.

"Nothing else. He was in a hurry and left after that. He was scared. He knows people are after him."

"Did he say where he was going?"

"No."

"If he knew that you knew so much, why didn't he cap you?" Mr. Mafia asked.

"He seemed to think you people would take care of that."

"What did you tell the cafone outside about the kidnapping?" he asked.

"Like he said, you came in right after he did, so I didn't have time to tell him anything, even if I'd wanted to, which I don't."

"But it looks like you had time to pour him a drink," Fearless interjected, holding up the whiskey glass. "You must have been getting ready for a long conversation."

"I didn't pour him anything. He poured it himself. This has been a day for the uninvited to come in and make themselves at home. Do me a favor and take him with you when you leave."

I'd had enough. Hauled in by the LAPD and FBI, having a gun pointed at me by Marino, and now pushed around in my own office by two gangs of thugs. I felt as helpless as that morning in Afghanistan, lying on the ground, more dead than alive, barely able to move, watching my buddies getting shot and dying. Only this time, I wasn't helpless, and I could move. I was fed up and mad.

Maybe a smarter man would've thought things through and decided on a wise course of action or at least kept his mouth shut, but I was beyond that. It was time for me to make a move and just go with it. It's amazing how fast the mind races when you're "in the shit."

I leaned forward as if I was trying to get up, only I didn't. The gorilla holding me down in the chair moved forward with me to keep me down, just as I'd hoped he would. I only feigned getting up to bring him closer to me. I then gave him a quick head butt to the nose, which caused him to loosen his grip on me just enough to let me stand up.

I spun around quickly and threw him a right cross to the nose. It wasn't much of a punch, but it was enough to send him reeling back to the wall and then down to the floor. He sat there with his legs stretched out in front of him, looking ridiculous.

"That's just a down payment on what I owe you," I said to the gorilla. I was about to turn around and say something just as clever to Fearless and Mr. Mafia when I felt the butt of a pistol on the back of my head.

The fact that I was beginning to recognize when I was being knocked unconscious disturbed me—it meant it was happening too often. Maybe I should start wearing a crash helmet. That was my last brilliant thought before the lights went out for me once again.

*****

"What the hell!" I said, coughing.

"It's just water," Curtis said.

He had gotten water from the kitchen and poured it on my face to rouse me. He handed me a glass of water and a hand towel.

"Wipe your face. And you may wanna wipe the blood off the back of your head."

Memory was returning slowly. "What happened?" I asked.

"Your visitors left after putting you to sleep. Nice people you associate with. They told me, if I printed anything about what happened here just now, you and I wouldn't live to see the next edition. The woman also said to tell you that you already have two strikes against you. One more and nobody could protect you or keep you from being put to sleep permanently. I wanna know what the hell is going on. I think you owe me an explanation."

"I don't owe you anything. If you hadn't come here uninvited and stuck your nose where it didn't belong, you wouldn't have gotten yourself involved in a mess you couldn't possibly understand or handle. And more importantly, you wouldn't have cost me what you just did."

I made my way to the desk chair as I spoke and downed my unfinished drink. I'd forgotten about being slugged in the jaw and my loose teeth, and I winced when the alcohol burned my gums. I poured myself another and lit a cigarette. I wiped blood from the back of my head. The bleeding seemed to have stopped, but I wondered if I needed stitches.

"What did I cost you?" Curtis asked as he sat down on one of the chairs in front of the desk and took a sip of whiskey.

"They were just as interested in Marino as you were. I wasn't going to tell them anything, because I need to see him again before they get to him. But Mr. Mafia told one of his boys to put a bullet in your ear if I didn't tell them what they wanted to know. Since I hate mopping up blood, I had to tell them something."

Curtis was unmoved. "Come on, Mig, this is Pulitzer Prize material here. What the hell is going on?" He leaned in closer. "If those people are who I think they are, this is big. Really big."

I shook my head slowly in disgust and massaged my jaw. "I guess you have trouble expressing gratitude. I save your life, and you're still asking for more."

"You can trust me. And you wouldn't have saved my life if you didn't like me at least a little."

"Like hell I like you. Bloodstains are bad for business, that's all."

As much as I hated to admit it, some press might be necessary—but not yet.

"I'll make you a deal, Curtis. You keep your mouth shut long enough for me to complete my investigation, and I won't kick your ass. I might even throw you a bone."

Chapter 55

Quid Pro Quo

The rest of the evening was uneventful. Alison didn't call me, and I had to work hard to stop myself from calling her. I couldn't help thinking about her and caught myself sighing like a lovesick teenager more than once. I knew I should remain suspicious of her, but I had dived in headfirst the moment I saw her and was too far down to recognize rapture of the deep.

The next morning, I tried to contact Marino again at his home and office, with no luck. Under the circumstances, I didn't expect to find him at either place. But he was the only one who could answer all the questions that needed to be answered and had a reason to do so. I had to get to him before Fearless Female or Mr. Mafia did. Susan Russo said she'd also been trying to get ahold of Marino, without success. She seemed genuinely concerned about him, and I told her he was in great danger and I was the only one who could help him. She agreed to call me if she heard anything.

I'd delivered on Canino as promised, and now it was time for Sachetti to come through. Given the direction things had taken, I also needed more information from him.

I went to see Sachetti's girlfriend and told her I needed to meet with him again. A blank stare was her only response. She didn't even blink. I wondered if there were more than two marbles bouncing around in that pretty little head. I tried to be as friendly and unthreatening as I could be, but I still couldn't tell if my message or benevolence got past those beautiful yet vacant sky-blue eyes. I began to wonder if there was even one marble in there. I had the urge to shake her, just to find out. But even if there wasn't much brain activity going on, there was no need to worry about her. When Sachetti got tired of her, she could always get a job as the weather girl for one of the local TV stations.

*****

Although Sachetti was now undisputed heir to the throne in L.A., he was still concerned about being seen with me in public. He called and told me to meet him in a parking garage near his girlfriend's place in Marina Del Rey at an hour much later than I liked. Since he didn't need me anymore, the late hour and location had me worried—it was a perfect set-up to get rid of a loose end. Me. He arrived in a Maserati but chose to talk in my car. With Canino out of the way, Sachetti looked more relaxed and confident than ever. He was on top of the world and dripping with audacity.

I tried to hide my nervousness with an assertive toughness. "I held up my end of the bargain. Canino's dead, and no one knows where Marino is. Now I want to know where to find Rachael Ginsberg's body."

"Don't be so cocky. There're a lotta people who'd like to see you dead. You got a way a' pissin' people off, and your guardian angel can't protect you forever."

"Be that as it may, I still want the body. Where is it?"

"You're a smart college boy. Did you ever hear the story about the guy who hid something in plain sight so nobody would think to look there?"

"Yeah. Edgar Allan Poe."

"Whatever. Anyway, keepin' that in mind, smart guy, where would be the best place to hide a dead body?"

I thought out loud. "Where a dead body is supposed to be... Where there're other dead bodies... A cemetery."

"Very good," Sachetti answered.

"There are lots of cemeteries. Which one?"

"In a small town called Realita, halfway between here and Vegas, there's a little cemetery called the Mountain View Cemetery. A ninety-year-old spinster named Mary Knudsen was buried there last year. She was just a tiny little thing and didn't weigh much, so there was plenty a' room in her box for another stiff. She didn't have no livin' relatives or friends, so there were no nosey people or funeral to be worried about. You get my drift?"

"You're absolutely sure about this?" I asked.

"I wouldn't waste such a valuable asset if I didn't have to. You think it's easy gettin' rid a' dead bodies? You can't stick a shovel in the dirt anywhere between Barstow and Vegas anymore without hittin' bones. Now, we'll never be able to use that cemetery again, will we?"

I nodded. "Speaking of dead bodies, what happened with Canino? Did you handle that?"

"Not me. I told you I couldn't do anything about Canino myself. You're as much responsible for whatever happened to him as I am. Maybe more."

"How could I be responsible?"

"I told you what would happen to Canino if the bosses thought he was a problem. Once it was known that you were on to him for the kidnapping and were gonna approach him with a deal, they couldn't let him have the chance to become a snitch to save his own ass. All the capos are old men, and no old man wants to die in prison. I told you, they're all crazy paranoid and got snitches everywhere spying on everybody."

"You make it sound worse than life under Hitler or Stalin."

"You got that right. They don't take any chances. So, when Florian found out you had the goods on Canino, he went to the other bosses, and they had to give him the okay to take him out. Simple as that. Problem solved. It was a no-brainer."

"But you're the one who pointed me to Canino in the first place."

"You're the only one who knows that. Are *you* gonna be a problem?"

"I gave you my word. You know I won't tell anyone. But I know you haven't told me everything. So, what's the rest of the story? How did Florian keep the FBI and everybody else from knowing it was his organization?"

"Fuhgeddaboudit. The less you know, the better."

I had brought a pint of Old Forester and a couple of plastic cups. I thought we might have a drink to celebrate his success, if he didn't whack me first, and I wanted to loosen him up to get more information from him. I handed him a cup, opened the bottle, and poured us each a drink. I lifted my cup and toasted, "Success to crime," as facetiously as Spade would've done.

Sachetti smiled that perverse smile of his, nodded, and returned the toast. I knew he wanted to tell the tale as much as I wanted to hear it, so I pressed him.

"I was involved in the investigation, and I know how it was handled. I know the agent who handled the investigation and everything that was done. The FBI and LAPD hit your people and our informants hard, but nobody was able to come up with anything to tie your people into the kidnapping. How did Florian do it?"

He was hesitant.

"Come on, spill it." I took out a couple of cigarettes, gave him one, and lit them.

"What the hell, it's a good story—proves the feds and cops aren't as smart as they think they are. But if one word a' this gets out…"

"It won't."

Sachetti took a sip. "Here's how it went down… Florian's wanted a piece a' Marino for years, cuz he's a gold mine, right? When he heard how Marino was in over his head in Vegas, he sent Canino to play him and get him in deeper. He got the casinos to hold off on calling in the markers and even got them to increase his credit. Canino wines an' dines him, and Marino likes having everybody thinkin' he's connected. Now, Florian's always been smart about sharing the action, so he got some a' the other bosses to go in with him on Marino's markers and got Atlantic City to use the bimbo to really hook him. Once Marino's hooked, Florian sent Canino to put the screws to Marino to pay off the markers *or else*. What makes it even better is, this is when Marino needed big cash from the banks to move on his L.A. and Vegas projects or he'd be busted. And Marino thinks he's in love and wants to start over with his new bimbo, but he's in the deepest shit a' his life, so he comes up with the idea for the snatch to solve all his problems at the same time. When Canino went to Florian with Marino's idea for the snatch, Florian knew we owned him."

"And Florian didn't know the wife had to be killed as part of the deal?"

"No way. I told you that already. Canino didn't even tell him about snatching the bambinos." He took another drink, refilled his cup, and handed the bottle to me. He was clearly enjoying telling the story.

I stared hard at Sachetti and went for more. "I find it hard to believe Florian didn't know, or that Canino thought he could keep it from him."

Sachetti answered with more Italian hand-waving. "Look, you gotta understand, this is business. Big business. And big business comes with big risks. Canino had the balls to go all-in on this one. It was the caper that would put him on top for good. But he knew Florian and the other bosses would think twice about snatching the bambinos and would never okay whacking the wife. You gotta get the okay to go after a high-profile target like the Ginsbergs, cuz it can backfire bigtime. A kidnap can go to shit fast, or it can really pay off, but there's no guarantee. You never know till it's over.

"What you do know is that it can bring a lotta heat and bring down some made guys, even the top boss, if anybody sings. And a caper like this takes a lotta dough up front just to get off the ground. But like I said, Florian's a smart guy and offered the other bosses a piece a' the action to get the okay and get 'em to pony up some dough to get the ball rolling."

I took a drink. "That's quite a complicated business arrangement. There are few lawyers with the brains or balls to negotiate a deal like that."

"You got that right. This is work for businessmen, not lawyers. In our line a' business, nothin's on paper, but everybody knows what the deal is and what happens if you break the deal or if it goes to shit. And Florian was smart enough to cover himself. He ordered Canino to use only outside muscle and not tell anybody about it. None a' our L.A. people were in on it. Florian didn't even want anybody Italian in on the snatch, so we'd be completely off the radar and in the clear. So, Canino brought in muscle from Kansas City, Dallas, and who-knows-where else. He just put the word out he was looking for help with a big caper and promised a big payout. Nobody in the Family, nobody that had to be protected, was brought in. And he made sure the guys he brought in didn't even know each other."

I nodded, refilled my cup, and put the bottle on the dashboard.

Sachetti continued, "But while Canino's settin' up the caper, Marino's givin' him hell, cuz it's takin' so long. That's when Canino gets the big idea to use the Turk and pull off the caper before it was supposed to go down. I told you about that part already. So, when it does go down, it goes even better than Canino expected. Everybody buys that it was the towelheads, and the Ginsbergs and Marino pay up a lot more than anybody expected. Now, *there's* somethin' the Feds should be lookin' into. Where'd they come up with all that green? And so fast? Canino and Florian couldn't believe it. The Ginsbergs and Marino didn't even try to negotiate. They just coughed up all the cash the Turk asked for."

Sachetti shook his head and took a swig. I nodded again, and he continued. "The only problem was when the wife had to be wasted. Florian was pissed cuz he knew that was trouble, but what could he do? Canino was payin' off the other capos with ransom money, and if anybody had to go down for the snatch, it woulda been Canino or Florian, not them. All Florian could do was order Canino to pull a *Goodfellas* routine and whack all the muscle he brought in, after they all went home, back to their own hometowns, so there'd be nothin' to connect them here."

"*Goodfellas* routine? What the hell is that?"

"I know you're a brainiac and spend all your time with your nose in a book, but don't you ever go to a movie once in a while?" Sachetti asked, flicking his hand and dropping ashes. "In that *Goodfellas* movie, after the big heist at the airport, the crew chief whacked everybody on the crew, so there'd be nobody left to talk—get it?"

"Got it."

"So, now, the only people in L.A. who were in on the snatch are Florian, Canino, and the Turk. Months go by, and things heat up between Florian and Canino. Like I told you before, I only found out about it when Canino bragged about how he got the schmuck to pay up another five mil vig on the loan for the last ransom payment. He thought he was solid gold and bulletproof, and he wanted everybody to know he had the brains and the balls to be top boss already. But then the Turk gets pissed, cuz he hears how Canino's been braggin' and throwin' cash around. He starts tellin' everybody that playing the A-rab angle was his idea and the snatch never coulda happened without him. He gets wound up and tells Canino he wants a bigger share a' the loot or he'll make a stink about it with the boss here and New York. Can you believe that shit? What balls! A fuckin' camel jockey talkin' like he's a made guy and owed any respect!" Sachetti shook his head in utter disbelief.

"Anyway, Canino goes through the roof and wants to whack him right there, but he can't cuz he's an earner and belongs to New York. Then you come along and botch a simple burglary. The cops arrest the Turk, and Canino has all he needs to get the okay to whack him before he can talk. So, that leaves only Florian and Canino, right? One a' them's gotta go anyway and might as well take the fall for it to close it off, cuz every wise guy in the country's scared it's gonna hit CNN sooner or later and a lotta heads could roll. So, who's it gonna be? You come along and finger Canino, so it's sayonara Eddie."

Sachetti bellowed with laughter and slapped his thigh. I couldn't help asking, "So, how did that go down?"

This time, Sachetti didn't hesitate, answering with another laugh and more hand-waving.

"That was beautiful. Poetic justice, like you smart people say, and it makes me laugh every time I think about it... I told you Canino always bragged about how he was a New Yorker, and New York wise guys are smarter and tougher and know their shit better than anybody else. Well, once Florian found out you were gettin' close, he brought out four Nuyoricans nobody out here knew about and put them up till he got the okay from the other capos for the hit. That was smart. Canino woulda found out if any local guys or known hitters from back East had come out here and were on a job. That's the same reason why Canino had the bikers come after me, instead a' any a' our own hitters.

"Anyway, once Florian got the word that even Canino's friends back East were okay with it, all it took was two phone calls, and the job was done in a couple hours. Serves him right to be whacked by a New York crew, and spics, no less. That must a' really fried his balls. He hates— *hated* spics more than he hated niggers."

"Why's that?"

"Cuz a' his name and dark skin, he was taken for a Mex a lot, and he hated that. Drove him up the fuckin' wall," Sachetti replied with an evil laugh. "Or did. He broke a spic waiter's jaw once just for callin' him *señor*. I mean, the guy was just being polite, right? Well, Canino won't have to worry about that anymore… And people say *I* have a bad temper."

"Didn't he have bodyguards or any of his own people around to protect him?"

"Of course. But you gotta remember, to us, this is just business. Just business, nothing personal. After Florian got the okay from the bosses back East, he called Canino and told him that he and the other bosses had decided it was time for a change in L.A. He sent for Canino cuz he wanted to tell him in person. He wanted Canino and everybody to think he was gonna retire and make Canino boss peaceful like. Show there were no hard feelings. What else would Canino think, after all his kissin' up to the other bosses and kickin' up all that green?"

Sachetti looked out the window and chuckled long and low. "The schmuck was so sure a' himself, he couldn't see he was being set up. Man, I wish I coulda been there to see his face when he knew he was fucked and gonna get clipped."

Then he got serious again and turned to me. "Canino never even made it to see Florian. Once his people were told there was gonna be a change in management and had been sent home to wait for the word, they got outta the way. It's not like anybody was gonna stand in front a' Canino and take a bullet for him. As soon as Florian got the hit confirmed, he named a new captain to take his place, so everything was settled. It's business as usual already."

"Very efficient. But why was Canino laid out so publicly? Florian could've just made him disappear."

"I'm sure he wanted everybody to know what happens to snitches, and he made sure everybody knew that's why Canino was whacked. That's what he wanted everybody to think, anyway."

"And how did Florian know I was ready to go after Canino? Did you tell him?"

"No way. How many times do I gotta tell you? I couldn't be seen havin' anything to do with you or bringin' him down. If anybody knew that or even suspected that, it woulda been open warfare. Canino coulda had me whacked, and nobody woulda said nothin', cuz that's just business. And I need to be pristine and clear a' any trouble when it comes time to name a new boss."

"Talk about being used. Now I'm the one who feels like a five-dollar whore."

"You got what you wanted. Everything has its price, remember?"

"Yeah, but if you didn't tell him, how did Florian know I was ready to go after Canino?"

"You don't make capo and stay capo for very long unless you know things—a lotta things. I'm sure he's got people reportin' to him about you and a lotta other things that you and me don't even know about. Don't any a' your big shot philosophers got somethin' to say about that, college boy?"

I nodded. "'Knowledge itself is power,' Francis Bacon said." I finished my drink, took a drag, and blew it out slowly as I thought about what Sachetti had just told me. I couldn't help wondering why he'd told me everything he did. I also couldn't help wondering why he didn't tell me all this at our first meeting—it might've made my job a lot easier.

I turned to him as he finished his drink. "Well, I wish you had told me everything you knew the first time we met and talked about this. Things might have turned out better."

Sachetti gave me a thin, icy smile and slowly shook his head once. "Everything turned out just fine," he answered.

*****

Not wanting to look like a fool if I'd been misled, I did my own due diligence before passing on the information about Rachael's body. I drove out to Realita, about two hours east of L.A. and another twenty minutes north of the Interstate.

Realita is one of those nondescript little towns that looks like all the other nondescript little towns between Los Angeles and Vegas. The only way to tell it apart from the rest of suburbia is its ostentatious *Welcome to Realita* sign proudly erected on the side of the road.

My drive through Realita reminded me of the town I grew up in, where the class and racial distinctions were as clear as geologic strata, and childhood memories came back quickly. Mexicans and Blacks lived south of the railroad tracks and bus station; poor Whites, just above; and the upper-middle-class Whites, north of them all.

As a child, I once made the mistake of riding my bicycle to the north side of town one afternoon, where I was quickly stopped by two cops who jumped out of their patrol car, its lights flashing and siren wailing. I was held for half an hour while the senior cop demanded to know from which house I'd stolen the bicycle. The younger cop went around the neighborhood, checking to see if anyone had seen an eight-year-old Mexican boy where he shouldn't have been. After half an hour of my being poked, pushed, and threatened, the older cop told me to go home where I belonged and to never come back to this side of town.

This aggressively racist policing wasn't only tolerated, it was rewarded. By the time I was in high school, the senior cop had been promoted to chief of police. This was still a part of America I had trouble understanding, as it was the America I'd gone to war for as a soldier and defended as an FBI agent… *"O patria! dolce e ingrata patria,"* as Rossini's soldier, Tancredi, would say.

I drove straight to the Mountain View Cemetery and spoke with the manager. He was new, as was the entire cemetery staff, according to him. The prior owners, a business partnership, had sold the cemetery a few weeks ago. The manager found Mary Knudsen's file and told me she'd been buried on December 24, 2016, which was only two days after the last ransom payment and the bombs went off at the bank. There was nothing in the file to indicate anything unusual or peculiar in connection with the handling of Knudsen's body or her burial. Knudsen had made arrangements to pay for everything twenty-five years ago, just after retiring from teaching at a local elementary school. There was no indication there had been any services or that anyone had attended the burial.

I went out on the grounds and located Knudsen's grassy plot, situated among trees with a view of the mountains. I couldn't explain why, but I knew for certain Rachael was buried here… I just knew she was here, and emotions welled up inside me. I fell to my knees and cried…

> *Sweet voice, sweet lips, soft hand, and softer breast…*
> *Faded the sight of beauty from my eyes,*
> *Faded the shape of beauty from my arms…*

Although John Keats had it right, Proust needn't have worried—love is not lost in death…

It was the first time I'd cried like that since my last counseling session at the VA hospital, fourteen years ago. I hadn't even cried when I learned Rachael was getting married. I had hardened my heart and willed myself not to cry, then or ever again…

But now I cried. Cried like a baby…

Then I did something else I hadn't done in more than fourteen years…

I prayed.

Chapter 56

The Thin Woman III

The drive back from Realita was a time for thinking and soul-searching. Why I cried and why I prayed I may never understand, but I was okay with that for now. As Augustine said, a finite mind can never grasp the infinite.

But some questions could be answered, and I knew I had to speak with Magda Ginsberg again, before anyone else. I was reluctant to do so, because I was certain my every move now was being watched and my telephones were being monitored. I wasn't sure if my phone conversations were being monitored in real time, but I was sure my call records were being reviewed daily.

I called her to arrange it.

"We have to meet," I told her. "There are things I need to know from you and things I have to tell you that I'm sure you'll want to know."

"What *chutzpah*! Enough, already! Can't you just leave it alone? Don't you understand you're going to get us killed with your *fakakta* investigation and all your *fakakta* questions?"

She was obviously very angry and very scared. Toil and trouble must have bubbled up for her also, but I insisted. "We have to meet."

"*Oy vey.*" She sighed. "Well, not at your fleabag motel again. If I'm going to be killed, I want to die in luxury. Meet me at the Langham in Pasadena. Tomorrow morning, 11:30."

"I know I'm being watched, and I would assume you are, too. Try to avoid being followed."

*****

I dry cleaned as best I could and arrived early at the Langham. I waited in the lobby for Magda, trying to be as inconspicuous as possible. I sat behind a large palm, hiding behind a newspaper, just like Spade or Marlowe would've done.

When she arrived, it appeared she was known to the hotel staff, who welcomed her obsequiously. She signed in and was given a key card. I met her at the elevators. As always, she was elegantly attired and looked very chic in her designer duds. She must have paid an early visit to her beauty parlor for a quick touch-up, as she was also looking professionally "done." This couldn't have been for my benefit, so I wondered if this was just to throw anyone following her off guard or if she had another assignation planned for the afternoon. In any case, today was very obviously emerald day, and she was wearing a full set of the green gems to go with her two-tone beige outfit—the emerald green piping knocking it all up a notch.

"I gather you've been here before," I said.

She gave me a wry smile. "From time to time. The staff here is very efficient… and discrete."

We went to a luxury suite, and she immediately ordered drinks after allowing me to light her cigarette.

"Now then, *boychik*, what's so important, other than accusing my husband of involvement in murder?" the matriarch asked, taking control of the situation.

"You've been misinformed. I didn't say he was involved in murder. I only said he might be seen as having information relevant to a murder investigation."

"A very diplomatic way of saying the same thing. Get on with it already."

"I wanted to let you know I've resolved the kidnapping. I know who did it and how it was done."

"Well, *mazel tov* to you, the great *shamus*," she said sarcastically. "I told you I don't care anymore."

"I think you do care. I think you have to."

"Well, don't expect me to start singing 'Hava Nagila.'"

The drinks came—gin and tonic for her and Scotch for me. The waiter brought full bottles and a bucket of ice. It was a bit early for me to start drinking, but I didn't want her to feel self-conscious about drinking alone, so we exchanged *l'chaims*, and I had a sip, just to be polite.

"You have to care because the secrets you've been hiding still need to be kept hidden. I know you haven't told me everything, but you're going to tell me everything now. If you don't, I'll have no reason not to tell the

FBI everything I know, and they'll have to investigate further and dig deeper. I won't mention your name, as I promised, but they'll still have to dig deeper because of what I tell them. If you don't want the FBI to do that, you'll have to tell me why I shouldn't tell them everything."

"I've told you everything already," Magda said. "There's no point in airing out the family secrets and humiliating us in public. Or do you intend for that to be your revenge for my keeping Rachael away from you?"

"I'm not interested in revenge or humiliating you in public. But I know there's more to the story that has to be kept hidden than the philandering. The thugs your secret investors sent out before came after me again, and this time they were ready to commit multiple murders of innocent people. No one would commit multiple murders just to keep Aron on as bank president or hide the Ginsbergs' indiscretions. And they're not mere thugs. It's obvious they have military training, military discipline, and military capabilities. Who are they, and what's really going on here?"

Magda finished her drink and ordered me to make her another. After I gave it to her and lit her another cigarette, she fiddled with her jewelry and stared at the obtrusively large emerald ring on her finger before answering. "Okay, Señor Quixote, you want the whole enchilada? I'll finish the story I told you before."

"I don't want a story. I want the truth. All of it."

"We're just talking, so I'll finish telling the story. It doesn't mean anything, so it's not worth repeating to anyone. You didn't even hear it from me. It's just between us, okay? It will be the most astounding *megillah* you've ever heard, and I say that knowing you've probably heard many astounding things in your time as an FBI agent. See what this does to your idealistic battle with windmills."

"Go ahead."

"Everything I've already told you is true. But you're right. It's not all of it. There's more to the story, and the more is very simple. Very simple and very, very illegal. What I didn't tell you, partly for your own good, is that, many years ago, we found out who our secret investors were. We found out by accident. We weren't looking to find out who they were, but after another one of Aron's adventures went too far, we found out there was really only one investor and that our secret investor was actually the State of Israel. The Israeli government, hidden behind many layers of shell corporations and partnerships, overseas and in this country. They had provided the capital to get our bank started."

Another stunner, and I was done with the polite sipping. I downed my Scotch and poured myself another. After it sunk in, I was disappointed in myself for being surprised by it. I'd fought my way out of the barrio, been to war, and been an FBI agent for many years, so I shouldn't be surprised by things like this. "Okay, but why would they do that?" I asked.

She smiled wryly again and nodded, accepting my naïveté and need to have the maven spell it out for me. "The Israeli government knew it was totally dependent on the United States for its very existence and also knew how fickle and corrupt American politicians are. Just think about recent history, and you can see how often America breaks its promises and turns its back on its allies. Israel needed a way to fund American politicians and political causes that were favorable to Israel. Israel also needed to undertake activities in this country to protect other Israeli interests. All this takes money, big money.

"American laws make it illegal if not just difficult to do these things and to bring money into the country to do them. Having a bank in the United States overcomes all those problems. You don't have to deal with the problem of bringing money into the country, if the money is already here. And you don't have to worry about how the expenditure of money on these things will look, if it's all hidden behind charitable or non-profit organizations or private individuals with no direct ties to Israel."

"So, you and they were afraid, if the FBI looked too deeply into the bank, it would be discovered that it was funded by the government of Israel and laundering money that was being used to influence American politics and carry out secret activities in the United States? And that you were an accomplice to that?"

"Yes, but we didn't have to worry when things were going normally. Our lawyers and theirs are the best. Very crafty. The flow of money is hidden in expenditures that appear legitimate and could be justified in one way or another. The problem is only when large sums of cash are needed in a hurry and the expenditure can't be hidden—*that* draws attention from the bank examiners. The Ginsbergs are very wealthy, but even we don't have millions of dollars in cash lying around. We had to take the bank's cash to make the payments the kidnappers demanded. And then we needed that cash reimbursed immediately to avoid problems with the bank examiners. And we needed still more cash to fund that *gonif's* downtown L.A. project and the bank's own regular activities, all just to make it look like it was business as usual.

"All that cash came from the shell entities. Funds laundered through our bank in the first place, from the profits of our investments. It may sound complicated to someone not familiar with high finance, but it's really very simple. Illegal money is laundered into legal investments, and some of the profits are laundered into secret accounts that are then used for whatever is needed—legal or illegal."

"Diabolical," I said, taking a sip and admiring the genius of it.

"*Feh*! Again with your fanatical idealism," Magda said, waving an emerald fist at me dismissively. "Grow up, *luftmensch*. Life isn't black and white. It's all a matter of perspective. And motive... Don't think Israel is the only country doing this. And don't think American politicians aren't aware of what's going on. It benefits too many people here for it ever to be exposed or done away with. What politician wants to lose a thousand contributions from a thousand voters, just because the money comes indirectly from the government of Israel?"

"Well, if I wasn't cynical before..."

"Do you still feel like jousting with windmills, Señor Quixote?"

"I'm still going to expose the kidnapping."

Magda shook her head slowly and sighed, now exasperated. "You're already on very thin ice. Didn't you get the message? They won't stop at anything to keep this secret and protect their interests. I'll tell you something else for your own good, since we're just talking and telling stories... We found out about this years ago, the first time Aron was being blackmailed. Being the *schlemiel* that he is, he tried to handle it himself, at first. All he did was get himself in deeper. He went from *schlemiel* to *schlimazel*. What else can I say?

"After he lost hundreds of thousands of dollars of the bank's cash in just a couple of weeks, they found out about it and took over. The last thing they wanted was a *schande far di goyim* that would bring in the bank examiners. They have a way of making problems go away that is very final and without any publicity—I don't have to tell you how. Over the years, we and the bank have had other problems, not so big but just embarrassing, and they made those problems go away, too."

"Do you know who the thugs are?"

"Not exactly. Probably Mossad. That's what we assumed, anyway. They come and go, different people every couple of years."

"If they were able to handle Aron's blackmail problem and those other problems, why didn't you call them in to handle the kidnapping?"

"Because Aron and I believed the kidnappers really were Palestinian military, like they said they were. We were sure the kidnappers would've found out if we brought in anybody, and they would've killed Rachael and the children immediately and run away. That's how those *klovim* work—they don't take risks. Again I tell you, the Mossad agents, or whoever they are, work for the Israeli government, not the Ginsbergs. We don't know who they are or what they do, and we have no control over them. They only care about protecting the bank and their secret ownership interest. They don't care about us. Aron and I had to do what was best for Rachael and the children. And we had to keep all that from that *gonif*, Richard. Who knows what that *mamzer* would have done, if he knew about our secret investor and the Mossad?"

While Magda explained the situation as she understood it at the time, I couldn't help thinking about all those subatomic particles bouncing around, seemingly at random, creating events and connections that were totally unpredictable, with consequences that were completely unfathomable to anyone—anyone except perhaps Laplace's Superman, to whom past and future were always present. It would've taken a superhuman intellect capable of comprehending the minutia of all existence to have figured out how to handle the kidnapping and save Rachael.

"I imagine the lawyers and the Mossad agents weren't very happy when they found out about the kidnapping and your use of the bank's money to pay the ransom."

Magda shook her head as she finished her drink and waved an emerald finger at me. "No, you *can't* imagine." She held out her glass for me to fix her another. "The only reason I called you to tell you about the kidnapping when I did was because I was afraid they would find out before we got Rachael back. I needed to bring in the FBI and someone who cared about Rachael more than anything else. If they found out first, they would've sacrificed Rachael just to end it and then cover everything up as quickly as possible."

I nodded, understanding Magda's reasoning now. "And when they did find out?"

"They were through with us. We had to agree that Aron would resign— *retire*, they called it, once the L.A. project was fully underway and the kidnapping was put to bed. We had to agree to fade away quietly—*or else*."

"Do you really think they'd do anything to you? How could they? You and Aron and your entire family are very high-profile, despite your efforts to avoid publicity."

"They're sick of us and all the trouble we've caused them. It was suggested to us, through their lawyers to our lawyers, of course, that if we didn't avoid further scandal and go away quietly, the Palestinians might come back to finish off the Ginsbergs, because we brought the FBI into the kidnapping when they told us not to. It would be a simple thing to make our murders seem like the work of the Palestinians, especially because of our support for Israel over the years. It would be an easy story to sell. Who could deny it?"

I had to ask, "Given everything you've told me about Aron, why didn't you leave him years ago?"

Magda gave me a look of piteous affection. "What? Leave my *nebekh* husband? That would be like leaving a baby in the middle of the street. How could I do that? My children would never forgive me. Despite what you must think of me, I have always put my family first… So, for the sake of my family, be generous, and let it go. If you really care for Rachael, think of her children now. If the Mossad even suspects I told you all this, they would put on their Palestinian keffiyehs, and that would be the end of the Ginsbergs. It might be ironic justice, yes, but who needs it?" She shrugged.

She'd made a compelling argument. "Okay, I won't tell the FBI everything I know. But there is something I'll have to tell them, and I *am* thinking of Rachael and her children, which is why I have to tell you this now. I wanted to let you know before I told anyone else and before it becomes public…" I hesitated and looked at Magda with all the compassion I could muster. "I know where Rachael's body is. I'm going to tell the FBI, so they'll be handling the exhumation."

The uncertainty of Rachael's death was now a fact, and Magda began wailing, as any mother would. She pounded the table with her fist, crying, "No! *No!*" then reached into her handbag for a handkerchief. Her entire body shuddered as she wept. I fixed her another drink and lit her another cigarette. When I put my hand on her shoulder, she allowed me to console her for a minute.

"When the FBI is done with the forensics on the body, it will be turned over to you. You can arrange for the proper services and burial. Rachael can rest in peace, and you and the children will have a place to honor her memory. But remember, when the FBI comes to talk to you about this, you must act surprised, as if you never heard anything about it before."

Chapter 57

Habeas Corpus

I had learned from the new cemetery manager that Mary Knudsen arranged to pay for her plot, casket, burial vault, and other associated expenses years ago, when she'd retired from teaching. Although she had no living relatives or anyone else who'd care, a court order was still required to exhume the casket.

Having told Magda Ginsberg what was coming, it was time to get things moving. Under the circumstances, I knew I couldn't tell anyone the whole story, but I'd have to reveal enough to call for an exhumation.

The story Bart and I worked out was that I'd call Bart to report I'd developed the Turk, Ahmet "Adam" Ozan, as a suspect in the kidnapping of Rachael Ginsberg-Marino and her children. Bart would say that I called him in consideration of our past friendship. I had confronted Ozan, and he'd agreed to cooperate with me and tell me all he knew, if I could arrange for him to be accepted into the witness protection program. I had told Ozan I wouldn't help him unless he gave me a sign of good faith, and I asked for the location of Rachael's body as that sign of good faith. Ozan had told me exactly where Rachael's body could be found. However, before I could act on Ozan's information or even verify the existence of the cemetery and burial plot, he'd been arrested by the Long Beach PD, released on bail, and then disappeared.

Bart would follow up on this and contact LBPD. As was its standard practice, the police had videotaped the arrest, intake processing, and initial interview of Ozan. Bart obtained a copy of those videotapes and had Aron and Magda Ginsberg listen to the audio separately. Richard Marino was still in hiding, so it couldn't be arranged for him to listen to the tapes, too. Despite the lapse of time, both Aron and Magda were certain the voice on the tapes was the voice of the kidnapper who'd made the telephone calls.

Although my hearsay information provided insufficient legal or factual justification, Bart prepared an affidavit to support the FBI's request for the exhumation. Since the senior echelon at FBIHQ has no idea what constitutes good management or leadership, promotions are based on how much publicity field managers can generate for themselves, and Norton, Brunette, and Rolfe were anxious for their press conference. This time, no questions were asked about the source of information, and the Ginsbergs' influence made judicial approval a cinch. The FBI and U.S. Attorney's Office requested that the affidavit be sealed in the interests of justice—mainly to hide the fact that there was little justification for the exhumation.

After all the interested parties were well on their way to the cemetery, I called Tom Curtis and told him where the FBI would be exhuming a body. I wanted the publicity, because I was hoping the exhumation would bring Marino out of hiding, but also couldn't help worrying what new troubles this revelation would unearth.

A second body was found in the coffin along with Knudsen's. It had only been a matter of months since the kidnapping and the coffin had been sealed and placed in its concrete vault for burial, so the remains of the second body were well preserved. The Ginsbergs identified the remains as their daughter. A full autopsy was immediately conducted on Rachael's body. The Ginsbergs insisted a rabbi be present during the autopsy, to comply with Jewish custom.

After the results of a preliminary examination had been verified, the FBI called for a press conference to take place a few days later, when more detailed forensic results would be available, but they didn't specify what the press conference would be about.

Chapter 58

PBR Street Gang IV

Immediately after the autopsy and forensics were completed, Bart called and arranged to meet me and Jason the night before the FBI press conference. He would only say that Rachael had been positively identified through her DNA and he wanted to go over the case and give me the full results in person.

We met at Club Mallard, and I noticed that Bart had brought Jason with him in his car. We sat at a dark corner table. The bartender recognized me but didn't let on. He was my kind of guy. We ordered beers.

"Nice place you picked for our meeting. I'd be surprised if there was one person in here who didn't have a criminal record or a gun and a knife on him," Bart said. "I take it you've been here before?"

"Maybe," I answered.

"Looks okay to me," Jason said then raised his voice. "'If I say it's safe to surf this beach, Captain, then it's safe to surf this beach!'" We chuckled. "Some neighborhood, though. I haven't seen so many junkies and street whores since my agent days." He got back into character and added, "'This sure enough is a bizarre sight in the middle of all this shit!'"

"L.A.'s got it all," Bart said. "You can expect to see anything and everything in la-la land."

"When I got up this morning and thought about my day, I didn't expect to run into a double amputee in a wheelchair hooking," Jason said, then turned to me. "'You're in the asshole of the world, Captain!'"

Our beer came, and Jason lifted his in toast. "'Buddha time!'" He noticed an ancient jukebox, walked over to it, and dropped some quarters into the machine. "Suzie Q" began to play over tinny speakers.

Bart got down to business. "I wanted us to go over the case to this point, because Mig said we're getting close to the end, and I wanna make sure we're all on the same page and have our asses covered."

Jason shook his head sadly. "Close to the end, huh? I knew 'someday this war's gonna end.'"

"Will you cut it with that lame-ass, *Deer Hunter*, Vietnam War shit? It's gettin' old," Bart said. "Why don't you watch a comedy, so you can at least contribute something funny once in a while?"

Jason turned me and, with a nod toward Bart, said, "'The man is clear in his mind, but his soul is mad.'"

I looked from him to Bart with raised eyebrows. "Ooo-kay... I promised you guys I'd give you the whole story. I'll tell you what I've come up with up to now." I went over the case step-by-step, again leaving out Sachetti's and Magda Ginsberg's names and a few other details I thought they were better off not knowing. We couldn't help laughing as I went over the meeting with Bureau management.

"You definitely 'put a weed up Command's ass.' 'A bunch of four-star clowns who're gonna end up giving the whole circus away,'" Jason said. "As much as I love the Bureau, I'm glad I'm not taking orders from soulless idiots like that anymore."

I told them about being shot at in my car and then hauled into LAPD, my encounter with Detective Bureau Chief Gregory, and his accusations. Again, Jason couldn't help himself and, shaking his head, said, "'He's operating without any decent restraint, beyond the pale of any acceptable human conduct. And he's out in the field, commanding troops!'"

"Satisfaction" started up, and Jason shouted, "Yeah! *Workout!*" He closed his eyes and began jerking his head and shoulders, waving his arms, and kicking his feet, ostensibly in time to the music.

Bart asked, "You having a conniption fit, Big Boy?"

Jason ignored him and continued his seated dance for a few moments.

I told them about Marino's visit to my office and how he didn't deny coming up with the idea for the kidnapping or deny wanting Rachael murdered as part of the deal.

"'He's wacko, man!'" Jason erupted. "'He's worse than crazy. He's evil!'"

I sipped my beer and told them about the subsequent visit from Tom Curtis, Mr. Mafia, and Fearless Female. Jason got into character again and said in all seriousness, "If you had people like that working with you, your troubles would be over very quickly. People who're 'able to utilize their primordial instincts to kill without feeling, without passion, and without judgment. Because it's judgment that defeats us!'"

"No," I said. "I'll take you guys over that bunch any day. But with the Turk and Canino gone, that leaves Marino as the only one who knows the whole story, the only one to go after, unless you guys have any other ideas."

"I think you're right," Bart said, nodding in agreement. "Marino's the one to go after at this point."

"Yeah, I agree. You were lucky you got on to the Turk," Jason added. "That's what made everything else fall into place."

"Yeah, but even that came at a price," I said and told them about my encounter with the very large and unfriendly rottweiler.

"'The horror! *The horror!*'" Jason shrieked. "You're lucky it was only a rottweiler that came after you. I hate those big fucking dogs. If it had come after me, I'da said you can have 'the whole goddamn fuckin' shit, man! You can kiss my ass in the county square, cuz I'm fucking bugging out!'"

We laughed again, and then Bart became somber. "Back down to business, and it's pretty bad business." He hesitated, took a long drink, and fixed his eyes on his beer. "The autopsy revealed that Rachael Ginsberg-Marino had been shot twice in the back of the head. The first shot would've killed her instantly. The second was just to make sure."

I knew Bart thought less of me for taking things personally, so I tried not to show any reaction, but I felt myself breathing heavily.

He continued, "The wounds are consistent with forty-five-caliber hollow-points. Probably at point-blank range. There were powder burns at the back of the head. The bullets went through completely, so they weren't recovered from the body. You know what hollow-points do. I don't know anything about Jewish funeral services, but I can tell you they wouldn't want any open-casket ceremony."

I thought of Rachael's beautiful face and called the bartender over to order a double shot of Old Forester.

Bart looked at Jason then turned and looked directly at me. "You always take these things personally. No matter how many times I've told you that you have to be dispassionate and objective to be a good investigator, you always get emotionally involved in every case. Every victim was your father or mother or sister or brother or your own child. That's why I wanted to give you the autopsy results in person. Since you seem to be taking this one extra-personally, for some reason, I thought it'd be a good idea to bring Jason with me, too."

"Okay," was all I could think to say, not knowing where Bart was going with this, but already feeling torn apart from the inside out.

"There's one more thing," he said, as the bartender set the double shot in front of me. Bart waited for me to take a sip. "Rachael Ginsberg-Marino was four months pregnant at the time of her death, and preliminary DNA testing revealed that Richard Marino was not the father of the child."

I finished the shot of whiskey and raised my glass in the direction of the bartender to ask for another.

"The pregnancy will be revealed at the press conference. But the medical examiner, me, and a couple of others in the Bureau are the only ones who know about the DNA results. We need to keep that information secret for purposes of the investigation, but I thought you should know."

I did the math in my head, swilled the second double, and slammed the glass on the table… After learning of Marino's engagement to Rachael, I had wished him dead a thousand times. After learning he was responsible for Rachael's death, I wanted to beat him to death myself another thousand times. Now, I *had* to do it. "I'm gonna kill him," I said. "I'm gonna *fucking kill him!*"

"'Terminate with extreme prejudice,'" Jason said, shaking his head. "He deserves it, but don't do it. You're not an assassin or an errand boy collecting on a bill. Seriously, my friend, don't do it. Don't even think about it."

I stood up. I was going to find Marino and kill him, but someone stopped me. Someone ordered me another double, and then another, and another. Maybe more. Someone got me home and into bed.

Chapter 59

The Empty Suits Have Their Day

When the FBI held its press conference the next morning, Norton spoke, with Brunette and Rolfe positioned behind him so as to be clearly visible in every camera shot. The Assistant Special Agent in Charge must've still been out doing whatever it is ASACs do. Although I knew Bart was there also, he wasn't allowed to take up any space in front of the cameras—after all, he was only the case agent. As always with Bureau management, Norton spoke as if he'd led and been personally involved in every step of the investigation and was responsible for its success.

In order to maintain the integrity of the evidence and not taint any further investigation and potential court matters, Norton said he could only reveal that kidnap victim Rachael Ginsberg-Marino's body had been found and that she'd been murdered. The FBI's investigation had identified a suspect in the kidnapping and murder from a confidential source who couldn't be named. That suspect had been in hiding and wouldn't turn himself in until a deal was reached and he'd been accepted into the witness protection program. However, as a sign of good faith, the suspect had agreed to provide the location of Rachael Ginsberg-Marino's body.

Norton went on to say that the body of Rachael Ginsberg-Marino had been exhumed pursuant to a court order. A rapid yet thorough autopsy and forensic examination had determined she'd been murdered and was pregnant at the time of her death. The suspect had since disappeared, and it was believed his former accomplices had done away with him in order to avoid prosecution. Norton assured the public the FBI would continue its relentless pursuit of the criminal perpetrators and bring them to justice.

The press asked for more information about the suspect and wanted to know if it was still believed that Palestinians were behind the kidnapping and murder. Norton would say only that the suspect was not

Palestinian, but since he'd disappeared before he could be debriefed, it wasn't known who his accomplices were. Norton repeated that he couldn't reveal any additional information, because it might jeopardize the ongoing investigation.

Brunette and Rolfe were each allowed a minute in front of the microphone to repeat Norton's statement and add an inane comment or two of their own. With brilliant bureaucratic backstabbing, ass-covering, blame-shifting, and spotlight-stealing, Brunette drew a head-jerking look of surprise from Norton when he revealed that the suspect was from the Middle East but not Palestinian, and was known to have been involved in narcotics trafficking, as well. He added that the suspect had good reason to fear for his life, since drug traffickers, like Hezbollah terrorists, often eliminate the people involved in their major operations to cover their tracks. Because of this, he pointed out, the actual perpetrators might never be identified.

The press demanded more, but Brunette only left them with the likelihood that the kidnapping and murder would never be fully resolved. No one from the LAPD had been invited to speak at the press conference, something I couldn't imagine the LAPD brass was very happy about.

The Ginsbergs, like everyone else, had been surprised to learn of Rachael's pregnancy. However, other than a very few people in the FBI, no one knew that Marino wasn't the unborn child's father. Rachael's body was subsequently released to Aron and Magda Ginsberg.

Chapter 60

Rachael Ginsberg-Marino – Deceased III

Richard had some good qualities, but I always knew he wasn't daddy material. I knew who I wanted to be the father of my children.

David just happened—I didn't plan it that way. I found out I was pregnant when Richard and I were dating, and I told him he was the father. He believed me and asked me to marry him right away. Mother quickly made all the arrangements to have our wedding before I began to show, to avoid scandal.

The funny thing is, Richard wasn't at all suspicious. He was too arrogant to think that any woman who had his attention could want any other man. But Mother was suspicious, though she never said anything. I think she was afraid of the truth.

With Sarah, it was different—I planned that. The first time Richard and I separated, I did it on purpose. I stopped using birth control, because I knew who I would run to again. Since the only two men in my life looked so much alike, I knew there would never be any suspicions raised.

I knew it was wrong, but I wanted it all—for my children. All the best both my men had to give.

Chapter 61

Invitation to a Murder

I woke up late the morning after my meeting with Bart and Jason with a beauty of a hangover. Bright sunlight was already streaming through my bedroom windows, so the day had begun, and there was no avoiding it now. I made myself a cup of coffee and turned on the morning news. The publicity surrounding the exhumation and the anticipated FBI news conference was extensive, making all the papers and TV stations.

I was still disappointed that it hadn't brought Marino out of hiding. I was beginning to wonder what all the news would cause him to do, or cause others to do to him. I got myself cleaned up and went to the office.

I felt sick after watching the FBI's press conference. Sick of the pretentiousness, the mendacity, the hypocrisy, the outright criminality, and the immorality of everyone involved in the case, including my own. I didn't want to think about it too much—it was just the way the world was—and I didn't want to think about that, either. Nietzsche might have been able to deal with the despair and meaninglessness of life and laugh about it, but I was too close to the problem to see any humor in this situation. My hangover didn't help my mood and wasn't conducive to deep thinking, either.

I stayed in the office, hoping to hear from Marino, but neither the exhumation nor the press conference brought him to me. I tried to reach him at his home and office, but no one had seen or heard from him since the morning of the L.A. project press conference. Susan Russo was very worried and wanted to call the police because he had called her several times, sounding frantic and wanting to know if anyone had been looking for him. She'd called the Ginsbergs, and Magda told her not to call the police. I didn't tell her he had come to my office, but I, too, asked her to hold off calling the police. Since the FBI had cut the LAPD out of the information loop and press conference, I knew Daryl Gregory would be livid and looking for any excuse to jump back in and muddy the waters just out of spite.

I went to my gym for a steam, hoping it would clear the alcohol out of my system. I brought a take-out lunch with me back to the office and waited for Marino or some other bolt of relevant information or insight, but nothing came through the door. I alternated between staring at files and staring out the window.

Maria came in after lunch, cheerful as always, and I wondered if it was just the fortunate alignment of good genes that made some people naturally happy, despite all the general shit in the world and the particular shit in their own lives. She said she'd been in the area, visiting a friend, and had come in just to check on things and see if there was any work for her to do. I didn't know she had any friends in this part of town and wondered who it could be.

I saw she'd made use of Alison's gifts of cosmetologist and hairstylist—she was looking quite sophisticated. Gone were the purple eye shadow and black nail polish, never to be seen on her again, I was sure. She was still relegated to budget dresses and modest costume jewelry, and her language skills still needed much improvement, but it was clear her days as an East L.A. *chola* were behind her—at least, I hoped they were. She was young, attractive, and hardworking, but even all that didn't guarantee her a ticket out of the barrio. I wondered what Oso thought of his little sister now and if he would stand in her way.

With her natural insight and growing maturity, she sensed I was in a dark mood and asked if I was okay. I nodded unconvincingly, and she came around to give me a sisterly hug. She said she'd work on getting the files in order—her mastery of the alphabet having grown enormously, also.

*****

A little before five, Fearless Female and her gorilla walked in.

"May I help you?" Maria asked.

"I'm here to see Dehenares," Fearless answered brusquely.

"Please, have a seat. I'll see if he's available."

With the door to the inner office open, I could hear the exchange and called out, "It's okay, Maria. I'll see them."

Fearless Female said to her gorilla, "Wait here. I'll speak to him alone for a minute."

I came out of the office and, with a nod toward Maria, said to Fearless, "She doesn't need to be a part of this." I couldn't help grinning when I saw Fearless in yet another pantsuit and the gorilla still sporting the remains of the shiner I'd given him.

Fearless looked at Maria and said, "Okay, she can go."

"You've done enough for today," I told Maria. "And it's getting late. You can go now and work on the files the next time you come in."

"Are you sure?" she asked, obviously aware something not good was going on. "Is there anything you need me to do?"

"No, please go. I'll see you soon."

"Are you sure?" she asked again.

"Yes. Please go now."

Maria left, and Fearless again ordered her gorilla to wait in the outer office.

In Jack's office, I sat down in the chair behind the desk, and Fearless sat in one of the chairs in front. She looked as cool and in command as always. "Your secretary is pretty but a little young for you, don't you think?" she asked.

"I like young things, if they're nice to look at. But she's not my secretary. The boss hired her, not me. And we were all young once and had to learn the ways of the world from someone."

"What has she learned from you?"

"I haven't taught her anything, yet. But I hope she learns that a woman doesn't have to wear pantsuits and be bossy to be the boss."

Fearless dropped her guard and gave me a hate-filled look that said I'd struck a nerve. I attacked again. "If the Scots could go into battle in kilts, I don't see why a woman has to resort to pantsuits to show she means business. Or why a woman has to be a bully to prove she's in command."

"What you don't know about women could fill volumes, I'm sure. But I'm here to find out what you do know. I want to know all you know about the kidnapping and the murders you claim Aron Ginsberg had something to do with."

"Don't you need your gorilla and the other two stooges in here to handle the physical labor for you, while you interrogate me?"

"I can handle you myself."

"I doubt it. I don't hit women very often, but when I do, I hit them as hard as I would hit a man."

"If that's your Latino machismo talking, save it. I've seen you hit a man. I wasn't impressed, and I'm certainly not scared."

It was my turn to be offended, but I had to let it slide for now. "Why should I tell you anything?"

"Because you like living, I assume. Come on, you're going for a ride."

"Where?"

"Someplace more conducive to conversation."

"The place where you keep your whips and chains, Madam? Or do you prefer *Mistress*?"

Fearless scoffed with a small smile. It was the first time I'd seen her smile, and it was a nice smile. It made me want to see her really smile.

She answered my innuendo, "You wish. You can only handle the tame, compliant type. You phony macho men couldn't handle a real woman even in your wildest dreams."

I was beginning to like her. "Why should I go anywhere with you? Why not have it out here?"

"You said you wanted to speak with Marino again. We found him, and we have him. Your Italian friends and my people are holding him for you. You can ask him all the questions you want. You get to live a few more hours, and when it's your time to go, you'll go with all your questions answered."

I had wanted to confront Marino, and this was my chance. He and I were both prisoners of our fates now, with circumstances well beyond our control, so I'd face him on an equal footing for the first time. If I had to die anyway, I might as well go knowing the full story, and there was no point in leaving a bloody mess for Jack and Maria to clean up.

Chapter 62

The Grand Inquisitor

The gorilla waiting in the outer office had screwed on his silencer and was holding his pistol on his lap, ready for the word to do his duty. As Fearless and I exited Jack's office, he pointed it at me, and Fearless told him to put it away, as I'd agreed to go see Marino. He seemed disappointed. I wondered if he worked on commission or got a bonus for each killing.

We walked to their car in silence, with Fearless and the gorilla on either side of me, their right hands in their coat pockets. The gorilla got in the driver's seat, and Fearless put me in back with her. She handcuffed and blindfolded me and insisted in her usual charming manner that I get down so as not to be seen.

"I knew you were one for the cuffs and blindfolds, but why bother if I'm not going to be around much longer?" I asked her.

"Standard procedures are like habits—very hard to break. And your guardian angel may save you yet. You could be lucky enough to see another sunrise. Who knows what might happen after that?"

"Maybe I'll even live long enough to see you in a dress."

She didn't answer, but I was sure she smiled.

The gorilla dry cleaned without having to be told, and about forty-five minutes later, we arrived at what I guessed was a large warehouse or factory. Rattling metal doors were rolled open, and the gorilla drove in. Fearless walked me into a sectioned-off room within the warehouse or factory and removed the blindfold. Opaque tarps had been placed on the floor and used to cover most of the walls and ceiling. I knew what that meant.

Richard Marino sat looking like a sack of potatoes thrown on a chair by the far wall of the kill room. His wrists and ankles were zip-tied. His bloody face and the urine and vomit on the floor around his chair told the story of what he'd already been through. I knew the feeling.

Fearless sat me down on a chair in front of him. I swallowed dryly and asked for water. There were several plastic bottles of water in the room. Fearless opened one and handed it to me.

Mr. Mafia was also in the kill room and spoke first. "You can see he's softened up and ready to talk. Even an ex-FBI agent should be able to get the whole story out of him now."

Fearless was the only other person in the room. I assumed their underlings were standing guard outside. Fearless said to me, "You wanted to talk to him. Now here's your chance. Interview him as if you were still an FBI agent questioning a subject to get a full confession. I want to know everything he knows. *Everything*."

I stared at the beaten man. "Not like this… Why should I?" I asked no one in particular.

Mr. Mafia came up behind me and slammed the muzzle of his pistol on the back of my skull then cocked the hammer. "Because, if you don't, I'll blow your fucking brains out. Now start asking questions, and you'd better do a good job of it."

*****

I did do a good job. It was a complete and thorough interview. My instructors at Quantico would've been proud. Mr. Mafia and Fearless sat behind me as I questioned Marino. Knowing I was under their watchful eyes, I felt my every word and move scrutinized, and that I was putting on a performance for them, one upon which my life depended.

After the usual initial reluctance, I gained Marino's trust and cooperation and convinced him to be honest with me and tell me everything. It was for his own good, I said. In a way, it was true—it *was* for his own good. I told him I couldn't promise him anything myself— even if I was still an FBI agent, I wouldn't have the authority to make any legally binding promises. But if he cooperated and told me the whole story, I'd try to convince the powers that held us both to take it easy on him. And if he had to be killed, to kill him quickly and painlessly. That was the best he could hope for. I told him I knew what I was talking about, because I was in the same boat. A quick and painless death was all I could hope for, too.

Half delirious, he told me everything he knew, from his point of view, of course. He said that he told Canino to set up the kidnapping of his wife to come up with the money for the Vegas project and to pay off his gambling debts. He admitted that he'd demanded his wife be killed as part of the deal, because he'd wanted out of the marriage without the pain of a divorce and the financial ruin it would bring. He denied knowing Rachael was pregnant. Canino had told him Florian would never approve of killing Rachael, so that had had to remain just between the two of them, until it was all over.

He said he'd never agreed to the kidnapping of his children and had really believed the Palestinians had been behind the kidnapping, after Canino denied his people had taken his wife and children ahead of schedule. When he repeated what I'd told him about Canino and the Turk, he cursed them at length for double-crossing him. He blubbered like a baby when he talked about Lola Valento, saying he really did love her and had wanted to marry her. I pitied him for that, but it was the only time I felt any pity for him, and my pity quickly turned to rage.

Marino then said that Canino had told him they would've had to kill Rachael anyway, because the men holding her had raped her repeatedly, and there was no way to cover that up, short of murder. Florian would've been furious, as would the other bosses. Apparently, there are some things even a mob boss can't stomach, especially if it brought unnecessary heat.

I jumped out of my chair and lunged at Marino's throat. I would've killed him, if Mr. Mafia and Fearless hadn't pulled me off him and held me down until I calmed down and agreed to continue with the interrogation.

When Marino regained his composure, he became his old arrogant and egotistical self again and tried to bargain his way out. I let him ramble on, as any good investigator would, knowing his words would only serve to dig him in deeper. He repeated that he had money stashed all over the world and would give them some. Hundreds of thousands of dollars, he said, maybe millions. He reminded us he was a brilliant businessman and could make money from any country in the world. All they had to do was let him go, and he'd go away quietly and nobody would ever know. He seemed to think, in offering to leave the country, he was offering something that anyone would think was of value and that his presence here would be missed. If they accepted his very generous offer, they would all benefit and everyone would live happily ever after.

Like a good agent, I went over his story several times, to make sure I got it right and there were no contradictions or unanswered questions. When I was done, Fearless and Mr. Mafia looked at each other and nodded, apparently satisfied we had the truth, the whole truth, and nothing worse than Marino's self-serving embellishment of the truth.

Marino sat, despondent, alternately crying and whimpering, already suffering in the hell he'd made for himself. He had committed vile acts of evil for money and a woman, and he'd ended up with neither.

Mr. Mafia leaned over to speak to Fearless. "You wouldn't take the boss's word for it, so we got you Marino. Now you heard it straight from him, delivered by an FBI agent no less, here where the woman and kids were held. You satisfied you got the whole picture now?"

"Yeah," she answered.

Mr. Mafia got up, walked over to Marino, and shot him right between the eyes. Then he shot him again. A life ended, simple as that, and business done with. *And where the offense is, let the great axe fall,* I couldn't help thinking. Marino had been right about one thing, though: he didn't get the bullet in the back of the head.

There's always some blowback in a shooting, and Mr. Mafia and I were close enough to get some of Marino's blood and brain fluid on us. Mr. Mafia took his silk handkerchief out of his breast pocket and wiped his face as nonchalantly as if he'd just blown his nose. Then he turned to Fearless and said, "Canino, the Turk, and the rest of the crew are already taken care of, and you got the papers signed for the money. Now you got Marino, just like you wanted. You satisfied with everything now?"

"Yeah," she answered again.

I guessed it was my turn next.

Mr. Mafia walked over to me, put his gun to my head, and said to Fearless, "We're done with this jamook. Do I take care of him, or do you still want him?"

Fearless said, "Leave him to us."

Mr. Mafia decocked his pistol and holstered. "Since you wanted it all done here, it'll be up to you to clean up the mess. We delivered on our end of the deal, so we're out of it now," he said and left.

Fearless and I sat looking at Marino's lifeless body, and I wondered if Marino could ever have imagined his life would end like this. She remarked, "You've just seen justice delivered in its purest and best form."

"How do you figure that?" I asked.

"If a truly good and innocent man is tasked to serve justice, that man will carry the guilt of it with him for the rest of his life precisely because he is a good and innocent man. If a crusader like you serves justice, there's always the element of self-righteousness or revenge, which taints the act of justice. But when an evil man exacts justice upon another evil man, the evil man gets exactly what he deserves, without the act of justice being tainted or harming the good man."

Yes, there are times when even justice brings harm, as Sophocles said, but I didn't think this was the situation he'd had in mind. "That's a very philosophical and eloquent way to rationalize murder," I answered.

"Hypocrite," Fearless responded.

She was right about me again, and again I didn't like it.

We heard Mr. Mafia and his men leave the building and the big doors roll closed behind them. The gorilla came into the room and confirmed the Italians were gone.

I got up and turned my chair to face Fearless. "You promised me all the answers. Are you going to tell me what the hell is going on here?" I asked her.

"A deal was made to avoid a war and the disclosure of damaging information. My people wanted the full story, the return of all the money, and the lives of those who were responsible for the kidnapping. The Italians wanted a guarantee that it would go no further than Canino and that all else would be forgotten," she answered.

"How very businesslike... I'm surprised they agreed to return the money."

"It didn't cost them a penny of their own. They transferred an interest in the Las Vegas project with a value equal to the ransom, paid to a partnership of private investors—my people. We both got into the Vegas project, which we couldn't have done otherwise, and without it costing either of us a penny. It'll bring us both millions every year for many years to come."

"It cost several people their lives, including one completely innocent woman. And her two children will be scarred for life."

"The children will get on with their lives. Real life isn't a fairy tale existence for anyone."

"That seems rather cold, especially coming from a woman."

Fearless looked me straight in the eye. "I was a nineteen-year-old soldier on routine patrol duty in Tel Aviv when I saw a busload of Israeli schoolchildren blown to bits by a Palestinian IED. Seeing tiny arms and legs strewn all over the street forms callouses on one's heart. It also gave me a reason to do what I must do with my life."

We had both seen too much too early in our lives to have any illusions about humanity. And, although our interactions had been few and unpleasant, I couldn't help feeling sorry for her because of that. Perhaps it was just my paternalistic chauvinism, but I wanted women to have some illusions.

I sipped some water and reached into my shirt pocket for a cigarette. Lighting it wasn't so easy with my wrists still in handcuffs. "Well, so much for sentimentality. What do you plan to do with me?" I asked Fearless. The gorilla snorted, smiled, and looked hopeful.

"That's up to you. Your guardian angel can't help you anymore. But if you agree to do a few things for us, you get to live. If you refuse or screw things up, you die. I hope you make the right choice. I'd hate to have to kill someone I knew so little but was beginning to like."

The gorilla sneered. "Why waste time with this *mamzer*? Let me have him. I won't have to waste a bullet on him."

"Your gorilla is anxious to get rid of me, and you seem to have everything under control. What could you possibly need from me at this point?" I wondered out loud.

"We still need more information from you. And we need you to sell a story for us. A false ending to a sad tale. One that will tie up all loose ends and bring an end to all the questions."

"Meaning exactly what?"

"First, we need to know what you were talking about when you told Marino about Aron Ginsberg's involvement in two murders."

"I didn't say Ginsberg was involved, only that he had information about two murders. I just threw that out to get Marino's attention and deliver a message to Ginsberg."

"You're lying and making it difficult to let you live."

"Damn right," the gorilla said and snorted again.

I stood up again and faced the gorilla, flicking my cigarette at him. "You won't find me such an easy punching bag without the other two stooges holding me back."

"Nobody hits me and gets away with it," he growled as he stepped toward me. "I'm gonna tear you apart with my bare hands."

"When I hit you, you'll take it and like it," I answered. I've always wanted to use Spade's line—my favorite. I wondered if I'd live long enough to brag about it.

"Enough macho posturing!" Fearless commanded us both.

I sat down and got back to the question at hand. "As far as those two murders go, I never said he was involved. I only told Marino that Ginsberg *might* have information relevant to the motives for those murders. I'm sure you know more about Aron Ginsberg's proclivities than I do. If the Santa Monica Police Department doesn't believe he was involved in the murders of the boy and his pimp, I don't see any reason to make any of that affair public."

"What else do you know about Ginsberg's proclivities and that *affair*, as you call it?"

I thought fast. "Not much. I only learned about those murders after I followed up on what Ginsberg's secretary—former secretary—told me. And she only came to me because you and your gorilla scared the crap out of her. She didn't know who Ginsberg was seeing or if that person and your visit had anything to do with the kidnapping. She did know I was still investigating the kidnapping and wanted me to know about Ginsberg and your visit." I had to lie. What, I should tell the Jews about the Iranians and start another war?

"Why would she want you to know about any of that?"

"You saw her—she's a pathetic old maid. She'd been secretly in love with Ginsberg for years and had delusions about the two of them running off together. And she cared greatly about Rachael and the children. Part of her delusion was that she'd be accepted as their loving stepmother and grandmother someday. She was concerned for them all and wanted me to do whatever I could for them, despite your threats."

Fearless nodded. "That's just crazy enough to possibly be true."

"It's true, all right. Love makes fools of us all. Just look at what it did to Marino… What else is on your mind?" I asked, wanting to get off that subject as quickly as possible.

"We need you to be Richard Marino tonight. You and he look remarkably alike. You'll put on his clothes and be seen carrying his personalized overnight bag onto his cabin cruiser at the yacht harbor. There's only one old night watchman there. He spends the night sipping cheap whiskey and is usually pretty well soused by two a.m., if he's even still awake.

"Marino is on the board of directors and a major contributor to the yacht club, so he has his own set of keys and comes and goes as he pleases. He's been known to take his *shiksas* on late-night cruises, so it won't be unusual for him to be seen arriving there in the middle of the night. You'll pass by the night watchman's little office on the marina, wearing Marino's captain's hat low over your face, and wave at him. Let him see the bag with Marino's name stitched on it. Hopefully, the watchman will be soused enough not to notice that you're not Marino, but not so soused as to forget to make an entry in his activity log that Marino came to the marina that night.

"You'll go to Marino's cabin cruiser, where we'll have a man waiting. He'll take the boat out and meet up with another boat at sea. You'll get on that other boat. Marino's body will be dumped overboard, and his boat scuttled. Neither Marino or his boat will ever be found."

"Why would I help you with that when I know getting on that boat would only make it easier for you to get rid of two bodies?" I asked.

Fearless smiled. "Don't worry. We need you to sell the rest of the story we want told."

"What story is that?"

"Tomorrow morning, Marino's secretary will find a typewritten suicide note on his desk in his office. The Italians couldn't get him to handwrite it or sign it, but his fingerprints are all over the paper. That should be enough to sell it as genuine. The night watchman will verify that Marino took his boat out in the middle of the night. You're going to tell your friends at the FBI and your reporter friend, Curtis, that Marino came to your office tonight, that he was despondent and suicidal about the exhumation of his wife's body and the news that she was pregnant. You'll say he threatened to commit suicide."

"Why would he come to me?" I asked as I had a sip of water then got another cigarette and lit it. "Everyone will want to know."

"That's a disgusting and unhealthy habit. I'm surprised anyone with your brains would smoke so much," Fearless said.

"It's nice to know you're concerned about my health."

Fearless smiled again. "You'll say Marino came to you because he knew you'd been investigating the kidnapping and had suspicions about his possible involvement. His secretary will confirm all that, as well as the fact that he'd been away from his office for days, which will further establish his despondence. You'll say Marino wanted you to know that he loved his wife and children and didn't have anything to do with the kidnapping. He wanted you to make sure everyone knew that. Then he said he had other people to see and things to do. He had a gun and said he'd shoot you, if you tried to follow him."

"Okay, that sounds plausible."

"That will be enough to close the door on Marino. You'll also tell the FBI and Curtis and anyone else who'll listen that your investigation of the kidnapping couldn't come up with any suspects after the Turk disappeared, so you couldn't be sure who was responsible for the kidnapping. Since the FBI hasn't been able to come up with anything different, that'll be enough to close the file on the official investigation."

"Don't the Ginsbergs deserve to know the truth? All of it?"

"They've already gotten more than they deserve. And they're better off not knowing the whole truth. It would be too painful and leave things unsettled for them. Leaving the Ginsbergs and the public believing the trail ends with the Turk provides a sufficiently satisfying explanation that everyone can live with."

My despondence must've been palpable. Fearless offered this. "If it makes you feel any better, you should know that Aron Ginsberg will be retiring soon. We're sick of cleaning up after him, so he had to go, one way or another. We gave him and Magda a choice. Either they could go out on a high note, or the Palestinians would come after them again. They were smart and chose retirement. Aron Ginsberg will be given an extravagant retirement dinner, which will be attended by the elite of Los Angeles and covered by the media. He and Magda will announce a scholarship to USC in their daughter's name. They will then act surprised when the new bank chairman announces that the bank will endow the Aron and Magda Ginsberg Chair for Jewish Studies at USC. So, the Ginsbergs will leave with their reputations not only unblemished but enhanced, and they'll go on to their comfortable retirement and see their sons and grandchildren flourish."

I nodded. "That's nice for them, but if I do all you want, how do I know I won't have a fatal accident in a few months?"

"That won't be necessary. If you do what's asked, you'll be an aider and abettor to murder, an accomplice after the fact, and will have made several false statements to the FBI. You're looking at twenty years in prison, and that's where you'll have your fatal accident, if you don't keep your mouth shut. You'll live as long as you keep my people and the Italians out of it."

She stood to go and then added, "Besides, you have your own reasons to keep quiet. Given your sense of ethics, I don't think you want *all* the truth to come out. It would hurt too many people."

Chapter 63

Richard Marino – Deceased

Y ou're all bastards...

Chapter 64

Teachings of the Master

I did my part, and everyone bought the story. The kidnapping had been resolved to the extent it would ever be, and everyone involved was as satisfied with the resolution as they could ever be. My work was done.

But not all of it. There were still some questions bouncing around my brain like marbles in a pinball machine that just couldn't find the right hole to drop into. I knew the questions would continue to bang around in there until I got my own answers.

Question number one was simple: why was I still alive? It would've been in the best interests of several of the parties involved for me to be dead. The old adage, "Dead men tell no tales," remains as valid as ever. So why was I left alive to talk when killing me could've been accomplished so easily?

Question number two was harder to deal with: who is Alison Grayle? She's apparently connected to Florian, but how *exactly* does she fit into this mess?

I was staring out the office window late one morning when Jack came in and caught me deep in thought. He asked about my pensive mood, and I told him what I'd been thinking about.

"Grab your fedora and let's go," Jack said. "There's only one place in L.A. to have the adult version of the birds-and-bees talk."

With that, we were off to Musso & Frank and the first of several extra-dry martinis.

"Unfortunately, thanks to a bunch of third-rate novelists and directors, this place has become a hangout for yuppies, hipsters, and wanna-be-seen-here-sters. Be that as it may, there's still no better martini west of the Carlyle," Jack said as he took his first sip. "I feel sorry for your generation. You and those who come after you will never know the sublimity of a perfect martini while listening to Bobby Short."

"Tell me about it."

"That's just it. You can't tell about it. It's magical—something you have to experience. I should say *was* magical. It's different now. Bemelmans Bar in the Carlyle is still nice, but not quite the same. Anything could happen back then. You expected the unexpected. That's why you went there. One of the reasons, anyway. I was having a drink there one night, and Sinatra came over and asked me if he was being investigated again and if I was tailing him. He recognized me because I had interviewed him a couple of times, and the last time was just a few weeks before, in connection with a case that wasn't going anywhere. I tried to convince him I was on vacation, and there was no investigation that I knew of. I had to get Bobby to vouch for me that I was a frequent visitor there, and then we had a couple of drinks. Sinatra ended up apologizing and gave me his number in Palm Springs. Invited me for lunch."

"Did you go?"

"When the Chairman of the Board invites you, you don't refuse. Those were grand times, my boy. Not like now. You can't even have one drink on duty these days. The Bureau is run by a bunch of pencil-weenie, momma's-boy, bureaucrat geeks who've taken all the fun out of the job. But enough about me. Now then, my boy, what exactly is on your mind?"

"Well, for starters, I've had a strange feeling ever since I got out of prison and began working the kidnapping. I knew I was being followed, but that didn't bother me too much. What did trouble me was that I felt someone was watching over me and I was being manipulated somehow. I've been beaten up and had guns pointed at me a few times, but there were times when I could've been hurt a lot worse or killed. I don't know why I wasn't. It would've been just as easy for them to handle it that way, and their problem would've gone away. A few of those times, someone mentioned that my guardian angel was looking out for me. I thought they were just using an old phrase—*guardian angel*—but now I'm not so sure. Maybe there really was someone looking out for me without me knowing about it."

"So, you want to know if you really did have a guardian angel protecting you, who it was, and why they were doing it?"

"Yeah."

"Who do you think it could've been?" he asked.

"I don't know. I'm not important enough to know anyone who has that kind of pull. And what's even more sad, I don't know anyone who likes me that much."

"Your problem is you can't see the trees for the forest," Jack said. "You're too close to the answer to see it. It's right in front of your nose."

"I'm going to need a lot more of these martinis for that to make sense," I replied as I took a sip.

Jack's expression became thoughtful. "Bart told me a lot about you when he asked me to bring you into the office. Although he could never get you to talk about it, he told me what he'd found out about your military record and how you'd saved his life twice. He thinks very highly of you, and when a man like Bart thinks highly of someone, that's as good a recommendation as there is."

"Bart thinks very highly of you, too."

Jack took a deep breath and let out a long, slow sigh. "I was a good agent in my day, but good is all I ever was. I made up for my lack of skill by working harder than most. Bart, on the other hand, is the real deal. He knows what he's doing and does it right. He says you're even better."

"Bart's been known to exaggerate."

"No, no. Don't be modest. He's got a keen eye for people. I've never known anyone who could read people better than Bart. He said you're the best man he's ever known, but he also said your best attributes as a man were also your biggest deficiencies as an investigator, and maybe as a man, as well."

"I've no idea where you're going with this," I said.

"Your sense of integrity, your sense of honor, your sense of right and wrong… Bart said, with you, it's always all or nothing, black or white. But that's not the way life is. In the dark, all cats are gray, and in this life, it's always midnight. Even the worst of people have a little honor and integrity in them, and even the best of people are a little corrupt and immoral. Until you learn to look for the good in the bad and the bad in the good, you'll never see the whole picture, the real picture, and you'll never be a great investigator. More important, you'll never see people as they really are, and you can't be a real man, a humane man, until you do. I say *humane* because, when you do find some bad in a good man, you'll see it's not really so bad, and maybe not bad all. That's something you have to know before you can accept people for who they are."

"Now you've really lost me. Maybe I've already had too much to drink."

Jack looked disappointed by my ignorance and spelled it out for me. "Stop thinking of the bad guys as bad guys and the good guys as good guys. You have a good mind. Apply all the curiosity and discernment your mind is capable of on the good guys as well as on the bad guys, and try to see things from their point of view. You don't have to agree with it or accept it, but you'll be surprised at what you can learn about the world."

We had another martini as we ate lunch and another one after lunch. I asked Jack for more of his experiences as an agent and DA's investigator, and he regaled me with stories involving some of the most well-known people in L.A., tales I wouldn't have believed if I'd heard them from someone other than a man like Jack. His stories made his point about people and the world not being as simple as black and white, with a good deal of irony and comedy thrown in the mix: A well-liked former mayor who did a lot of good for the city but had a penchant for cheap prostitutes—and the uglier the better. A revered actress with a long and distinguished career who would've made Messalina seem like a cloistered nun. Etcetera, etcetera.

Jack finished his storytelling and got serious for a moment. "I answered your question as best I could," he said. "Now, I'd like to ask you a question. Bart told me you were quite the Latin Lover. So, why haven't you taken Maria to your bed?"

I hesitated. Normally, I wouldn't answer such a question with anything other than a fist to the nose. Maybe it was the martinis. Maybe I felt I owed him an answer for all he'd done for me. Maybe I knew he was asking because he was a wise man whose question would make me think about things I wouldn't otherwise think about.

"I've seen Maria grow a lot, thanks to the chance you've given her. I think she can make something of herself and have a good life. But I've known too many Latinos who never had a chance to get out of the barrio. I don't want to do anything that might hold her back."

"A roll in your hay wouldn't necessarily hurt her chances."

"She's been through a lot, but anyone can see she's never been in love. She's never had her heart broken. I don't want to be the first one to do that to her."

"Do you think you're so wonderful that a woman couldn't recover from the pain of losing you?"

"Not at all. Women have found me easy to forget, I'm sure. I just don't think a woman could be friends with the first man who broke her heart… I like Maria. I'd like us to be friends."

"Interesting," Jack said. He stared into the depths of his martini as if staring into a crystal ball. "If I were a gambling man, I'd bet that someday she'll break your heart, in one way or another."

We went back to our drinking, smoking, talking, and laughing. All the while, I couldn't help thinking in the back of my mind about who could be responsible for me not getting whacked to eliminate a problem in a very simple way, and I tried to see things differently, as Jack suggested.

I realized that, although I had never thought of myself as an adherent of Manichaean Dualism, my good-versus-evil outlook must seem very narrow-minded and naïve to people as worldly and wise as Jack and Bart, and certainly Magda. Maybe it was just that fifth martini, but I did begin to see things differently, and a new picture of the world emerged, one that clearly revealed that what I had failed to see had been right in front of me all along.

Chapter 65

The Deposition

I drove Jack home, and then I went home to sleep off lunch. The picture of the world that had begun to appear during Jack's lesson was completed as I slept—it's amazing what dreams reveal. When I awoke, I called Bart and arranged to meet him later that evening. After we dry cleaned, we met at the parking garage by the Santa Monica Promenade. We were both tired of sitting in bars and garages, so we walked along the Promenade.

"Will you be leaving the Bureau now, old man?" I asked after lighting up, as usual.

"Yeah. I've done everything I was ever gonna do in the Bureau. No point in sticking around, especially since I don't have to worry about you causing any more trouble."

"Have you decided what you'll do when the Bureau finally kicks you out?"

"I plan to tear up the turf at every first-class golf course in the world," he replied. "The ones that'll let me in, anyway."

"Remember to send postcards," I said.

"What about you? Norton, Brunette, and Rolfe all seem satisfied now that the kidnapping is as done as it's ever gonna be and won't get in the way of their next promotions. You don't have to worry about the grand jury anymore. You can practice law now. It's a lot safer than being an agent or private dick. And I hear there's big bucks in it, that is if Señor Quixote can stand to get his conscience a little dirty now and then."

"I haven't decided yet. I'll let things percolate for a while before I decide what to do. And although the kidnapping investigation is done with, there's still one last piece of the puzzle to put in place."

"Like what? I thought all the loose ends were tied up."

"Well, I promised to tell you everything I found out, including things no one else knows about."

"You don't have to explain anything to me. But if you're gonna tell all, don't you think Jason deserves to be here? After all, he did contribute a lot to the investigation."

"I don't think you'd want Jason or anyone else to hear what I have to say."

"What do you mean?"

"I mean, I know why I don't need to explain anything to you. There's no need to explain anything to someone who already has all the answers. Someone who knew what was going on from the beginning."

Bart remained poker-faced and didn't say anything, so I continued.

"There was only one person who knew everything I was finding out about the kidnapping as I went along with my investigation. That same person had the brains and experience to figure out things I may not have even told him about. That person must also have known things I didn't know and, for reasons of his own, chose to be a guardian angel and save me from getting whacked by people who could've easily done it, people who would've been better off if I were dead. There's only one way that person could've known those things."

I continued to stare at Bart, but he remained silent, so I went on. "For that person to be in that position—to know those things and be in that position of power—he'd have to be connected to some very important and dirty people. He'd have had to be in the dirt up to his neck himself, and for a long time." I stared at Bart and waited for him to respond.

Bart finally spoke. "It's not that simple. Haven't I always told you the world isn't black and white? Haven't I always told you that you have to be practical and deal with the world as it is, dirty and corrupt and messy, and not how you want to believe it is? I learned to swim in the dirty water like everybody else. I don't try to walk on top of the dirty water, like you do."

"You were always honest about that."

"I deal with the real world on its terms, not a fairy-tale, comic-book, make-believe version of it, like you do. And I never put myself up on a pedestal or pretended to be a hero. That was all in your head."

The disappointment on my face must've been evident. Bart continued to explain. "I knew Vincenzo Florian way back when he was just Vinnie Florian, working his way up the mafia ladder, and I was just a green GS-

10 rookie agent. Because of the nature of our work, we crossed paths several times. For some strange reason that neither of us could understand, we just got along, but we knew we could never be what regular people would call friends or have a normal friendship."

We passed by a Starbucks and Bart said, "Let's get some coffee. I got a feeling we're gonna need it."

We got our overpriced caffeine, lit up again, and walked as Bart continued with his story.

"He started to pass along information to me for no reason. Information that couldn't be verified in any way but was always one-hundred-percent accurate. It was information that could be used to start an investigation or steer an investigation in the right direction or just to put the screws to the right person and get him to talk. His information was usually historical, after the fact. And it was information about everything, not just the mafia. Keep in mind, the mafia is like the CIA and FBI—they have people everywhere and pick up bits and pieces of information about all sorts of shit. Street punks, cops, judges, lawyers, politicians, actors, movie moguls, diplomats, housewives—you name it, they all talk to the mafia when they have to, just like they talk to us when they have to."

"He never asked for anything in return?" I asked.

"He didn't have to. A lot of the information he gave me served to eliminate his rivals and enemies, sometimes directly and sometimes just by making them look bad. A wise guy who gets arrested or who can't earn and kick up to the boss gets stepped on and stepped over. The only thing Florian asked was that I never reveal his name, and I agreed to that. I used him like an unofficial, hip-pocket informant. That's why I didn't have a problem when you wouldn't give up your source about the kidnapping. I understood that. Some things are sacred and you just don't fuck with."

"I find it hard to believe you never did anything for him," I said. "Things just don't work that way."

"He was a valuable source of information, and I did protect him once or twice by telling him to stay out of some things, but that was it. And I told him on the condition that he not interfere with the investigation. But don't get the wrong impression. At first, we only connected four or five times a year, and after he became a captain, only two or three times a year. It wasn't like we confided in each other on a regular basis. It wouldn't have been safe to meet too often. It was only when he had something important for me or when I needed him to fill in the gaps on an investigation. Even then, he only said what was absolutely necessary and nothing more. Sometimes, we couldn't help each other, and we understood that. We also understood, if the shit ever hit the fan, we'd each do what we had to do—and we knew what that meant."

"So, when did you find out the truth about the kidnapping and who was really behind it?"

"Not until you got out of prison and started pissing people off. We all bought that it was the Palestinians, remember? I was all set to retire, and then Florian called me and said he had something important to talk about. He invited me for a round of golf at Torrey Pines, down in La Jolla. He's a member and can play there whenever he wants. We've met there several times over the years. It's the only way I could ever get in there.

"Anyway, he knew you'd find out sooner or later that it was his people who pulled off the kidnapping, if you didn't get whacked first. We talked about how to handle the situation between holes, and we made our deal. He wasn't worried about you finding out it was his people, because he was insulated and had a way out for himself. In fact, he wanted you to find out about Canino as soon as the money was laundered and made legit, so he could get rid of Canino before Canino got rid of him. His only concern was that he had to know when you were gonna make your move against Canino. He needed to know in advance, to protect himself. The only way to do that was for me to stay in the Bureau and keep watch on you."

"So, if you knew it was Canino, why didn't you go after him yourself? You could've been the big hero and retired in a blaze of glory."

"When did I ever care about glory or being the hero? And I didn't know it was Canino behind the kidnapping until you told me. Like I said, Florian always told me as little as possible and only what was absolutely necessary. It was safer for both of us that way. All he said was it was his people behind the kidnapping—that one of his captains came up with the idea and ran the operation.

"Besides, I couldn't be the one to nail Canino, because it would've raised questions about how I came by the information to go after him. There wasn't anything to connect him or any mafioso to the kidnapping. In order for Florian and me to be safely in the clear of any suspicions, it had to look like someone outside the mafia and FBI had figured it out and gone after him. It was risky enough just asking for that telephone information you wanted, but I was able to pass that off as just routine follow-up. Even after the connection was made between Marino and Edward Hawkins, and Edward Hawkins and Canino, there was still no way to connect Marino directly with Canino. You were the only one who could make that connection, and, for some reason, you didn't want anyone else to know why, did you?"

"I have my reasons."

"It doesn't matter to me what those reasons are, but you can understand now why it had to be you to go after Canino. Since you'd already started causing trouble, you were the perfect candidate for the job."

"The perfect fool, you mean."

"Señor Quixote was made to order for this one."

We sat on a bench and watched the movie theater crowd come and go as we sipped our coffee. I thought about what Bart had told me and asked, "So, after you drove me back to my office from the federal building, you went to Florian and told him I was going to confront Canino and put the screws to him?"

"He was keeping his part of the deal, so I had to keep mine," Bart said.

"I don't understand. What was his part of the deal? What did he promise that was so important to you?"

"He promised that the Bureau would have its fall guy and that my best friend wouldn't get whacked, no matter who he pissed off."

I stared at him for a few seconds.

Bart answered my stare and said, "The way I see it, if a man saves your life once, you owe him your life. If he saves your life twice, you owe him *his* life. We're even now."

Although I never felt Bart owed me anything, I understood what he meant. I nodded, and Bart continued.

"It actually turned out better than Florian expected, since, the way you handled it, the trail ended with the Turk as far as the Bureau and the public are concerned. Like I said, he didn't care if you figured out his people were behind the kidnapping. He needed you to, but he needed to know when you were ready to go after Canino, so he could take care of him and put a stop to the investigation right there, with him. He didn't care if you got both Marino and Canino, so long as you fingered Canino for the kidnapping, and it ended there."

"He wanted to take care of them himself, you mean. Have them killed before they could talk."

"It's not like either of them is a great loss to the world. If they both had been arrested and tried in court for all their crimes, they both would've been convicted on all counts and would've deserved the death penalty. That's assuming you didn't kill them yourself first. Florian did you a favor by doing them before you had a chance to get yourself charged with two counts of murder."

"I'm supposed to be grateful?"

"You're supposed to see that it worked out for the best for all concerned, under the circumstances."

"The best for all concerned? In view of all the people who've been hurt, you'll have to explain that to me."

"Okay, I will," he said, as annoyed with me as Jack and Magda had been. "Start by accepting the fact that there's evil in the world and bad things happen to good people. Innocent people like Rachael Ginsberg and her children have bad things happen to them. It's done by people like Marino and Canino. Those two got what they deserved. You got to keep your informant out of it and go on jousting with windmills. And you managed to solve the kidnapping and murder, even though the FBI got the credit for it and pricks like Norton, Brunette, and Rolfe get promoted. Florian gets the benefit of Marino's L.A. and Vegas projects for himself and his partners and the millions in legitimate income they'll bring them in the future. His choice for successor gets to take over the L.A. business, and his daughter makes partner in her firm."

"Wait, wait." I needed this crystal clear for my own peace of mind. "Spell it out for me. Who exactly are Florian's successor and daughter?"

"I'd have thought you'd figured that out by now. Florian's choice of successor is Michael Sachetti, and his daughter is Alison Grayle."

I stared at Bart and then shook my head, stunned yet again—but it all made sense now. We got up and continued talking as we walked.

"Florian wanted Sachetti to take over because Sachetti was the only L.A. captain who wouldn't try to force him out and who'd even offered to protect him in retirement. But Canino was a big earner and too well-connected with the wise guys back East for Florian to show any favoritism, especially since Sachetti is known to have a bad temper and fly off the handle and do stupid things, like beat up his girlfriend and that loan shark that got him sent to prison.

"Florian promised to help Sachetti, but he couldn't help him openly. All he could do was give Canino enough rope to hang himself. Since

Sachetti was in prison, he had to let Canino handle Marino and the kidnapping. But Florian was smart and cut Sachetti in on a piece of his action on the kidnap on the q.t., just to give Sachetti a stake in the project and keep him from going after Canino until after it was all over. The last thing Florian wanted was to have two of his captains going to war while he was trying to feather his own nest.

"When the kidnapping was over and done with, Florian let Canino take the credit for the kidnap and brag about it to all the other made guys and pay out the tribute to the other bosses. He told Sachetti to make friends with the Turk on the q.t. and tell him to claim he was the real brains behind the kidnap and demand more of the ransom from Canino. He knew that would be enough to light Canino's fuse."

I felt a wave of nausea as if I'd been punched in the gut again. Sachetti had manipulated me and done a great job of it. I had swallowed his cliché-spewing, mafia goombah routine hook, line, and sinker, as he would say with a laugh—telling me just enough to be believable, just enough to point me in the right direction, and just enough to keep me doing his bidding.

"Fortunately for Florian and Sachetti, you came along, and Canino was too greedy for his own good and not smart enough to protect himself when the shit hit the fan. Or should I say, when Quixote hit the windmill?"

"*Hmph*," I scoffed as Bart laughed, shaking my head and angry at myself. I didn't see anything funny in my having been played.

"When Canino became witness protection program material, the other bosses had to let Florian get rid of him. All the capos are old men. They want their Metamucil and comfortable slippers by their bed and the soft butt of a twenty-year-old bimbo under the sheets to keep them warm. No capo wants to die old and sick in prison, which is where they would've been, if Canino had been allowed to sing."

"And there was only one way the bosses could've known I was on to Canino and was going to approach him with the chance to get into the witness protection program even before Canino himself did."

"Yeah, but don't be so angry about it or for the way things turned out. Try looking at it a different way."

"Which is?"

"To the mafiosos, it was all just business, nothing personal. You're the one that was on a personal quest for justice, whatever that is. They got what they were gonna get anyway. You just helped move things along.

And this way, it saved your dumb ass and the taxpayer a lot of money, don't you think?"

"Yeah, right... What about that second grand jury subpoena that was never issued? Did Florian have anything to do with that?" I asked.

"If you don't know, I sure don't. Florian never mentioned anything about that, and I didn't expect him to. You're the lawyer, what do you think?"

"I don't know. DOJ and the U.S. Attorney's Office have guidelines covering second subpoenas to recalcitrant witnesses, but that wouldn't have stopped them. Somebody must've put the brakes on it. Does Florian have someone in the USA's Office with the power to stop a subpoena from being issued? It would have to be someone high up."

"I wouldn't be surprised if he did, and it makes sense. You couldn't have done what you did if you were back in jail for contempt. He needed you out, digging up dirt and pissing people off, to get the goods on Canino. Which means, if you decide to practice criminal law or stick with being a private dick, you'll have to be careful who you deal with in the USA's Office and who you piss off."

We finished our coffee, tossed our cups, and continued our walk. I took a deep breath and hesitated before asking the next question. I wasn't sure I wanted to know the answer. "What about Alison Grayle?"

"She's Florian's illegitimate daughter. She may be a bastard child, but he loves her like crazy. Always has, for some reason—go figure, Mr. Psychology Major. She's just another bastard kid from one of his mistresses, but he took a shine to her since the day she was born.

"The funny thing is, he doesn't even know if she's really his kid. The mother wasn't exactly the Immaculate Virgin, and he's never asked for a DNA test. But none of that's ever mattered to him or stopped him from doing all he could for her." Bart shrugged and shook his head. "I guess she just brought out the daddy in him. She's always been special to him and had the best of everything. Nannies to take care of her and the best private schools, college, and grad school. When she was little, he even hired— What's that word for those special nannies from other countries?"

"Au pair?"

"Yeah, that's it. He hired a bunch of them and bragged about how they taught her to speak four languages by the time she was twelve, and how she'd been all over the world a dozen times before she even went to college. He pulled the strings to get her a job at that big investment firm and promised her the L.A. and Vegas accounts, too, once the deals were done and laundered clean. With the money managing those accounts will mean to her firm, she'll make partner and be set for life… By the way, you should be proud of yourself. Florian wasn't sure he could count on Alison to handle you. He wasn't sure she liked men, but, apparently, she goes both ways or made an exception for you."

I wasn't feeling very proud. I'd have to think about that one. "He's very enlightened and accepting, for a mob boss," I said.

"Her *orientation* came as a shock to him, at first, and nearly ended their relationship, but he had to accept it when she told him it was all his fault. She said he'd warned her about men, alcohol, and drugs but never about women."

We both laughed. "Yeah, that sounds like Alison… What about the Mossad? Who's your friend there?" I lit another cigarette and offered Bart one, but he shook it off.

"I don't have a friend in the Mossad. All I know about that is what Sol Abrams gave me on the Iranian FCI angle. At first, he said he couldn't give me a name, because he didn't want an FBI agent making direct contact with the Iranians. He was afraid it would blow years of investigation. I told him about you, and he said it would be dangerous for you to go digging into the top-level Iranians. He said the Iranians, the Mossad, and a half dozen U.S. government agencies would be all over your ass. But apparently, you managed to get the Iranians to point you in the right direction without getting your ass in a ringer or blown away. And then you really stirred the shit when you started digging into the Ginsbergs and the bank and looking into things that had nothing to do with the kidnapping."

"It was all tied into the kidnapping," I said.

"Well, I don't know what you found out, but whatever it was is what really brought the big boys down on you. Maybe it was the Mossad who put pressure on the lawyers to stop the U.S. Attorney's Office from issuing another subpoena for your ass. You knew too much, and they could've been afraid of what you might say in front of the grand jury."

I nodded—that possibility also made sense.

"Apparently, the Ginsbergs and the Mossad are connected, but I don't know why or how, and I don't wanna know. Even Florian was afraid of what was going on there, and that's why he told me more of the story after the Bureau's press conference, when it was clear the kidnapping was as resolved as it was ever going to be. He wanted me to know things had gotten beyond his control and he couldn't protect you anymore.

"Sol's a smart guy and must've figured it out, or someone told him what was going on or what you were up to. That's probably why he helped with that doctor's name and with keeping you out of trouble. But it was the kind of trouble I couldn't help you with like I could with Florian. Sol came to me and said you'd gotten into shit that was beyond Top Secret, and you were close to having a fatal accident or being made to disappear without a trace. Each game is played according to its own rules, he said, and you'd gone beyond a criminal investigation and into spy-versus-spy, so there were different rules. He said he'd do what he could to keep you alive, if I kept him informed every step of the way. He couldn't help you unless he knew what you were doing and planning to do. He made me promise to stop you from doing anything stupid, like pissing off the Agency or Mossad. But he couldn't guarantee anything, because the Mossad had their own marching orders and would deal with you in their own way. I guess you managed to stay on their good side."

"So, is Abrams working for the Mossad?"

Bart sighed, looked me in the eye, and shook his head, *very* annoyed with me now. "Sometimes, you really disappoint me, Mig. You still don't get it, do you? It's not all one way or the other. After all this time and all you've seen, all you've been told, you still think it's all either black or white. The world doesn't work that way…"

I shrugged, admitting my ignorance.

"To answer your question directly, I don't think Sol is a Mossad agent or informant. He probably gets and gives information on the q.t. as the need arises for him to do his job. Could he be charged with espionage? Maybe, but that would be a mistake for all concerned. He's walking on that razor's edge, like I was. I trust him to have his priorities in order and do the right thing, like giving us the right name and doing what he could to keep your sorry ass alive."

Hard to argue with Thoreau, especially since I'd been marching to my own drummer lately and not playing by the rules. And impossible to disagree with Sartre, as the events of the last year had proved there was no man more courageous than a man who made his own choices and lived a life of moral heroism in a world of moral meaninglessness and chaos… A man like Bart, who believed that giving his all and doing his best was what he owed the world.

I doubted if Bart thought of himself as a hero or an Existentialist. He just did what he believed was right, regardless of the danger, cost, or any other consideration, and he was ready to accept the consequences, whatever they might be.

"So, what do *you* get for thirty years of walking on that razor's edge?" I asked.

"Same as any other agent. I get to retire and collect my pension. I get to know that I did some good in the real world when I could, like keeping my idealistic partner from getting his dumb ass blown away by any of the dozens of people he'd pissed off on his quest for something that doesn't exist."

Chapter 66

Farewell, My Lovely

I drove home looking forward to sipping Scotch and listening to Bach while contemplating the events of the last year and drifting off to sleep. I now understood most of what had happened and why. But the more I thought about it, the more I realized there was still more to the story. There remained many unexplained acts and omissions, and none of the people involved could be trusted to have told me the whole truth—not even Bart.

My experience had taught me that there were always unanswered questions in every investigation, but my inner voice told me there was more digging to do—and that I had to keep digging for my own good. I understood why I'd been allowed to live to finish my investigation, but that didn't explain everything, and the fact that Mr. Mafia and Fearless Female showed no reluctance to kill me as the case came to its conclusion made me realize my hold on life was tenuous.

I began to drift off to dreamland, finding myself in the Labyrinth, in search of the Innermost Cave of Hidden Truth, where I would find the Holy Grail containing the Magic Elixir that would reveal the Secret Knowledge that would allow me to live long enough to collect Social Security—important now that I no longer had the guarantee of a government pension.

Before I could get very deep into "the Dreamtime," as the Australian Aboriginals called the parallel world of dreams, my phone rang, and I was surprised to hear Alison's voice. I hadn't heard from her for several days. She hadn't called me, and I wasn't about to call her. I was done going after unattainable women, especially after what Bart had told me about this one.

"I didn't expect to hear from you again," I said.

"Why not?"

"Since the kidnapping was resolved to the satisfaction of all the parties that count, I'd assumed your assignment was over, and you wouldn't be bothering with me anymore."

"I wasn't raised to be a whore, you asshole. It's a good thing you're at the other end of a phone call. I'd scratch your eyes out for saying that to me, if you were here."

"So, the kitten has claws."

"Do you always have to be such a sarcastic jerk?"

"It's my nature. Like getting involved with the wrong women."

She gracefully ignored my jibe and took a moment before responding. "Are you busy tonight?" she asked.

"I was just going to look over my fingerprint collection."

"I've missed you. I'd like to see you tonight—if you can be civil."

"Why? Are you going to throw me one last one for old time's sake? Or is there still something more your father needs to find out from me?"

She sighed. "I guess it was a mistake to call you. I'm sorry, for everything. Goodbye—"

"Wait, wait. What did you want? I guess there's no reason not to tell you whatever else you wanted to know at this point."

"I don't want to know anything. I just wanted to see you again."

It was my turn to sigh. I wanted to believe her. I needed to believe her. "Okay. When?"

"I have work I need to finish here at the office. I can be at your place by 10:30, if that's okay."

I told her it was okay, even though I knew it would be painful—I knew I was getting dumped for good. Maybe I should call her back and cancel. Maybe we should meet at a bar or some other public place. I couldn't decide, so I changed the bedsheets instead.

*****

Even after a long day, Alison was just as desirable when she walked in as if it were a dewy spring morning. Her marvelous presence in my rundown shack was as incongruous as a supermodel in a prison camp.

"Would you care for something to eat or drink?" I asked, trying to be civil.

"No. I just want you."

So much for civility and self-restraint...

*****

It was a little after midnight when we took a break for orange juice, and I lit a cigarette, which we shared. "Will this be the last time we see each other?" I asked.

"Yes," she said. "But not for any of the reasons you think."

"Then, why?"

"Because, if I keep seeing you, I'll fall in love with you, and we're just not right for each other. The sexual chemistry is there, obviously, but I wasn't raised to be the wife of a man like you."

"What kind of man is that?"

"A man who believes in things like honor and integrity the way you do."

Rachael had said the same thing to me years ago. I still didn't understand. "I've always thought those were good things."

"Not the way you see the world and your role in it."

"And how is that?"

"You're a knight errant. I told you that before. What you don't realize, Mr. Quixote, is that the real world is a kingdom of knaves. Those imaginary windmills you're always fighting have real villains behind them, and one day, they're going to get you. I wasn't raised to be the dutiful little wife who's willing to wait for that phone call from the police in the middle of the night. Depending on the kind of people you've pissed off at the time, they'll either find your bullet-riddled body in a dark alley or with one shot to the back of the head on the side of the road."

"You don't give me, or us, much of a chance."

"We never had a chance."

"Because of your father? Is he the only reason you came on to me in the first place? And now that he doesn't need anything from me anymore, you're free to dump me and go on with your life?"

"You came on to me, remember? But no, it's not just because of my father. He only asked me to meet you and find out what I could, and only if I wanted to. He already had other people watching you. I could've gotten all I needed from you with just a smile and then strung you along. But after I met you, I really did want to get to know you. And I've come to care about you. A lot."

"How did you know I was going to be at that bar the first night we met?"

"I didn't know. My father's people had been following you. They told him other people had been watching you, too. At least two other groups of people. You were responsible for causing traffic jams all over L.A. His people called him that night, and he called me when you went into the bar. He thought it would be a good place for us to meet, if I wanted to. And if you can be honest, you'll admit I owned your little beastie the first time I smiled at you."

"You're very sure of yourself."

"The only thing I wasn't sure of was if I had the patience to wait for all the losers to get lost before you made your move."

"I'm glad you did wait for me."

"So am I. The things my father and other people said about you made me want to meet you. And when I did, I really liked you from the start, though I expected you to be taller. I've come to like you a lot more since then. A whole lot more."

We were sitting up against the headboard, and I looked away. I took a sip of juice and lit another cigarette. Some might think it awkward if not upsetting to be in bed with a woman who's just told you she couldn't love you for the man you are, but I remembered some philosopher or writer said it's best not to be too comfortable in bed with your lover—it ruins the passion and the surprise.

"Does it have to end now?" I asked, still looking away.

"I told you… if I keep seeing you, I'll fall in love with you… I can't let that happen. The night you spent at my place was bad enough."

"What do you mean? What was so bad about it?"

"The call I made that night was to my father, and I told him what you'd told me. He said he already knew everything, but he was concerned that Canino might get to you before he could deal with him. He asked me to keep you at my place for a few hours, so you would be safe. He knew Canino wouldn't dare come to my place looking for you… I was glad to be able to do something for you, and I wanted you to stay the night anyway. But it was horrible, thinking of what might happen to you." Alison shook her head slowly. "I can't go through that again."

I was stunned. Again.

"I know you think I've had it easy and all handed to me by my father, but that's not true. I've had to work hard to get to where I am. The life I've worked hard for is finally within reach, and I *want* the good life. A suite at the Ritz and chauffeured limos and luxury homes all over the world and private jets to parties with the rich and famous. But you couldn't care less about things like that. All you'll ever need is a quest, and for you, there will always be windmills. I know how it will end for you, and I can't live my life waiting for that to happen." She shook her head slowly, saying, "I can't. I won't."

She was right. Themistocles's advice to women, to choose a man of integrity without money rather than a man with money but no integrity, wouldn't be of any help to me now. Alison may not have been of the *sang royal*, but she was to the manner born. She was a woman who needed *things* as much as she needed to be loved... But love was the only thing I could ever give her...

I tried to picture the kind of man she wanted and didn't like him any more than I liked the man Rachael had given herself to... I could never be that kind of man. Nevertheless, I couldn't help wanting her in my life—eight days a week. I wanted to say her name fifty times a day and have her come to me every time I called her name... If I could have that, maybe, just maybe, Rachael, the war, and all those other wounds wouldn't hurt so much...

We sat quietly, staring at the bedsheet, avoiding eye contact, each of us lost in our own thoughts... I had committed more crimes in the last year than I'd ever imagined myself capable of, all in the hope of seeing justice done for the unattainable Rachael, but what good had come of it? And I'd been just as ready to break every commandment for the equally unattainable Alison from the moment I first saw her. Perhaps it was time to forget about windmills...

"I could practice law," I said.

"No, you couldn't. Not enough action in it for someone like you. Even if you did practice law, it would have to be at a legal aid office in Boyle Heights. And, sooner or later, you'd be disbarred for punching out a judge or DA."

"Maybe I could learn to like garden parties."

"No, you couldn't do that, either, and I wouldn't want you to. You wouldn't be you. You need the thrill of danger and the pursuit. You're the psych major, not me, but it seems to me you rationalize your need for danger by seeking out righteous causes to fight for. That's just who you are. You'd be a lost soul otherwise, and it would be a lost world without the real you."

I hate it when someone thinks they know me better than I know myself. But maybe she was right...

My mind was racing again, thinking a thousand thoughts, as in all those prior moments of sheer terror and fear and "in the shit," when life was at stake and truths came to light, and I realized I could never have her, nor could I ever have had her to myself, any more than I could've had Rachael for myself. Despite all the love and desire, all the hopes and dreams, some things were never meant to be.

We both turned and looked at each other, but there was nothing more to say. We made love one last time. It was coarse and quick, and as soon as it was done, she got up and dressed. Despite the lateness of the hour, she didn't want to stay the night. It would've been too painful for the both of us, and the morning goodbye would've been worse.

"I'll miss you," she said as she left.

Chapter 67

To Make an End is to Make a Beginning

When the autopsy and forensic examination had been completed, Rachael's body was released to the Ginsbergs, and they made funeral arrangements. Given the unusual circumstances of the situation, allowances had to be made for the ritual cleansing, purification, and shrouding of Rachael's body prior to burial, and special prayers were recited by a rabbi in the presence of the *chevra kadisha*. For the sake of appearances, and to avoid any speculation or scandal, no mention of Richard Marino was ever made during any of the services.

The majestic coastal bluff overlooking the Pacific was an idyllic setting and perfect outdoor stage for this production. In keeping with strict religious tradition, Rachael's body was placed in a plain, unfinished wooden casket and carried in seven stages from the hearse to her gravesite. The traditional prayers and psalms were recited with the gravest solemnity at each stage and at her gravesite. This was Grand Opera—every detail was important, and every word and movement a performance.

After the casket had been lowered into the grave, family members and mourners walked past and used a spade to toss dirt over the casket. It was announced that the traditional shiva observances would be held at the Ginsberg estate in Holmby Hills, and mourners would be welcome to visit and participate. Those who couldn't attend were asked to pray the mourner's Kaddish.

The final scene of Act III was coming to a close, and it was time for the curtain to fall. The scale of this opera had been Wagnerian and epic, leaving me feeling very small in its midst. And, despite the heat of the day, a chill ran down my spine when I felt the presence of all the other now-deceased actors whose roles had been to forfeit their lives to bring us to this inevitable conclusion.

Every man was used as he deserved, as Shakespeare would say, and none escaped his whipping, not even me. Although Bart had said I should take some consolation for solving the crime, the truth was I hadn't solved anything. I had been a bit player in a minor role, used only to speak a few lines and present a false story for a tidy conclusion—a lousy and heart-wrenching conclusion for me. Unlike traditional grand tales, this story would end without a hero to admire and applaud, only villains to despise. I wasn't sure there had been any real justice done, and I couldn't even say what true justice would have looked like in this case. You think about it and tell me.

When the burial services were finished, Magda sent her driver to go bring me to Aron's Cadillac. When I hesitated, the driver confided that Magda corrected her initial command and said, "Tell him that Mrs. Ginsberg *requests* to have a word with him."

"Requests to have a word" is as close to begging as that old woman will ever come in this life, I thought. Even so, given all that had happened between us and my own contentious nature, I was inclined to deny her "request." But what the hell—it was her only daughter's funeral, after all. I nodded and followed the driver to Ginsberg's Caddy.

I wondered what Magda could possibly have to say to me at this point. I had gotten past all the lies and hypocrisy to reach the truth that had brought me to this finale and wondered what good it had done me or anyone else. *How terrible it is to know, where no good comes of knowing...* Sophocles again, right on target.

The rear window rolled down, and I bent down to speak to Magda, my left hand on the roof of the car. Aron Ginsberg was seated on the far side, staring out the other direction, lost in his sorrow and despair, but holding Sarah's little hand. She already resembled Rachael to a remarkable degree. David had his head down, holding back tears; he resembled his father somewhat.

"My deepest condolences, Mrs. Ginsberg," I said sincerely.

Magda spoke in a low voice, so Aron and the children, if they were capable of it, wouldn't hear what she said.

"Thank you," she answered as she leaned toward me and hushed her voice even more. "Although it wasn't made public, that other FBI agent told me that Richard wasn't the father of the baby Rachael was carrying. He said the FBI wasn't able to identify who the father was, either. He said you are one of the few people who know this also."

"Yes, I know," I replied.

"He asked me if I knew or had any idea who the father could be, and I said I didn't have the slightest idea… Some things are best not known or made public, even if they are known," she stated emphatically. "For Rachael's sake, I trust you can understand that."

"Of course," I replied. "We wouldn't want to ruin her, would we?"

Magda sat back and gave the order to drive as she pressed the button to raise her window.

They say the fiercest beast on the planet is a mama grizzly bear protecting her cubs, I thought to myself as I walked back to my car. If a mama grizzly had to go toe-to-toe with Magda Ginsberg, I'd feel sorry for the cubs…

Maybe true justice doesn't exist, but true love does—love in all its crazy, mysterious forms that each of us feels and expresses in our own unique way and that makes us all think and do crazy, stupid things no one else could possibly understand. Maybe that's the one and only true thing we humans are capable of…

Focused on these thoughts, I didn't notice the motorcycle that slowed down as it drove behind my car. I didn't see the biker stop and pull a pistol out from under his vest, and I didn't feel anything until the first bullet tore into my chest.

Acknowledgments

First and foremost, special thanks to editor extraordinaire, Kathryn F. Galán. Once again, her expertise, advice, and patience were essential to the creation of this book.

A very special thanks to a very special friend, Glenda R. Cole, whose opinion and insight I greatly value and count on.

What could be better than a sister-in-law who is also a friend? One who is Jewish and reads and speaks Hebrew. Thank you, Sharon Sax Regalado, for your help.

Once in a great while, the Universe bestows an unexpected and undeserved blessing. Thank you, Marcia Trainor, for your excellent and invaluable advice and assistance.

Many thanks to the Yiddish Book Center of Amherst, Massachusetts (yiddishbookcenter.org), for their assistance with some of the Yiddish used in this book. Any Yiddish I got wrong is due to my own misunderstanding and entirely my fault.

And although I've never had the privilege of meeting either of these gentlemen, I must thank John Milius and Francis Ford Coppola, writers of the screenplay for *Apocalypse Now,* truly one of the great films of all time.

About the Author

Martin R. Regalado is a graduate of Amherst College and U.C. Berkeley-Boalt Hall School of Law. He practiced law in the San Francisco Bay Area prior to entering on duty as a Special Agent with the FBI. He retired in 2011, after serving for more than twenty-nine years in several offices across the country and overseas as an investigator, legal instructor/advisor, and firearms/tactics instructor. In addition to various awards received during his career, in 2017 he received an award for law enforcement from the United States Attorney's Office in Los Angeles.

His first book, *In the Still of the Night (A Fictional Biography)* was published in 2019.